THE LAIRD OF DUNCAIRN

A FEY MATTER NOVEL

CRAIG COMER

CITY OWL
PRESS

THE LAIRD OF DUNCAIRN
A Fey Matter Novel

CITY OWL PRESS
www.cityowlpress.com

Cover Design by Muhammad Asad at Photo Arena. All stock photos licensed appropriately.

Edited by Heather McCorkle.

For information on subsidiary rights, please contact the publisher at info@cityowlpress.com.

Print Edition ISBN: 978-1-944728-16-8

Digital Edition ISBN: 978-1-944728-26-7

Printed in the United States of America

For Martina,

who inspired this book, and whose love, support,

and patience I could not do without.

I love you always and always ever more.

PRAISE FOR THE WORKS OF CRAIG COMER

"For a heroic fantasy novel written by not one, not two, but three authors - Garrett Calcaterra, Craig Comer, and Ahimsa Kerp - THE ROADS TO BALDAIRN MOTTE is a surprisingly well-structured, remarkably cohesive tale that actually benefits from the different voices, without seeming fragmented."

— Bob Milne, Beauty in Ruins

"In THE ROADS TO BALDAIRN MOTTE, three perilous adventures are tied to the same epic war, with different people from different walks of life, but, clearly in the same lands, at the same time, speaking the same language, right down to the swear words. It was graphic and captivating. I couldn't put it down."

— GoodReads Reviewer

"In THE LAIRD OF DUNCAIRN, each character is unique and has a back story that allowed me to develop attachments to them. The story is very well developed and is told in a way that grabs you from the beginning. As the heroine, Effie, comes to know her race's past, she develops abilities that surprise herself, her companions, and her enemies...This book was a great read. I cannot wait for the sequel!"

— Rita Cline, ARC Reader

"Excellent story-telling and well-rounded characters makes this a thoroughly enchanting tale of a strong yet compassionate female protagonist in a man's world. I was particularly enthralled by the geography and the period, incredibly well researched and invoked. Loved THE LAIRD OF DUNCAIRN, couldn't put it down."

— Gillian Balharry, Reviewer

SCOTLAND, 1882

CHAPTER 1

Effie exposed her hand to the growling bear. Her fingers found Rorie's head and gave him a few soothing strokes behind the ears. A rumble came from deep in his gullet, as fierce as his wee body could muster. Frigid wind blasted them as they hid behind a large boulder atop the crown of Ben Nevis, the highest peak in the Highlands. A stranger had come to speak with her employer, Thomas Stevenson. Not an odd occurrence, but for a fortnight Rorie had groaned and whined, pawing for her attention as if disturbed by dark thoughts, trying to plead with her that something was amiss. And now that the stranger had come, Rorie's discomfort had turned into malice.

"If only I could peer into that head of yours and see what the fuss is about," she said, planting her hands firmly on her hips.

Rorie squatted on his haunches with a big huff, turning his head away. Though preferring the wild of the forest, he behaved himself around others when she asked. And only because it was she who asked. The bond had something to do with her Sithling blood, but Effie couldn't explain how it worked. It was as much a mystery to her as any of the uncanny bonds she'd made with woodland creatures, lazy housecats, and goofy hounds over the years. As much a mystery as why the queen and all the lords of London abhorred her kind, though she'd done nothing to warrant their wrath.

Rorie had been loyal to her ever since she'd convinced Stuart Graham to rescue him from a carnival the prior year, saving him from a brutal—and probably short—life of baiting. But he'd never acted so ill-tempered. Had the stranger come to take him away? Or was it she who should be fearful? By sight alone, the stranger wouldn't know her for a Sithling. Short of stature, with a young woman's curves and chestnut locks clipped about the shoulders, she lived her life amongst the Scots all but unnoticed, the truth of her mixed fey blood hidden.

Yet such reliance on appearance was a false safety.

Her hair whipped about her face, blinding her until she swept it back. The lodge of the Scottish Meteorological Society perched only a short distance away, a cozy, timbered house well-weathered from years of driving gales. Its chimney puffed white smoke, teasing her with thoughts of hot tea and honeyed biscuits. But that was where Mr. Stevenson had taken the stranger, and he'd instructed her not to return until he bade her. She blew into her hands for warmth, vexed by the riddle of the strange visitor, unable to contain her curiosity any longer.

"I'm going for a closer look," she said to Rorie. "Wait here." Hoarfrost crunched as she shifted her weight and slunk forward. The frozen dew crusted the fern and bracken around the lodge, radiating a cold that sank into her bones. Her olive-colored dress and drab woolen coat were serviceable enough, but they did little against the cutting winds atop the mountain, winds that drove in the damp air as if she wore nothing as all.

She understood why Mr. Stevenson wished her to hide. He was a man who believed in prudence. He would not jeopardize one of his great works, nor his reputation nor her safety, on the off chance a stranger would find her out. There were some who could recognize her fey nature if they stood close enough. The scientists of the day, many of whom had their pockets lined by London's coin, said fey blood corrupted the flesh, giving off an odor that some could smell. Catholics and Protestants alike said it was the sins of the fey that radiated a cloud of evil around them, allowing those pure of heart to perceive them. Other tales held that a fey's eyes glowed in the dark or that they would burst into flame if they touched iron. All of it seemed foolish to Effie. She drank her tea and let it pass the same way as anyone she'd ever met, regardless of their blood. How some knew her for a Sithling while most did not was as random as why some seeds took root and others wilted.

A whistle shrieked, drawing her attention. Next to the lodge, Mr. Stevenson's plans for a great observatory were coming to fruition. Steel beams braced half-raised walls as masons slathered on stone and concrete by the ton. The pipes of a steam crane shuddered, and a burst of gas exhaled as another beam was lifted into place, soaring thrice the height of a man to the workers waiting above. The construction was what had brought them to Ben Nevis, and Effie guessed the stranger would not have come if he weren't involved with the great project in some manner.

She stalked forward, half-crouched so the wind wouldn't stagger her, and reached the sill of one of the lodge's thick windows. Grabbing the smooth, lacquered wood for support, she peered through the glass into the lodge's main room. It held several tables of a dark and sturdy teak, and a stone hearth large enough for a royal estate.

The stranger stood with his back toward her. His coat and polished shoes bespoke a city, but not the odd leather cap with its flaps that clung tight around his ears. She didn't recognize the tartan on his trousers: blues, greens, and purples all jumbled together as if shouting at her. She recalled he'd driven his own steam carriage up the winding road, working the levers and knobs as if he were used to the task, an odd thing for a wealthy man.

"I will take your concerns into account, Mr. Crofter," said Stevenson. The window's frame had warped over the years, allowing her to hear him clearly. He stood by the hearth. A dark coat fit snugly around his stout frame, its wool threadbare from years of rugged service. His balding head held tufts of hair around the ears, yet they served to dignify his face rather than embarrass it.

"They are not just my concerns, Mr. Stevenson. They carry the weight of the Society. It is time to distance ourselves from such relations. Lord Granville will have his way, and you must choose where your loyalties lie—with the Society or with your fey friends."

Stevenson's face darkened. "We have pushed back these threats before and should not wilt so easily to tactics of hatemongering. Parliament has no grounds, and Lord Granville not enough allies."

A shadow moved from the corner of the room, and Stuart

Graham's stocky frame came into view from where she crouched outside. The man's knee-length boots were coated in mud, a workman's badge he wore proudly, and his white locks curled in ringlets atop a face as cheery as it was round. "Bah, let us speak plain, Mr. Crofter. You knew of Mr. Stevenson's associations before you funded the observatory. It was his name alone which brought in enough benefactors to ensure the completion of construction."

Mr. Crofter grunted. "Do you think any of these benefactors will stand against the threat of an Inquiry? No, Mr. Graham, they will scatter like rats." The stranger turned to Stevenson. "You will do as we ask, or we will sever ties and throw you to the wolves. One noted engineer is easily replaced by another. Now I bid you good day." He slapped his gloves together and strode for the door.

Effie recoiled. The news from London must be dire for Mr. Crofter to speak to Stevenson as he had. She crept to the front corner of the lodge and watched the small yard of trampled grass where the stranger's carriage sat. Graham emerged from the lodge's main door. He pulled a worn and battered watch from his pocket and studied it before casting his gaze to the skies. Mr. Crofter came out on Graham's heels, walking cane thumping the dirt as he ambled. The pair exchanged a cordial nod, similar to one shared by passing gentlemen in a city street. Effie didn't understand such manners. It was clear Graham was in a foul mood and Mr. Crofter the cause of it, but they pretended like nothing cross had occurred between them.

Rorie wasn't as polite. A low growl came from behind the boulder where she'd left him, and the bruin's head popped into view, teeth bared. She waved at him to stay back, but the noise had already drawn Mr. Crofter's attention. He peered at the boulder, his eyes growing wide. He muttered something, a scowl on his face, before clambering into the waiting steam carriage. Graham stood stiffly while the other man brought the boiler into action. The carriage's engine was a monster of steel and wood, with copper tubes lashed in a lattice across its flank and a charred snout thrusting upward from its roof. With a parting nod, Mr. Crofter threw open the valve, and the carriage sputtered forth with a burst of burnt coal perfuming the air. Only when the squeaking of the carriage's axles had faded down the mountain road did Graham turn to stare right at Effie.

As he beckoned her, brooding clouds rolled over the surrounding hills, darkening the sky. The wind gusted, flapping his leather coat about his legs. Neither were good omens. She stood and crossed to him, her cheeks flushed in embarrassment. He greeted her with a grin forced from pursed lips, and he spoke in a rushed manner, barely taking a breath.

"Och, lass," he said. "You took a risk. If my waistcoat weren't as round as an ox, ye'd surely been seen. It's like to piss down any moment. Let's get into the warmth before it does. Mr. Stevenson wants a word."

Effie nodded sheepishly as the steam crane's whistle shrilled again. Black smoke belched from its boiler, the engine fighting the strain of the wind. But she needn't watch the work progress to know the shape of the observatory. Its structure had long been affixed in her head from the drawings she'd rendered of the project. That was her place in the endeavor. Stevenson had discovered her talent for depicting his designs years before when she was just a lost girl sheltering under his protection. She'd sought him out after the death of her mother, the famous lighthouse engineer who designed edifices powered by stardust—the glowing azure silt, forged by Fey Craft, that burned hotter than oil and slower than coal. Her eyes grew glassy. The time was a blurred memory that still haunted her dreams. She'd come close to starvation and almost succumbed to exposure. Worse, she'd been captured and beaten by the queen's Sniffers, those who hunted fey, and only managed to escape by sheer luck. Yet none of those trials compared to the sorrow of isolation, the sense that all her warmth and cheer had fled. That she was alone, the last of her family, nearly the last of the Sithlings.

Alone and yet not alone. She glanced at the dark shadows of forest sprouting from the hills ranging beneath the peak of Ben Nevis. How many of the other fey races hid there watching them? Pixies and brownies, gnomes and hogboons all still dwelt within the Highlands. The remnants of a Seily Court existed, yet her mother had taught her to be as wary of it as of the Scots. She could count on a single hand the number of fey she'd ever met, and none were likely to take her in if the need arose. Such was the way for many Sithlings. Despite their appearance, they lived between races, not quite human and not quite fey. Their blood derived from a sect of the Daoine Sìth interbred with the Votadini, an ancient human clan whose might had receded under an onslaught of Scoti tribesmen. What remained centuries later could claim neither as kinsfolk.

Effie followed the man she considered an uncle into the lodge. Heat from the hearth enveloped her the moment she stepped inside, soothing away the bite the cold wind had left. Laid out on one of the tables were Thomas Stevenson's plans of the observatory, his lines and notes as formal and stiff as he was. On another perched the casing for one of his famous screens, a protective box for meteorological instruments. Its sides were angled slats designed to keep moisture from the instruments contained within, allowing them to collect data for weeks on end unattended. Her own worktable rested in a corner. A collection of colored charcoals, neatly arranged within a tin, sat atop a rendering of the observatory. Her drawings always held more flora than the bleak locations Stevenson chose to build on, and the observatory was no exception. Ben Nevis' crown boasted none of the hearty pines and spring flowers her depiction held, but that never seemed to bother her employer.

Stevenson greeted her with a curt nod and gestured to a chair by the hearth. He didn't make her wait long, once settled. "Our caller was Mr. James Crofter, a noted engineer whose father worked with Thomas Telford on the Great Canal." Effie's lips tugged at a smile. To Stevenson, names were always linked to matters of accomplishment. His own noted a long family line of engineers. "He came to us in haste with news from the coast. Murder has been done in the village of Duncairn."

Effie started. If given a dozen guesses, it was not the news she'd expected to hear. She read Stevenson's face, but it remained a stone mask. "Was it someone you knew?"

"A fisherman," answered Graham, bringing her a cup of tea, "An Ewan Ross. His boat capsized in the Bay of Lunan."

She took the cup, piping hot and full of sugar the way she liked, and breathed in its sweetness.

"The importance is not whom but the how," said Stevenson. "Fishermen in the area swear a host of rabid seals tipped Mr. Ross' boat, accosting it in unison. Not normal behavior to say the least."

She stifled a laugh. The poor fisherman deserved better, but the image of a group of seals harassing his vessel, barking and slapping the water with their flippers, was comical to her. "Surely these fishermen are mistaken in what they saw, or perhaps Mr. Ross agitated the seals in some manner. Perhaps they were trying to help the man." She glanced between the two men, wondering if they were jesting with her. "Yet I fail to see how one could call it murder."

"That's what I did say," said Graham. "The Scottish folk are long known for tales of fancy. Any dark bed of kelp becomes the Kraken in their minds."

Stevenson cleared his throat. "Putting Mr. Ross aside, there is a second account Mr. Crofter related. A week ago, a young lass was accosted on the road to Montrose, just outside of Duncairn. She suffered woefully and is much delirious, but describes her attackers as hairy imps slight of stature, with sharp ears and wicked fangs. They battered her as she fled. She recovers now from a fractured skull and other wounds." Stepping to the table, Stevenson rested his fingertips on it. "Short, devilish imps with pointed ears. These creatures have a name. The Shetland folk call them trows."

"Bah, bollocks," spat Graham.

Effie blinked, taken aback by the certainty in Stevenson's gaze. "I had not believed trows real." Her cheeks flushed at the admission. Her knowledge of the fey races, and of Fey Craft, were scarce at best. Much that she knew had come from Stevenson.

"Real enough," said Stevenson, "though not seen in the Highlands for centuries. They are fell creatures not of the Seily Court."

She frowned. "I thought all fey were bound to the Seily Court, before the Leaving at least. The binding is what gave Fey Craft power in this world." That power had dwindled ever since the Daoine Sith abandoned Sidh Chailleann, their ancestral home.

"There are some fey the Seily Court cannot control. They form their own covenants, Unseily Courts they are called, though decades have gone since the last rumors of one's appearance."

"Oh," she said. She stared into her cup, feeling a bit lost. It seemed, every time matters of fey lore arose, she understood the least.

Graham read her expression. "Don't fret, lass. You still ken more of your blood than all of us together. Mr. Stevenson's just got more years of hearing tales than you." He winked. "Many more, by the top of his head."

She forced a smile. Graham often reminded her how young she still was. For all her curves, she was still recent to adulthood by human standards, let alone fey. Thinking on the accounts of Duncairn, she drew the simple connection. "You believe the two attacks are linked, and if these trow creatures did the one, then the seals were really—"

"Selkies," affirmed Stevenson.

"But that doesn't make any sense. Selkies are not wicked creatures. They shed their sealskins in favor of human form to lure men and women into loving them. They don't work in packs, nor accost fishermen at sea."

"I have never heard tale of such a thing either," said Stevenson. "Just the same, fey sightings have grown in past weeks across the Highlands, enough to reach the ears of Her Majesty's Fey Finders, and now with these attacks it is almost certain there will be an Inquiry."

Effie blanched. There hadn't been an Inquiry by the Sniffers in almost fifty years. Most in London called the fey hunters relics, the funds used to support them better used elsewhere. Yet as dire as the news was, it did not follow why Mr. Crofter had spoken of such immediate threats. There was more to the stranger's visit Stevenson wasn't telling her, something she hadn't overheard. She studied his face. Her foot tapped impatiently. Cheeks growing red, she forced herself to still and sip her tea. She could be more stubborn than a stone when it fancied her, but secrets foiled her patience. As much as anything else, curiosity had driven her into the world of man after the passing of her mother, the need to explore the enigma of their society. Yet even as a girl she had always quested after knowledge. Her mother had often scolded her, reminding her life wasn't a puzzle to be solved but a great riddle to be savored.

The lesson had rarely stuck.

She would need to pull the truth out of the man. "Rorie is in a foul temper," she said. "He wants to warn me of something, but I can't understand what. I thought it might be Mr. Crofter."

Graham traded a glance with Stevenson. "She's a woman more than twenty years grown. There's no sense as treating her like the girl she was."

Running a hand over his chin, Stevenson worked at the muscles of his jaw. "Parliament pushes for legislation to formally outlaw any association with the fey. That would include the use of Fey Craft—stardust, precisely—and the harboring of those with fey blood."

"Bah!" Graham cursed. "That kind of nonsense comes up every odd year. They'll make no ground with it. We've still friends enough in London."

Pain flashed in Stevenson's eyes. "That is not the worst of it, you well know, Mr. Graham." He turned to Effie. "The Society feels a sacrifice is in order, something to appease the crown and end talk of an Inquiry. They instructed I draw up a document listing the fey I am in contact with and hand it over to the crown."

Stevenson drew up his weight into a rigid posture, clasping his hands behind his back before speaking. "That is why Mr. Crofter came to us—to demand I betray dear friends."

Effie's blood ran cold, and she had to swallow hard to keep the tea in her stomach from surging upward. So that was it—the missing piece. To protect their investments, the Society wished to send her and Stevenson's other fey allies to the gallows. It was not strictly illegal to harbor pro-fey sympathies, but neither was it fashionable, and those who did often found themselves in prison or their fortunes waning. She sensed Rorie's seething hatred for Mr. Crofter and felt a fury of her own spring to life.

"Do they all know of me, then?" she asked.

"Not directly," answered Stevenson. "But they know I have enough involvement with the fey that I could perhaps influence the crown's good graces."

"You wouldn't!" Effie exclaimed.

"Of course not," Stevenson snapped. He turned from her to cool his temper, yet she thought nothing of his outburst. His benefactors had placed him in a horrible position. They would not let their investments fail; they had too much money at stake. Either he sacrificed the fey known to him, or they would find an engineer to run their projects who would. She had heard Mr. Crofter threaten as much, she now understood.

"It's a fool plan," spat Graham. "I should've skinned the man alive for suggesting such a cowardly thing. The Fey Finders would hang the fey and still seek an Inquiry in Duncairn. Better if this observatory falls to ruin."

Stevenson shook his head. "The Society will not allow that. But they do underestimate the devastation of an Inquiry; they see only what it would mean in London. Her Majesty's Fey Finders care naught whether a fey is good or fell, peaceful or sinister of purpose. Their aim is to demonstrate their own worth. Without check, they'll scour the coast and put to the question all they find, as they did during the Potato Famines a few decades ago. They'll use the Inquiry as a grand stage and propel these legislations through. From there, their wrath would spiral out of control." He pressed his palms against the table, though it appeared he would rather knock it over. "We cannot let that happen. We must strive to show the world that fey and human can coexist."

"What will you do?" Effie asked, eager to hear his thoughts. Part of what drew her to Stevenson was his work, always seeking to blend science with nature. He was a pure naturalist who used stardust to power his famous lighthouses, promoted harmony with the fey, and sought to canonize their lore.

"We must sap the hatemongers of their advantage," said Stevenson. "I will stall them as best I can, but we must find the true motive and intent of these attacks before their Inquiry can come to bear. If the truth is known, there's a chance the Fey Finders will find no allies north of Edinburgh. The Scots have no fondness for London's authority."

Effie considered his words. She had no stomach for politics. Large crowds and public debate went against every fiber of her nature. But that did not mean she would wither away like some English violet. She could not let innocent fey fall victim to such a scheme as the Society planned. If Stevenson meant to unravel the truth of the attacks rather than appease his benefactors, it would take all his resources to hinder their enemies in Parliament, leaving nothing for Duncairn.

So to there she must go.

She rose, her mind settled. "If an Unseily Court exists in Duncairn, we must know of it before the Inquiry. It may be our best chance of gaining leverage, and our only chance to forestall Mr. Crofter's designs." Her words were heavy, but she stiffened her back against them. "I will go there and uncover the truth of the matter."

"What!" Graham barked. "You can't mean to go near that village. The queen's bastards will be crawling over it before the fortnight is through."

Effie swallowed to keep her voice from trembling. "There is danger, but to do nothing is to guarantee more fey will suffer." She faced Graham. "I can do nothing here to help; my presence might even bring greater danger if Mr. Crofter returns."

"You can do less against an Unseily Court!"

"If one exists," she reminded him. She tried to keep herself steady despite the knot forming in her gut. Graham and Stevenson had risked their lives and the fortunes of their families to let her in and give her a sheltered life. She would not balk at doing the same for them. "You are both needed here. At the least you cannot be seen in Duncairn. The scandal would link your names to whatever judgment the Inquiry handed down."

"There are others," huffed Graham. "I ken a man near Montrose who often trades with the fishermen of Duncairn." His tone was more tired than she had ever heard. "He knows much of the fey and has befriended a few in the area. I would have him handle this."

"If you could reach him," said Stevenson. "The man is a drunkard and hasn't responded to your missives in weeks."

"I'll speak with the fishermen and the girl's family," said Effie, "and if an Unseily Court exists, we will throw them to your benefactors and limit the crown's hand. It is the least either party deserves. Please, Mr. Graham, I must do something to protect the lives of the fey. I will not run and hide when I can offer aid instead."

"Bah!" Graham stammered, but his shoulders sagged in defeat. He spun on a heel and stormed out, slamming the door behind him.

The cold gust that rushed in made Effie shiver. She smoothed her coat and stepped closer to the hearth. Stevenson's face fell as blank as unmarked parchment, and he bent to scour over the observatory's designs. Effie knew Stevenson well enough to leave him be. Silent brooding was his nature, and she didn't take offense. To others it might seem he didn't care, but she knew he cared perhaps too much.

"Mr. Graham left his coat," she said. "I'll go after him."

She found Graham watching as the workmen set the observatory's giant lens in place. It was a moment they had planned for weeks. She knew a few of Graham's crew by name, but they all recognized her, giving her a cheery nod or word of greeting. Mr. Stevenson thought it a risk, yet she took that sentiment with a grain of salt. Where Stevenson placed prudence above mirth, Graham naturally exuded an honest warmth. He treated the crew like family and didn't employ a man he didn't trust.

"He should be seeing this." Graham had his arms folded across his chest. His cheeks and nose were rose-colored, as if he'd been nipping a few drams, but it was only from the wind.

"He has more pressing matters on his mind," said Effie, handing Graham his coat. She was not in a mood to speak in circles. "How dangerous are these creatures?"

Graham raised his eyebrow and stared at her askance. "If they're real? Dangerous enough you shouldn't go messing with them. It's a thick lad who pokes at a badger and doesn't expect to get bit."

"But you doubt trows exist?"

Graham stomped his boots for warmth. "I think Stevenson's nose has sniffed after funding for so long that it doesn't know a fart from a flower." Her eyes narrowed, and he held up a hand for her pardon. "This observatory is funded by landowners hoping its weather data will lead to better crop growing. They don't give a cuss about Acts of Parliament or the stars or the fey or any other bit of science that doesn't put more money in their pockets."

He pointed down the road. "That man, Crofter, is from Newcastle where the Hostmen lord over the coal trade for the entire empire. They aren't the type of men one should meddle with, and I wouldn't doubt the bugger is afoul of them."

"And Mr. Stevenson has been led down this path before." Effie finished Graham's thought. The affair with the lighthouse engineer, John Wigham, had left Stevenson accused of reckless slander, his name tarnished forever in the eyes of many in the scientific world.

"He's blinded by his own interests," said Graham.

"It is the fey's interest too," said Effie. "We are also his benefactors and have no other voice. The constabularies will not defend us. The magistrates of Edinburgh are bought and paid for by men who proclaim us the offspring of Black Donald." She stopped short of mentioning Graham's own interests, those of the French merchants who stocked his warehouses full of goods.

Graham gave her a cheery smile, but she saw the doubt and fear behind it. "We have enemies, lass. Too right. Some we know of, some we don't. I can't say as I understand what's going on myself, and that's what frightens me most. There's a strange feeling to this whole ordeal." The smile dropped from his face. "Robert Ramsey is a good man and no drunkard."

She rested a hand on his arm. "I will inquire after him."

He squirmed in frustration. "The tale of this Mr. Ross being killed by selkies is foolishness, and no doubt the other attack was carried out by some drunken rogue. The lass is just mistaken in what she saw or embellishing the tale for some reason." His skepticism made her love him more. It was the concern of a father not believing night had fallen, if only so his child could play in the sun a little longer.

"I've lived a happy life these past years, sheltered from those who would do me harm. That was your doing, yours and Mr. Stevenson's. It's time I repaid you the favor."

Graham's eyes grew moist. "Be careful, lass. The queen's appointed a new Fey Finder General, the man called Edmund Glover. I fear you know him, and he knows you."

Effie's stomach dropped to her toes. The name made her skin crawl. The last time she had heard it, she'd almost died.

CHAPTER 2

A misting rain harried Effie down the slopes of Ben Nevis to the train station at Fort William. Stevenson's coachman doffed his cap and left her on the platform, her only luggage a worn leather Gladstone and a nearly-empty reticule. She clasped her hands in front of her, trying not to fret. It was silly to feel so alone. There were others milling about, of course, but they could've been birds for the comfort their squawking brought. When at home—her small cottage nestled in a village to the north of Glasgow—there was at least the expectation of seeing her friends again before long. But those hopes seemed ethereal now, something she couldn't grab hold of, like the vapors of a steam engine.

Her mother had taught her never to meddle in the affairs of humans, and with good reason. Humans were dangerous. Her eyes wandered over the faces on the platform. Not many waited to join the train to Aberdeen, but the compartments would fill as they made their way along the Great Glen, cutting a path eastward at Aviemore. A woman huddled with four children, trying desperately to keep them seated on a bench rather than racing up and down the platform. Two men in tailored suits sipped their morning tea, their arms resting on a giant trunk well-tarnished from travel. Within was a modern contraption of some kind, no doubt. Tinkerers often peddled their devices throughout the Highlands, as technology changed the world by the day.

On the opposite side of the platform, a slim fellow's gaze lingered on her. She bristled when their eyes met and looked away. Men often found her attractive, but she'd never gotten used to their attention. It was a base instinct to shrink into anonymity. Anyone could be an agent of the queen, or at least willing to sell her out for a bit of coin. And in the Highlands there those whose mothers had told them enough tales of the Black Donald that they would rouse a mob to chase her away if they didn't burn her first. Sometimes she wished she were a gnome or a pixie; then she would always have to hide. Hiding was safe. Hiding kept you alive.

Hiding these past years had made her happy.

Her hands refused to still. Fear of discovery brought on the aching dread of loneliness, but it warred against her eagerness to prove her worth to the men she loved. They were more than her surrogate father and uncle. They were her family, more so than the blood relations she'd never known. She'd helped them before but never in a way that really mattered. They had never relied on her. The work she did for Stevenson could be done by others, including himself. Her neck tightened. The weight of emotions threatened to crush her like a stone on a dried leaf.

Rorie had sensed her discomfort. The bear had gnashed its teeth and whimpered, refusing to come near. She'd chased him down and hugged him as tight as she could. Thomas Stevenson had been more stoic. He'd wished her a safe journey, his gaze lingering for only a few moments before turning back to a matter with the foreman. She didn't begrudge him the lack of display; there were more emotions bottled within the man than could fill a loch. His eyes had spoken enough.

Graham had worried over her as if she were still in swaddling. He didn't need to remind her of the dangers. She'd lived long enough amongst their society to know how to conduct herself. It wasn't like before she had come to them, before they had taught her. She checked her reticule, thumbing through a number of coins. It was the details that would put her in jeopardy, as much as some passerby being able to sense her fey blood: wearing the wrong type of clothes or not using the correct courtesies, anything that would make a stranger pause and take notice. Coins had sparked her first confrontation with the queen's Sniffers. She'd barely left girlhood, starving and alone, when the man called Edmund Glover overheard her speaking with the matron of a wayhouse. The matron had scoffed when she'd used an ancient coin to pay for her meal, the only one she had left to her from her mother's meager belongings. Glover had beaten her unconscious and bound her for the dungeons in Edinburgh because of the simple mistake.

She touched the back of her head, remembering the throbbing welt the encounter had left. If it weren't for Glover's overconfidence and a scrap of fey lore remembered from her mother, she'd not have survived the ordeal. Glover was now the Fey Finder General, the leader of their ranks. She shuddered. She'd hoped never to hear the man's name again.

The minutes passed until she heard the distant shriek of the train's smokestack. As it approached, the platform bustled into action. Porters gathered luggage carts while conductors blew their whistles. A shadow fell over her, and she started, recognizing the slim figure who'd leered at her. The fellow doffed his hat, his other hand clutching a cane capped by an ivory bust of some Roman general.

"Do you need assistance, miss?" His voice was kind, but his gaze held little doubt of the other thoughts behind it.

Effie shrank under the gaze and stepped away before her wits told her to freeze. It wasn't uncommon for a woman to travel alone, not like fifty years prior, but untoward advances still hounded the vigilant and unmindful alike. She met the man's wolfish eyes. There was no glimmer of recognition in them. He didn't know her for a fey. He was a common lech, acting on nothing but his own base desires, and she would not run from her mission before she'd even boarded the train. She would certainly not let this man defeat her.

"I believe the porters are sufficient to my needs," she replied, then gestured. "Perhaps the woman there requires your help. Four little ones are many to handle alone."

The man sneered. "Children are such noisome beasts. I hope they don't spoil our entire journey with their prattle."

Effie furrowed her brow, hoping the man would take her annoyance as a firm rebuke. The man might not know her for a Sithling, but his attention might draw the eyes of others who would.

Handing her case to a porter, she pressed past the lecher and boarded a car near the middle of the train. It was as far from the noise and smoke of the engine as possible without entering the polished compartments reserved for the rich. To her chagrin, the slim man followed and took a seat at a table where he could face her. She ignored his leer but couldn't help feeling trapped as the train lurched forward under a squeal of metal scraping metal. He wasn't a Sniffer. Their lot were ruthless in the hunt. Yet the man was proving almost as irksome.

"…fifths the kinetic energy," spoke a husky voice. The two men with the trunk, having stowed it, took their seats across the aisle from her. They were deep in conversation and barely registered her with polite nods.

"Well indeed," replied the other. "And yet its efficiency is beneath that of coal, at three times the cost. I don't believe he'll be applying for a patent just yet."

"Coal." The first man shook his head. "In twenty years we'll all be laughing at the silly things we used to do with it. I can guarantee that." He scanned the car. With a lowered voice, he started off again. "The Germans have this compound they're testing…."

Effie turned to stare out the window, shifting on the hard, wooden seat. Normally, her curiosity would have her hanging on every word. An efficient fuel source for boilers, one to rival coal, was one of the great pursuits of the day. If the bluster in pubs and coffeehouses could be believed, the very fate of empires depended on it.

But she was in no mood for such discourse as the chugging motion of the train propelled her further from the safety of her friends. It only served to remind her that these men of science didn't trust the eldritch lore of her kind. Though some befriended the fey, and men like Stevenson sought to blend fey lore with modern knowledge, those in the cities branded her kind as devils.

She didn't need to read the broadsheet the husky-voiced man held folded across his knees to know the slant of its ink. The newspapers of London and Edinburgh slandered the fey, blaming them for fomenting dissidence against the crown. They were blamed for pestilences and freak storms, when a mine collapsed or a fire raged.

Those in power wanted to preserve their empire, and men seeking control needed villains to cast down. The fey were a target easily agreed on. It had started during the time of the Tudors, when witches, pagans, and non-converters were burned at the stake.

The Seily Court took no part in those religious wars; the Scottish fey had long since retreated into the hidden places of the realm: the Songsmiths to the Isle of Skye, the Star Readers deep within the timbers of the Trossachs, and the Spae Wives to simple cottages along the Great Glen. Yet the crowns of England and Scotland branded them as traitors all the same. Over the following centuries, England's armies rooted the fey from their ancestral homes in the southern shires. Even in the Lowlands of Scotland, the fey were hunted. A Spae Wife of Lothian was hanged and burned the past summer, her neighbors turning her over to the magistrate for leniency against some debt. Effie shuddered as an image of the poor Sithling woman, struggling against the rope, flitted through her head. The newspapers had proclaimed the sentence a righteous protection of the realm, despite the lack of any committed crime.

Only in the Highlands did the fey survive, for the Highlanders had themselves felt the harsh lash of London during the wars of the Auld Alliance and later during the Highland Clearances, when they were forced from their ancestral homes by greedy landowners. They resisted the crown's laws out of spite, while mistrusting the fey as much as they did the tax collector.

The slim man continued to leer at her. Effie could feel it pulsing with a fetid energy, enveloping her like a shroud. For a time she ignored it, but the persistence of the man unnerved her. She glanced over her shoulder and swallowed. The man's lips twitched into a smile. It was a disgusting thing, misshapen and toothy. Patches of hair spotted his cheeks, growing as unevenly as thorns in a briar patch. His gaze intensified, a beacon focusing attention on her like the lamp of a lighthouse. It sent anxious tremors down her arms, and suddenly she couldn't ignore its scrutiny any longer. Panic overwhelmed her. With each breath the car shrank, the air growing thinner. The man leaned forward, as if to rise, and she bounded to her feet ready to bolt.

The two men across the aisle broke their conversation, turning to stare at her. Her blood boiled, and she cursed to herself. She'd lived so long under the shelter of trusted friends that the faintest brush of attention had ravaged her nerve. She would have to do better in Duncairn, or the whole business would become a grand failure. Nodding to the men, she took a breath to slow her movements. She couldn't sit again, not and endure their notice. Collecting her reticule, she made her way to the door at the car's end, her dress rustling against wooden armrests as she passed the rows of benches. If she could stay calm, they would all soon forget her.

The next car held only compartments, she saw through the window, but it was too late to return to her seat. She reached for the handle, but another hand beat her to it. "Allow me. These things can stick." The man's warm breath coated her neck.

"I beg pardon," she hissed. "You are too forward." She felt her face grow cold as the blood drained from it.

"Apologies. My only wish is to give you service." The lecher flicked his wrist, and the door opened. The outside air from between the cars whipped at her dress and hair. The ground sped beneath her, a blur of rock, steel, and wooden ties.

He placed a hand on her waist to steady her and pressed against her bustle. The touch was sickening. She snatched the hand away and bolted through the door, slamming it against him as he tried to follow. She was rewarded by a satisfying yelp. Thoughts of the small dagger she kept in her reticule flooded her mind, but it was no use. Violence would only draw the authorities. She had to keep moving and hope he would find her too difficult a prey. Her only solace was that he wanted as little attention as she did.

She shut the next car's door before he managed to reach it, and hustled past the first two compartments. They were both empty, offering no sanctuary. The third contained a single occupant. She ducked inside as the car door banged open.

The occupant made to rise as she entered, but she barely registered the movement. "Good morning, miss," came a handsome tenor.

"Oh, please don't bother yourself." She heard the strain in her voice and forced herself to swallow. If the man took any offense, he ignored it.

"Lovely day, isn't it?" This time his tone held a note of mocking. Outside, the sky warned of a downpour as winds gusted clouds as dark as night across a murky horizon.

She struggled for the correct response, something clever to acknowledge the jest, but the lecher crossed by the compartment, and she sucked in a startled breath. The slim man's eyes flickered between her and the rest of the compartment before he continued down the corridor.

"Are you disturbed, miss?" asked the occupant. He craned his neck to track the retreat of the lecher.

Effie shook her head. "No, thank you. I'm quite all right." The words felt as absurd as they sounded. But her racing heart started to slow, cooling into a seething anger. Nearly undone a mile from Stevenson by the lust of a man. Her hands balled into fists. She should've brought a pinch of stardust to throw in the man's eyes and blind him. It was no worse than he deserved.

"Pity; I make for a dashing hero. And that scoundrel appeared in need of a good dashing."

She danced her gaze over the occupant. The young man lounged in a frock coat of dark wool, a starched shirt popping out at the neck. His boots were polished to a sheen, his hair more so, though the black curls gave his cheeks a hint of ruggedness. Not a man used to a day's labor, but not a dandy either. His manner put her at ease. It held no hint of danger, only a restless mirth that appeared to welcome her company.

He raised his fists, with a boyish grin. "Pugilism is my specialty. At University, I recorded no less than fifteen knockouts." He rubbed the back of his head. "The last one hurt like the devil. I broke my opponent's fist, and my ears rang for a month."

Despite the awful wit, Effie couldn't help but smile. Her anger lessened. "You make a good impression of yourself, sir."

He made to doff his hat, but it rested above on the luggage rack, so he wound up running a hand through his curls. "Mr. Conall Murray, lately of Edinburgh."

The name gave her pause; it didn't match his accent. "But you're not Scottish."

"Alas, I am. Born of Dunkeld but raised in the south.

Portsmouth, to be precise."

"Educated in the south as well," she guessed.

"Aye, at Warwick, much to my family's great vexation."

She laughed. In a way, Murray's jolly mood reminded her of Stuart Graham—a more fetching, younger version, but with the same carefree demeanor. "You are very forward with your shortcomings."

"I do apologize. You have caught me in a rather awkward state, Miss—?"

"Elisabeth Martins." She extended her hand. The name came easily; they had agreed on it before her departure. Stevenson's prudent nature had dictated a separation between her involvement and his enterprise. It was far better to be careful and wear a name without note than risk tying her to his benefactors.

Murray took her hand and gave it a firm but delicate shake, then settled back into his seat, leaning on an armrest. "Well, Miss Martins, have you traveled through the Cairngorm Mountains lately? If not, you are in for a treat. There are great works progressing near Glen Avon. A town has sprung up within the past month, full of carpenters, miners, and engineers. Cooks and seamstresses, smiths and grocers are flocking nigh, and there's even a weekly broadsheet in circulation. Some big discovery by Sir Walter Conrad, the geologist."

She hadn't heard of the discovery, but the name of the geologist sounded familiar. "He must be rich to afford such an expensive operation." The tension in her neck relaxed. A dashing hero Mr. Murray might not be, but he made for pleasant company, and there was no danger in joining the man in conversation. That she had barged in on his solitude didn't seem to upset him in the least, and she saw no need to remove herself to another part of the train.

"Word is he owns half the royal jewels," said Murray, tapping the side of his nose. "But it isn't his coin supporting the works. Talbot and Gersh have that honor."

Effie's brow furrowed. "The bankers from Newcastle?" She recalled Graham's warning. The Hostmen of Newcastle were rich and powerful coal barons who held a stranglehold on Britain's trade. They surely controlled the city's banks as well and no doubt had their hands in any investments.

"The very ones." Murray accepted her knowledge without

patronizing her, she noted. The younger generation were certainly different than the old. He checked his watch. "We should reach the site within the hour."

She showed polite interest as Murray explained the mining tools Sir Walter's men used, from the giant steam-powered hammers that ripped the earth asunder, to the rock hammers wielded by delicate hands with deft touches. His knowledge was impressive, if not overly interesting. Just the same, it was nice speaking with a man she'd only just met. It made her feel more like a Scottish lass free to dance with the village lads rather than hide at home in the shadows. His smile was certainly nice. It lit up the compartment as he spoke, despite the storm swelling outside.

As Murray had promised, the great worksite of Sir Walter Conrad came into view before the hour passed. Even with forewarning, Effie started at the sight. Hundreds of men hustled about a patchwork of buildings. They flooded the gentle hills with a hive of activity. Some of the buildings were built of stone but most were timbered, quickly thrown up and simple. A few rows of canvas tents dotted the area. They looked cold and frail under the threatening sky. Fires roared in cast-iron pots, and in open pits, for washing and cooking and just to keep warm. The men were a rough sort, covered in muck and sweat, their clothes tattered by heavy labor. Every few carried a pick or hammer, but she did note a tailored suit here and there, and a surprising number of women and children.

Further on, the tall stacks of steam hammers thrust high into the air like steel trees that would dwarf a giant. Beneath them, other contraptions lay about for the moving of dirt and sifting of soil. Their knobs and levers made them look like hedgehogs. Murray tried to point them out, but there were too may for her to follow.

"Wondrous, isn't it?" he asked.

She watched as a weather balloon rose above the worksite, tethered by a thick cord. Two other balloons were already aloft, dancing in the Highland wind. Behind, the slopes of Ben Avon rose in a haze of browns and purples. Its crags brought forth the memory of one of her mother's tales.

"I know of this place," she said. "There was a yellow stag...." Her voice drifted off; she couldn't quite remember the details. Had the stag saved the local clan chief from murder? Or had it tricked him into following it into the snow, leading the warrior to starvation and death? Effie couldn't say. Most of her mother's tales were vague and jumbled in her mind, scraps of knowledge half-remembered from her childhood.

"A stag?" Murray looked at her quizzically. But before he could say anything further, a large blast of steam exhaled from the train's engine and the brakes began to squeal.

"They've built a station," said Effie, as the train shuddered to a halt.

A host of laborers hoisted barrels and sacks from one of the forward cars, piling them on carts fastened to the backs of steam carriages. A few passengers also detrained. She chilled as she noted the lecher was one of them. He marched off through the buildings, not once looking back, his cane piercing the churned-up earth with each step.

Her impression of the worksite distorted. Suddenly, all she noticed was the sundered land and barren hills, the piles of refuse that bled into the soil, and the black smoke that choked the air. Sir Walter Conrad's camp was a far cry from the renderings she depicted for Stevenson.

She feigned a smile. "Wondrous," she said, for the sake of politeness. Murray studied her, unsure, and the urge to continue became overwhelming. "I don't mean to offend, it's just, I can't help but imagine the clans of Glen Avon raising their sheep and harvesting from the forest here on this very land. Before the Clearances, some of your kinsmen may have dwelt here for centuries."

"Ah, a romantic." Murray's eyes saddened. "I used to be one."

Effie bristled. "But do you not think their blood belongs here and not in some far-off village or on another continent? What is a crown's worth if its greed drives honest men from their homes?" Her tone bit harder than she'd intended. Worse, the argument was not a wise course for her to remain unnoticed. Folk remembered those who spoke openly against the crown. At least no one else was within earshot.

Murray raised a hand in defense. "The Clearances were an ugly business. I will not defend them. But to muddle their cruelty with the wonders of this Industrial Age is perhaps unkind." He repositioned himself as the train began to chug forward once again.

"Did one not propel the other?" She could not seem to find a comfortable position on her seat, either.

He weighed the matter before responding, tapping a finger to his lips. "Technology propels the very world. Think on the greatness it's brought the British people in the past few centuries: the medicine, the living conditions, the freedom of travel."

"An empire."

"Yes, an empire, and why not?" He shrugged. "If it means staying on a course of progress and discovery, why shouldn't Britain seek to remain the dominate realm of Europe?"

Effie cast her gaze out the window. She had no good argument other than the sorrow for what used to be. "I apologize if I've disturbed you, Mr. Murray. It was not my intent."

He shook his head, oiled locks springing to and fro. "Never. I enjoy your candor, but perhaps we should discuss more of mutton and less of the empire."

She laughed. "In the Highlands, I believe the two are much the same." He grinned, and they held a lighter conversation for the remainder of the journey.

At the Banchory station, she gathered her things and bid Conall Murray well. He rose and nodded kindly, extending a hand. As she reached for it, the train lurched, its brakes settling against the strain of the steam's pressure. Effie stumbled forward, clutching his arm for balance.

Conall's face caught fire, cheeks glowing red while his dark eyes danced. "You are a pleasure, Miss Martins," he said, taking a step away for propriety. His breath smelled of mint, his coat like the smoke of a warm hearth. Effie realized she'd enjoyed grabbing his arm and that the thought didn't embarrass her. Perhaps she'd spent too much time with Graham's workmen, to have such a coarse notion. She felt her face light up with mischief as she turned away, leaving the young man blushing.

A local service took her south through Montrose and on to Duncairn. From the vantage of the station, it was clear the fishing village had outgrown its roots. Its village green sprawled over a pair of knolls with a burn trickling between them. But unlike those in the Highlands, the stream's water was thick with foam and stank from abuse. Cobblestones paved only the High Street, and many of those were poorly laid. The buildings were shabby, in need of paint or a good scouring, their plumbs crooked and rooflines sagging. A tang of salt hung thick in the air, mixed with rotted fish and molded wood. Through the buildings, Effie could make out jagged cliffs and the cobalt waters of the North Sea.

A dirigible floated above the coast, moving slowly against the wind. This one's design was tame, built for function over aesthetics, most likely transporting goods for the army. Effie found herself staring. Flying machines weren't a new sight, but she marveled at how quickly they'd become common. Perhaps it was the viewing distance, but they'd always held more beauty to her than the sputtering, smoky contraptions on land.

There were those about the village, too. A few steam carriages teetered along the streets, horns blaring at the carts that lumbered in their way. The horses drawing the carts eyed them anxiously, while their masters barked curses and shook their fists. She glanced at the shop signs as she strolled the High Street. Some were etched on storefront glass in gold leaf, their lettering precise. Others were scrawled in paint on rotted planks that creaked as they swayed in the breeze. Bruce and Sons: Carpenters boasted chairs machine-crafted in Manchester, each one perfectly alike, while the Blind Poet smelled of sour beer and pipe smoke. At one end of the street, a fish market was set up where hawkers sold cod and whiting from carts.

The villagers were a mix of hearty fishermen in stained, worn clothes, and well-dressed businessmen whose coats and vests were layered over starched shirts. The former grinned and winked as she passed, the latter doffed their hats, but none offered to carry her luggage. She didn't mind; she would rather tend to herself. The fewer strangers she met, the better. She tried to stay clear of as many as she could, walking wide around them without appearing odd about it. She didn't know how close she would have to be for one to sense her fey blood but discretion was the better part of valor.

Her mind lost in wander, she almost passed the hotel before its velvet drapes caught her attention. The St. James appeared as frail as its neighbors, but the carpets and décor were inviting, and the flower boxes beneath the windows were full and blossoming. In stark contrast, the attendant at the counter was as stiff as the banister, greeting her with pursed lips, almost a smile except for the annoyance in his eyes.

"Miss Elisabeth Martins," said Effie.

"Room for just one?" The man pushed his spectacles back with a finger, scanning the ledger. "I do believe we can take you if you'll just rest a moment in the parlor." The dismissal was clear in the man's tone. Effie bristled but kept her composure. Such rudeness she expected in a city, though Duncairn was far from being called that.

She took a chair near the hearth, facing the window. Gazing out at the market, she wondered where she should start. She didn't have the Fey Craft of divination to rely on, not like Star Readers. She was a Grundbairn; a child of the forest. It was a rare affinity even in the days of her ancestors, and the Fey Craft of Grundbairns sprang from the earth, not the stars. She knew a handful of rhymes her mother had taught her, but nothing of use to her now. She could call on the families of those attacked but thought it better to glean some knowledge of her surroundings before intruding on them. It was said fishermen spread tales faster than a crow could fly, though they could also be unsavory company for a woman traveling alone. Still, it was better than wasting time in the hotel.

She glanced at the attendant. The man busied himself at the ledger. He hadn't moved to call a porter or a maid since she arrived. "Are the fishermen in for the day?" she hollered. Surely they would do her no harm in broad daylight.

"Just a moment, Miss Martins," the man replied, not taking his eyes off the ledger.

Her brow narrowed, and her foot began to tap. She'd wanted to freshen herself up after the journey, but she refused to play this man's game. It was times like these she wished she had some of the Fey Craft spoken about by the country folk. Perhaps she would give the man a tail or set him to wandering after snarks until he starved himself.

She gathered her reticule and marched for the door. "I am stepping out for a walk," she said. "Please see to my luggage." With a grunt of acknowledgment, the man waved her out the door.

The docks were easy to find. A stair cut into the cliff face zigzagged its way down to a collection of short piers. A longer, broader ramp led off to the south for carts and horses to drag goods up to the village, but it appeared largely unused. Instead, the dockworkers loaded the day's catch into a gondola that ran on a cable straight up the cliff. An engine at the top powered a wheelhouse that drew the steel box up and down the slope.

Boats of all shapes and sizes crowded the piers. They bobbed on the tide, as fishermen mended nets and swabbed decks, or merely sat and watched the sea. A few shoveled coal into holding bins aboard their decks; others tinkered with engines. A breakwater ran behind the docks, with an old lighthouse perched on its head. It was a small, stone tower powered by a whale-oil lamp, a relic of old technology. Much like the men around her, Effie thought.

She approached one of the boats. The man aboard was packing a haul of cod into a crate of salt. He took her in with a shake of the head. Gesturing, he gruffly told her no sales were allowed on the docks. She needed to go up to the market.

"I beg pardon," she replied, "I'm looking for acquaintances of Mr. Ewan Ross."

The man glowered at the name. His tone left no doubt of its warning. "What needs you with them?"

"Nothing untoward, I assure you." Effie smiled and relaxed her bearing, trying to appear friendly. The man spat and turned back to his work.

She met the same response from the next fisherman. The two after that gave her a shoulder cold enough to skate on. It seemed the mere mention of Ross cut their tongues short, but whether they were frightened or obstinate she couldn't tell. Digging into her reticule, she wondered whether coin would loosen them a bit.

She felt for a sixpence. Before she could reach it, a bellow startled her. Heavy boots thundered her way. "Away with ye!"

The fisherman towered over her, hulking shoulders as wide as Graham's. His cheeks flared red beneath a coarse black beard. He charged her until they were inches apart, his breath pouring over her in huffs. "Ye didn't ken Ewan Ross. Git yer gob shite away afore I give ye a good dunt!" He raised his fist as if his threatening gibberish weren't clear enough.

She paled and dropped the coin, snatching hold of her dagger instead. It was a keen blade, but one swat from the fisherman would likely take her head off. Work on the docks froze as dozens of stares turned her way. Above, the seabirds circled, crying out in mocking. She'd been a fool to think to the riddles of Duncairn would unravel so easily.

CHAPTER 3

"You have no business here." Another fisherman joined the first, shorter but no less stout.

Effie stepped back, keeping a firm grip on the dagger. If she drew it forth, it would end badly for her, but she wouldn't cower and give them the satisfaction of an apology. She had done nothing wrong. She felt the eyes of those on the docks glaring at her and winced under the scrutiny. The sensation that they were prying under her skin made her dizzy. Too many faces had burned her visage into their minds, too many strangers would now recognize her. Fishermen told tales. She knew that. How could she have been so careless?

Without a word, she marched for the stairs. The larger man stormed after her, but the other held the brute at bay. Curses followed, choice words fit for the docks. She could think of a few more and directed them at herself. It had taken less than an hour to fail at discretion.

She needed to take better care. And hurry. Word of her inquiries would spread through the village like a rampant fire, and any who would do her harm could find ample loose tongues to guide them. Worse, if any fell creatures did roam Duncairn, they might discover her before she could uncover them. The thought chilled her bones more than any curse the fisherman could utter.

She paused on a landing halfway up the stair and surveyed the docks. A few fishermen watched her, but most had returned to their work. Their severe reaction vexed her. She could understand the hesitation in speaking with a stranger—she kept a wary tongue herself—but their aggression had felt more like that born of fear. Mounting the final steps, she heard the cries of the fish market and headed there. She would need to try a different tack with these men. Perhaps they would know of Robert Ramsey, Graham's friend. Asking after him would be less intrusive.

Late in the afternoon, the market had little trade, and the morning's catch had begun to stink despite the salt used to preserve it. Cats wandered about the carts, mewing and stretching as if, having woken from a long nap, they were expecting dinner. That the fishmongers didn't shoo them away spoke of a normal routine.

The fishmongers were an older lot. Three were hunched and leaned on canes, and the other pair were not far off.

"A good price for you, miss," said one as she approached. He patted his gnarled hands on his cart. His eyes were a kind blue, his coat mended by several patches.

"Good day," she said. She scanned the fish for a moment before deciding on one. A purchase couldn't help but put her in better graces. The man plucked it out and began wrapping it in a sheet of coarse paper. "I beg your pardon, but I've just arrived this afternoon and was looking for an acquaintance of mine. I was told he may have come by the High Street. His name is Robert Ramsey."

The man pinched his lips and shook his head. "No, not today, miss."

But another fishmonger perked up. This one had a bulbous red nose which Effie guessed didn't come from the cold. "Rabbie ain't been in the village at all today. He's up in Montrose, I ken."

"Aye, but meant to be here on the morrow, ain't he?" asked a sturdy-looking man wearing an apron over his coat. He was younger and towered over the others if only because he stood straight, yet his hair was gray and face lined with wrinkles.

"Maybe," replied the man with the red nose. "But who's to say these days?"

"What do you mean?" asked Effie.

"No offense to yer acquaintance, miss, but Rabbie's been acting mighty curious of late." He rubbed at his cheeks. "The whole village's been acting curious, truth be told."

"Ach," cried the man with the patched coat. "Enough with your aching." He handed Effie the wrapped fish, and she dug into her reticule for some coins.

"It's not just me saying it," said Red Nose, "Archie McEwan had his whole catch spoil the other morn afore he could get it from the docks, and Davie Gavin had his nets rot straight through." He stammered while the others threw their hands at him in disbelief, shaking their heads and chuckling. "An me own wife, Maisie, almost had a train run her down."

"Aye, after she'd been a dozen nips into the whiskey," said the younger man. Laughter filled the market, and the poor drunkard could only scowl.

"But there have been odd occurrences, haven't there?" asked Effie, carefully. "I heard rumor of an attack on the road north of here, not a couple of days ago. Some terrible thing to a poor girl."

The laughter died, and several of the fishmongers found they had a great need to inspect their carts. The drunkard hobbled closer until she could smell the whiskey on his breath. "It's the fey." He motioned at the other fishmongers. "They don't want a hex on their homes by saying it, but the wee folk have turned dark and cursed the village with their devilish ways."

Effie kept her face a mask of kindness, despite her excitement. The man might not know the full truth of things, but at least he was talking freely. "You don't seem to fear them."

"Me wife fashioned me a ward against them." He opened his coat. A sprig of heather was pinned on his vest. Around it, a leather chord was tied in a braid of intricate knots. "Her grandmother were a Spae Wife who kept the village clean of fey and their tricks."

Effie nodded, pressing her lips together. It always amused her, the befuddlement of the country folk. True Spae Wives were fey whose Fey Craft lay in healing, yet it was common to hear of elder women— those who could tend to an ache or two—called the same.

"You're as bad as them Sniffers," said the man with the patched coat. "Soon you'll be talking of bonfires and chimes and dancing shadows in the night."

"I cannae...." The drunkard's breath caught. Effie followed his shocked stare, her eyes widening in horror. The cats! They sat around her feet, straining their necks and flicking their tails. The whole lot of them, lulled as if she had brought them under a trance. So intent had she been on the conversation, she hadn't noticed their gathering. But they sat now, awaiting her to address them. It wasn't the first time such an uncanny reaction had occurred to her presence. Sometimes birds would perch on her shoulder, and dogs would often follow her for hours. Her fey blood beckoned them in some way. But never had an entire pack acted in such a manner.

It was said that before the days of the Romans, Grundbairns had tended the forests and gardens of the isles, but she understood little of what that meant or how it called to the animals who dwelt on the land. Her mother had raised her alone, teaching her simple rhymes about roots and flowers, and singing to her of giants and the stars. When she'd died, she'd left a great void in Effie's understanding of her own kind. It left her woefully unprepared for such bizarre encounters.

The fishmongers eyed her warily. She hoped none had any ability to sense her fey blood. But even without it, there was no hiding something was odd about her, odd enough to inform the authorities. That they were likely as afraid of the queen's agents as they were of her brought little comfort.

"They must smell a gentle heart," she said, hoping for levity. Swallowing down the urge to flee, she proffered her wrapped fish as evidence. Then she scolded the cats in a stern tone. "But you'll get none from me. Shoo, now; go find somewhere else to eat." She tittered, the trill sounding forced and anxious.

A slim, coal-colored tom crept to her and rubbed its head on her boot before scampering away. The gesture reminded her of Rorie, of his natural affection toward her. The rest remained an awkward moment longer, then dispersed, stretching and looking away as if they had meant to be somewhere else all along.

"Er, aye," the drunkard muttered.

"You can tell the Sniffers all about your fey and grandmother on the morrow," said the younger man. "There's one coming on the train from Edinburgh."

"Er, aye," repeated the drunkard, blinking.

Effie's breath stopped, and she glanced at the hour. Over the

High Street, the sky had darkened, and a row of gas lamps sprang to life casting the storefronts in a pale yellow. She had less than a day. The queen's minion would surely hear of her and be curious who else was asking after the strange events of Duncairn.

Less than a day. She wanted to laugh at the fear. Already half the village knew of her. How long would it take for them to run her out, Sniffer or not? She could worry about the Fey Finder later, once the man arrived. With luck, she would be on her way home by then.

"Where might I find Mr. Ramsey, if he does come to the village?" she asked. She pointedly ignored the cats stalking in wide circles around her.

The drunkard regarded her with suspicion, but the younger man tipped his hat. "The Blind Poet, miss. But I daresay it's not a place for someone as yourself."

Someone as yourself.

Effie started, though he hadn't meant it that way. He referred only to her sex. The business with the cats and news of the Sniffer had put her on edge. She thanked him and retreated down the High Street. She had tarried long enough with the fishmongers.

Turning at a broad intersection, she wandered through the heart of Duncairn. The shops sprawled for a few crisscrossing streets before giving way to tidy rows of private homes. She left the fish unwrapped in an alley, knowing the cats would find it. Perhaps they had known a gentle heart after all. Near the edge of the village, she paused at a shop nestled on a narrow street. Its neighbors slanted from it, as if trying to avoid its reach. Someone had painted a large pentacle on the door in thick strokes of blue paint. Beaded glass hung in tendrils over the windows, and chimes caught the breeze in a soft melody.

The door groaned open, and an elderly man shuffled out. Orange patches spotted his blue frock coat. Its sleeves and his plum trousers were dusted in chalk. A bundle of parchments peeked from beneath one arm, notations in a precise hand scrawled on them.

He examined her with a clouded and lifeless eye. "Be open again in the morning, lass. That's as far a future as I can give you until then." His voice was crisp, far from the thick grunting of the docks.

Effie tried to decipher the man's face. True Star Readers could pull omens from the heavens, but their Fey Craft had long since faded. All Fey Craft had faded since the Leaving, when the Daoine Sith fled the world. But that of Sithlings had always been lesser, born from a diluted blood. The water of an azure sea turns clear when cupped in a bowl, her mother had once said. Fey Craft existed now more in fable than in truth. If the man had any uncanny ability at all, it came as a charlatan. Besides, no Sithling would risk such exposure, even in a small fishing village. The man was undoubtedly human and his livelihood a ruse.

"Wandering stars bring luck," she said, feeling courtesy demanded she speak. It was an old rhyme. The elder fey were said to have traveled to the stars when they left. One could see them shooting across the skies, on some nights.

"Hark closely, and duck!" finished the man. He chuckled. "Aye, they do indeed." Nodding, he tottered a few feet before turning back. "Best be careful after dark, lass."

Effie tensed. "Why is that?"

"Drunken louts on the High Street. The constable keeps threatening but does nothing about them." He shook his head in disgust. She watched him amble away, wishing she could confide in him. But that would be folly. A man who lived a lie treated others as kindling, readily tossed into the fire as the need arose.

A waft of charred meats and spices, coming from one of the homes down the street, reminded her she hadn't eaten in hours, and her stomach began to gurgle. She'd seen a dining room in the St. James and hoped they had something warm in the kitchen. At the least, she was eager to kick off her shoes and remove her bustle.

Daylight vanished as she headed for the hotel, and Duncairn quickly became a crypt full of shadows cast by the moon. The silvery orb brought an uneasy quiet with it, and the eerie transformation made Effie's gut tighten. Hers were the only footfalls, but shadows near her jumped along the narrow street under a cold silence that froze the air like a blanket of winter frost.

Something followed her.

Or somethings. A tickle formed in her bowels, oddly pulsing like a pinch of lit stardust. It was a sensation she'd felt once or twice before, never knowing what it was. It reminded her of a tiny silver bell ringing an alarm on some distant hill.

On top of that was the fear, a distinct dread of the dancing shadows. It pulled at her feet, turning them into heavy stones that slowed to a crawl even as she urged them to go faster. She started to sweat, biting her tongue to keep from calling out.

She peered between buildings and along the rooflines but saw no one. Not a soul stirred in a window or along the street, and only the heavy tramp of her heels filled her ears. Where had everyone gone?

A vague shape emerged from the shadows, too dark to make out, but enough that she could feel its leering gaze. Her skin crawled as others joined it. The shapes slunk in the darkness, something foul stalking her, hunting her, hungry for her. The pulsing tickle in her bowels swelled, tiny bells clanging furiously. Her fear spilled forth in quaking gouts, robbing her of her balance, and she stumbled.

A flash darted across the street. She ducked as it whistled past. Wood clattered against the wall near her head. Gripping the hem of her dress, she found her feet and bolted. Freed from the confines of cloth, her legs were swift, used to running in the forest.

Gas lamps blazed ahead, their amber light offering a hope of protection. Beyond, she spied the broad avenue leading back to the High Street. She rounded the corner in full flight, fear pushing her faster than a harried rabbit, and smacked into the red-nosed fishmonger. The drunkard oofed and tumbled to the ground. She caught herself barely, flailing her arms like a lunatic.

In a blink, the odd tickle fled, the ringing echoing off into nothing. The shadows stilled, warmed by the hissing lamps. She trembled, her breath short and ragged. The drunkard gaped at her. His eyes were a mirror of her own, only his fright was directed at her. She stammered an apology and reached to help him up, but he shied away.

Guilt twanged, but there was nothing for it. She spun and scoured the street behind. Nothing stirred; the village was tranquil, its rough edges silvered under the moonlight. The uncanny feeling of a crypt was gone. Behind her, the din of the High Street beckoned like the crackle of a warm hearth. Duncairn yet lived, its folk carousing among the taverns and public houses, shrouded by a thick, salty mist that rolled in off the North Sea.

Her nerves had settled by the time she reached the hotel, enough so she could speak without her voice breaking. The amber glow of the St. James' gas lamps spilled onto the cobblestones, cheery and inviting. A soup of leeks and tatties perfumed the dining room, but she no longer had an appetite. The snooty attendant ushered her to her room. Her luggage had already been brought up, and the man left her with a warming pan of piping hot coals. She gave no comment to his rudeness; she wanted only to crawl into the sanctuary of a soft bed, to pull up the covers and remove the chill that gripped her spine.

But with the doors and windows locked tight, the walls throbbed tighter and tighter around her like a cage, shrinking until she could barely move. The room was no sanctuary, only a reminder that she was not safe outside. She never had been, not since the moment she'd left Ben Nevis. She'd wanted to remain unnoticed, to unravel the fanciful tales of fisherman and bring word to Stevenson of hope for their cause. But the confrontation on the docks and the shock of the fishmongers were of little concern. Fiends infested Duncairn. True devils from the darker parts of fey lore.

She blanched as awareness came. They had stalked her through the village. But they hadn't stumbled on her; they had known where she was the instant the sun had set. They had probably known the moment she arrived.

CHAPTER 4

Within a dark dream, hunger had seized her wits. A lass of barely twelve years, she huddled in a gully near the old Highlander's Way, drenched by summer rains. The heathered crags of Glen Coe sprawled around her. Moss-coated peat lay like a sponge beneath thorny bracken, thick with water trickling down from the munros above. Across the roadway stood a wayfarers' public house. Smoke billowed from its chimney, bringing with it the savory aroma of boiled cabbage, onions, leeks, and salted lamb.

Her mother had cautioned her against the dealings of man, but she was tired of being hunted. She was exhausted from weeks of foraging, living under damp rocks, roaming the glens, and not knowing where to go. Lost without her mother, who'd faded from life and abandoned her with nothing but precious memories. Not a home or sense of place. Not a purpose other to go on and live as she always had. At first it had been enough, but the days grew long and lonely as they tallied into months, and Effie didn't know how much longer she could live as a hare scuttling around the wolves' den.

Scampering across the roadway, Effie pulled her cowl tight around her chestnut locks. She spied a steam carriage in the yard on the far side of the house. A man in a gray suit shoveled coal into its rear hatch. Another lounged against a low fence, fiddling with a chronometer. His arms were sleeved in boiled leather plated in bronze. Effie found herself staring. She'd seen such things before, but always a curiosity overcame her to know more, to study every little knob and lever.

The man with the shovel glanced at her, a hard stare from a hard man, and she hurried inside. The common room of the wayfarers' house held a trio of long wooden tables. A fire warmed the air from a stone hearth, over which hung the cooking pot. Withered beams sagged so low Effie had to duck to clear the threshold. A pair of highlanders huddled in a corner, all brawn and scruff. Their tartan trews were red, striped with black and yellow. They'd thrust a dirk into the table between them, an old custom for requesting privacy.

Perched before the hearth, like a sow spitted and put to roast, was a red-cheeked gentleman. His coat and vest were finely woven. A golden chain looped from a pocket at his gut to a button on his chest. A small wooden box lay open on the table next to him. Stems of iron, topped by tiny metal disks, sprouted from its innards like a field of dandelions. He squinted through spectacles of purpled glass at a ledger on his lap.

"Well, there's a lass," boomed the voice of a southerner. The speaker and his companion were the room's only other occupants. They sat at a table near the door, cups of a frothy ale in their hands.

"Ah, let her be," said the man's companion. He smiled at Effie with kindly eyes. Both men were city folk, but neither was richly dressed. The starched shirt of the kindly man spoke of an office, while the tattered coat of the boorish man spoke of travel. She ducked her head in greeting and sat at the end of their bench, closest to the door. Her gaze flickered to the gentleman, but he was intent on the book before him and did not stir.

The southerner leered at her chest, despite its slight budding. "You from Invercoe? Talard here is looking for land to purchase and a comely wife to settle down with."

"Welsh stone is what I said, Harrington." Talard smirked. "His lord of Invercallie requires a hundred ton to beautify the Fern Tower."

Harrington waved a dismissive hand. "Eh, his lordship will have his stone. The steam hammers of Swansea will sing their thundering tune, and the stone will be on the Great Northern Rail within a fortnight." He leaned toward Effie. "Have you ever seen these contraptions of James Nasmyth's? Powerful enough to topple mountains, they are." When Effie shook her head, he patted her arm and took a gulp from his ale.

"The 'ol Colossus of Roads would've liked to make use of them back in his day," said Talard. Effie knew that name. Thomas Telford had built the great Caledonian Canal that linked the east coast with the west. He'd invented ways of melding stone with iron plate, built bridges and aqueducts and roadways, altering the very face of the High- and Lowlands.

"To be sure," Harrington agreed.

Talard took a draught of his own, then blotted his lips with a kerchief. "Have you heard of the work done near the Ross of Mull? They say Thomas Stevenson, of the lighthouse Stevensons, is using stardust to fuel the lamp. A thousand times as powerful as those gas pumps of John Wigham."

"Lofty, that man is. He's got patronage from lairds all over the empire." Harrington put a finger to the side of his nose. "Guess it pays to wear a cloak and mask in the right company."

"Ah, I don't believe it," said Talard. "All this talk of dark fraternities sprouting up all over London."

Effie blinked. "He's using stardust?" Her mother had told her of the vapors the Star Readers inhaled as they foretold the fates of the world, but she had never heard of men using its properties.

"Dust of the Aether," said Talard.

"Meteorology is Stevenson's true passion," said Harrington. "He's even got that society he founded looking at building an observatory atop Ben Nevis."

"The giants will knock it down if the winds don't first," scoffed the matron of the wayhouse. Effie jumped. She hadn't heard the woman approach. The matron was a stunted crone whose curved spine shortened her even further. Wispy gray hair fell to her waist. Grease and blood stained her apron. "There's lamb in the pot. A cup for three pence, and a pint of ale for three more." Effie dug into her pocket and pressed the few bits she'd scavenged into the woman's hand. The crone's wrinkled brow furrowed, and Effie's gut lurched to her throat as she realized her mistake. One of the silver coins was embossed with the head of James VII of Scotland. An old coin from an outlaw king.

"Tsk, I canna take this, lassie." Effie's cheeks flushed, and her head rushed. She had to snatch the coin quickly, before Talard and Harrington saw it. Then she could flee into the forests and not look back. There would be no questions if she ran fast enough.

She reached out, but the crone jerked and the coins spilled to the ground, plinking across the stone. Talard lurched to his feet, while Harrington exclaimed. Effie scrambled to the floor, scraping her hands along the stone to scoop up the silver. She'd just reclaimed the last when a command thundered from the hearth.

"Bring that here." Effie raised her head. The gentleman studied her from behind his purple lenses. Malice seethed from him like a carrion bird circling a wounded prey. She froze for only a heartbeat before leaping for the door.

But his man from the courtyard, the one sleeved in plates of bronze, blocked the threshold. A backhanded swipe sent her reeling to the floor, her head ringing and jaw pulsing in agony.

"Now, I dare say," stammered Harrington.

"Most untoward," said the gentleman. "But you'll find I have little love for the queen's enemies." He stood and beckoned for his man to bring Effie closer.

Harrington's eyes grew large at the thinly veiled threat. "Yes, yes. Well, I think we can all agree on that count."

The room spun. Effie tried to struggle, but her arms were pinned and her legs wobbled as she was dragged toward the hearth. "My name is Edmund Glover," said the gentleman. "I have the privilege to hold Her Majesty's employment. If you are a loyal subject, I will apologize on behalf of my valet and will make restitution. But I do not believe either will be needed." He grabbed Effie by the chin. "I can see the fell glint of the fey in your eyes."

Talard gasped. "A fey? Surely not."

Glover gestured to the valet, who locked her arms behind her back. He searched within a leather satchel, pulling out a long syringe and a vial of clear liquid. Effie squirmed but couldn't free herself. She heard the crone's wheezing and Harrington's heavy breath behind her. She glanced at the highlanders and saw that the dirk had disappeared. Both men watched intently, hands folded with their cloaks. One nodded slightly when she met his gaze. The old ways,

Effie thought, for the little good it did her. But she would not dishonor her mother by cowering. She stared back at the Fey Finder with a snarl on her lips. "I am an honest subject who has done no wrong."

Glover's smile was a foul thing. "So we shall see," he said. He filled the syringe and tapped the needle. "This serum I've concocted turns emerald when mixed with human blood. Let us see what it does with yours." The valet forced one of her arms forward. Glover sneered. "Regrettably, I'm not sure of the exact location of your veins."

A bead of flame raced across her wrist as the valet's knife cut into her. Effie sucked in her breath but refused to scream, even as her blood welled and dripped to the floor. The Fey Finder dipped the tip of the syringe into the flow and pushed out a half-dram.

The fluids swilled liquids together, and the serum turned black.

"Most curious," said the queen's man. He tossed the syringe into the hearth and repacked his things. "We'll take her to the magistrate," he told the valet. "His lordship can decide the manner of her execution."

Effie howled. Outside, hunger had reduced her to sobbing fits, but now it seemed such a trivial thing. She kicked and scraped, trying to win free from hands that held her firm. Tears streaked her cheeks from the pain. Her blood sprayed from her wrist as she tried to claw her way loose. Glover danced out of reach, a look of disgust on his face. She could see drops of her blood coating his glasses and chin. Then something hard crashed into her skull. A grunt escaped her lips, and she collapsed to the stone floor.

When she woke, she was in Duncairn, the mound of wool blankets and goose-down bedding tangled and pinning her arms. She started upright and nearly fell from the bed. Scrambling free, she relit the bedside lamp. Her hair was damp with sweat, her pillows twisted in a jumbled mess. The nightmare's horrors had been real enough, years in the past. She had been a girl then, yet old enough to know better. Entering the wayhouse had been a foolish thing. And yet, she wondered some nights what would've become of her if she hadn't. It was, after all, the first time she'd heard the name of Thomas Stevenson.

The memory of that later meeting brought on a sense of joy, and she shook off the last scraps of panic. She had survived the day, and dreams, however horrible, could not touch her. It was still dark outside, so she sorted her blankets and lay back, determined to remain vigilant. But heavy eyes soon pulled her back into slumber.

This time piercing eyes chased her through an endless maze of streets, winking in and out like devilish fireflies. They swarmed around her, filling her with dread, flitting in to leech from her flesh and dancing back to leer with bloody fangs. She raced away, ducking down alleyways and across broken cobblestones, only to find them waiting, always ahead of her.

She jolted awake a second time, having gained little rest, but daylight spread through the curtains, and she decided there was no use wasting the morning with more foul dreams. Her gaze fell on her luggage as she pondered what to do with the early hour. The wisest course would be to keep the doors locked until the next train to Banchory departed. Graham's warnings echoed in her head. Foolish lass, she agreed. What had she mixed herself up in?

She grabbed a brush and yanked it through the knots in her hair. She had to assume the previous night's attack deliberate, a planned ambush. If it had been a random thing, then she had no more to worry from the imps as any other stranger in the village. Any one of them could be a danger at any time. But the things had surrounded her quickly, as soon as night had fallen. Perhaps they weren't brazen enough to strike within the village under the daylight. Or perhaps these creatures could only show themselves at night.

"Foolish lass," she repeated aloud, plucking a mirror from the nightstand and staring into it. The imps were not the only danger. The Sniffer would arrive in the afternoon. Best she be gone before either of them found her. Against fashion, she selected a slim bustle to wear beneath a sturdy dress the shade of tallow. She wanted her legs free, unhampered by the silly wire frame.

Her stomach begged for morning tea. She checked her belongings one last time before taking a deep breath and opening the door. By the time she'd closed it behind her, she knew she was going to do a reckless thing. Her mind was set, a force of iron that would not bend under the pressure of those who wished her ill. She'd felt fear before, and while she had no desire for heroics, neither would she cower and allow her friends to suffer for any lack of courage on her part. She had little time to be of use to Stevenson, but she would not return to Ben Nevis with mere tales of shadows. She refused to fail so easily, so utterly. The morning remained, and she would make use of it.

In the dining room, she sipped honeyed tea and worried a piece of toast slathered with berried jam. From what the fishmongers had told her, Robert Ramsey would not be found until later in the day. The fishermen had provided scant information at all, and she gathered the shopkeepers would offer even less. But she didn't need further confirmation something was amiss in the village. Not anymore. She needed evidence the imps were part of an Unseily Court and what their purpose was, if any existed, in coming to Duncairn. That left her with few options, but perhaps the Munroe girl would be more forthcoming than the men of Duncairn. If she could keep the lass talking, something useful might slip out.

The desk attendant was in no better mood when she found him in the lobby. His expression made it clear he would rather she didn't exist, but he provided concise instructions on how best to find the road to Montrose, if one so desired. And soon a crisp breeze buffeted her as she strolled from the village along a broad carriage road. Open fields rolled away to either side, spotted by copses of rowan and oak. The road was well-rutted and stony, cleaved into the countryside like a scar. The Munroe house lay a short walk from the village. The cottage was squat and ruffled, its stone walls weathered, its thatching disheveled from years of wind and icy rain. A low wall of stone ran along the road for a while, only to give up short of the pasture's end. Sheep bleated and shat, huddling in pockets for warmth.

Effie picked up the hem of her dress, though it was already well-soiled with muck from the road, and stepped carefully around the sheep's leavings. She'd not reached the door when it swung in and a ginger-topped head popped out. The man's cheeks were round and chapped. His eyes were sharp, peering at her as if she were a leper come to kiss him.

"What can I do for ye, lass?"

"Good morning, sir." Effie curtsied. "Can you tell me—is this the Munroe house?"

The door closed slightly. "Might be. And who's doing the asking?"

"Miss Elisabeth Martins. I've come…." She read the man's face and knew what would come if she mentioned the girl. She licked her lips, her determination wavering. "Come to…."

"I don't treat with solicitors, if ye've come to hawk some contraption from the city. Got no need for soot on my clothes or steam burning my hands. I keep me land with me own hands, as the good Lord did intend."

The wind stirred a tiny bell that hung over the threshold, causing it to chime. She studied it for a moment, noting the sprig of primrose wrapped around its handle. "I've come regarding the matter of Mr. Ewan Ross," she said, as a new tactic came to her. "I've heard queer talk of the events, but none in the village would relate such rumor."

His eyes narrowed. "Ye be kin to Ross?"

She shook her head. "No, but I was told your family has also met with unfortunate matters."

The man growled. "Be gone! I don't want any of your trouble," he snapped.

Effie pointed. "I didn't think primrose grew this far south. Do you have some in the fields nearby?" He blustered, staring at the sprig, and she knew he didn't. "It holds no power over the fey, despite its rarity. Some charlatan has sold you a useless ward. Did you pay a handsome price for it?"

Munroe glowered. "What would ye ken of it?"

"I know much of fey lore and would gladly share it with you. All I ask is a few details of your daughter's misfortune, all the better to help your family avoid such dangers in the future." Heavy lines formed on the man's brow as he considered. It was clear worry had plagued him for some days, and that he'd slept little over that time. "A simple iron cross would be enough to ward against the mischief of sprites and pixies," she added. It was a common device many of the country folk believed in, and though it panged her to lie, her words took root.

"That's what Father Murphy did say," said Munroe, nodding. The door opened a crack. "But alas, there aren't many details for ye to hear. My Sarah's not been right since the attack. All she can do is babble nonsense and drool herself aplenty. She keeps trying to wander off, but I keep her tucked tight in bed."

Effie deflated but tried to keep her tone pleasant. Her heart panged for the poor man and his unfortunate daughter. "How then do you know of the beasts who set upon her?"

"Oh, she had a spell afore falling into the stupor. Frightened and crying out, twitching at the sky as if the stars were to come crashing down, but lucid in her account. She were taking the path along the cliffs on her way home from Duncairn. She'd gone to the village to collect on some debts owed me for my wool. It was dusk, or as near enough as makes no matter. The beasts weren't tall, she said, but had heads too large for their bodies, and wicked fangs sharp enough to…." He fell quiet and his stare went blank. He turned to something inside the cottage Effie couldn't see. When he turned back, his eyes were moist. "They bit her, you know. Tiny marks ravage her arms. She gets in uncanny fits. I've tied her down, or she'll open her wounds again."

"How ghastly!" Effie recalled her own encounter and shuddered. "How did she manage to flee?"

"I don't know. When she didn't come back, I set out to find her. She wasn't far, lying in the fields at the edge of our croft. Thanks be to God I found her in time." He crossed himself and turned his gaze heavenward.

The pop and shudder of a steam carriage drew both their attentions to the road. The carriage rocked as its wheels found the ruts. Puffs of smoke trailed it like a tail rising toward the clouds. "Father Murphy attends her daily. It brightens her mood to see his presence."

Effie twinged in frustration. "Then I should leave you to your devotions and call at a better time." She had no intention of meeting with the good Father. Though the Church's teachings on the fey were often misguided, their beliefs and superstitions were closer to the truth than those proffered by most men of science. But it would not be wise to enter into discourse with the man, who would most likely ask questions she wouldn't want to answer.

Munroe started, as if coming out of a trance. His gaze focused on her. "Och, I've said enough," he barked. She felt his pain and almost reached for him—a simple gesture of support, yet one she knew wasn't proper.

"The Lord grant your daughter good health," she said, instead.

Clutching her dress, she retreated through the mud, ducking her head as the carriage wobbled past. The driver ignored her. He was too intent on keeping the wheels from sticking in the muck. But from within the carriage the priest's wizened face peered at her like an owl staring down a cornered field mouse. She refused to meet the man's eyes. It felt too much like all the doors in Duncairn were closing, trapping her without answers to its riddle, her options evaporating as the day slipped away like morning dew melting under the warm sun.

She didn't fancy herself a great detective, not even a passing one, but that didn't mean she was devoid of skills. She relished games of wit and deduction, playing them often with Graham. She considered that for a moment. Perhaps it would help if she spun the riddle into one she could play. She was an artist by trade and a Grundbairn by birth. Fey lore said the latter attuned her to the natural forces of the Isles, but she had barely any knowledge beyond that—other than her fondness for animals and theirs for her.

But she could render a picture in her head, keeping all the details in place as she layered different elements over one another. As a girl, she'd assumed everyone could do such a thing and was surprised to learn it a talent. A riddle was much like a rendering, with certain facts in focus and others distant or vague. The trick was to determine their correct order and significance in the overall composition.

She fell into a brisk stride. The assault the previous night left little doubt the other accounts of Duncairn held a strong merit of truth, so she would treat them as fact. Selkies had harried and killed Ewan Ross. Trows had battered Sarah Munroe, breaking her skull yet allowing her to live. Sarah's father and the poor drunken fishmonger were the only ones willing to speak of the fey, yet neither had much to offer beyond common superstition. Neither named trow or selkie as an assailant, nor a conspiracy between the attacks.

But they had to be related, intertwined within some cabal, if not an Unseily Court. They were too random for it to be otherwise. And to bind selkie and trow together would take intelligence or a large amount of power, or both. She therefore had to assume whoever led the cabal also knew the repercussions, the response London would send. That meant there was a greater game afoot, something worth the danger of an Inquiry. Another thought struck her, and she stopped short. Her focus on the attacks had omitted an obvious question, one the villagers wouldn't have an answer for regardless of how long she pestered them.

Why Duncairn?

There were eldritch places with mystical energies all throughout the Highlands, and yet this cabal chose the small fishing village to set their roots. Were they local fey or a wandering troupe? She scanned the withered cliffs and barren road. It seemed an odd choice, either way.

Perhaps that was the key, what she should've been contemplating all along. She had come to uncover those responsible for the malicious attacks, not root out gossip from the locals. They wouldn't know an Unseily Court from a spoiled potato. She didn't need a definitive account from them if she could find the imps on her own. Following her logic, there had to be a connection between Duncairn and the attacks. If she could only find it, the whole riddle might unravel. But the thought of prowling the countryside seemed as useless as an easel made of flower petals.

She planted her hands on her hips and let out an impatient huff. At least she could start by retracing Sarah Munroe's footsteps. Her father had mentioned a path near the cliffs, and Effie headed in that direction. Leaving the road, she strode up a tufted hillock and picked her way toward a giant oak.

A few birds fluttered around the tree, dancing from branch to branch. She considered them as she approached. It was said Grundbairns once communicated with woodland creatures as if they could speak the queen's tongue, but Effie couldn't recall her mother ever mentioning such a ridiculous feat. Rorie certainly appeared to understand her, and she was apt at guessing his moods—normally grumpy—but their interactions fell far short of conversation. Yet who was she to say what was once possible? Fey Craft had dwindled in the years since the Leaving, when the Daoine Sith abandoned their ancestral homes, and they had left long before Effie was born.

The market cats had certainly acted oddly around her. Perhaps whatever sense her fey blood imparted was as apparent to them as the scent of the daily catch. The notion held a sort of logic. Before Rorie, there'd once been a red squirrel who'd left acorns for her each morning for a fortnight. She'd never been able to thank the little fellow, but it'd been pleased to serve her just the same. A crow had once warned her of a sinkhole as she tramped near Glen Coe, and the dogs of her village often wandered by when she was at her baking. The last she chalked mostly to a hound's nature, but the others were tales similar to those spun about her ancestors.

She approached the oak as softly as she could. Would the birds warn her if the imps were about? They squawked and hopped among the leaves. One settled a bit lower, its coloring hazel and spotted. It eyed her and scooted closer, staring right at her. She stepped forward and held up an arm for it to perch on. The bird chirped and shuffled its feet, but in a rush of feathers the other birds took wing, and it followed. They soared away, back across the road to a distant copse of trees.

Feeling foolish, Effie trudged on. She might as well ask a worm to shake her hand. She crossed a small glen of muddied grass before mounting another ridge of hillocks. On the far side lay the path Munroe had described. It hugged the cliff top, the pounding crash of waves signaling the coast beyond. She reached the hard dirt of the path and tracked it to the horizon. She had no idea how far the site of the attack lay, nor in which direction. Yet guessing she hadn't come very far from the Munroe house, she started toward Duncairn.

She hadn't taken two steps when the bramble rustled. She yelped, then relaxed. Feeling the eyes of some gentle critter on her, she squatted down to appear less threatening. The bramble shook again, and a fox's head popped out. Its body was sleek and furry, its coat as ginger as rust.

"Hello, there," she said. She glanced around. The closest shelter beyond the bramble was some distance off. "You're a bit far from home. Hunting?" The fox yawned with a small squeak, stretching its front paws. It seemed amused by her.

"I don't suppose you can tell me more about the trows or the selkies?" she quipped, feeling absurd.

The fox whimpered, shying back. Its fur bristled as it sniffed the air.

Effie tensed. Her head swam as a jumble of thoughts crashed together. "Can you understand me?" The fox wriggled its maw and dashed into the fields, fleeing without looking back.

"Wait!" she called, but it was too fast. She stared after it, stunned. She'd seen understanding in the critter's eyes, the same glint of awareness Rorie often held. Maybe it hadn't comprehended the words, but it had trembled when she mentioned the trows. Her lips pulled back almost to her ears—or so it felt. A sliver of her ancestors had shown through, an echo of the blood that flowed through her veins. There was no doubt about it.

Another realization came. If the fox knew of the trows, their warren wasn't in the village. It wouldn't prowl such a crowded area unless forced. A gust from the sea buffeted her arms, washing away the warmth of the sun. Suddenly, the shadows around her stretched across the path as the clouds above shifted. The crash of waves below masked a disturbing quiet that hid underneath like an asp in the grass.

Effie calmed herself. She knew the trows harbored nearby; she'd been looking for them, after all. The fox's confirmation changed nothing. Determined not to let fear rule her, she continued on. The dwellings of Duncairn sprouted from the horizon, their rooftops coming into view far in the distance. Every so often smoke billowed on the water, puffing from a passing vessel. The path followed the cliffs, narrowing at times, rising and falling as the hills slouched toward the sea. She studied the ground as she walked, hoping for some sign of the attack—a marring in the dirt, or the thicket smashed and disheveled. But she spied no trace of an encounter, not even footprints scuffed the path.

She wondered if she wouldn't be better off chasing birds and foxes through the fields when she came across a ring of cairns surrounding a long barrow. The mound rested atop a wide bluff, its banks overgrown with grass and diminutive white blooms. It rose to her own height and stretched twice as long. The rocks forming the cairns were coated in moss and battered from the sea winds.

Goose pimples rose on her flesh. Fragments of fey lore flooded her head—dark tales of fey who guarded the dead, of ghouls and wights and other foul things meant to scare children. She stepped off the path and entered the circle. The barrow marked the resting place of some ancient warlord, perhaps. The Isles were full of them.

The underbrush crackled. Effie leapt from her skin, stumbling backward as the fox sprang into view. It stopped and stared, flicking its bushy tail. "You shouldn't do that!" Effie heaved. It regarded her in silence, and excitement replaced her fright. She stammered, her tongue not heeding the words she wished to speak.

The fox grumbled and darted across the path, halting on the far side. There it stopped and watched her. She edged nearer, taking each step carefully, but the fox showed no interest in moving, and she realized it waited for her patiently, wanting her to come.

It wasn't until she stood over it that she saw the cut in the cliff face that lead down to the beach. "There?" she asked, peering along the sand. The fox glowered as if she were as thick as stone. She huffed and glowered right back. There was no reason to be rude.

She spied nothing below, only a narrow stretch of sand. The fox yipped and pawed at the dirt. She almost asked what was below, and snorted. The poor thing was right: she was being dense. It had already shown her what it could. There was nothing left but to ignore the wee critter or trust it.

She scanned the barrow again, deciding she'd gone mad. There was no time to listen to foxes. She'd miss her train and be stuck in Duncairn another night. But wasn't uncovering the imps why she had come? Hadn't she asked the wee thing to guide her? Where was her courage if it stopped short of anything useful?

Her foot tapped.

"Och, all right," she said finally, hefting the hem of her dress. The cut descended steeply. She stumbled a few times on the trek down, her dress snagging on thorny grass, her boots skidding along exposed stone. By the time she reached the bottom, her gloves were torn and her hair tangled like a puffin's nest. The fox hadn't followed her down. It had no interest in the sand or crashing waves. It watched her from atop the cliff, as still as a pointing hound.

The beach led south toward Duncairn a short distance before petering out. A tumble of boulders halted the other direction where the cliff had given way at some point. The largest boulder was as big as a carriage, the smallest came near to her waist. Water lapped between them, swishing about in a foamy bath. As she stepped closer, a cleft in the scar darkened.

She stepped onto the first boulder, soaking her feet in the process. The added height revealed the cleft was an opening large enough for her to pass through. She gasped. Her heart thumped, pounding at her breast and sending a rush of blood along her limbs in skin-prickling waves. Thrill raged against fear, holding it back as a smile reached her lips. Spinning to face the cliff top, she found the path empty.

The fox had already gone.

CHAPTER 5

The surf zipped across the beach, waves dashing against the boulders in an echo of the salty wind buffeting Effie. She stood on her perch, again questioning her sanity. A fox had led her to a cave, a cave no doubt filled with devils bent on causing her mortal harm—those who had assaulted her the previous night, cracked the skull of a young girl, and killed one man. And yet, she wanted to go inside. The key to the riddle of Duncairn must lie within, and her curiosity wouldn't let her back down despite the danger. Graham would call her fool-headed. She had a few savory words for herself, too, but they were no reason to stand around wasting time.

Hiking up her tattered dress, she clambered forward, knowing she must look a state. Hair clumped to the side of her face, her boots were scuffed and laden with muck. She dared not glance at her dress; the hem had snagged so many times during her descent that she was surprised she remained clothed. A crazed woman sneaking into a cave. That was how tales of disaster began.

Bare sand stretched beyond the last boulder. Sea water lapped into the cave's entrance, a narrow defile that would become impassable at high tide. She dropped into the sand with a wet *thwomp*, and stepped gingerly across the foamy rush, trying to move as silently as possible.

The cave was large enough for her to enter without ducking, though a man like Munroe would've had trouble. Its innards came into focus as she left the bright of day behind. A passage sloped toward a shallow pool, one she had no choice but to slosh through, before it widened enough for several men to walk abreast.

Climbing from the pool were footprints, several sets coming to and fro, trailing deeper into the cave. They were human sized without evidence of claws—one good sign, at least—and a few days old by the pungent water welling in them. The sunlight dimmed as she pressed on but remained plentiful enough for her to see other shallow pools dotting the cave's floor. Clumps of seaweed stank of damp and mold, the stench hung thick enough to taste. But there was another scent, too. Effie stopped and breathed. It took her a minute to identify the smell—the putrid tang of rotting flesh.

A dark shape caught her eye, half-slumped out of one of the pools. She gagged and choked back her breakfast as she stalked closer. It was as she guessed—the carcass of a selkie, dead in its sealskin. Its tongue lolled from its mouth, its eyes vacant. Flies swarmed the bloated carcass. Effie frowned at the puzzle, glancing around. Footprints trailed from the entrance, yet the ground was barren of drag marks. The selkie hadn't washed into the cave, nor had it waddled in on its belly. It had walked in, succumbed to some malady, and been left to rot.

Covering her mouth, she stooped closer. The skin hadn't yet deteriorated. The thing had obviously died recently, certainly within the week. A black clump of sand spread beneath one of its flippers. The flies buzzed there thicker than anywhere else. She reached out a gloved finger and ran it just above the dried blood, feeling the crust atop its sleek fur. The trail ended at a puncture wound the size of her thumb. It was too large for a bullet, but perhaps a harpoon had done the creature in. She couldn't judge the size of one of those. Maybe the thing was stabbed in the attack on Ewan Ross, and wandered in afoot, only to collapse.

She rose from her haunches and started. Another corpse lay in the shadows a few feet away. Spinning, she scoured the cave in the dim light. Flies led her to a third and fourth selkie resting against the cave's wall. A chill ran through her bones. Harpoons would not have done this, not to all of them.

After stealing to the second corpse, she needed only a moment to spy the circular wound under its flipper, the blood staining the sand beneath it. The others had the same, but it was the last that froze her breath. A jagged piece of wood jutted from its wound, as if snapped off from a longer shaft. The memory of clattering wood rang in her ears, rebounding from a stone wall as she fled through the streets the previous night.

An arrow had slain the selkie. And its master was no doubt the same murderer who had stalked her.

She held her breath and yanked on the splintered shaft. The stone arrowhead slid free in a burst of pus and maggots, sending the flies swarming. She leapt clear and waited for the cave to stop swirling and surging bile to flush from her throat. She took the stone to clearer water, as far from the stench of decay as she could find, and washed the blood away. Beneath the grime, layers of runes were etched, their intricate lines woven together in a pattern with no end. Their meaning baffled her, but the level of craftsmanship was well beyond that of a common stonecutter.

A hunter of some sort, and a craftsman. She bit her lip but could only form more questions and no answers. A large, thundering wave shook her alert. In the dark, amongst the corpses of selkies, was not a time to dally over theories. She dropped the arrowhead into a pocket. There would be time for it later; the cave continued deeper under the cliff.

When she reached its rear, only the faintest crashing of the waves carried to her. The cave itself was deathly silent. She plucked the dagger from her reticule, not sure what good it would do against anyone, or anything, that lay in wait, but its weight steadied her nerve. The ceiling had tapered until its height lowered to just above her head. Against the rear wall, a blackened section spread above the remains of a campfire. The ash was days old, but it appeared the fire pit had been used frequently and for some time. Scattered about were a handful of blankets, all soiled and worn thin. Fish bones littered the area, crunching underfoot, and on a flat stone rested a kettle and jar of tea.

The selkies. She'd found their home, the cave where they lived in human form before setting out on foot to the countryside above. The blankets and kettle were meager, but from the tales, they preferred to live as seals, coming ashore only when a primal lust overcame them, stealing away the young lassies who caught their eye. The cave was more of a wayhouse than anything else.

She turned to the bodies, though she could no longer make them out. They hadn't been dragged into the cave. No, they'd been ambushed here, slain by one who knew their lair. The entrance was a distant globe of light, like a gas lamp at the end of a street. The daylight beckoned to her, its safety like a warm blanket, and she repelled the urge to sprint toward it and abandon her lunacy.

Ash stirred at her feet. She yelped, losing grip of her dagger. It thunked to the ground, and she scurried to snatch it back up. As she did, she felt the kiss of a frigid draft. The clue brought a thrill of excitement. Holding out a palm to gauge its direction, she followed it to a narrow defile a dozen yards from the fire pit. The cleft was perhaps large enough to store a chest of clothes, but it was too dark to see anything beyond her outstretched hand. Her legs trembled, the hair on her arms stiffened.

Both warnings she ignored.

The draft flurried into a gust, billowing her dress. The wind had to come from the surface somehow, and another entrance. She crouched and patted forward with her hands. As she guessed, the cleft continued onward, wide enough for her to shrug through.

She stared at it, knowing she'd come far enough, that she could return to Stevenson and tell him what she'd discovered, and he'd think none the less of her for leaving Duncairn. He'd likely praise her, and he and his fellow sympathizers would determine the best course of action. There was an Unseily Court lurking in Duncairn, or at least some dark cabal. The crown would make no distinction between the two. It had turned on its own, trows ambushing their selkie allies. There was no need to place herself in further danger. Except that the cleft held more riddles, perhaps a clue as to why the trows had butchered their cohorts, or even why they were in Duncairn at all.

A quiver sprang to life in her gut much like the night before, only its tickling was softer, more rolling, like being adrift in the ocean, spilling down swells only to rush up the next rise. The tiny bells of warning were so distant they sounded like droplets pattering from leaves after a summer rain. The sensation puzzled her. Was it her fey blood telling her to flee? She didn't think so; it felt different from fear.

Maybe her fey blood urged her to go on. She snorted and rolled her eyes. That was only what she wanted it to mean. Leaving now felt too much like fleeing. It was prudent, what Stevenson and Graham would beg her to do, yet at the cost of feeling powerless, the cost of knowing she needed their protection more than they needed her friendship. That cost was not something she could live with. It would plague her more than any of the nightmares from her youth.

She clenched the dagger in her teeth and shimmied forward, waving her hands before her. Crawling in a dress made for an awkward, jerking progress, but the ground remained smooth and level, hard dirt compared to the floor of the cave. The cleft snaked for what seemed like miles, leaving all trace of light behind. The wind whispering through the passage no longer stank of the sea. It smelled of the earth, of root and the metallic tang of buried rock. Her hands scuffed along until they met stone sealing off the passage. But still she felt the draft. She reached higher and found the passage continued, only to end a foot beyond. The pattern repeated itself, and she realized she was at the foot of a stair. Not a natural one, either. The angles were too precise, the spacing near symmetrical. Someone had carved the steps.

Clambering on hands and knees, she tried to keep her labored breath quiet, and after a sturdy ascent the walls sharpened into focus. Light peered down from above, its illumination allowing her to stand and creep forward. The stair dumped her onto a small landing. Its walls were chiseled into a smooth surface. Sunlight beamed from an archway to her left bright enough to reveal the base of another ascending stair a few paces to her right.

She gasped. Through the archway lay a chamber the size of a lord's bedroom. Within, the glint of silver and gold made her shield her eyes. A dozen mirrors reflected a sunbeam from a shaft chiseled through the ceiling, scattering the light like a prism. The beams washed over a treasure hoard fit to ransom a king. Silver plates were thrown in piles, many dented as if beaten. Scattered around them were gilded cups, trinket boxes, larger chests clasped in bronze, necklaces, broaches, and bracelets. Fragments of carved stone cluttered the center of the chamber as if broken from a single, larger piece, while shelves pressed against the walls held iron pots and jars blown from colored glass. Roots dangled from the ceiling, poking down from damp earth.

She guessed at her bearings. The barrow. The cleft's stair had led her under it. Her eyes flitted back to the shattered stone. The sarcophagus must have been large when intact; its width appeared to equal her height. She thought again of the tales of ghouls and wights, and dismissed them. They were only meant to scare children. The gnawed-on carcasses of small rodents cluttered the center of the chamber, and the stench of piss wafted from every corner. No spirits had risen from the grave. The chamber was a warren, and a recently used one at that.

Footpaths cut across the floor in a web. She padded forward, her eyes still getting used to the light. On one of the plates balanced a pile of coins. Of all shapes and sizes, some had their faces worn away while others held visages of Robert the Bruce and earlier kings. The coins were centuries old, their minters long forgotten. Near the pile, flutes, pipes, and metal chimes were strewn about. Hearty sticks lay atop some of the plates, which were so dented they could be used as bowls. A rusted sword lay forgotten on a cloth-of-gold cushion, its blade rusted and brittle. Effie doubted she could lift the thing without it falling to pieces.

In the corner of the chamber, a large bundle of canvas caught her eye. She picked her way to it. The canvas was lashed to a framework of bone and wood, which fanned outward from a sturdy central pole, shrinking in size as it went until the tips were the thickness of a flute. The bones must've come from a cow or horse, for they were larger than any bird she knew. The wood appeared to be yew, strong yet very flexible. She pulled on one side of the contraption and saw the wing take shape. Dumbstruck, she felt a grin yank back her lips. Not one wing, but wings. It was a contraption meant for a single flier. At the heart of the thing, a steel box banded in leather was sewn to the canvas. An organ's worth of miniscule pipes ran a hectic pattern across the leather, with a pair of trumpet-like horns projecting to the rear. Effie squatted and ran a hand along the propulsion system.

She'd heard of such devices before. Graham had told her of one the Americans were trying to manufacture, and every few months the newspapers would speak of a day when people would travel primarily through the skies. The thought of swooping around the clouds like a bird enthralled her, but Effie couldn't fathom a world like that. The weight-to-thrust issue was the first problem. In order to achieve solo flight, one needed to bring enough coal to maintain a constant boiler pressure, and the heavy load would keep grounded any aircraft unattached to a gigantic lift system like a balloon. The only means around such an issue was to use a different fuel—one that was lighter, burned hotter, and still didn't melt the contraption itself—and the only fuel known to fit those criteria was one most wouldn't touch.

She lifted a small latch on the propulsion system and uncovered the substance she'd predicted. Stardust was difficult to obtain and existed only in small quantities, making its value greater than that of the richest metals. Yet for all its rarity and wondrous properties, it was not coveted by more than a handful of engineers. Proper society frowned on any substance born of the fey, and most would have it outlawed if the choice were given to them. In the great universities, men of learning debated theories and devised plans for great machines, but for all their advancements, bigotry still infected the great circles of power that held in stranglehold the nations of the world.

Stevenson used stardust in his lighthouses and suffered for it. Though as maritime beacons were no longer at the cutting edge of technology, the matter was not as scandalous. Naturalists considered his work more art than science, and the blending of the natural setting with architectural principles was esteemed. Shunned by men of science, Stevenson was lauded by those on the outside looking in. He wasn't alone. Other men of art and nature, and a few rogue inventors, used stardust to power their devices. Their exploits, failures, and crimes were sometimes noted by the newspapers, though often Effie would hear of them from Graham.

Her wonder overwhelmed her. She tugged and prodded at the contraption, identifying the throttle mechanism and straps for a flier's arms to control the wings. She deduced how the thing achieved lift and imagined the wings soaring over the cliffs like a giant bat.

Eyes closed, she was lost in a dream when chittering echoed from the edge of the chamber. Her heart hammered, and she had to catch

herself from toppling over. The noise came again, this time answered
by a chorus of grunts and cackling. It rebounded against the walls,
emanating from a wolf-sized hole on the far side of the chamber
from where she had entered. She scrambled backward, kicking over a
stack of plates. Their clatter rang louder than the bells of the High
Kirk of Edinburgh. Terrified, she shrank back against the chamber
wall, frozen like a trapped rat. Beneath the guttural chittering, clawed
feet scraped across the earthen floor. A host approached, the fiends
of the warren.

Effie tore her gaze from the hole and forced it to the ground
beneath her feet. Focusing on each step, she staggered from the
chamber. She passed under the archway and flung herself into the
shadows of the landing, just as the beating of a drum began. The
thump, thump, thump boomed to the fey pulsing in her gut, which
wound into something immediate, the herald of something she
couldn't understand. A wail of pipes joined the drum, blown in
piercing notes. Shadows played against the mirrors as figures entered
the chamber from the hole in the wall. Effie caught sight of one in
the glass. It stood like a piglet rearing on its haunches, with the snout
of a boar and the eyes of a hawk. Fur as dark as peat coated the
creature, who spun and hopped, dancing to the clamor made by its
fellows.

Trows.

Naming the imps did nothing to calm her. She fell against the
stone, not daring to breathe. A dozen entered the chamber. Some
snatched up dented plates and began beating them in discord to the
drum. Chimes crackled against the shrill of pipes like the howling of a
beast stuck in the moors. A fiddle started, a banshee's wail ripping at
the tendons of her neck. She wilted under the terrifying melody. She'd
abandoned her dagger back into her reticule but didn't dare move to
fetch it out. The drums thumped faster and louder. Some part of her
knew in a moment they would cease, and she feared the silence that
would follow. Her small measure of safety would be ripped away,
exposing her to them. She had to flee while she had a chance. Sliding
a foot along the wall, she scuttled her rump after it.

She eyed the stair descending to the cave. But the drums stopped
her. The way they echoed reminded her of the cramped passage

below, of crawling through the dark. She trembled. It was too easy to imagine the trows skulking after her, raking with their claws, biting with snapping maws. They were smaller than her and could move faster. Next to the descending stair, the second stair continued upward. If she was wrong, she would be trapped. But years of poring over Stevenson's designs had taught her how to picture how spaces fit together, and she knew the surface of the cliff was not a dozen feet above her.

Sucking in a breath, she dashed across the landing. The second stair curved widdershins as it ascended. Each rise shrunk and roughened until she bolted along an earthen ramp. The ceiling crushed down, forcing her to scramble on hands and knees until the ramp ended at a blanket of peat thick enough to trap out most of the sunlight.

The drums boomed louder. Chimes gnashed together in a high-pitched squeal. The peat above stunk of putrid mold. Effie punched it aside and thrust her head through, gulping in fresh air. She shimmied out of the hole and patted the peat back down, scraping her hands raw in the flurry. A rock would block the entrance better, but if she'd managed to escape unheard such an action would surely alert the trows.

She picked up a smaller stone anyway, ready to fling it at anything that poked through the hole. It had opened next to one of the cairns, on the far side of the barrow from the coastal path. Ready to pounce, she waited, listening. If she'd escaped without their knowledge, she had no cause to race blindly along the cliff. Confined within her dress, she stood no chance of outrunning them anyway. An instinct told her it was better to stand and fight than allow them to drag her down from behind. Her gut still reeled as if it could hear the uncanny cacophony below. In her head, trows danced around her, hunger etched on their demonic faces. She could almost sense them and point to where they stood in the warren beneath her feet. The cool evening air that kissed her cheeks tormented her with its malevolence. The tang of sea salt, so welcome as she burst through the peat, soured into the rotted stench of four selkies decaying before her.

Selkies slain with arrows etched with runes, in a warren where trows sprang from dark tales of centuries past, bent on mayhem and murder. Stevenson's investors were scared of the Hostmen of Newcastle, as matters of money scared many in this age, but their fear was misplaced. In Duncairn lay the true horror. Effie swallowed. When the Sniffer reached the village, he'd have to be a simpleton not to start an Inquiry. And he'd be justified in doing it, too. Stevenson's hopes of keeping the matter contained had quickly evaporated. Silence would not keep them safe.

Despair nipped at her until her mother's voice wafted through the fading sunlight, a calm lullaby summoned from deep in her memories. It was not her fey blood but the steel of her heart, that given to her by the love of family. It reminded her to hold strong, and it banished the haunting visions that plagued her thoughts. She glanced over the mess her clothes had become and ran her hands through her hair. Disheveled and trembling was not how she had been raised. Thoughts of her mother's scowling disapproval warmed her a bit, and she was finally able to steady her breath. The fey pulsing dimmed until it was only an echo at the back of her thoughts.

The sun was near to setting. The distant crash of waves and the buzz of midges darting about the grass were the only sounds. Nothing emerged from the warren. They hadn't followed her. She rose and fixed her appearance the best she could. With the stone clutched in her hand like an anchor against the oncoming darkness, she hurried toward Duncairn, eyes darting to every shadow as if Black Donald were at her heels.

CHAPTER 6

Effie leapt from her skin. The rustle came again, and she froze, peering into the alleyway. It was only a stray mutt digging through refuse. A night bird had set her to fits a moment before. Since the barrow, every scrape or squawk had become a trow stalking her, its thirsty little eyes leering from the shadows; its tongue salivating, lolling over jagged teeth, claws like a raptor's talons ready to rip into her flesh.

She scurried through Duncairn, shying from anyone who passed, until the St. James loomed before her. Its windows were filled with amber light, and she wanted nothing more than to rush into its warmth. But ice gripped her spine and brought her up short. Within the hotel, the attendant hovered over a man lounging in one of the sturdy leather chairs near the hearth. The man smoked a pipe, a newspaper held crisp before him. The attendant poured coffee, setting the cup next to a plate of biscuits. The pair spoke: the guest with terse gestures, the attendant replying with courtesies Effie didn't think him capable of, bobbing his head and deferring to the other man's inquiries. Something about the new guest gave her pause. His coat was of a stiff, gray wool, well-kept but simple. His shoes were polished, glinting off the flames from the hearth, but not expensive. The way he barked at the attendant spoke of position, but the clothes displayed little notion of wealth.

The word barked in her head, and she jumped as it was repeated aloud. "Sniffer," whispered a voice behind her.

She spun and found the younger fishmonger strolling past. He stopped and nodded to her. "Came in on the afternoon train like the flux, giving the constable what for and needling others as he passed."

Effie pursed her lips. After what she'd encountered under the barrow, she wasn't sure the queen's man had it wrong. A thought passed her to slip the man a note, but she cringed at the treacherous notion. Their involvement had never done an ounce of good.

"Nae worry, Miss Martins. He'll not bother you none," said the fishmonger, misreading her expression. He bobbed his head again and started off before jerking to a halt. "Bless me brains for porridge, I almost forgot. Rabbie Ramsey's in the Poet, if you're still looking for him. Though I'd get there afore he gets too far in his cups, I was you."

Effie brightened slightly. It seemed the first bit of good news she'd heard since leaving Ben Nevis. She wished the fishmonger a good evening before turning to study the queen's agent. Like making a sketch of one of Stevenson's projects, she made a mental note of his appearance. It might be she'd need to recognize him in the future. For all her time living amongst the Scots, she'd only run into three other Sniffers, yet she supposed that had more to do with the waning of their profession rather than any skill or luck on her part. As the decades passed and the fey population dwindled, London's Parliament found it increasingly difficult to justify the expense of the queen's Fey Finders. Now, only an odd dozen remained for the whole of the empire. Still, each encounter had left its mark on her, the run-in with Edmund Glover most of all. Her eyes narrowed to slits at the memory of that disgusting man. No, she would certainly not have any involvement with their ilk. She wouldn't trust them to scrub her boots.

The hotel was closed to her while the man lounged in the lobby. He would sniff her fey blood the moment she stepped inside. And even if he didn't have the natural ability, she wouldn't risk a casual conversation with him. Their ilk had other means to root her out. She'd seen firsthand the use of their serums and the brutality of their methods. That left one place to go: the Blind Poet and Robert Ramsey.

She found the public house near the station. It was lively so close to dusk, as the denizens of Duncairn retired from a long day's work. The reek of sour beer had not lessened since her arrival, nor the haze of pipe smoke billowing out of the narrow entrance. Inside, dingy, olive drapes clung to walls of dark-lacquered oak. On the wooden panels between, scraps of poetry were scrawled, some legible, most not. The chalk had faded where drunken shoulders had rubbed it, and smeared where drinks had spilt. A panel above the bar read, "Gie me ae spark o' Nature's fire, That's a' the learning I desire." Another, high on the far wall read, "And on distant echo borne, Comes the hunter's early horn." The words flickered under the light of two giant chandeliers.

The only women present were a pair of hags in tattered shawls and stained dresses. Effie felt them appraising her, and when she glanced their way, they laughed. The men weren't any kinder. The drunk ones gawked at her openly, while the rest scowled or whispered to those next to them. She recognized one of the fishermen from the docks; the man's stare made her throat run dry. The drunkard from the fish market perched at the bar, but when she nodded to him he turned away.

"Are ye sure ye wanna be here, miss?" asked the bartender. His meaty arms were bigger than her neck. "There's a braw coffeehouse down the street what serves the gentler folk. Ye'd find better custom there."

She leveled a cool gaze at the man. She wouldn't be so easily intimidated, not by a bunch of ornery louts, not after the horrors she'd encountered only an hour earlier. She strode to the bar. There was no need to shout her business for all to hear, even if every eye already watched her. But she'd only taken two steps before a chair scraped on the floor behind her and a calloused hand snatched her arm. The man flung her around and pulled her close, his whiskey-drenched breath spilling over her.

"I hear you've been asking after me." The man swayed as he spoke. Though his face pointed at her, his eyes were unfocused and cloudy. "What does one of your kind have to say to old Rabbie, eh?" The hand tightened and her arm began to go numb. "I bet a pretty lass wants to use him, convince him to do himself harm. What says you to that?"

She gagged at the stench of him. His clothes were soiled from days of use. His shirt was ripped and what looked like dried blood splotched one side. Dried sweat perfumed the dirt and grime, overpowered by the stink of something rotting. She fought the instinct to struggle and lowered the hand she'd meant to slap him with. She doubted she could win free, and even if she did, she had nowhere to go. Besides, Graham wouldn't have placed her in harm's way. There had to be more afoot in the man's appearance than what it seemed.

Studying Ramsey, she tried to breathe without her nose. "You are recommended to me by a dear acquaintance, but perhaps in error. I was not informed I would meet with such a rude welcome." She spoke softly, so others couldn't hear.

"Rude!" he spat, cackling. In his mirth, he staggered backward and almost pulled her over. She regained her footing only by snaring the back of a chair, causing its occupant to snipe at her.

"Och, leave off," boomed Rabbie. He wasn't the largest man in the room, but Effie guessed even the brawny fishermen would be wary of him in a fight. Something about him spoke of a steeled wolf. "Over here, then, trickster." He waved, releasing her. She followed as he ambled to a table shoved up against the back wall.

He slumped into a chair and gulped down the thick, black beer from the pint in front of him. He seemed for a moment to forget she was there. Then he rounded on her. "Dear acquaintance, is it? Don't hold back on Rabbie, now, or I'll know it. Give us a name."

The other denizens had resumed their conversations, but Effie still felt their attention on her. She leaned forward and lowered her voice. "Stuart Graham."

"Graham, is it?" He rubbed at the scruff on his cheeks. "Aye, he consorts with the like. Well-known in those circles, he is. He could do."

She frowned at the odd words. From the far-off cast to Ramsey's gaze, she wasn't certain they were addressed to her. Something was clearly wrong with the man. Trying a gentle tack, she asked, "You accused me of wanting you to do harm to yourself. Why? Is it common for young women to offer you such propositions?"

He sneered. His lips pulled back to reveal teeth as putrid as his breath. "They call you tricksters. Always mocking, yer kind is. But you won't mock me any longer. Aye, no one pulls the wool over Rabbie Ramsey. I have too keen a wit." He tapped the side of his head with a thick finger. As he raised his arm, she noticed again the dried blood on his shirt. A small patch looked wet.

"Are you injured, sir?" She reached across the table. Ramsey jerked backward, slapping her hand away and nearly tumbling from his chair.

"I won't have it from you!" His head started twitching about, as if he were tracking a midge in flight. "You'll get yours soon enough," he mumbled.

Her gut tightened at the threat. He knew she was a Sithling. Trickster was a common moniker the Scots gave her people. And perhaps he meant her harm, but she didn't think so. The man's murmurings and twitching tugged at a memory from her past. She'd seen someone bewitched once before. A Star Reader from the Trossachs had put a friend of hers in a trance in order to rob her. The songspell had crept over her friend like a silky web and caused her to act out of sorts, as the man before her did. Effie had foiled the spell without realizing it by singing a counter-rhyme her mother had taught her. But there was no music in the public house, and the cacophony the trows raised was surely too far away to affect the man here. Yet Ramsey's far-off gaze and strange actions left little doubt he was not fully in control of himself.

She needed more time to decipher how the Fey Craft was accomplished, so she fumbled in her reticule. "I have a bit of a thirst," she said, pulling out some coins and offering them to Ramsey. "Would you?"

He held up an empty pint glass and grimaced. Begrudgingly, he scooped up the coins and swayed toward the bar. She scoured his clothes as he went. Perhaps there was some contraption about his body winding a soft tune only he could hear, but she couldn't fathom something so small as not to be noticed. She thought again of the Star Reader, and of her friend, Gabus Säurbaum. Her friend's precious gems were at the center of that affair. What was wanted of Robert Ramsey? If he'd stumbled on the trows, why hadn't they slain him as they'd tried to slay the Munroe girl? Or as they had the poor selkies?

Or as they had her?

She started, her eyes bulging wide. Digging into her pocket, she fetched out the tiny arrowhead she'd pulled from the dead selkie. Its runes seemed to glisten under the flames from the chandeliers. Selkies weren't known to hunt in packs; they weren't known to hunt at all. And each was wounded in the flank. If they'd worn shirts, she was sure they'd be as soiled as Robert Ramsey's.

The arrows weren't how the selkies were killed; it was how they were bewitched! The trows had forced them to attack Ewan Ross. The knowledge seeped in, knotted riddles untying only to reveal tighter, more complex ones beneath. Cold sweat beaded on her flesh. The room spun as another realization dawned. A trow had shot an arrow at her, not to kill her but to make her do their bidding. The realization brought more questions than she had time to consider.

Ramsey returned, a jug of whiskey tucked under one arm, a trio of pints clutched between his hands. His clothes were ragged enough for him to have spent days in them, and the stench confirmed the same. She studied the blood crusting his flank. The ointments and cloves in her reticule, used for treating wounds, were of no use. She needed to pluck out the arrowhead, and there was no way the man would let her do that while awake. Getting him to pass out from drink was one option, but it would do her little good if he did so within the Poet. She could barely lift one of his arms.

He squatted back into his chair, sloshing beer onto the table as he set down the pints. "Generous with your coin, don't think I didn't notice." He swilled from one of the pints, for the moment content, though she harbored no illusion she had won the man over.

She cast her gaze about, trying to think of any reason they should leave. By the bar, she caught the stare of a man who'd just arrived, the angry fisherman who'd accosted her on the docks. He was alone, the scowl on his face forming deep gullies in his cheeks. Her eyes lit up. A plan formed in her head. Not a good one, and certainly not a smart one, but it would have to do.

"Do you know that man at the bar?" she asked. She indicated the fisherman. When Ramsey turned, she forced a smile for the fisherman's benefit and added, "He told me all about Ewan Ross."

"Ross?" barked Ramsey, loud enough for the whole public house to hear. The fisherman flinched. She chuckled, holding the man's gaze for a moment before turning toward Ramsey. She clopped a hand over her mouth for good gesture, feigning embarrassment. Ramsey shook his head. His brow furrowed. "What of him? What're you getting at?"

She peeked and found the fisherman stalking toward them, his eyes burning with fury. Her heart pattered faster. "Tell me of Ross. Did you know him well?"

For a second, clarity reached Ramsey's eyes. "Aye, he was a good man. What happened...." He drifted off, then started and reached for a beer.

"I bade ye to leave," said the fisherman, hovering over their table. "Ross were me best mate, and I will not have a spectacle of his death. Not by the likes of ye."

"Och, quit your whinging, Calum," said Ramsey.

"Mr. Ramsey has been very generous in his accounts," offered Effie. "Unlike your rudeness, sir."

The fisherman bristled. "What have ye said?" His fists clutched, knuckles whitening. "Ye should keep your gob shut."

Ramsey thumped down his pint. "It's my business, ain't it? Bugger off!"

Calum raised a fist, balking. As he did, Effie kicked the table. Two of the pints toppled, spilling beer over Ramsey and herself.

"Bloody arse!" howled Ramsey. He shot to his feet, gripping Calum by the shirt. A string of curses flew from his lips along with a jug of spittle. The fisherman returned them, his face going red, the veins of his neck bulging. He snatched Ramsey's arm, and the pair grappled, staggering about the room and knocking into chairs and tables.

Ramsey swung wildly, his attack feral but hindered by too much drink. Calum held his ground better. He clouted Ramsey twice across the temple and drove a fist into the man's gullet. Ramsey grunted in pain and dropped to a knee.

"Oi, out!" roared the bartender, waving a truncheon and storming forward. Effie calmly pulled out her chair and picked up the jug of whiskey. Shame followed her, but she couldn't afford such emotion. Besides, the result was without doubt a better one than what the bewitched Ramsey had intended for her. She only wished it hadn't come at the expense of so much attention. Word of the scuffle, and her part in it, would spread through Duncairn like a fire on a pool of oil. She snorted. For all the attention she'd already received, she might as well worry over a broken branch on a felled tree.

She reached Ramsey's side and slung one of his arms over her shoulder. "Help me, please," she asked Calum. The fisherman stood dumbstruck, as if uncertain how he'd come to stand where he was, with blood on his fists and a bruise welling on his cheek.

"Out!" barked the bartender. Calum started and dropped his fists. At Effie's gesture, he bent and scooped up Ramsey's other arm, hauling the man against him. Ramsey moaned as he stood, but he allowed Calum and Effie to walk him outside. She directed them around the side of the public house, to an alley lost in shadows.

They laid Ramsey on the cleanest spot of ground they could find. Blood ran wet from underneath his shirt. The wound had opened during the scuffle. He clutched at it feebly, his moans growing softer and weak.

"I never struck him so hard." Calum blinked at her. "Ye put a spell on me!"

"Don't be ridiculous." She dropped to Ramsey's side and started rooting through her reticule.

"Are ye some trickster come to hex the entire village? Looking to trade our jewels for our souls?" He retreated as he spoke, his face contorted, his stare locked on her hands. He signed a cross over his chest.

She drew out her dagger, unstopped the whiskey, and doused the blade. "Of course I'm not." After pouring a healthy dose over Ramsey's wound, she took a swig. It burned down her throat, tasting heavily of peat. Ramsey shuddered, trying to roll about, but she held him firm.

Calum's shriek was louder. "I'm off to fetch the constable. He'll ken what to do with ye!" He stumbled backward out of the alley and raced away.

Effie cursed. As if all the denizens within the Poet weren't enough of a bother. A clock started in Effie's head. She hoped the constable wasn't near. She needed time to work. Precious seconds to flee, her primal self screamed, but she wouldn't leave Ramsey in his current state—ensorcelled and bleeding in an alley—even if she didn't need the man. She ripped open his shirt and propped him until she could see the puncture in his side. It looked shallow enough but inflamed, like a ruptured boil grown to the size of a tea biscuit. Blood leaked from it, and a yellow-ish pus that stank of decay.

"This is going to hurt, I'm afraid," she told him. She held a breath to steady her hand, and probed with her fingers. Ramsey cried out, suddenly lucid. He thrashed against her and she almost toppled over. She put her weight against him and clung on until he steadied.

With the dagger, she made a quick slash across the wound. In the dim light, she couldn't see anything but the blood that welled into the opening. He clawed at her, trying desperately to win free. From the street drifted the mumble of gossipers. Soon someone would seek them out. Calum would return with the constable. She had no time for delicacy.

Tossing the dagger, she plunged her hand into Ramsey's flesh. Her fingers slipped about, prodding and digging, until at last she found hard stone. Clutching the arrowhead, she yanked, winning it free just as Ramsey's fist crushed into her jaw. She flew back, arms and legs flailing, and landed hard on her rump.

Ramsey roared and fell limp. Scrambling to her reticule, she snatched up a small vial. Inside was a thimble's worth of Salt of Hartshorn. She unplugged it and put it to Ramsey's nose. Jerking awake, he winced as the pain returned to him. He took her in, with his bloodied shirt and throbbing wound, the dagger thrown nearby, and shouts growing louder from the street. With a clear gaze, he blinked.

"Beg pardon, lass, but who the bloody arse are you?" He rose to his elbows as she handed him a cloth to press to his side. Her jaw felt as if a horse had kicked her. A welt had already begun to form, and she was thankful none of her teeth felt loose.

"Can you walk?" she asked, unsure how much of his prior state was from drink, from Calum's fists, or from the bewitchment.

"Need we?" he asked, though she could see a cunning in his eyes that hadn't been there before. He reached for the whiskey and chugged a mouthful. Clenching his teeth, he heaved himself upright.

She gathered her things, then helped him gain his feet and let him lean against her. "I'm a friend of Stuart Graham's. You brawled with a man called Calum, the constable is on his way, and there's a Sniffer at the St. James set to hound anyone who knows anything of the fey. There's also a host of trows skulking about, bewitching any they come across if they don't kill them outright. As their victims go, you were lucky."

He belched and drained more of the whiskey. "Sounds about right," he grunted. "I ken a place. Let's get there before I pass out again." She nodded, and together they staggered away from the Blind Poet, deeper into the gloom falling on Duncairn.

CHAPTER 7

R amsey left a trail of blood, droplets painting an unsteady line,
until Effie grabbed a blanket from a wain they passed and
wrapped it around him. Not many were about as they hobbled
through the streets of Duncairn, and those that were hustled about
their business with only a curious glance. The streets were dark, lit
only by gas lamps spaced every dozen yards. Ramsey wheezed and
shivered, but his steps were sure and his stare hard.

Effie left him to his thoughts. She had enough of her own
battling within her head. Could she trust the man now that the
bewitchment had apparently dissolved? How much would he know of
the occurrences around Duncairn? And more so, how much would
he be willing to share? On one hand, Ramsey represented an ally she
sorely needed. On the other, he already knew more of her than she
liked of any stranger, and she risked everything if he were caught by
the queen's Sniffer or bewitched again.

They looped through a series of alleyways and side streets, each
turn taking them farther from the heart of the village, until they came
on a quiet lane that ended at a stone wall broken by a single wooden
gate. The wall rose to near the top of her head. The backside of a
three-storied building loomed on its far side, timber-framed and
sagging with age. Ramsey unhitched the gate and ushered Effie
through. A patch of weeds stretched from the wall to the building, lit
only by moonlight. A small stable hugged the wall to her right, the
quiet huffs of sleeping horses coming from within. As Ramsey led her

across the barren earth, she caught a whiff of roasted pork and some salt and leek affair, with a hint of warmed bread swirling in the background. They carried from a door someone had propped open on the main building, which let out warm torchlight in addition to the rich scents. Her stomach rumbled in approval.

Ramsey strode for the door, and they entered a hallway that was clean and cheery, if not worn and narrow. The walls were splashed a deep burgundy, with vibrant gold trim, and adorned with paintings of hunting scenes from the countryside. The clank of pots and dishes came from an opening to the right, but Ramsey led her through to a room off the opposite side. It was a small serving area for the staff. A sturdy table crowded most of the space, and a matching cupboard filled the rest. Through the wall toward the building's front, the din of fiddle, chortle, and conversation could be heard.

"An inn?" she asked.

"The best in Duncairn," replied a man, popping his head into the room from the hallway. He wore a black apron over a white shirt, his sleeves rolled up past his elbows. A thick mustache billowed as he spoke, though his hair was greased and well kept.

"The Tattered Grouse," rasped Ramsey, sinking into a chair. "A fine and honest place, despite its owner."

The man snorted. "Ah, Rabbie, always a charmer. I heard ye shuffle inside." He looked closer and started. "Oi, yer bleeding all over the floor!"

"We have need of assistance," said Ramsey. "A pull of some thread and a needle." He winced. "And drink—a dram for medicinal purposes, and another to keep the spirits up. Maybe a third to keep the chill off."

"I'll fetch Bessie." The humor fell from the man's face. He took them both in with a grim nod and hurried away. His shouts echoed down the hallway.

Effie went to Ramsey's side and tried to study the wound. He shied and waved her away. "It's not bad, not that deep."

"You've lost a lot of blood." She planted her hands on her hips but felt awkward glowering at him. She wasn't the man's schoolmarm, after all. She found a chair of her own and slumped into it, her feet thanking her for the privilege.

He pushed back into his seat, trying to hide the wince as he did. "Now what did Graham assure you I'd assist thee with?"

"Only that you'd help in some manner befitting a friend. That he'd tried to contact you but hadn't heard anything in quite some time."

"Ah, I see the way of it." Now that they were focused, Ramsey's eyes held a sagely depth. She could see now why Graham accounted for him. "You're Stevenson's lass." She bristled at the insinuation, and he put up a hand in apology. "No offense meant. I've heard of you, is all. The Sithling who tamed a bear. Graham didn't say as much, but he told me of the bear's obedience, and I worked out the rest from his account." He took a deep breath, thinking a moment. "It must be a dire strait for them to send you out here alone."

She pointed to his bloody flank. "I should think they were right in sending me." Her bark was as much to steady her own nerve as to scold Ramsey. Meeting a stranger could be bad enough. Having one know of you already was enough to drain the blood from her face.

"Och, I do thank you." He made to stand, eyeing the cupboard. "Do you have a thirst?"

"Stay," she commanded. "I'll get it." She found a couple of glasses and poured from what remained of their jug of whiskey.

"What do you remember?" she asked. She took the jug back to her chair and set it out of his reach. He would pass out soon enough, and she desperately needed answers before he did.

But Ramsey only sipped at his glass, savoring the whiskey's bouquet. "I've lived in these parts all my life. Had run-ins with many a hogboon and selkie before, even a pixie once. I ken most of them in the area and am happy they call me friend. But the fey had all been acting strange for a few weeks, I'd noted, so I set out to converse with a fellow I know, one of the skin-shedding persuasion if you get my drift. Only he never showed, and I woke up bleeding, staring at your lovely visage."

"So you know nothing of the trows? Or Ewan Ross?" His blank stare answered her questions. She related both accounts and continued on with her arrival and discoveries. He gawked and cursed, gripping his chair hard as she described the warren beneath the barrow, and their meeting at the Blind Poet.

"I ken the barrow you're describing. Folk have always spun tales of dark spirits there. I always thought them superstitious prattle." He took a sip and ran his tongue along his lips. "Trows, eh? They're supposed to be nasty buggers. Sure, a hogboon may give someone a fright, and pixies are known to laugh their wee arses off playing their little tricks—moving stuff about, a broom or cup or the like—but neither mean any harm. Attacks? Murder? No, never. I knew something darker were afoot. I knew it in me bones, and curse me for a fool for wandering about with blinders on."

"You said the fey were acting strange. How so?"

"Leavin', most of them. Those who've lived in these parts for centuries, packing up and trucking off as if the Black Donald were hounding them." He shook his head. "They used to speak of trows in the area, but not for three hundred years at the least. Dark times ahead, if they've returned."

Effie shivered, remembering firsthand the wickedness trows could enact. But something nagged at the back of her thoughts. "Trows are said to dwell where the dead are lain, haunting those who live nearby, but have you ever heard a tale of them crafting weapons to bewitch people?"

"Nay, it is curious, that," he said. "How is it you came to know I was bewitched?"

"It was clear in your eyes, and the wounds the selkies had matched the one in your side. Once I plucked the arrowhead out, the spell was broken."

"And if that hadn't worked?"

She swallowed and reached for the whiskey. "I hadn't really considered that. I'd seen someone bewitched before, but it was done with music that time. Stopping the music stopped the bewitchment."

"Can I see it?" he asked. She offered the pair she now possessed, one cleaned in seawater, the other still bloodied. He plucked one up and inspected it under the lamplight, rolling it about between his fingers. "Made of flint. I've seen fisherwives hang similar baubles on their hearths to ward away evil. Thunderstones they call them, the Lord knows why. But those are simple things with crude circles etched on them. Nothing so delicate as this." He ran a finger over the runes. "This took a master to carve."

"Or powerful Fey Craft," offered Effie.

"Aye," he admitted, setting it on the table.

Fire ran down her throat as she drained the rest of the glass. She relaxed as its warmth spread to her shoulders, working at the tension found there. "I'm afraid I've made a mess of my time in Duncairn. Soon those who were already wary of me will know of the Blind Poet. By sunrise, I doubt there'll be an ear in the village who hasn't heard the gossip. The Sniffer and the constable will be looking for me. Possibly for us."

He grunted. "It's not as bad as all that. A night doesn't pass without some bloke being tossed from the Poet. I know Calum and will set things right. He's not a bad man, only scared. They must all be, for them to be as tight lipped as you say. Usually they're flopping their tongues about faster than a fish hauled on deck."

He paused long enough to take another drink. "But it would be best if you stayed from sight. The queen's man is not a danger to scoff at. The villagers fear their kind more than they do the fey. None want the London government meddling in their affairs. Things get printed in papers, trade gets disrupted, the village becomes the butt of jokes. The men of Duncairn only want what all men want: to have their word taken seriously. Their rude welcome was no offense meant to you."

Effie smirked at the irony. She and the Sniffer, two strangers who'd come to take their word seriously, shunned under the fear they'd turn the village into a mockery. "What do we do now?"

What felt like a year passed as Ramsey contemplated. He hefted the stone. "We find out why they didn't kill me, and if more folk are bewitched. That is the heart of the matter."

Ramsey's advice was sound, but Effie wasn't as certain they saw the whole picture. "From the tales I've heard, trows are cruel, but it isn't their way to plan and scheme. It's possible they aren't the ones behind the attacks. Where did they even come from? Could they have been drawn here by some greater power?"

"Bah," Ramsey scoffed, a little too forcefully. "If it were more sinister a plot, why draw the government's attention? Ross and the girl, those attacks were clumsy. I'd wager the trows aren't playing at anything more than havoc. The stones could've been in the barrow to start. They might not even ken what the things do."

Effie crossed her arms about her chest. She raised an eyebrow. "Do you really believe that?"

"Nay," he spat. He grimaced as he wriggled into a more comfortable position. But he'd barely stilled before starting and slapping his hand on the table. "I'd near forgotten. Twelve days afore I was to meet with my acquaintance, I heard word of a theft in Montrose. A regiment, passing through to drill in Aberdeen, swore a quarter of their munitions had gone missing while they were billeted overnight. Not enough to warrant more than setting the constable out to question the local toughs, but two days later I hear of a silversmith whose coach breaks down outside the city. By the time he's got it fixed, his pistols have disappeared.

"I don't ken if it fits with this business of the trows, but it doesn't sound good. You may be right, bugger it all." He slid his glass toward her and she refilled it, pouring another for herself for good measure. She needed something to kindle her temperament. It felt like the cold from outside had crept into the small room, tendrils of darkness snaking forth, entangling her in an icy clutch.

She bit her lip, not caring for what she was about to suggest. It was a direct betrayal of Stevenson's wishes, the opposite of why she'd come, but if it would offer a measure of protection to those in Duncairn, it was worth the sacrifice. "Shouldn't we send word to the queen's agent? Tell him of the trows and their warren? Surely, whatever detriments the government would bring to Duncairn would be outweighed by the protection granted."

Ramsey balked. "As at Stonehaven, where a trio of hogboons were lined up and shot; or at Arbroath, where two lasses were hanged as Songsmiths, despite the cries of their parents. Nay, the government would only bring force of arms. With fire and blood, they'd come, and never mind what fey or human they'd kill. And in the end, they would know nothing of trows or selkies, or of any greater plot afoot."

She leaned forward, pressing. "Are we then to let the trows roam about as they please?"

Ramsey's eyes narrowed. "There will be a reckoning, but one of our determination. We have more friends than you might think, yet it is foolish to act without first rooting out the danger we face. The full brunt of it."

Begrudgingly, she conceded the point. It had Stevenson's voice in the logic of it. He always warned against the dangers of acting in haste.

"The stones are a place to start, then," she said. "Perhaps a Spae Wife could tell us more."

Ramsey shook his head. "Theirs is a knowledge of healing, not bewitching. What we need is an expert in stone lore." He sighed and studied the table. "There's a prospector I ken who may be able to help." He pulled his gaze up to meet hers. "He dwells in London."

She read his face, recognizing the same cast she'd seen only a few days before atop Ben Nevis. Stevenson had worn it then. "You want me to go," she said. It wasn't a question. He nodded, and her neck tightened. She was being sent away, having done little and nothing to help Duncairn, nor Stevenson and his investors. They'd hardly be thrilled to learn an Inquiry was justified. Her voice softened in shame. "What will you do?"

"I'd best start warning the local fey, those who haven't fled, that is, and searching for any under the trows' bewitchment." He waved her away when she started to protest. "I know you wish to help, but it's for the best I do it alone. The trust they've shown me is theirs to give, not mine. And as you've said yourself, there're too many who can point the Sniffer in your direction."

She cringed as the words rang true. It was best if she left Duncairn. But she stifled the sense of guilt, the creeping fear of lacking that imbues defeat. Before her sat one man saved by her actions, and she would assure more joined the tally. They needed knowledge to unravel the greater conspiracy, and that knowledge was in the distant hands of an expert.

An expert in stone lore.

A grin played at her lips. "You said we needed an expert in stone lore. I may be able to do one better than your prospector. The last I'd heard, a friend of mine was in Edinburgh, a gnome and master of stonecraft."

Ramsey's brow raised. "If he's in the city, there's a librarian who would ken where he is."

"She," Effie corrected. Gabus Säurbaum, the very gnome she'd found bewitched in the Trossachs not so many years ago. She knew the librarian Ramsey spoke of too, a kindly woman who worked at the University. The woman was known to aid the fey, secreting them tomes of knowledge that were otherwise sealed to non-students. Effie had met her only once, years before.

"I can take you south to Inverkeilor," said Ramsey, "to catch the train to Edinburgh. It's only a short ride, and there's no sense in risking Duncairn again."

She frowned. "You're wounded. I'm sure I can find the way."

Ramsey grunted. "Bessie'll see me stitched up by morning, and I know the shortest route. I needs be setting off anyway." A throat cleared from the doorway. The matron of the inn hovered there, her eyes narrowing on Ramsey. "Speak of the woman," he muttered.

"I'll nae have it from ye," she snipped, folding her arms under a formidable bosom, "dragging blood and dirt and who knows what else into me inn." She turned to Effie and gave a fleeting smile. "There's a bath and clean frock in the room down the hall. I'll have a supper for ye as soon as you're done." To Ramsey, she barked, "Come on then, the needle is waiting."

Without waiting for a response, she spun and stormed away. Ramsey followed, as meek as a scolded schoolboy, shuffling along with his hand clutched to his side. Effie retrieved the stones and tucked them away, then found the bathing room and latched herself within. The warm suds melted away the grime and soothed her sore legs. She gave herself to the bliss, letting go of her thoughts and worry over the day's events. She meant only to rest her eyes for a moment, but when she opened them the water was cold and her fingers puckered.

The dress the matron had found for her was simply cut, of a hearty gray wool. She shrugged into it and tied a ribbon about the waist. She thought of her things left at the St. James and wondered if Ramsey would be able to retrieve them. There was nothing of value, only a few garments and paper for sketching. Her dearest possessions she kept within her reticule.

She found a stew waiting for her in the room near the kitchen. As she set about it, the inn keeper returned and told her Ramsey had already eaten and departed. "It was best for me if folks didn't see the pair of you leaving together. But he'll be waiting for you just down the road, at the southern edge of the village. I lent him one of me best horses to go along with his own."

Effie thanked him for his generosity as he bobbed his head and left. When she'd licked the last of the stew from the bowl, she rose and slung her reticule over her shoulder. The thunderstones she tucked into a pocket of her dress. Her feet protested at having to move again, but she ignored their tenderness and the dreariness behind her eyes. As she stepped out the backdoor, her gut quivered as if someone ran a feathered duster along the inside of her belly. She gripped it and begged the stew to settle. She took a few more steps before her wits awoke. The tickling was not her dinner.

Tiny bells clanged furiously, appearing as if the warning in her head had been somehow masked.

A form emerged from the shadows near the gate. Wood clacked against stone. A soft cackle breathed across the courtyard. "Clever lass, come to bend knee to your master. The Laird of Aonghus, I have styled myself. Fitting, I believe, for the master of chattel." She peered into the darkness, barely making out the crooked shape hunched over a thick cane. It rapped the cane against the stone wall, each strike crawling under her skin.

"I've decided you may live and serve me, Sithling," said the creature. The yard flexed, and trows skittered forth, crunching weeds and scuffling the dirt like the herald wind of a maelstrom.

She didn't wait for them to reach her. She ducked her head and ran.

CHAPTER 8

Manic cackling filled the yard. Effie's gut lurched at each rasp. Her heart thundered. Her legs churned as fast as she could manage, but the heavy wool dress entangled them. It made her feel as if she ran against a stiff wind. Trows sprung into her path, raking with jagged claws. Hopping in glee, they chittered, teeth glinting under the starlight. There were so many that she couldn't keep count. From the stables came a terrified screech. The poor horse's panic exploded within her, its clarity like a painting of one of her own memories. She forced it out of thought and focused on the gate. If she could reach it, the night might protect her.

Might. A whimper passed her lips.

The gate loomed within reach, but the ground was a mire from constant treading and the damp weather. Her foot slid as she stretched for the latch. She lost balance, and her momentum slammed her into the gate's wooden planks. Fire exploded at her knee. Claws snared her arms as she clung to the gate, scraping her flesh raw. She swatted at them and fell backward, splashing into the muck.

On her rump, she scrambled from the trows. A pair darted between her and the gate. Three more encircled her as she spun toward the inn's door. The distant beacon of light was at the edge of a cold abyss, as unattainable as the barred gate. A cold thought told her that her life hurtled toward its end.

Gulping in cold air, she forced her eyes to remain open. She would not give in to the terror. She would find a way to make the vile creatures pay for their prize. She screamed, hoping those in the kitchen would hear, but only a meek croak uttered forth.

"Quiet." The self-proclaimed laird hunched as he walked. His features were hidden by a dark cowl wrapped over an emerald cloak, but the hand clutching the cane was gnarled and tufted with white hair. He stood no taller than the trows, a head at least beneath Effie, yet there was no doubt he ruled their every action.

"I did not give you leave to speak," he continued. "You will learn your place, Grundbairn, or be a feast for my pets." He gestured toward the trows.

"What are you?" Effie spat.

The laird's eyes narrowed. He wiggled his cane and a trow leapt forward, sinking its teeth into her shoulder. She shrieked, flailing at the creature, but it skittered out of reach. Its lips curled into a foul grin, blood dribbling from them.

The laird clicked his tongue. "You will learn of your master in due time. As we slay our enemies, the minions of that southern bitch, you will come to adore me, as all my pets do. But first you will pay for the slave you stole."

Effie steeled herself against the pain. Despite the leering trows and the steely glare of the laird, she managed to calm herself. Stevenson had long chided her that stubbornness held little value if her wits were left behind. An asp doesn't lurk in the grass to strike at a rolling stone, after all. "The queen's regiments will root out your Unseily Court," she probed. "They will come with rifles and torches and hang you from a rope. You've been foolish, letting these creatures attack so blatantly."

She braced for another assault, but the laird's body jiggled as he laughed. "Unseily Court, is it? The Sidhe Bhreige do not hold to your lowly courts. We are Ri Sith, your masters. And I give no credence to that human woman and her metal crown. Let her come with all her warriors."

Effie's jaw worked, but she had no words. Pieces of a puzzle fell into place. The laird wanted an Inquiry. He coveted the attention. But did he truly mean to challenge the might of London? The notion was ridiculous. It felt as if she'd solved a riddle only to realize she'd toiled at the wrong one.

"Your arrival brought me great joy. I hadn't seen a Grundbairn in some four thousand years," said the Laird of Aonghus. A distant sadness crept into his voice. "I thought perhaps you'd come to join me of your own accord, the desire to cast down the whelps who betrayed your forebears burning furiously within you. But you are as weak as they were. I see now you must be led to vengeance like a lamb to shelter."

He wiggled his cane again. A trow emerged from where the laird had beckoned, a bow drawn between its claws. A stone head tipped the nocked arrow. She didn't need to see the runes to know they were there.

Her resolve slipped as memories of horror flooded her. Rotting selkie corpses moldered under a swarm of flies. A drooling Ramsey barked at her, eyes vacant and dead. Graham warned against her coming to Duncairn; like a fell spirit, his words carried on the wind. Searing pain throbbed at her shoulder, the breath of the trow and bite of its teeth still kissing her flesh. The light of the inn paled and swam away into the stars. Only a black void was left for her.

The laird cackled. "Bend the knee, and you will no longer feel such despair. Bend it, and you will know only victory."

She started at the creature's knowing look. He knew what was in her head. Had he forced it there? Anger swelled in her chest at the invasion, and she shoved against the dark thoughts. But she'd as soon crumble a stone wall with her breath. The images of death and fear would not fade. They only strengthened. Gritting her teeth, she abandoned the effort for a new tactic.

A flower lay crushed in the muck a few feet away, yet still it lived. She focused on it, something beautiful and pure, and tried to clear her head. The flower shone bright for a moment before sliding away. Again she tried, and again it slid. Gasping from the effort, she pulled harder, reaching out across the yard, straining every muscle.

And something else snapped into focus. Something unexpected that had been in front of her the whole time.

It had been so obvious. Her first night in Duncairn and again at the warren—she should've figured it out. The odd throbbing sensation in her gut, with its tiny warning bells, was a projection of the trows cast by their fey blood, an internal Knowing of their foul presence.

She could sense them!

Each trow throbbed in her mind like a beacon. She could even point to those behind her. But that was not all she sensed. A tendril of something rich and earthen came from the stables. She clutched at it and yanked, and smelled a sweet bite of hay undercutting the vileness of the trows. Within the stable, the terrified horse bucked against its stall; its powerful rear haunches battered the gate. Wood splintered, shattering as the horse won free.

The image flashed in Effie's head as if she watched it happen, but it was a moment before the loud crack rang through the yard. The horse, a gray mare spotted with puffs of white, bolted across the muddy ground. Effie blinked, not understanding how she'd seen what the horse would do before it occurred.

The laird hissed and trows recoiled in surprise. Primal instinct took over, and she thrust her confusion aside. Snatching up a pebble, she hurled it at the trow wielding the bow. It flinched as it loosed. The arrow whistled through the night, snaring her hair, the shaft whipping across her face.

She yelped and batted the thing away. Her cheek burned but was undamaged. The trows frenzied, some fleeing the galloping mare, others rushing toward her. The bowman drew another arrow and put it to the string. Effie lurched to her feet and charged the laird. She smashed her knee into the crooked figure, pummeling with her fists. Pale flesh and ivory hair glimmered as the cowl was knocked aside. He grunted and toppled to the ground, glaring at her with fiery eyes shielded by a bulbous nose.

"You cannot hide," he roared. "I know your scent and will loose my hounds on you!"

Her hands found the gate's latch as the bow twanged again. She spun through the gate and heard the shaft clatter against the stone wall. A trow lunged at her. She slammed the gate on its outstretched claws. It squealed and drew back. She rammed the gate closed.

Her legs felt like solid stone. She wanted nothing more than to stop and curl up in a shadow and hide, but her feet were already fleeing down the street. She grabbed the hem of her dress, raising it so she could run faster. Darting down an alleyway, she fled into an adjoining street, casting about for anyone who could help her.

But the streets were silent in the early morning. The sun had yet to brighten the sky, and the village slept. Her lungs burned. She slowed, knowing she couldn't keep up the frantic pace for long. She needed a safe place to hide. Ducking into the shadows of a garden, she searched and listened.

Across a narrow alleyway, a carriage house stood. Its large front door was barred, but a side entrance was left ajar. She held her breath and peered back toward the inn. Nothing stirred. She waited a moment longer to be sure, then scampered over to the carriage house, slipping inside. The steam carriage within was marred by age, its copper tubes dented, its doors scratched, and the iron of its boiler caked with rust. She checked the front bench—drivers often kept a brace of pistols there, for protection on the road—but it was barren.

Next to the coal bin, she found the handle of a broken shovel. It was better than nothing, so she snatched it up and returned to the door, peering into the darkness. She had to find Ramsey. The man could be in danger. He also had horses, which seemed a better choice for flight than her own legs. She could pound on a few village doors, too, but what would she tell those she roused? If the constable were fetched, she'd as like be placed in shackles as believed, and the Sniffer would have her before the morning cocks crowed.

Fool, she thought, suddenly. Why didn't she try to sense them? She reached out as she had in the yard, trying to focus on their presence. But nothing returned to her, not even a faint tickle in her gut. Perhaps they'd abandoned their pursuit. She snorted. She'd grown thick in the head from all the running.

Her shoulder ached from where the trow had bitten her. She cast about for a rag. Finding a scrap clean enough, she pressed it to the wound. As soon as she did, her knee began to ache, and her arm. "Fine, then," she quipped, tossing aside the rag. She would just ignore it all.

The air outside had thickened by the time she returned to the door, becoming a damp sea mist. Darkened patches of street could hide a thousand trows, but she couldn't wait for them to come. She had to move or risk being frozen in terror of what might crawl out of the night.

Creeping along the outside of the carriage house, she forced herself to choose slow, deliberate steps. Shadows hid her as she worked her way up the street. But the village seemed larger, its outskirts ever distant. Surely, hours had passed, but still the sun refused to peek over the horizon. A horse whinnied somewhere off behind her, and her heart jumped, the jolt pimpling the skin of her arms and neck.

She giggled, letting out a slow breath. A few more paces took her to the shelter of a giant oak. There, she crouched and leaned against the solid trunk. She could finally spy the village's end, the rows of houses halting abruptly, the land beyond dipping so that a ditch was formed along the road.

But the road was empty. She cursed. Where was that blasted man? She contemplated for only a second before a fluttering sound, like a kite buffeted by the wind, swooped overhead. A shadow in the sky soared over the road and disappeared. It was too quick for her to make out more than the size of the thing, which would dwarf Rorie.

The laird could find her anywhere. She could not outrun him. Her hands shook, and she tried tucking them under her arms, but that only made her entire body tremble. The fluttering came again, closer. She sunk into the tree, making herself as small as possible. The thing swooped low. This time she followed it as it sailed along the road. Its wings had ribs and slats exposed. Its back puffed a blue exhaust, like a tail made of gas fumes. Strapped to its body was a trow, whose arms were lashed to the structure of the wings, giving direction and control.

She'd seen the contraption in the cave, but still her jaw dropped in wonder. She watched, dumbstruck, as the trow flew down the road and looped back up into the night, disappearing into the stars. It was beautiful: the grace of its movements, the brilliance of its engineering. She waited for it to come around again. If only Graham were there to watch as well. The man shared her enthusiasm for modern devices, but especially so when it came to flight. He would've pointed out just how the wings gave lift, what better materials could be used in the structure, how to tweak the design to make it more efficient.

The fluttering grew louder as the trow came around for a third pass. The hairs on the back of her neck bristled, and she realized with a start how long she'd been distracted. With its arms lashed to the wings, the trow couldn't do anything to her directly, but its circling was a beacon for the others.

She whipped her head about and caught movement on both sides. Hefting her dress up, she lurched forward, bolting from under the tree. The winged trow shrilled. An arrow whistled from the darkness, sailing behind her to thunk into the giant oak. She dashed away, not looking back. The edge of the village flew past in a blur, the empty road loomed ahead. But it was too open, too dangerous.

She slowed and lumbered into the ditch beside the road, gasping for breath, trying to swallow and wet her throat. The winged trow whipped overhead. She couldn't remain where she was, but she couldn't go back. She cursed the trows and cursed Ramsey. The latter had barely escaped her lips when one of the beasts came scampering out of the dark. Its teeth were daggers, its chittering an unnerving siren.

The trow launched at her. She swung the broken handle of the shovel, cracking it against the beast's head. The thing cried out, wobbling on unsteady legs. She cracked it again, and it dropped. She refused to think about the wet crunching sound of her strikes.

"It attacked me," she whispered, arms shaking.

The winged trow arced toward her, hurtling down the road from the edge of the village. But she knew not to pay it any heed. She scanned the ditch and road, and her eyes locked on another trow. The one clutching the bow, an arrow nocked and sighted on her. She braced herself to leap aside. Cold sweat ran along her neck, each bead a tickling hand of ice. The fluttering wings whooshed, darting at her in a deafening crescendo. The claw wielding the bowstring relaxed, letting loose the arrow.

A pistol barked. Its report echoed through the night. Effie dove as the trow crumpled. The arrow wobbled in flight, sailing wide. She hit the ground and rolled, coming to a crouch as the winged trow barreled overhead. The shot had startled the creature, and it dipped low enough she could make out a wart on the thing's nose.

Her arm reacted without thought. She swiped at the trow with her shovel haft. The jolt from the strike shot fire up her arm and numbed her flank from hip to ear. The trow's head snapped back and twisted, its arms falling limp as it darted past. The wingtips hit the ground first, cartwheeling the contraption several times before it slid to a stop among the grass.

Effie tasted blood and realized she'd bit her tongue. The shovel haft had ripped from her grasp and was lost in the dark. She rubbed her quivering arm, feeling naked without the weapon. A horse stomped nearby, and a mounted figure materialized from the dark. Relief came as she spied the second horse in tow.

"Bloody hell!" spat Ramsey. "Where did a little shite like that get such a wonder?" He trotted the horses forward until she could make out his face. He held the reins in one hand, a six-barreled revolver in the other.

"The Laird of Aonghus, I'd imagine," she replied. His brow furrowed in confusion. She ignored it. "And I had thought the beasts had ensnared you again, or worse." Her pain and fear turned her tone to steel, but she had no mind to apologize.

"Time be for talking later," said Ramsey. If he'd taken any offense, he didn't show it. "Let us press on from the village. Some would've heard the shot and will be out to see what's happened. Best we not tarry and be forced to answer any questions." He alighted and held out the reins. "Here, take hold of these while I collect the creatures."

Effie climbed to the road and snatched the reins, holding her tongue. Anger wouldn't serve at the moment, and Ramsey needed to deal with the trows, not assuage her fury. It came from abandonment, she realized. A part of her had believed the man had fled, leaving her to face the trows alone. She took a deep breath. Well, he hadn't, and crying over milk that hadn't spilt was childish. Still, her nerves were raw, and grasping onto indignation was helping to keep her on her feet. Without it, she feared she'd crumple into a ball.

Ramsey had shouldered the one he'd shot, and after he flung the body over a saddle, she pointed at the trow she'd clubbed. "There's one just there." Ducking his head, he scrambled into the ditch. He groaned as he hefted the trow's body, and winced with every step as he trudged back to her. The beast appeared like a child in the man's arms. Long ears flopped with each step, and its lanky arms hung limp.

She marched to his side and winced, putting a hand to her mouth.

A stench rose from the trow's tattered fur that would rival the worst privies in Glasgow. "I hope you haven't opened your stitches," she said, trying her best to ignore the smell. "Let me take a look."

"Och, they're fine." He waved her away. "Let's go and see what's become of the poor flier. You smarted him right with that club of yours."

She smiled as he led the way. They found the winged trow sprawled across the road, still harnessed to the contraption, its tongue lolling from an open mouth. Blood trickled from a dozen cuts and scrapes, but its chest rose in shallow breaths.

"Out cold," mumbled Ramsey, nudging the wings with a boot. "Don't know if that makes me happy. Guess I'll figure that out when it wakes."

"Can these things talk? I've only heard them hiss and gnash their teeth. Hellish noises but nothing sensible. I wonder what it would have to say?"

"We'll see on both accounts." Ramsey tucked in the trow's wings, and with Effie's help slung the trow over the second horse, contraption and all. With no room for them left in the saddles, they walked the horses down the road until they were hidden from the village by a small knoll.

Ramsey circled back a few times to ensure they weren't followed by beast or man, and when he finally returned to her he planted himself with his arms folded. "Now what's this about a laird, and what's befallen you?"

She told him of the crooked fiend and her escape from the inn, how the laird had spoken of chattel and controlled the trows as if they were his hounds. Ramsey listened with a grumpy intensity, his nostrils flaring as he grunted and spat curses.

"I don't ken anything of the Sidhe Bhreige. Some fey coven, perhaps? I'll need to check on the Grouse. Bloody hell, I didn't think they'd be bold enough to come into the village, let alone rampage through it! Who knows who could've seen the creatures?" He shook his head. "This laird is none too subtle. He'll have the queen's men on him within the week, if not sooner."

A chill ran down Effie's back. "It appears that's exactly what he craves."

"Och, I can't make sense of it." Ramsey dropped a hand to his pistol and glanced around. "But no sense squawking about it here. Dawn's coming and you've a train to catch. I've a friend we can dump these critters with, though I can't take you to his place direct. He'd not appreciate me giving up his secrets as you wouldn't yours."

She shook her head. "I understand, but with this laird, and these attacks, why should I go on to Edinburgh while you stay in peril?" He stammered, but she cut him off. "And not just you but all of Duncairn as well? I won't flee when others stand and fight."

Ramsey shook his head. "I don't mean to call any to arms, only to warn the local fey. Besides, how can we win if we ken nothing about the trows?"

Effie huffed. Ramsey's logic was sound, but it still ground at her to leave him surrounded by devils. "This laird has revealed himself. Whatever his plans, he's a greater threat now than before. He'll hunt until he catches you." She ignored that the statement could be said for her as well.

"Aye," said Ramsey. Through the gruff tenor, she could hear fatigue. He stood tall, but his face was sallow and eyes heavy. She studied the horses and thought of all the long miles he would need to ride before his task was done. It seemed foolish that he would take her all the way to Inverkeilor when he could instead steal a few hours of sleep. But she would not risk returning to the Duncairn station, not with a Sniffer and trows about.

Her arms prickled in excitement, and she realized she stared not at the horses, but at something on one of the saddles. She could ride well enough, but there was another option. She forced herself not to grin as she turned back to Ramsey. "Well, if you'll accept that danger, then the best I can do to aid you is to ensure you get some rest. Help me unstrap this thing." With giddy hands, she began undoing the harness of the wings.

"What?" barked Ramsey, realizing what she intended. "If you think...Look, there's no chance I'll let you...." He blinked and clenched his fists.

"It's no more ludicrous than you spending the night escorting me when you should be recovering your strength. No more ridiculous than riding about with a trio of trows slung from your horse and no idea what else is about to jump at you. True, I could take one of the horses and go by myself to Inverkeilor, but what would I do with it once I reached the station? And we don't know what's out there waiting for me, or for us. With the wings, I can fly over any danger and stash the contraption before anyone's the wiser."

"But you've no idea how to work the controls!"

She grabbed the throttle and tested it in her grip. "I've studied it enough. And if these dimwitted creatures can figure it out, I'm sure I'll do the same. I've worked with stardust before and know its properties. You know that I have."

His snort was so loud it could've come from one of the horses. "Stubborn as a goat, you are, and like to get yourself killed for it."

"I don't need to make it very far, and I won't be seen. By daylight I'll have hidden this thing and be well on my way to Edinburgh."

His body stiffened, preparing another argument. Then he swatted a hand and relaxed. "Your health be yours to ruin," he mumbled. He turned to one of the saddles. Digging out a pair of coachman's goggles, he offered them. "To keep the wind from blinding ye." She accepted them with thanks, and they worked to strap the wings onto her back. The harness wrapped around her shoulders, chest, and waist. The trow who'd worn it had been a deal smaller than her, and it took some doing adjusting all the lengths. But the weight was surprisingly manageable. The compartment housing the stardust felt no heavier than a tramper's rucksack, and the wings folded out like she had a few extra coats draped over her arms.

With the goggles fitted snugly over her cheeks, she knew she must've looked like a giant moth as she turned to Ramsey. "Fare thee well," she said. "I will return as soon as I can."

Ramsey's eyes turned soft, and he placed a hand on her shoulder. "Keep your head down in the city, Effie the Sithling. The strangers you find in the pubs there aren't the kind, generous souls you've found out here."

Grinning, she gave him a wink and wheeled about so she pointed south. An open field and the blanket of night stretched before her, with the stars above fading toward dawn. A lump clogged her throat, and she knew if she stopped to think it would only threaten her resolve. She hit the throttle and felt the wings push forward, the straps of the harness digging into her shoulders.

The contraption whistled on her back, shoving her forward. But the force did not free her from the ground, and she had to stagger across the field to keep from toppling over. Catching her balance, she hit the throttle harder. Her stagger became a sprint, wings spread wide, each step lighter than the last. After a few paces, her toes barely kissed the ground. She leapt and felt the wings catch the wind, pushing her further into the sky.

A giddy scream escaped her lips. The wondrous sensations of the ground shrinking beneath her, of whipping through the air, of feeling light as a feather, erased all memory of the evening. She ducked her head to try to find Ramsey, but the view straight down was dizzying as she sped along. She jerked her arms, and the wings wobbled and spun. Crying out, she lost all sense of direction. Thrusting her arms out wide, she forced herself to stare ahead. The wings corrected, helped by the wind, and she found again the stars and land.

Taking a deep breath, she resolved to never do that again. Instead, she moved her arms a hair, in unison, and felt herself begin to bank in a circle. She corrected and turned the other direction, then pulled her shoulders back and climbed, giving the throttle more power. The lights of a village sparkled in the distance. She set a course to avoid it, her body relaxing as her confidence grew. If Graham could witness her now! She could almost see the pride, worry, and marvel warring across his brow.

Time melted away, and for a long while there was only the caress of the wind and the fluttering of the wings. The black void of the open sea spread out to her left, and soon she could make out pockets of dark and light shadows outlining the trees and hills. Dawn was less than an hour away, and with it the end of her flight. She yearned to stay aloft all the way to the city but knew that for folly. Even under different circumstances, she would need to make a less conspicuous approach.

Another village emerged from the night, and she angled toward it. A thick wood surrounded the set of buildings, which nestled against a hill. She searched for an open spot in the foliage and wondered if it wouldn't be easier to continue on to the next village. Or was that only her desire to carry on up in the air?

The notion elated her more than anything had in a great long while, but the feeling was short-lived. Suddenly, a lance of pain seared her spine as if a hot knife ripped the muscles there free. She screamed, her body contorting and arching backward. The ground blurred as she flipped head over heels. Her arms slipped out of place, and the wings thrashed. Cold sweat gripped her as she plummeted. The pain made her body lurch from side to side. The trees screamed closer, the wings refusing to catch the wind. She could smell pine, and then she was crashing.

CHAPTER 9

The intense pain vanished as quickly and oddly as it had arrived, leaving her flushed and trembling. She yanked hard on the wings, jerking the throttle down, straining to gain altitude. The wings flipped vertical. For a moment they seemed to lift, but her feet slid forward and she spun in a circle. One wing caught in a branch and tore, the ripping sound draining the blood from her face. She tucked as her momentum hurled her past the tree, shoulders scuffing through the needles, pulling the smaller branches along with her. Wood splintered in sharp cracks. The wing's fabric screeched as it came apart, muffling her panicked howl.

The ground raced to meet her, sharp stones jutting at her like daggers. Steeling her mind, she fought to brace herself. With luck, she would only break bones and not puncture any organs.

Her arm dipped, rebounding off a branch, and the world flipped over again. Then she jerked to a jarring halt, as if a giant had snatched her from the air. The fuel tank shattered, but the straps bolting it to the wing structure held firm. Stardust exploded outward in a shower of glittering light, raining over the undergrowth. Where it fell, the leaves sizzled. The straps dug into her chest, driving the breath from her lungs. Her vision swam. She tried to blink it clear, but her body won out.

And it wanted only to rest awhile.

She swayed, and her eyes closed.

Darkness swallowed her before pain brought on a nightmare. A memory sprang to life of her wrist on fire, the back of her head throbbing as Edmund Glover's steam carriage rocked back and forth, trundling down the road to Edinburgh. Her hands were bound behind her. The wayhouse of Glen Coe, with its food and warmth, was left far in the distance. At least she was dry. Her snort turned into a snarl that drew the Fey Finder's attention. She sat on a bench of red velvet, opposite the man. The carriage bounced and shuddered over every rock. Its engine popped and sputtered. The stench of burning coal hung thick in the tiny compartment. Outside, the gnarled crags rolled slowly past as they made their way out of the Highlands. Creeping toward her doom. There would be no hope for her once they reached the city.

Effie yanked against her bonds, crying out as the rope slid across where the valet's blade had slashed. It burned more than it should, as if she held it within a crackling hearth. She grimaced, her eyes watering.

Glover stared at her, cheeks wobbling as the carriage swayed. "Your kind are ever strange. Would that I could study you further." His calm demeanor and cold tone enraged Effie.

"What kind of creature preys on an innocent child?" she spat. Her head ached and her wrists were raw, yet Effie yanked again against the ropes. Her hands slid further apart, growing slick with fresh blood from the effort.

"Innocent? I think not. A wolf who savages a farmer can claim innocence because the beast understands no better morality." He folded his hands in his lap and shifted his seat as the carriage lurched. "But your kind do understand. Fey have always been crafty devils. Crafty and foul."

Sharp pain blossomed in waves as Effie continued to work her hands free. But she held her face stern and refused to cry out. Instead, she thought of the rhymes her mother used to sing when she was injured. Her mother had ways of singing the hurt away, of making everything right. Of protecting her. Her mother had taught her many things: salves to cure inflammation and poultices to stave off infection. She had even taught her how to sear a wound closed with an unction. An unction of crushed petals and blood.

Effie's eyes lit up. Oh, how it burned. "Purple bells steeped in burn; blood and petal knit flesh in turn," she whispered, as the knowledge came back to her. Her mother's lilting voice echoed in her head, singing the rhyme as she often did when Effie had a cut. The unction turned black when mixed properly. In small doses, it would tickle and crust after burning a minute or two. Applied in quantity, the unction was kin to an acid.

"It was twinflower in the serum," she said.

Glover nodded. "A simple flower, harvested from the pinewoods of Strathspey. Simple, yet rare." He reached into his satchel and pulled out the vial. It was almost full. "It likes your foul blood not."

"It burns," Effie agreed. The petal and the blood, to sear the flesh. It was a poison she could use to her advantage. Her eyes narrowed on the vial. Her wrists were slick yet almost free. Another painful yank was all she needed.

The Fey Finder frowned. His mouth opened, but before he could speak, a rifle shot cracked, echoing through the glen. The chimney shrieked, letting out a long hiss of steam, as the carriage jerked to a halt. A thumping sounded on the roof, from the coachman.

"Highwaymen on the road," came a shout from the valet. "Masked and armed."

Glover drew a pistol from beneath his bench and pointed the barrel at Effie's head. "Do not move. Pray these brigands are no kin of yours, or I'll bury you along with them." Throwing open the door, he leaned out.

Effie's heart pounded. She yanked hard, and the bonds fell away. Her arms tingled in joy, but she had no mind for them. She lunged for the vial, snatching it from atop the satchel.

Grunts and clacks of wood and steel rang outside, mixed with the shuffling of feet on the road. The carriage rocked as something slammed into it. Glover turned and cursed when he saw her. He brought the pistol to bear, but not quick enough. Effie smashed the vial into his face. The serum mixed with the blood trickling along her arm and turned black. Glover tried to shove her, but she drove her fist into his throat. The pistol fired, and her ears rang with a high-pitched squeal.

She smeared her slick wrist along his cheeks and jaw. The serum hissed, drinking in her fey blood. Wisps of smoke rose from his flesh, and he began to shriek. His hands clawed at his face as his legs thrashed.

"Most curious," said Effie, repeating the man's words from the wayhouse. She took up his pistol and cracked it against his skull.

Glover slumped. Effie re-cocked the pistol and sprang from the carriage. Beside the road, the valet struggled against two brawny men who were hooded and masked. The coachman lay sprawled across the driver's seat, a welt forming at his brow.

Effie hesitated. Her mind screamed for her to run, but her legs were rooted in place. One of the men swiped at the valet with the butt of his rifle. It clanged against the man's bronzed arms, and the highwayman staggered back.

The other darted in low, thrusting with a dirk. The valet dodged but stumbled in the bracken and fell to a knee. His assailants set on him in a flurry that left him motionless.

When they turned to regard Effie, she found her pain and fear and rage had gone. She recognized the men before they lifted their masks. They were the same highlanders from the wayhouse.

One raised his hand in a calming gesture. "We mean no harm, lass. Our Good Auntie were a Maid of the Trees, a lady who ken the giants our father said."

"I know little of giants," said Effie. "But my mother sang of them sleeping amongst the munros. Perhaps your Good Aunt could tell me more."

The highlander shook his head. "Alas, she's dead of the flux. Still, we couldn't let one of her kin be bundled away to Edinburgh. The dungeons there are worse than the streets, and them has got a stink and rot not fit for a Campbell, black as they may be."

"Aye," said the other. He tugged at his trews, red striped with black and yellow.

Effie glanced up the road, then at the carriage. "How did you get ahead of us?"

Both men laughed. "We ken these lands as we ken our own legs. No road of the queen's is quicker than the trails of a Highlander."

"You put yourself in danger for me," said Effie, as a tug of guilt overcame her. "And I have nothing for you."

"It is us as should give. We remember the tales of the auld days when the fey tended to our clans and lent their Fey Craft to our hearth and home."

Pride welled within Effie for the first time she could remember. "I am Effie, daughter of Adeleyde," she said, standing a bit taller.

"The brothers Croy, Colin and Donal, of Kinlochy."

She curtsied, the gesture feeling a bit formal after the brutal scuffle. But her emotions overwhelmed her when they returned stiff bows. "If it wouldn't trouble you more," she asked, "could I perhaps count you as friends?" Her heart clenched. She hadn't meant to be so bold, but the men were the first who'd shown her a kindness in months.

She didn't think it possible for Colin's face to become anymore cheery, but somehow his cheeks rounded more, and the glint in his eyes shone brighter. He bowed again, then laughed. It wasn't a rude thing to insult her but a bellow of mirth.

"Of course ye can, Effie, and we'd be honored to do the same of you."

She almost hopped in excitement. Despair had been a lonely thing, but now hope had rekindled. Despite the queen's wrath and society's shunning, there were those who would trust and favor her.

"We best take to the hills," said Donal. "The Sniffer and his lackeys will wake soon enough, though he has no hounds with noses good enough to flush us from the glen. We'll be safe."

"Aye," said Colin. "Where are ye headed, lass?" he asked Effie.

She thought for a moment before deciding. "West, to find an engineer named Stevenson," she answered. She had never been more certain of anything in her life.

The dream faded as Effie blinked awake. More than a dream, really; a memory. The near-encounter with the Sniffer troubled her almost as much as her flight from the trows. Both had stolen a measure of safety, but the former touched on horrors held deep inside. Wind buffeted her, and she swayed back only to rush forward. A night bird chirped, snapping her alert. She struggled for a moment, not sure where she was, until she realized she swung from a branch, still lashed to the trow's wings.

The forest floor was only a short drop, but the effort of pulling her arms free of the straps made her lightheaded. The skin at her shoulders had rubbed raw against the straps, and the sockets behind felt like a blacksmith had taken a hammer to them. The wound from the trow's bite bled anew, blood trickling down her back. Landing, she crouched for a moment, hands working at the opposite shoulder to loosen them and staunch the cut. The pain lessened some, enough that the tremors stopped.

The foliage around her was thick and the undergrowth heavy, but she could make out the moon beaming through a clearing a short distance away and recalled the lights of the village not too far beyond. The forest was silent except for a breeze kissing the bracken as it swept low through the trees, and the occasional chirp of a night scavenger.

She marveled at the wreckage above her. By the heavens, it all seemed so foolish now, the thought of flight. But she'd mastered the controls quickly enough before the onrush of pain. The timing of it was more than passing strange. Perhaps she'd climbed too high? Learned men wrote of the curious vapors and other oddities found at higher altitudes, yet she swore she hadn't gone any higher than the dozen or so munros she'd capped with Graham. She contemplated the matter, but it refused to offer any better answer. The night grew long, and her arms began to shake, this time from the cold, so she turned her thoughts to carrying on.

The wings were a lost cause. Even if she could free the salvageable parts from the tree, without a power source they were only extra weight to carry. She tested a step, wobbling on unsteady legs, yet thankful nothing felt broken. Slinging her reticule over an arm, she marched toward the moonbeam, the only source of light piercing through the trees. Hopefully she'd run into a stream, something cool to soothe her throat and wash the sap from her hands and face.

She passed through the clearing, stopping only to gain bearings from the remaining stars, and trudged along at a plodding pace until the sky grew bright enough for her to gaze through the canopy of trees. The early morning turned colder as frost built on the undergrowth. She wished desperately for her coat, and was thankful when she found a road winding its way through the forest.

She followed it toward the village. The lights she'd seen when soaring above the hills had seemed so close to her then, like she could reach out and touch them. Now her ankle burned with every step and the scratches on her back itched something awful as her tattered dress rubbed against them.

She smelled the smoke first, before turning a bend and spying the outlying cottages. Made of thatch and stone, their chimneys puffed away, sending out scents of the morning meal being prepared. She passed the first few without noticing any signs of movement, but by the time she reached the village proper she could hear the scurrying of each household as it went about its daily routine. She considered knocking on one of the doors but feared she'd have few answers for her current state.

The clop of hooves and trundling of a wagon came up the road behind her, a farmer hauling his goods to market. Her stomach rumbled at the sight. Mounds of carrots and potatoes filled the wagon, and she wondered if he might sell her a spud or two. He eyed her cautiously, taking in her wretched appearance, until his dog leapt from the bench and scampered over to her. The hound wagged its tail and rubbed against her legs, dancing in happy circles as it beamed up at her.

"Whist, Harold, enough of that," said the man. "Give the lady her space." He stopped the wagon and said to her, "Beg pardon, miss."

"Oh, it's no trouble at all," said Effie. She bent to scratch behind Harold's ears, trying not to wince too much as she stooped.

The farmer bit his cheek for a moment before asking, "If it's none too forward of me, I was wondering if I may ask whether you're quite well?"

Effie smiled at him. "My horse threw me and bolted," she said, relating the tale she'd come up with while walking. It was a weak premise but believable enough. "I was trying to get an early start so I might press and make a good distance today, but I got turned around in the woods, and now I'm not really sure where I am."

"Ye coming from St. Andrews?"

She blinked but managed to nod. St. Andrews? She hadn't realized she'd come so far south during her flight. She'd expected to be north of Dundee, with the Firths of Tay and Forth still yet to cross. If she was south of St. Andrews, she was almost to Edinburgh.

He blew out a long breath. "Well, ye must've started right early, then. Not even this one's up at that hour." He pointed at Harold, who looked at him and barked, tongue lolling out. "Aye, ye, ye lazy bugger."

"Do you suppose I might trouble you for a bit of food? I seem to have lost all my things." She opened her reticule and started to dig. "But I do have some coin. I will pay a good price."

"Eh," said the farmer. He glanced around, but the villagers were still tucked within their homes. "It's not the money, miss, only I wonder what sort of affair would cause ye to ride alone at such a wee hour. I'm not a man for trouble."

"I wished to surprise my father," she blurted without thought. "He's in Edinburgh for the fortnight. I should've taken the train, as Mother suggested, but it seemed like such nice weather the past few days not to enjoy a long ride." She held out a few shillings for him to inspect, enough to purchase half the food in his wagon. Harold did his part, too, whining for his master to take pity, tail wagging merrily all the while.

The farmer looked them over and chuckled. "What a pair, as if straight from the mouth of Dickens!" Harold yipped and spun a circle. "All right, then, I can do you better than a carrot. Ye can climb on back if ye wish, and we'll go fetch me son, Ben. He'll take you as far as the ferry."

Relief flooding her, and she thanked him. "I'll accept, but only if you let me pay for the service." He protested but not too ardently. Once it was settled, she stooped and hugged Harold, getting her face licked in return. "And thank you, Harold," she laughed.

The man's wife wasn't happy to see him return home with a full wagon, and she was even less happy to see Effie. But she changed her tune at the sight of the coins, and found Effie yet another dress to borrow while Effie scrubbed herself clean and wolfed down a bowl of porridge. The warm meal doused any worry over yet more strangers knowing her face. The matter of Duncairn was greater than the risk to her safety, and expedience outweighed any concern over the danger. Besides, she would soon be lost in a giant city, her face unremarkable to thousands.

CHAPTER 10

B en was a cheery fellow, quick to jest. He found almost everything interesting and constantly pointed out all he found along the road. They passed through towns and villages, lumbering along in an old buggy pulled by a horse better suited for plowing fields. Effie tried to provide pleasant company, but her thoughts kept straying to the crooked fiend of Duncairn.

The self-proclaimed laird was part of a fey bloodline she hadn't known existed. Her mother had never spoken of fey not joined to the Seily Court. A week before, she hadn't ever heard of an Unseily Court. Sidhe Bhreige, he had called himself. She didn't know if the term was a title or a race. Her own race were known as the Votadini Sith once, but that name hadn't been used for a thousand years. The term Sithling sprang from that origin, but it was easier still for humans to simply call her fey rather than bother with a distinction of the myriad races that spawned from the Daoine Sith.

She hoped Gabus Säurbaum could provide better insight, once Effie found her within the city. She would head for the University first and see if the librarian knew of the gnome's comings and goings. She would contact Stevenson as well. The steel-colored sky darkened as she thought about what she would tell him. The news was grim.

Her eyes grew heavy as the morning warmed, and her efforts to remain awake turned futile. She woke late in the afternoon stiff and sore but a little less groggy. Ben offered her some bread and salted fish, which she greedily wolfed down. It took them another hour to reach North Queensferry, a village on the northern shores of the Firth of Forth. Its ferries were the sole means to cross the great inlet, unless one wanted to ride clear around through Stirling where the waters narrowed to create fords across the River Forth. The skies had turned dreary by the time they reached the harbor. The wind whipped the waves of the firth into a fury, their tips white with foam. The harbormaster laughed when she asked if there would be another crossing, telling her it'd be too dark for a return voyage. "Best to keep yer belly from heaving, lassie." The man chuckled. "You'll be a better for it in the morning."

Ben shrugged and took her back into the village, offering to remain until she could sort out some kind of accommodation. But she wouldn't have him shivering in the dark when she could manage herself, so gave him her thanks and a little extra coin to see him well. She found a boarding house and paid a dear price for a meager dinner and private room. Her mattress was lumpy and stained, but her bones ached so much she fell asleep before the torches had been lit in the streets outside.

Morning brought with it a cold frost and the squawk of sea birds. She warmed herself over tea and wondered after Robert Ramsey, hoping the man been able to evade the trows. She had to return to Duncairn as quick as she could. Leaving the mess and its dangers to Ramsey irked her like a splinter she couldn't pluck from her finger.

The harbormaster was in a cheery mood when she found him again, and she booked a passage departing within the hour. He eyed her strangely when she told him she had no luggage, and he noted Ben's absence, but with a belly laugh he was off again on some other task, Effie already forgotten. That was the way of city folk. Their attentions never lingered. There were too many other sights and sounds to observe. She'd marveled the first time she'd lost herself in a crowd. For all her hiding, it seemed ludicrous that one of the best places she'd ever found to disappear was among a mass of humanity. Before Stevenson had taken her in, she'd lived in hovels, fearing anyone who'd happened by. In a city, one could hide in plain sight. Cutpurses and harlots dwelled among the shop keeps and factory workers. Bankers walked the same cobblestones as scullery maids. No one paid you any mind unless you caused a stir, and even then the crowds could swallow you up and forget you ever existed.

There were dangers, to be certain. The more people there were, the greater chance there was one with the ability to sense her fey blood. But the endless other sensations given off by the city seemed to mute whatever scent her blood imparted. It allowed her freedom to walk along the streets and wynds with no more fear than the open countryside.

The *Mary MacDougal* was a flat-bottomed barge with two tiers of benches. A housing toward the stern provided service and shelter, but Effie enjoyed the view from the prow. A decade before, the city had sought to construct a gigantic bridge over the firth, which stretched a mile and a half wide at the ferry's crossing. But the attempt had halted just after the footings were poured. She recalled reading about it. Another of the architect's bridges had collapsed into the Firth of Tay, killing seventy-five people, and the disaster had shocked the engineering community. The poor man whose faulty designs had caused the collapse, Sir Thomas Bouch, died within the year of a saddened heart, his reputation in ruins, and his bridge over the Firth of Forth never completed.

Effie stared into the murky water, straining to catch a glimpse of the abandoned footings. The firth was too deep, of course, but she imagined she could make out the shadows of Bouch's legacy, lost like Atlantis beneath the modern world. It reminded her of her own people, who had once dwelled on the shores of the firth. Their history was buried where none could find it, too, purposely eroded from the shores, a choice made when the Daoine Sith abandoned the Highlands.

She found a bench and rested her eyes for a time, letting the swaying of the ferry loll her back and forth. When she raised her head again, the sharp crags of Arthur's Seat and Castle Rock dueled before her as the city came into view. The latter lorded over tenements, ramparts, and spires; the former over the heather-laden cliffs and rolling pastures that spread to the east. A trio of zeppelins hung beneath the clouds, beasts of canvas and iron-banded wood held aloft by alchemy and propelled by science. Leaf-shaped blades protruded from the rear of each, spinning like giant wheels.

On her first trip to the city, her knees had buckled, such sights being wonders she had never imagined. But for all the wonderment, the city was a filthy place. Clouds of soot cloaked it. Steam puffed from trains, factories, and the trams that ran throughout the city's heart. Coal dust billowed whenever the wind stirred. The city folk left refuse in piles in the alleyways, and thought nothing of emptying buckets of waste out a high window to spill on the street below.

The clamor was also deafening compared to the countryside. Whistles shrilled, bells tolled, and gears creaked constantly throughout day and night. And that didn't include the noise from the city folk themselves. Hawkers, workers, and a thousand conversations formed a din as loud as a thunderstorm.

Effie stepped off the ferry and joined the queue for the steam-powered tram that would take her into the heart of the city. The light railcars were something of a marvel, a system of single-car engines that had become the envy of European cities. As her car tutted along, she watched the buildings grow larger and more industrious. The outskirts of the city still had the feel of a country village, with rows of cottages and markets filled with horse drawn wagons. The streets were muddy lanes, the denizens dressed in linen dresses and wool smocks, simple coats and tattered trousers.

Edinburgh was a city of hills and crevices. Up the Leith Walk toward the backside of Calton Hill, tenements began to sprout, some twenty stories in height, others shorter but perched on higher ground so that they loomed over their taller cousins. Each layer held a ranking of floors, so that lawyers lived over clerks, and they over the bakers and shopkeeps. The lowliest lived at the bottom, amongst the refuge and grime. Atop Castle Rock crouched the royal fortress, its ramparts bristling with cannons, the queen's colors flapping in the wind. Its ancient walls had been captured more than once, but the castle remained a stalwart defender of the city. Graham had told her its history while she was just a wide-eyed lass.

In the times she'd visited Edinburgh since, she'd learned more of the nooks and crannies, and of the city's painful past. The tales fascinated her, and she found it difficult to behold the modern bustle without attempting to peek beneath its current skin. The Old Town alone held more layers than an onion, and it stood more congested than any other city in the world. Walls, boggy lochs, and sharp cliffs had kept the city contained to Castle Rock since the earliest settlements, before even the Romans had come to the Isles. But as the population grew and the land reached its capacity, older wynds and dwellings were simply sealed up and built over, the newer tenements constructed higher and larger. A labyrinth of forgotten streets lay beneath the modern city.

Cresting Calton Hill, she could spy a few of the buried ways poking out from the sides of the hills, gasping for air, making the whole mess look like an anthill. That part of Edinburgh was ancient. Yet as time wore on, the need for defensive walls disappeared, and it was decided the city should expand to neighboring hills. The lochs were drained, and on top of forgotten structures seven great bridges were built, thrusting out from the Old Town. A planned New Town was designed for the rich and powerful, and the old heart was given over to the poor.

She shook her head, glancing between the New Town and the Old, as her tram rattled along. The divide of wealth shone in stark contrast, neat and orderly on the one side, dingy and slumped on the other. Instead of becoming less cramped, the Old Town had seen an influx of foreigners and Highlanders. Some were forced from their lands by the Clearances or the Potato Famines; others crowded into the city looking for work. The unemployed and destitute overwhelmed the streets, competing with their neighbors for a better life. In a place like Edinburgh, it was not unheard of for parents to sell their children into servitude—destined for the mines, to toil as chimney sweeps, or to work as household maids and footmen. Their parents were simply unable to feed them, and the offer of food became greater than the bonds of family.

"Great invention comes from great strife," Graham had tried to reason, but still she refused to believe that any mother with a good heart would abandon her child thus. Her own mother would've starved before gifting Effie away into the horrors of such employment, the bond between them stronger than any suffering in life. Even Stevenson, whose relationship with his own son had soured, had taken her in, fed her, and clothed her, when he found out she was an orphan. That others wouldn't do the same, more than anything else, made Effie distrust city folk.

She alighted on Princes Street, at the southern end of the New Town, and made for the Bridges. Dividing the old city from the new was a depression once filled by the Nor Loch, a foul smelling water made even worse by the city's sewage. But the land now was a hive of modernism, hosting the great coal bunkers that fed life to the city, and Waverly Station, the main rail terminal. Manufacturing plants, tinkers' shops, and the offices of engineers all huddled together in the glen. The men wore heavy aprons and goggles to protect their eyes from soot and sparks from forges. Some had bronze or steel plates sewn to their aprons, others marched in armor like the knights of old to protect themselves. Telegraph wires ran along a network of poles, the clink and grind of metal gears was constant, as was the heat billowing from engines, kilns, and forges. Contraptions of all kinds were constructed and tinkered with, from recording lenses to steam hammers, voice projectors to sleek airships.

North Bridge connected to South Bridge, the pair spanning from Princes Street to Castle Rock, though only a few of their arches remained visible. The rest were swallowed up by tenements and industrious buildings sprouting from the banks of the hills and atop the bridges themselves. It gave the city a sense of flight—as streets crossed, some lofted thirty feet above the other, hiding the very existence of the bridges.

Effie smiled as she walked and tried not to gawk. The streets were packed, and she had to keep herself from being pulled in odd directions by the masses. The women wore their hair in bonnets to keep off the soot, though a few sported richer hats and dresses of vibrant colors. Arcades and shambles spread out between the buildings. She passed a baker, a tailor, and a kinescope sharing the street level of one of the tenements before crossing the High Street, which led up Castle Rock to the castle.

A man in a bowler hat tapped her with a cane as she passed a shaman's shop. The unctions and ointments he sold proclaimed miraculous healing. "Do you have a boil that won't go away?" the man barked. "Or a souring of the stomach? Step in, step in, and you'll find the cure."

Racks of vials and glass bottles, some decorative and shaped in intricate detail, others simple and squat, filled the shop. Staves and totems from the Americas and Africa, and even a few from the Orient, hung about the walls adding to the level of mysticism. Effie shook her head and hurried on. A second hawker tried to persuade her to witness a steam-powered sewing machine, while another shop boasted that it held within it The Wonders of Electrical Devices. This one she almost entered but decided she'd best come back another time when her matters weren't as urgent.

The University stood at the end of South Bridge, a stone edifice perfectly proportioned, with fluted columns protruding from its front façade and an inner courtyard dominated by a tiered fountain. The shoes of students clacked against the cobblestones as they scurried to and fro, a marked difference from the scuffing of leather soles on the dirty streets outside.

Effie knew where to search for the librarian. She crossed the courtyard and passed through a thick, iron-bound door. Finding a stair, she wound down the marble steps until she reached a vaulted room stuffed with desks and cabinets overflowing with papers and files. Slender drawers in the former held cards detailing each cabinet's belongings, but most times those drawers were just as packed and confused. The few students she passed paid her no mind; they were too intent on their own work, some with their heads buried in books, others in terse debates, huddled in small groups.

Near the far corner of the room an odd angle in the wall created an alcove large enough for a longcase clock to stand wedged in its crevice. A gap allowed Effie to disappear behind the clock, and to the others in the room, she seemed to vanish into the walls. The University, like the rest of Edinburgh, had been built right on top of the buildings that lay there before, stacking the new above the old without bothering to do more than seal up any rooms or hallways that still remained from the previous dwelling. Behind the alcove, a rotted door frame jutted up from the floor, ending after a mere couple of feet, its portal cut in half by the room in which Effie stood. At some point, an enterprising soul had hammered a way through whatever stones had been used to seal up the chamber beyond, and a cool draft wafted through the old doorway, which was illuminated by a row of torches on the far side.

Effie had used the passage before. It was one of the known

entrances to the Town Below, the sealed up wynds, closes, chambers, and undercrofts that still existed under the modern city. These dark, dank places, sealed from the world above, were now the haunts of cutpurses and street toughs who used the underground ways to conceal their movements. It was not uncommon to find rogues hiding out in an old tanner's house or holding a clandestine meeting in the boarded-up remains of a dressmaker's shop. In the vaults beneath the city's bridges, a more civil form of thievery took place. There, traders set up as cobblers, drapers, and jewelers, selling stolen goods to the poor at a favorable price. Every few months, the constables and town watch would come and clear out the warrens, but they would not stay empty for long.

The fey used the Town Below for their own purposes. Those races who weren't Sithling could roam the ways without scrutiny, an unspoken pact of silence with the cutpurses keeping each group from disturbing the other. Effie's knowledge of the underground city was limited, though Graham had once taken her down Mary King's Close, under the castle, and into the catacombs snaking from the old dungeons to Waverly Station. He'd wanted to show her the escape routes dug into Castle Rock, and though she'd loved him for it, she'd felt the entire time like an apprentice footpad.

Under the University, she hiked up her dress and shimmied through the low opening. A stone table positioned on the far side broke the drop and allowed her to clamber down without fear of falling. The chamber was well-maintained. A few books were sacked on a teak desk, along with a pen and ink. Someone had kept the room clear of dust, and the torches were bright enough for her to make out three other exits. Two led to the Town Below. The third ended at a false wall, on the far side of which was a public house frequented by the University staff.

Rumor held that in centuries past, when human dissection was not as en vogue as it was currently, a pair of the medical school's professors smuggled cadavers through the public house, dug up fresh from the city's cemeteries. They'd drop the corpses through the false wall to be carted away to a clandestine classroom somewhere in the University. Such macabre tales were common in the Town Below, but Effie paid them no mind. What concerned her more were the Sniffers who sometimes crawled through the lost wynds. They were the real danger.

Effie ran a finger along the stack of books, selected one, and sat on a bench against the wall. The librarian would know she waited. The woman always knew when any of the fey needed her services, if they remained in that specific room. It had to be in a proximity of where the woman worked. She had the gift to sense fey blood, but Effie had never heard of the ability extending very far.

The book she picked related the history of the Goddodin, the tribe whose stronghold once perched on the same earth where the queen's castle now stood. She flipped the pages for a while, until her eyes grew heavy and she rested them for a bit. Fatigue took hold and by the time she woke, an hour at least had passed. The scent of tea, a strong brew infused with honey, wafted to her. She opened her eyes to find a slender woman sipping a cup while scratching out notes at the teak desk.

The woman turned as Effie stirred, her raven locks in a frazzled state. What remained in a bun atop her head threatened to spring loose from its binds as she crossed the room to offer tea. Ink stained the woman's fingers, and though her eyes were as dark as her hair, freckles spotted her pale cheeks.

"Good morning, Mistress Librarian," said Effie, accepting the steaming brew. "My name is...." She paused, unsure which moniker to give. "Well, I am called of late Miss Martins. You may not remember, but we've met before."

"Aye'ya, I know," said the woman. Her head bobbed with enthusiasm on every word. "You're the artist, the one who sketches those beautiful lighthouses."

Effie blushed at the compliment. "I was so young when last we spoke, I'm surprised you remember."

"Not so young as you say. Your aura did already yet beam. I remember it clearly, and I could tell it was you the moment you stepped on University grounds."

"From my aura?" Effie's cheeks turned a shade redder. "Mine is that strong?" She didn't know whether to be embarrassed or proud.

The woman's eyes lit up. "Oh, aye. As with all your lot, it's brilliant!" The librarian stared dreamily at the wall. "If only it weren't to cost me my livelihood, I'd pen a gorgeous paper on the matter."

"To instruct others? Is it a smell? Or something you see?"

She chuckled. "Oh, no, you feel them, lass. And you can't learn to feel auras. It's something already inside you."

Effie's brow furrowed, not following. She wondered if it was related to what she'd sensed of the trows, but that had come from the power of her fey blood. Or had it? She didn't know, only that it had felt at the time like she could feel every living thing around her, not just the trows and their master. And if she could do that, how was the ability different from the librarian's talent? Or that of the Sniffers, for that matter?

The woman waved her hand and chortled. "Best I don't utter too much. The University's secrets are their own, as they say."

A question caught in Effie's throat. She wanted to know more, but she was there to beg a favor, not to make demands. "I suppose mine are as well," she offered.

"None to worry, love," said the woman, patting Effie's leg. "I don't go gabbing where my tongue don't belong."

Effie nodded her thanks. "I have a favor to ask," she said. "I'm looking for a friend, a gnome from Bavaria whom I believe to be in the city."

The librarian rolled her eyes and huffed. Her demeanor suddenly soured. "The rocksoother. Aye'ya, she's still here. Been borrowing book after book, sending me all over creation without as much as a grunt of thanks." She shook her head. "'Tis her kind, I suppose."

Barely containing a laugh, Effie snorted into her tea. She knew the woman spoke of Gabus Säurbaum without a doubt. "Do you know where I can find her?"

"Beneath Marlin's Wynd, under the Tron Kirk, is where she is most often. Looking at glaciers, she keeps saying to me, though a simpleton could tell you there ain't any ice under the castle."

Effie politely agreed and gave her thanks. They spoke while she finished her tea, though Effie avoided all talk of Duncairn. She'd decided it best to learn what she could of the arrowheads without risking the start of rumors of trouble. Rumors could bring entanglements.

After the woman departed, Effie took one of the doors to the

Town Below and headed for Marlin's Wynd. Shades of the past coated every corner of the sealed city. Stains a hundred years old splotched the walls, and the dirt floor still held the churn of footsteps from those long dead. The reek of stale air reminded one of the Nor Loch, where centuries of sewage was tossed from the hills above.

Marlin's Wynd stretched from beneath the Tron Kirk down to the Cowgate, but it wasn't the lowest passage under the church. Effie followed the librarian's instructions, finding access to the levels below. She clutched a lantern as she went, loaned to her by the University. She kept it mostly hooded. In such darkness, only a flicker of light was enough to find her way.

Soon she reached a narrow passage lined by derelict row houses. Halfway down, a warm fire lit one of the dwellings, the crackle of its flames piercing the eerie silence. Effie took a few steps, then closed her lantern completely. She could see well enough without it.

"*Guten morgen!*" she called.

"*Mein Gott!*" yelped a startled voice, followed by a crash of what sounded like books falling. A shadow passed through the cottage as something moved about. "*Wie sind den da? Ich haben eine Pistole!*"

Effie laughed. "I don't think anyone will understand your threat, Gabus. You might as well shoot all who come near." She strode forward into the firelight.

"Ah, *gut*," grunted Gabus Säurbaum. Like most of her kind, she was an ornery sort whose hands were gnarled from years of picking at rocks deep within the folds of the Earth. A braid of dingy brown hair ran down her back. Her ears stuck out like saucers around a nose as bulbous as a mushroom. Effie had never seen her without a fine layer of dust coating frock and trousers, nor without her rucksack, which she spied on a table within the house. It held an assortment of tools: hammers of varied shapes and types, chisels, dusters, parchment, and a hand lens.

"Tea is for warmth, *ja?*" said Gabus, giving her a toothy grin. She tucked a fat-barreled pistol into her apron and disappeared inside. "I get you some."

"Good to see you again, too," said Effie. "Are your studies going well?" She wasn't surprised at the peculiar welcome. The gnome had her own way of doing things.

"Nay." Gabus waved her hand. She hunkered over a kettle, her meaty hands sloshing the water about as she set it over the fire. "Or *ja*, is fine. I can't complain." Her ears twitched, her eyes narrowing. "How did you know to come here?" Effie opened her mouth but was cut short.

"That woman!" exclaimed the gnome. "Always yapping, never working. It took her a full day to fetch me that." She thrust a finger at a large tome open on the table.

Effie read the title: A Survey of Drainage in the City of Edinburgh. "It sounds fascinating," she said.

When she'd asked Gabus about her work in the past she'd only received disjointed answers she could make neither heads nor tails of. It had something to do with the formation of Edinburgh's cliffs and glens, and the presence of volcanoes in ages past. That, or glaciers. Her friend had spoken long-winded on both topics as they hiked through the Trossachs over a decade ago. Robbed and bewitched, their first encounter had left Gabus in a foul mood far worse than her normal self.

"Gabus, I have a favor to ask and some news to relate. I've encountered trouble to the north, in a village called Duncairn." She took the cup of tea Gabus proffered her. "At first I believed the trouble to be the actions of an Unseily Court. But now I fear it is something far worse. Do you know of the Sidhe Bhreige?"

The gnome's ears wilted. Her grip on the kettle tightened. She glanced longingly at the tome, then started packing up her things. "I ken a cozier place where we may rest our feet," she said, dumping the fresh pot of tea onto the fire. The flames hissed and filled the cottage with an herbal-perfumed smoke.

Without another word, Gabus led them up Marlin's Wynd and down a small alleyway to the door of an old bookshop. Within, Gabus had stored a sack stuffed with wool to sleep on and a few tins of food. A collection of rocks lay scattered about, some chiseled and hewn, others as gnarled as the hands that had procured them.

"We have cake now, the best," said the gnome. Her voice was calm despite the intensity in her gaze. She checked the door more than once, and her hand kept straying to the butt of the pistol as if its presence was soothing. "Full of dates and nuts, from a baker on Clerk

Street. A greater value you cannot find." She pointed at a blanket for Effie to sit on, then dug at the food and came away with two plates, each with a slab of the cake. Once they were settled, Gabus spoke. "The Town Below is very quiet. Your Scottish folk have been leaving for weeks, looking as frightened as kinder. I have not heard of these Sidhe Bhreige, but they are something wicked, *ja*? Something bad from long ago. Tell me of them."

It dawned on Effie that she'd neither seen nor heard a soul as she'd traipsed through Marlin's Wynd. That in itself was passing strange. All of the fey who weren't Sithlings were forced to use the Town Below to move about the city, lest they be seen by human eyes. Those rogues who shared the underground had no cause to alert the authorities, wanting even less attention and more than willing to look the other way. And as for the Sniffers, there weren't enough of them to patrol the whole of the Town Below and the whole of the countryside.

"But why have the fey fled from here?" asked Effie, shocked. "Duncairn's troubles are too far away to cause such panic in Edinburgh."

Gabus shrugged. For all her inquisitive mind, the gnome was not one to care about matters unrelated to rock and soil. Effie huffed in frustration. The similarity between the fey fleeing Duncairn and those abandoning Edinburgh was obvious but left a gaping hole needing answers. Unless the Laird of Aonghus' reach was far greater than she'd imagined, there was some other disturbing plot afoot.

She gathered her thoughts and launched into the tale of Duncairn, starting with the stranger atop Ben Nevis and ending with her journey to the city. Her friend's brows rose at the mention of murder and turned to fury when she heard of Ramsey's bewitchment. "*Gott in Himmel,*" she rasped when Effie handed her the pair of arrowheads. Gabus studied the runes on the stones, her face more piqued with interest than Effie had ever seen it.

"Do you know what they mean?" asked Effie.

"*Ja.*" Gabus nodded, her gaze not rising from the intricate markings. "You've told me. They bewitch people."

Effie took a deep breath, biting back frustration. "Well yes, but can you tell me anything more? Who could've crafted such a thing?

What language is used?"

The gnome shook her head. "A master of Fey Craft carved these. I've seen the etchings before." She looked about the room. Spying a book next to the makeshift mattress, she snatched it and began poring through its pages. "*Ja*, this will help."

After waiting in silence for a few minutes, enough time to nibble through her cake, Effie asked, "Do you think it will take long?"

Gabus glanced up. "*Nein*," she said, waving her hand. "An hour or so. Perhaps more. I may need to go see that woman again and get another book."

Effie stared at the walls. When she started to hum, Gabus shushed her. Effie asked whether she should put the kettle on, and was ignored. But her hands wouldn't stay still. She needed to do something. "I'm going back above," she announced, uncertain her friend was listening. "I need to telegraph Stevenson and Graham. I'll come find you here later."

She stood and dusted off her dress. A bit of fresh air and a walk would aid her thoughts. She'd almost reached the door when Gabus said, "Avoid the castle, *ja?*" Her gaze rose above the top of the book and locked on Effie. "The Fey Finder General is in the city."

Effie paled, wishing she had a pistol of her own.

CHAPTER II

Effie emerged from the Town Below and decided there was no harm in finding a bite to eat before telegraphing Stevenson. She might even learn a thing or two of the city's gossip, if the tongues flapped in the Grassmarket as much as they had during her last visit there. Better, it was unlikely she would run afoul of Edmund Glover in such a vulgar corner of Edinburgh.

Gray clouds had blanketed the city by late afternoon. The wind off the North Sea whipped about the streets, stealing hats and accosting garments, forcing pedestrians to stroll along clutching their attire, lest it be taken away. Effie held her arms against her dress, keeping it from billowing up as she hustled through Potter Row and down into Grassmarket. The broad avenue nestled beneath the sheer cliff of Castle Rock, on the far side of the castle from Princes Street. Once home to a market boasting everything from livestock to tobacco, the area was now a quarter for the poor. But it still bustled with activity. The destitute swarmed about by the hundreds, some hurrying about mundane tasks, others milling along aimlessly. Tenements stacked like beehives along both sides, tilting toward one another, their facades sagging like the faces of old hounds—long jowls grayed and worn. Washing hung from drying lines cast out of windows, and ropes for hoisting buckets—sometimes twenty stories aloft—draped from rigging high above. The dirt near the base of the tenements was a cesspool of waste and stagnant rainwater, forcing the denizens toward the center of the avenue.

The steam trams never entered Grassmarket, and the few carriages that rumbled through the street were ragged and ancient. With the castle's ramparts looming above and the old Flodden Wall ringing the opposite side, the area felt like a prison. Effie glanced around and thought the notion not far wrong. The faces of more than a few drunkards and ruffians returned her gaze. With the draining of the Nor Loch and the construction of New Town, prosperity had fled the Old Town.

But despite its squalor, Grassmarket remained a vibrant part of the city, and what was hushed and secreted in polite society was pronounced with great zeal among the masses. Effie found a coffeehouse whose patronage appeared full of domestics from the rich houses of New Town. The wood inside was thick and stained. Heavy timbers ran like ribs overhead, while the stools and tables were simple and squat. The aroma of coffee fought with that of sweet pastries, making her stomach rumble with delight. She purchased a pie stuffed with minced meat and gravy, and added a few spoonfuls of sugar to her coffee before finding a table. An abandoned newspaper lay atop one of the chairs, and she picked it up, flipping it over to scour the headlines.

They almost stole her breath. Several reports of peculiar sightings, and of thefts and assaults plaguing the roads of Lothian and Fife, had warranted the crown taking action. A regiment of the queen's army mustered, supported by another from Newcastle. They were set to march within the week to bring order to the countryside. There was no mention of Duncairn, or of any of the events along the coast, but Effie could not fathom the sheer coincidence. She scanned the rest of the paper but found nothing else relating to the matter.

She needed to telegraph Stevenson. Surely the man had heard the same news and realized its importance. As she mulled the implications, she turned her ears to those seated near her. At a table next to hers, a podgy fellow barked at another about the construction of a new breed of zeppelin meant to ferry entire companies of soldiers faster than any ship.

"Munitions, cannon, even the horses, all in a go," said the man. His sideburns poofed from his cheeks, white whiskers spiraling in every direction. One of his legs was missing, a sturdy peg in its place.

"And the Transvaal is where it'll head, to reclaim what is properly ours. The Boers may have caught us once, but they won't again."

"Well needed, too," agreed the man's companion. "I don't care for how these other kings and queens in Europe speak of our empire these days. Put them in their place, we should."

"Aye," said the first fellow. "I only wish I were fit enough to reenlist." He tapped his stump with longing. "Zulu bastards."

Effie nibbled at her pastry as the men carried on. At another table, a woman moaned over the price of salted beef. It seemed merchants were hiring extra guards against the banditry on the roads. "One would think Rob Roy had come back from the grave," lamented the woman. "It's bad enough I can't afford to put food on me own table, but do ya' think Mrs. Florent gives me extra coin for her table? Nay, you must be mad! I'm to quit me whinging, she says, as if I can drop the cost with a wiggle of me arse."

Effie shoved the last of the savory pie into her mouth to keep from laughing. Its salty crust melted on her tongue, the sweet gravy rich with flavor. She thought about getting another but resisted. She was about to leave when a name boomed across the coffeehouse demanding her attention.

"Sir Walter Conrad," said a deep voice behind her. "He and that lackey of his have come to dine with the Duke of Edinburgh."

"The prince is in town?" asked a girl's soft lilt. Out of the corner of her eye, Effie caught tresses of ginger hair sprouting from a bonnet.

"His Royal Highness has come from London to inspect the city's defenses, so they say. Some nonsense about the threat from Germany. Bismarck is conspiring with the Russians again, and the whole world trembles at the man's power. But it's more likely the duke wanted a tidy holiday and a chance to milk the local gentry of their expensive wines."

"The duke's a German himself, isn't he?"

"Next in line to the duchies of Saxe-Coburg and Gotha, through his father. Married to a Russian Grand Duchess, too. But he's Her Majesty's son first. He'll stand proud for Britain if it comes to war. Not that it will. There's too much inbreeding in the monarchies for brother and sister and cousin to fight one another. It's just posturing over the African and Indian colonies, is all." He cleared a throat full of phlegm and sipped from his coffee with gusto.

"Poor Sir Walter, having to dine with the duke after such an embarrassment two nights ago." The girl's voice was full of an innocent sorrow.

"Och, explosions happen in the mining trade. It's dangerous work digging so deep underground. But don't you worry over Sir Walter. The man knows how to dance aside any mark society would lay against him, and his coin purse will quiet the matter afore the week is done."

Effie set her cup down and rose to leave. On her way to the door, she peeked at the timber-voiced man and saw by his dress he was perhaps a footman. The girl was at least a dozen years his younger and wore the garb of a scullery maid. She wished she could dream up some ruse to question the man over what he knew of Sir Walter, but her mind was stuck on an endless list of puzzle pieces, of which she could get none to intersect. An explosion at the Glen Avon mines, that was something. She thought of the lecher on the train and had to keep herself from wishing the disgusting man an ill fortune in the event.

Heading out of Grassmarket, she climbed the hill past Greyfriar's Kirk and made her way to a gardened square near the University. A telegraph wire strung along the lampposts led her to a cablegram company, though once inside she was overwhelmed. There was so much to recount to Stevenson that she could pen a novel. She settled on a few simple lines encoded in the architect's parlance they employed to disguise their messages. It was a trick they used frequently. Wandering eyes would only see comments regarding a fictitious lighthouse under construction.

She told Stevenson of the trows and the Laird of Aonghus the best she could, and of the random thefts across the countryside and her journey to Edinburgh. She hoped he knew enough from the newspapers to fill in any gaps. As she handed her missive to the clerk, the sense of failure she'd felt in Duncairn rose up again. She swallowed down the lump in her throat. Stevenson wouldn't blame her for sending bad news, nor would he accuse her of fleeing Duncairn. But that knowledge did little to lessen the turmoil roiling inside. The clerk grunted and tapped out the message, ignoring her. When he was finished, he handed the scrap of paper back and she shoved it into her reticule, tugging the drawstrings closed.

Retreating into the oncoming twilight, she studied the faces she passed. Each man and woman was lost in the haze of their own concerns, oblivious to the rumbling clouds storming to the north. A sinister force tickled the hairs of her neck, the wind feeling like the breath of a thousand devils.

She didn't want to return to the Town Below, not just yet. Her ignorance nagged at her, and she was determined to make the most of her time in the city. The Hostmen of Newcastle and Sir Walter Conrad were foremost in her thoughts, so she decided that was the best place to start. She made for Waverly Station, descending a wynd on the far side of the High Street.

The great coal bunkers of Edinburgh were dug into the hillside beneath the North Bridge. An endless army of coal porters shoveled and piled the coal that came in on the rail, loading and unloading to the shrill whistle of a supervisor. It was long days of grueling work, and the men were given little sympathy by their employers. There were too many starving mouths in the city, all eager for employment, for the workers to complain over an ailment or something as petty as exhaustion. Clouds of black dust consumed them, puffing like pipe smoke as they walked. Their hands were gnarled and backs crooked, and the few who walked straight were mocked by their elders.

A loading dock allowed private customers to come and purchase coal for their own needs. The queue of carriages and carts was endless. A few of the men stopped and stared at her as she approached, reminding her of the docks at Duncairn. One of the workers pulled down the soot-stained handkerchief tied about his face and hacked up enough spittle to drown a rat. The man next to him laughed and whispered something, his eyes never leaving her chest.

"You don't want to be round here, miss," said a man in a supervisor's jacket. A whistle hung around his neck along with his goggles. He tipped his bowler for her. "'Tis not a place for ladies."

Effie smiled and ducked her head as if embarrassed. She saw the gleam in the man's gaze and decided to act coy. "Thank you, I didn't know. I just wanted to see the bunkers I've heard so much about."

The supervisor ran a hand over his mustache. "Just arrived in the city, are you?" He glanced over at Waverly Station. "The last train to arrive embarked from Inverness this morning. You come from there? A pretty town full of beautiful things, it is. I've seen it with me own eyes when I worked the line as an engineer's apprentice. What brings you to Edinburgh?"

"I have a cousin who works as a secretary," said Effie, saying the first thing that popped into her head. "She's going to teach me to typeset and how to file. I know I don't belong down here, but my curiosity got the best of me." She put on a look of wonder. "It's so much coal. It must be from a thousand mines."

Chuckling, the man shook his head. "Nay, not as many as that."

She pointed at one of the bunkers. "Is there enough coal in there to power an airship? I saw them in the sky as we approached, but it's too dark now." She scanned the night, futilely.

"More than enough to fly a dozen ships to London. We build them here in the city, you know? Soon the entire horizon will be filled with them, shuttling folks around the Isles. Some say around the world, though not in a go, of course. Would need to land and re-supply quite a few times for all that."

"Heavens, what a wonder it'd be to fly in one of them!" She felt stupid reacting like a naïve little girl, especially as the memories of her flight with the winged contraption flitted through her head, but if she was overdoing it, the man gave no indication.

"Do you receive your coal from Sir Walter Conrad?" she asked. "I've heard much talk of his mines near Glen Avon, and someone on the train said he was in town dining with the duke."

"I fear you're a bit mistaken. Sir Walter isn't a coal miner. He's found some new substance, a highly volatile gas, but one he says is worth more than all the coal in the bunkers." He shook his head again. "Must be something for all the trouble they're having with it. Men dying in explosions, I hear. More than one." He waved an arm. "Stick with coal, I say. It's safer and easier."

Effie spied a soul or two in the bunkers who might disagree with that opinion as she digested the new information. She tried to recall the details of her conversation with Conall Murray, the Scotsman on the train, but could only remember how infuriated she'd been at the sight of the ruined hillsides, a reaction that almost embarrassed her now.

The man stepped closer to her. "You shouldn't dawdle too much without accompaniment. Evening's coming, and soon the bunkers will empty, the men heading home or to the public houses." The supervisor's jaw worked as if he were about to continue, but a shout drew his attention. His brow scrunched as he grabbed for his whistle.

Effie jumped on the opportunity to remove herself. She thanked him and hurried away, lest an awkward proposition arise. He stared after her for a moment, as if deciding whether to follow, then shook his head in frustration, barking orders at the coal porters.

She wandered for a few minutes, uncertain where to head next, until she passed the shop of a tinker. Through the window she could make out diagrams of lighthouses hung on a wall. The faint tapping of a hammer came from a corner of the shop where a jolly-looking fellow with red-chapped cheeks hunched over something on a table. Bits of metal scrap lay in piles across the floor. The shelves held vials and jars of different chemicals, and crates of what looked like glass tubes were stacked in the room's center.

Stepping past a pair of barrels, one of sand and one of water, she hollered to the tinker. "Pardon, sir. My name is Miss Martins."

"We're closed, lass," said the man, keeping his head bent to his work.

"I noticed your lighthouses. I'm a draftswoman, and…."

"Not hiring." He waved her off, his tone distracted rather than rude. He started tapping the hammer again, the rapping barely audible.

Effie bit her lip. Night descended quickly, and it was time she returned to see what Gabus had discovered. But she'd spent time with tinkers before and knew their ilk. If the man were worth his salt, he'd know all about Sir Walter Conrad and the operations at Glen Avon. She glanced toward the door to make sure no one else was within hearing. "I work for Thomas Stevenson," she announced. It was the only thing she could think of that might loosen the man's tongue without her having to explain her curiosity.

The hammering stopped. "Do you now?" His gaze rose to meet

hers.

"As I said, your diagrams caught my attention." She held her voice firm despite the weight of the tinker's sudden attention.

His eyes flitted to wall. "Beautiful things. A cherished form and function. I wish I could say the designs are mine, but they're from a Dutch fellow I met in Delft. Do you know them?"

She squinted, taking in the hexagonal shape and flat roof. Both were odd elements foreign to her. "No," she admitted.

"Never been built," he replied, appraising her. He set the hammer down and toddled over to her. Beneath his apron, the man wore the trews of a Campbell. One shoulder was protected by a thin plate sewn into thick leather, the metal corroded and scratched. "Genius, though. Uses a system of cells flooded with electrolytes to power the lamp. Stevenson still uses that fey powder. Good for some things, but Fey Craft will never be as elegant as science. Too much unpredictability."

"What of Sir Walter Conrad?" She jumped right in. There was no sense wasting time; she'd already told the man more of her secrets than was prudent. "Rumor has it men have died over this new gas he's discovered. Is it as unpredictable?"

"Not just a gas, but a new element!" The man's red cheeks lit up. "A substance of wonder he calls Aerfenium. His lads found it prospecting for iron. Poor souls breached the crust of a cavern filled with the stuff, and their lamps caused it to ignite. Brought the whole mountainside down on them." He shook his head, but the glee didn't fade from his expression. "A tough way to go, no doubt, and a shame for them to miss all the excitement. With a handful of his men dead, Sir Walter had to come up and inspect the goings-on. That's when he made the discovery. Within a month of the disaster, he's shocked the empire with the properties of this stuff."

"But I've seen no great announcement."

"You wouldn't, would you? They're trying to keep it all hushed up. But tinkers, engineers, and plain folks just looking for work are rushing up to the site. Word leaks out. Some say Sir Walter's found a way to control the gas and feed it into a boiler in small doses. It burns a fire ten times hotter than coal. Ten times, mind you. With that kind of pressure, engines will go faster than anyone's ever dreamed. Not to mention it's a gas, so there's no weight to it. What do you say to that?"

Effie blinked. If true, the implications of the discovery were astounding. Subtracting the need for heavy bins of coal would reduce the overall weight of any object using a boiler. Carriages could be made to hold more people, smaller and faster. Airships could travel further and would need less loft. No more coal bins would mean no more shoveling, and an end to filthy air. The world would indeed change.

"The gas would warrant stronger boilers, to handle the greater pressure," she said. She heard the excitement in her voice as her mind raced to catch up with all the possibilities the new technology would bring.

"Aye," agreed the tinker. "So you see, a few men dead don't mean nothing to a man like Sir Walter Conrad. Even that second explosion they're saying happened a couple nights past won't deter him. All in the name of science, he'll put it. And who can say he's wrong?"

"But how was this substance not discovered before?"

The tinker huffed. "The world's a big place, lass. There are probably thousands of elements yet to be uncovered, hidden away in the lands of heathens and primitives. We've only begun to dig at the Earth's riches. She'll yield more in the future. God will see to it, and those of science will hearken to the call."

Effie reined in her thoughts as the tinker rambled. She'd seen the worksite with her own eyes, yet had read nothing of it in the newspapers. "You said Sir Walter aims for secrecy. Why is that, if this is such an astounding discovery?"

"Ha! The money, of course! An announcement would send men scrambling to find the stuff themselves. You know what happened in California with Sutter's discovery. If Sir Walter can find a way to prospect for his Aerfenium before anyone else, and own that part of it, he'll make himself the richest man in the world. Him and his investors."

A gong went off in Effie's head, the vibrations of it staggering her. She grabbed the wall to steady herself. "The Hostmen of Newcastle."

"Aye, they're the ones." The man nodded. He toddled back to his worktable. "That's why my batteries are so important. Watch this!"

He hefted the object he'd been tinkering with, a metal cylinder the diameter of a cannonball and length of an arrow. A strap went around his neck to help hold the weight as he began turning a crank sticking out of the middle. Gears churned within the contraption, grinding loudly. At first Effie couldn't tell what was happening, until he swung the thing about and the beam of light it cast danced on the wall.

"Portable light without a flame," he said. "I built it for the mines. No explosions this way. One just needs to have a lad crank it continuously and you can illuminate any place you'd like. In a week's time I'll be making a hundred of these things for Sir Walter, and then every other prospector will want to follow."

"Spectacular," said Effie, trying to force enthusiasm into her voice. She was impressed but still reeled at the scope of Sir Walter's discovery. The man's designs and Stevenson's were at odds, yet a threat now loomed for them both. The Hostmen had no doubt played a part in calling up the regiment from Newcastle, wanting protection for their investment. Protection they could control. It meant they feared the sinister events befalling the Highlands just as much as Stevenson's investors.

The laird killed men out of some game he played. But the foe of her foe, Sir Walter, allowed men to die in the name of progress. The ground seemed to grow murkier by the day, leaving no safe path in sight.

She thanked the tinker and wished him luck with his Portable Flameless Torch. She forced herself not to run as she departed. She and Gabus had work to do, no doubt a long night of poring over tomes in the library. But by morning, Effie wanted to know just who this Laird of Aonghus was, and better yet, who his allies were.

A train pulled into Waverly Station. Even in the failing light, the puffs of black smoke filled the sky. New Town and Old Town teemed with life on the hills to either side, and atop those were the windows of tenements and offices. Many were illuminated, filled with men like the tinker, hunched over designs and devices, conjuring the future. She could think of a thousand things to do with Aerfenium if it proved stable enough.

Climbing her way up Castle Rock, she entered the Town Below through a portal in Lawnmarket and headed along Mary King's Close.

A few twists and turns took her beneath the High Kirk of Edinburgh, and from there to Marlin's Wynd. She found Gabus in a frantic state, rushing about the abandoned shop, throwing things into her rucksack. In went flasks and candles, a notebook and a hammer. Her pick and trowel lay next to the bag, ready to be lashed to the outside.

"Gabus, what is it?" Effie dodged to the side as her friend pushed past.

"Oh!" the gnome exclaimed, clutching her chest. "You gave me a start. I thought you a banshee! Good you are back, though. It's time we are leaving. The city is not a place for us anymore. Too dangerous." She swallowed and ran a hand over her lips. "A pity, though. I will miss the weather." She cinched up her rucksack and planted her hands on her hips, surveying the shop. "And those sausage pastries, crisped just right. I'd make them with a bit more spice, some chilies from the Americas, but for here they are okay. The best."

Effie stammered, trying to catch up with the frenetic gnome. "What danger?"

"You had things right. You Scottish fey are all heading north. To the sky, I'm told." She frowned and wrung her hands. "Is there some airship to fly them? How else to get into the clouds? Nay, you Scots make no sense." She slung her rucksack onto her back and hefted a stout walking stick.

Effie was more confused. "Wait. Slow down. Where are you going?"

Gabus stared at a pile of rocks left on the table. "I will miss the University. It has a wonderful collection of books." She wagged a finger. "Not as good as Heidelberg but useful."

"Gabus!"

The gnome blinked and looked at her. "What? Are you ready?"

Effie pushed out a slow breath and released her clenched fists. "No, and I'm not letting you take another step until you tell me what's going on." The gnome's eyes narrowed, but Effie didn't budge.

"These Sidhe Bhreige are nasty devils. Not an exaggeration, *ja?* Truly, they are fell demons from the tales of nightmares. Your folk cast them out centuries ago. Their return *ist sehr* bad. Their beasts will ravage the land, killing and enslaving. So let the humans fight them, *ja*? There are rocks aplenty elsewhere."

Effie stammered. "But...Who? How are they coming back?"

"The spell binding them has failed," said Gabus. "Perhaps we return to Bavaria. The Erbgraf should be warned." She paused, considering. "Or maybe we head to Vinland, across the ocean. But now, we must go. Any who stay are more fool than a pixie in the moonlight." She pushed past Effie, but they both froze at a sound from outside the shop.

The scuff of footfalls on the dirt echoed down the wynd. Effie met her friend's panicked expression and gestured for her to turn around so she could get at the pick. Reaching out, she'd just clasped the haft when the metal click of a pistol being cocked broke the silence.

A man spun into the doorway. He had a wide jaw and broad shoulders. A drab suit coated in coal dust hung on his gaunt frame. He leveled the small pistol in his hand, holding it at the waist. Devious glee shone in his eyes, at odds with the snarl of his lip.

A Sniffer. Effie had seen enough of the zealots to recognize their kind by the fanatical hatred seething behind their glares.

Gabus leapt aside, yanking the pick from Effie's grasp. Snatching a chair, Effie hurled it across the room. The pistol fired, and she heard a whoosh as the bullet ripped past her ear.

"*Gott in Himmel!*" gasped Gabus. The gnome ducked her head and bolted, careening through the pile of man and chair.

The Sniffer rose to a knee and leveled the pistol at her back, cocking it again. Effie lurched forward, driving her shoulder into him. They bowled over. Her feet found flesh and she kicked, scrambling to win free from the tangle. A hand yanked her hair back, the other snaking its way around her throat. Spinning, she flailed, cracking her elbow into the man's face.

He brought his legs over and kicked through hers, toppling them again. Effie flopped on her stomach and crawled forward. A heavy arm fell on her neck and crushed her to the ground. The man's weight followed. She wormed, reaching back with her hands.

The cold barrel of the pistol pressed against her head. She stopped cold, sprawled halfway out of the shop. In the distance, she could make out the shadow of Gabus. The gnome hesitated, watching the struggle.

"Run!" Effie screamed as the man astride her leveled his pistol at the gnome and fired. The shadow disappeared.

Effie's ears rang from the shot. A savage growl rumbled from her throat as iron shackles snapped on her wrists.

CHAPTER 12

Her body ached. Her backside was stiff from sitting on the cell's single bench, her shoulders sore from leaning against the barren stone wall. Her toes pinched from wearing her shoes too long, her feet swollen within the supple leather, and her knees burned from where she'd scuffed them trying to run from the Sniffer. The shackles still drooped from her wrists. She could move them only a little before they dug into her skin. A draft swept under the slats of the door, making the discomfort worse. The bite of cold froze her to the bone, making her shiver so horribly she bit her tongue.

She didn't know how long she'd been left in the cell, but her stomach had only begun to gurgle. A few hours at the most, she guessed. The Sniffer had pulled a hood over her head before leading her on an endless march up stairs and through covered arches, across slick cobblestones, and finally to a room where a fire had roared. There, a deep-timbered voice had jested at her appearance and offered the Sniffer a drink. She remembered the clink of glasses and a muffled conversation. Then a firm hand had grabbed her.

"Hold still," the Sniffer had breathed into her ear before jabbing a needle into her arm. The other man had laughed and made some rude comment as the room spun into blackness.

She'd woken to find herself in the cell. A red splotch puffed where the syringe had gone in. She tried not to look at it. Every time she did, it throbbed. She thought to call out, to beg for a drink of water, or better yet for one of whiskey. For some food. To demand to speak to a magistrate. But she knew what fate awaited her. Unless she could get word to Stevenson, her life would soon end at the bottom of a short drop. One attached to an even shorter rope.

At least Gabus had escaped. If only she'd listened and they'd left a moment earlier, perhaps they'd now be in some village outside the city discussing the matter over tea. She shook her head. No, the Sniffer had trailed one of them and lain in wait. There was no other plausible explanation. It didn't matter which of them it had been. Knowing which cow broke wind didn't help clear the air, her mother used to say.

She needed to focus. Ramsey was still in danger, as were the people of Duncairn. From the news Gabus brought, and from what she'd read in the newspapers, the whole of the Highlands spun into jeopardy. The troubles Stevenson feared had only chipped at the surface of a hidden iceberg. What frightened her most were the stories of munitions stolen from the regiment camped near Montrose. Were the trows arming themselves? Did they fear the regiments marching north under the queen's banners? Memory of their salivating grins made her flesh crawl. Perhaps it was the army who should fear.

A key clanked into the lock of the door, scraping along the metal. Effie's innards churned, melting into her legs. A lump clogged her throat. Despite her resolve to stand firm, she held her breath. The panic angered her, mostly from the lack of control it seemed to consent. She'd promised herself to rage against her captors, to show them they were not mistaken in treating her like a savage. She steeled herself and rose. Planting her feet, she leveled her gaze.

But the man who came through the door sucked all her bravado and anger away. She gasped. "You?"

Black, curly locks bounced as the man bowed. "Good evening, Miss Martins. I am sorry to meet you in such an unfortunate circumstance. I had hoped we'd run across one another again, but in some grander place."

"You're...." Effie started, but she couldn't find another word.

"Conall Murray, from the train to Aberdeen."

"Yes, I know," she snapped. "I meant to say...Well I don't know what I meant to say." She took in his fine dress. "Are you my barrister?"

"Ha!" He smiled, but his eyes remained without mirth. "No, though I wish it were so. I fear I am the enemy. I've come to ready you for an interrogation." He paused and studied his hands. "I did try to see you earlier, but you looked so restful sleeping."

She thrust her arm forward, the wound throbbing as her blood rushed. "Restful! This? I believe the word is abducted." Her brain spun, not quite able to make out what Mr. Murray's role was in her capture. Her enemy, and not a barrister. Certainly not a guard, either. Was the man a clerk of some sort? She tried to think of why a clerk would travel to Aberdeen.

And then it clicked. She slumped her rump back onto the bench. "You're a Sniffer," she said, her voice full of frost.

He ducked his head as if in apology. "I'm afraid you are correct, though my official title is Fey Finder. My colleague, Mr. John Thomas, contacted me when he brought you in. It is lucky for you that he did. Mr. Thomas is not well-versed in the manners of polite society."

She stared, denying she'd ever felt a moment of sympathy for the man. Denying the thrill his touch had brought as they parted. "You're a vile creature, to put on airs aboard the train. What game did you play, to treat me thus?" He looked down at her, and she lurched back to her feet, not wanting to give him the satisfaction.

"You must accept my apology," he said, with a sincerity in his voice that both confused and infuriated her. He leaned forward and lowered his voice. "I didn't know you were a Sithling then, and even if I had known you must trust that I wouldn't have acted." He tried to smile. "You see, I'm new to my post and not very skilled at it."

"Lies." Her blood boiled. "How could you not know? Your kind can sniff fey. It is the very nature of your profession."

"Not all of us. I can smell only the lovely flowers in your perfume." Murray's words stung as if he mocked her, some rude jest only he and his brethren shared. She eyed the door, judging Murray's size and the gap between him and the frame.

He caught her gaze and the smile faded. "You would not make it far, Miss Martins. There are guards within the corridors and along the walls, and I fear they would not be kind to one in your position. I beg that you do not make trouble, or it'll go worse for you."

Reaching behind the door, he pulled forth a set of iron chains. "I will also need to shackle your feet," he said, stepping forward. "The magistrate is not as trusting as myself." He looked on her with an expression of remorse and leaned forward to clamp on the chains.

She slapped him with all her weight. The sound was like the belch of a cannon. Her palm caught fire and arm went numb, and within a heartbeat a turnkey appeared with a club in hand.

"Filthy fiend," the turnkey sneered. His teeth were yellow and putrid, the stubble on his chin covering a patchwork of scabs and scars.

"Quite all right," said Murray, clutching his cheek. He held the other man back and continued his work.

Effie remained limp, seething as the chains were clamped on her ankles. The turnkey chuckled and slapped the meat of the club into his palm. She was grateful when Murray sent him away, but her fury remained pitched as the Sniffer ushered her from the cell, leading her down a hallway of stone and up a short, winding stair.

They emerged into the night in a courtyard dwarfed by a giant oak tree. A curtain wall cornered by rounded turrets enclosed the yard, and behind the tree a keep rose toward the stars. Its stone was illuminated by the warm light of gas lamps spilling from the tiny slits that fashioned its windows, and from torches spaced along the wall.

"We're not in the city," she said, breathing in the fresh air. Wood smoke filled her nostrils along with a hint of roasted fowl.

"Craigmillar Castle lies just outside its boundaries," said Murray. "A hunk of old stones no one has cared about for centuries. The crown procured it for special prisoners, those they wish to hold in secret."

"So they can hang them in secret without the messiness of an honest trial," she said. The notion scared her more than if they made a spectacle of her. At least then her fate would be known to her friends. Murray didn't deny the accusation, but the grip on her arm dropped. He strode toward the keep and left her to shuffle along behind, her chains jingling like the bells of a sleigh.

He led her through the great hall to a chamber warmed by a pair of hearths. Her skin prickled at the sudden heat, and she tried to will herself to absorb as much as possible. A large desk dominated the room. It sat atop a carpet with a muted floral design. A sideboard held brandy and whiskey, and a pair of chairs rested beneath a tapestry depicting a hunting scene.

Behind the desk sat a man in thick black robes, his beard neatly trimmed and fingers coated in ink. He worked at a stack of papers, reading each in turn, sometimes scrawling out notes in the margins. Murray stepped forward and waited until the man looked up. "Your Honor, I've brought Miss Martins."

The magistrate eyed her through a set of spectacles. "The Sithling," he said. "Very well." He rang a tiny bell, and a valet appeared. The magistrate gestured, and the valet bowed and departed on some errand, his master putting his head back to his papers. Effie and Murray were left to stand in silence.

Minutes passed, but each time Effie spoke she was either shushed or ignored outright, and all attempts at movement were halted by Murray. Her feet had grown weary by the time the valet returned. Holding the door ajar, he ushered in a pair of gentlemen dressed as if they were expected at a ball.

"Sir Walter Conrad and Mr. Edward Waite," announced the valet. Effie gasped as the room tilted. She stumbled and was grateful when Murray grabbed her arm to hold her steady. The man was making a habit of such action.

Sir Walter peered at her from dark orbs perched on gaunt cheeks. Raven-black hair cropped close to his head made his lanky body appear that much thinner. His pressed and starched clothes hung stiff about his frame, everything in its proper place. The other man stood a hand shorter, with a flowing mane of white tucked delicately behind his ears.

"Yes, very good." The magistrate set his pen down and rose. "Sir Walter, I'm sorry to have pulled you from your dinner, but you bade me inform you if we came across any fey while you were in the city. I'm not sure what this one was up to, but we found her beneath the Tron Kirk, no doubt plotting with the heathens that dwell there."

"Quite right for fetching me," said Sir Walter. He shook the man's hand and stepped aside. "You may leave now." The dismissal was sharp, like the crack of a whip. The magistrate's jaw worked. He was clearly not used to being dismissed, especially not from his own chambers. Yet Sir Walter gave no indication he'd given insult, and his tone left no doubt who commanded the room.

With a curt nod, the magistrate bade Murray to follow as he strode out. Murray shuffled his feet, his eyes flitting between Effie and Sir Walter. "Beg pardon, sir, but do you think I should stay so as not to leave the prisoner unattended?"

Sir Walter laughed. "Do you suppose she'll work some Fey Craft on us? Chained up as you have her, I doubt she could take a piss!"

The Sniffer bristled but conceded defeat. He found her gaze, his own with that same somber cast she'd seen on the train. Effie thought for a moment he might take her hand before he remembered himself. Turning, he fled without a word.

Sir Walter's smirk trailed him out the door. "Odd fellow, but I fathom it's in his line of work." Once they were alone, he crossed the room to stand before Effie. "Have you ever met a Sithling before, Mr. Waite? This one is quite attractive. Quite clean, too. She'd make for a good children's tale, the kind with gold dust and sweets."

Waite sneered. "Newcastle rid itself of their kind long ago," he said. He moved to the sideboard to pour them a pair of drinks. "Now, they're only kept as amusements at carnivals, though I've never seen one whose tricks were more than slight of hand. Bawdy nonsense, most think it."

"And you?"

"I call them an abomination of science."

"Tsk, tsk, Mr. Waite." Sir Walter's smirk returned with gusto. His eyes sparkled as if the funniest thing in the world had just occurred, but it was something only he could understand. "Don't you know everything is science? And science is everything. Isn't that right, Miss Martins?"

Effie had recovered from the shock of Sir Walter's arrival. Disdain for his callous sense of humanity warred within her against an overwhelming curiosity. A part of her wanted to wrap the shackles around his throat and snuff the smile from his face for treating her thus. But another part yearned to pick at his vast knowledge, for him to tell her everything of Aerfenium and their plans for its use. He was no friend of Stevenson's, but it seemed they now shared a common cause. She forced herself to relax, unclenching her shoulders and fists. Civility was always the best course when negotiating, Graham had taught her, and it now stood as her best chance at gleaning any information the man might impart. Not that the knowledge would do her much good if she couldn't manage to free herself.

"I certainly don't consider myself an abomination," she said.

"There you have it, Mr. Waite." Sir Walter sipped at his brandy. "And I believe her. To the contrary of the world's detestation, I believe the fey are perhaps the greatest scientists on Earth."

Waite snorted. "You won't be saying that in front of my trustees. Some are not as lenient toward open-mindedness as I am, and many are of the opinion that one noted geologist is as good as the next."

"I have not forgotten. They are a group stalwart in their principles, and yet what would the world be without greed?" asked Sir Walter. The two men exchange a look as weighted as an anvil. The silence seemed to last an hour before Waite broke his gaze. He moved behind the magistrate's desk and began shuffling through the papers.

Sir Walter turned back to Effie. "It dawned on me years ago that to Alcuin of York the works of the Greek mathematicians must've read like fables. Certainly to those lords within Charlemagne's court, they were a far cry from the Catholic superstitions that plagued their day." He leaned back and rested against the front of the magistrate's desk. "So I asked myself, how is that different than the lore of the Scottish fey? Could their Fey Craft be nothing more than an advanced knowledge of scientific principles, as yet unknown to man?"

"Such talk can get you killed," said Effie. "Or worse, shunned. Discredited."

"Quite right. So I am careful to discuss the matter only with those who will never be believed, or those whose pockets I line with gold."

Effie wanted to laugh at the man's hubris but kept her face a blank mask. "I'm sorry to disappoint you, but there is a great flaw in your logic. If Sithlings are humans putting some con upon the world, what of pixies and gnomes and hogboons? Not to mention the giants and the dwarves? Are they human as well, altered by science?"

"Oh, I have no doubt the different fey races exist. I see proof of that standing before me. It is the basis of your Fey Craft I question, your claims of mystical powers only your kind can possess. The druids once held dominion in these isles based on similar lies."

"And you expect me to confirm your suspicions?"

Sir Walter shook his head, his unyielding smirk giving her shivers. "No, I wouldn't imagine you would. Even if you held such knowledge, which I doubt—after all, the lie of your Fey Craft would work best if maintained in earnest by only a few of your kind, leaving the rest ignorant—you would deny me the satisfaction."

"Then why summon me? To discuss your Aerfenium?" She took a guess and was rewarded. His brow twitched, and in his gaze she saw him reevaluate her.

"Word was bound to spread," he mused. "There is only so long such a discovery can be kept quiet." He raised his glass in a mocking salute toward her. "Thousands will seek to harness the substance and turn a fortune on the labor we have done. But we will not let them. Aerfenium is ours to mine and ours to dispense."

"I'm sure the crown will see it that way," she scoffed. "What would they want with faster ships and machines that can fly through the air light enough to carry a battery of cannons?"

"They will have no choice if we can find it all first," barked Waite. He set down the papers and jabbed a finger into the desk to emphasize his point. "The Hostmen of Newcastle maintain their grip not by developing boilers but by overseeing the trade of coal. Let other fools invent what they will, as long as we see our share of the profit."

"So you see our predicament?" asked Sir Walter. "Time is running short, and we need to patent a way to prospect for Aerfenium before some other hoard is discovered. If we own the finding of the substance, we stand to profit from every invention that comes after."

Effie dropped her gaze and studied her feet, trying to process what Sir Walter was really saying. The man had some illusion she could find Aerfenium faster than he could. That meant he either thought the substance was of fey origin, like the stardust Stevenson used, or that Fey Craft had some affinity for finding it. It was why he'd sent the magistrate and Conall Murray away—he was desperate to keep his theories secret.

Her gut fluttered with excitement. She had no intention of

dissuading the man from his notions. As long as he believed she held the knowledge he sought, she would be safe from execution. Hardening her tone, she tensed her body, putting on the air of a coiled snake. "If you think I would help you, you're stark raving mad."

"Men have died for our cause!" barked Waite. "Good men, and I won't leave their work for others to pilfer. We need to know Aerfenium's properties, whether it is stable and how to safely extract it."

"Don't trouble yourself," said Sir Walter. "She will tell us her secrets, even if she doesn't intend to. There are means to see to that."

"And what of the attacks? They are coming dangerously close to the excavation."

Effie frowned. More news of attacks, and from the lips of a man who wouldn't bend to gossip. But near Glen Avon? How many minions could the Laird of Aonghus possibly control?

"The fey will do anything to protect their substance," said Sir Walter. He drained the rest of his brandy and tossed the glass onto the desk. It clunked and rolled across the blotter, forcing Waite to trap it and set it upright before it tumbled to the floor. "Unfortunately for them, the queen has more men and more bullets."

CHAPTER 13

Her audience with Sir Walter Conrad ended as abruptly as it had begun. Her efforts to pry out further information made Edward Waite bluster until his cheeks bulged like ripe tomatoes. Sir Walter's eyes only sparkled with amusement. From the cold tension between the two men, it appeared the Hostmen of Newcastle sought to keep their investment on a short leash. That was a nugget Stevenson could use to his advantage. She was glad his name wasn't mentioned, and she wondered how long she could avoid her captors making the connection. The thought made her fear what else the evening would bring. The geologist had made it clear: she would divulge her secrets or face torture.

She swallowed down the moment of panic and ran through her encounter with Sir Walter. The man believed the fey were mounting attacks to protect the secret of Aerfenium, something linked to the science they masqueraded as Fey Craft. But Duncairn was nowhere near Glen Avon, so Sir Walter couldn't have referred to those attacks. The unrest the newspapers spoke of was more widespread. Before the Sniffer had interrupted them, Gabus had said a spell had failed releasing the Sidhe Bhreige. The Sidhe Bhreige, meaning more than one. Effie bit her lip, feeling as empty as a whiskey cask on Hogmany. She didn't know fey could cast binding spells, let alone anything of the Sidhe Bhreige. With every scrap she learned, it felt like a thousand threads were missing.

Conall Murray marched beside her as they returned to the cell.

The Sniffer had withdrawn further into himself, his stare distant as he ushered her along. Something had hurt the man fierce to bring on such a melancholic disposition, but she had enough enemies to contend with not to worry over the happiness of one she should despise.

The turnkey threw the cell door open, the glee in his eyes making the chamber more frigid than it already was. She remained stiff as Murray took the shackles off her legs.

"I'll get you some food," he said.

"Can you take these off as well?" she asked, raising her hands. He glanced about the empty cell and at the sturdy door. Nodding, he unclamped her wrists. Her arms felt weightless after wearing the iron for so long. Red rings of pinched skin throbbed as she shook out her hands.

"And fetch me a blanket," she said, as Murray turned to leave. He stopped and regarded her. Some of the warmth came back to his eyes. She scowled. "It's cold enough to freeze snow in here," she added.

The corners of his mouth twitched. "I believe that's part of the charm, Miss Martins."

"It is, indeed," said a voice from the corridor. It had been a dozen years, but Effie still recognized the clipped brogue. It haunted her dreams on dark nights. Her gut watered at the sound. Her evening had just reeled into terror, and she felt herself spinning. She crumbled to the bench, her legs no longer able to support her.

Edmund Glover reached the doorway. "The strumpet of Glen Coe," he sneered. "I did not believe the news." His rotund form reminded her of a suckling pig. His coat and vest were as fine as Sir Walter's, though he wore them not as a gentleman but as an actor fopping about the stage. He squinted at her through purple-colored lenses. A pale scar of puckered flesh covered his cheek and chin, a reminder of their last encounter. Fissures ran through the flesh, red and dry and cracked. Seared was the best term for it, for it'd been acid that had done the work. Monster was the best term to describe the man, more so than even the trows. His brow hung thick over narrow eyes and a sharp nose. His hairline had receded over the years, and what remained was swept over to one side, wetted down against the scalp. He held the same black case he'd carried before, cruel instruments kept within.

"I fear you've tangled our professions," she said. She met his eyes but couldn't keep the tremble from her voice. "It is you who takes money for sinful deeds."

"As petulant as ever. I should've killed you the moment I discovered you in that wayhouse." He thrust a finger at his scarred face. "But now I have this to remind me never to trust your wicked race. I wear it as a trophy, did you know? When people stare and children startle, my chest swells. Their discomfort is nothing compared to the moral justification I've received from your hand." He leaned forward. "From your deformed blood."

Effie choked on his breath, but defiance flared, not allowing her to shy away. "Bring me some twinflower. I would be glad to bolster your resolve even further." It was the rare flower from the pinewoods of Strathspey, mixed with her blood, that had produced the acid which burned him. Her anger welled, fueling her will against the terror. "Perhaps until there is nothing left but the pool of slime that is your heart."

He clucked his teeth. "Already she speaks of murder," he said to Murray. "You see, young man, the vicious beast is best put down." He crossed the cell and set down his case. "Go see to her gruel, and lock the door on your way out." Murray ducked his head, appearing as unnerved by the Fey Finder General as she was. She felt his gaze linger as the door swung closed, but her eyes never left Glover. She flinched as the lock clicked.

Glover pulled open the case. Inside sat an assortment of needles and small blades, some curved, ending at sharp pricks, others flat with jagged teeth. A row of stoppered vials were strapped to the interior, and a white cloth dotted with blood was folded neatly atop a coil of clear tubing. Sweat beaded at her temple. She thought of Sir Walter's earlier threats, and the notion that she could fool such a man for more than a minute suddenly seemed ridiculous.

"It's illegal to kill me without a trial," she said without thinking. The objection was weak at best. Despite the calls for liberty and fair treatment made by labor parties across the empire, many prisoners still met with misfortune while incarcerated, and there were those who simply disappeared. Yet even if she had a trial, the outcome would be known before it began. By a simple compound mixed with her blood, Glover could prove she was a Sithling, and her kind was not granted any leniency. The best she could hope for was to stall, to buy time for Stevenson to act. But for that she would need to get him word.

"I am aware of the law," said Glover. "I am the eyes of justice, not the sword, though I'm sure the hangman will allow me the honor of placing the noose around your neck when the time comes." He took up the cloth and blotted his forehead. "It is a quick death for most, but not if the rope isn't positioned properly. Men have been known to struggle for almost an hour as the knotted cords choke the life from them, suffocating their will in a rather prolonged terror. They would cry out and beg the mercy of God, if only they could speak." He pulled out a wicked-looking blade and inspected it. "How is it you think you will die?"

She swallowed and clamped her lips shut, refusing to give him any satisfaction. Her fingers throbbed from clutching the bench, her legs felt like bundles of straw. "Alas," he continued, "that moment must be delayed, if only for a short while." He rounded on her, waggling the blade in her face. "I know you conspire to carry out a great evil near the town of Montrose, and that many have already fallen prey to your wicked schemes. But my agents there tell me of creatures even more fell sheltering along the coast. You will tell me where I can find your cohorts. The number of days you have left to live depends on it."

Her mind raced. What did the man know? If his agent had already placed her in Duncairn, she could tell him everything of the trows and the Laird of Aonghus. He already seemed to know something of them and could perhaps aid the people of Duncairn where she could not. But she would need to spin a tale of how she came to be there and her involvement in the matter. Else, she might endanger her friends. She grasped for a plausible explanation, but as she gathered the threads of her story, it kept unraveling. She couldn't keep the details straight. The cell was too cold, shrinking and expanding with every breath. Her shoulders shook and mouth ran dry.

Glover hovered over her, his flabby jowls swaying as he bent closer. He pressed the blade to her cheek. "I could use this and make us even. It would make you talk, but not before I ruined your pretty flesh."

She heard her breath grow louder, felt her chest heave. She wondered how quickly she could snatch the blade away, and whether he would simply kill her if she tried. Maybe such an excuse was what he wanted.

His eyes narrowed behind the purple lenses. He jerked back and tossed the blade into the case. "Do you ever wonder why the fey are so loathed? Civility is what separates us. I am civilized while you are a beast."

She gulped in a mouthful of air and slumped against the wall. "It was you who bound a girl, stealing her away for execution. You'll do the same now, once you get the information you want."

He snarled. "Like any huntsman with a prize." Snatching up a syringe, he filled it from one of the vials. "Don't worry. This isn't twinflower. I've experimented much since our last meeting, and I never make the same mistake. You'll find I've learned many things, tested many compounds on other fey. Some killed a few of your brethren before I realized the toxicity to your blood, but I've found a serum that will loosen your tongue."

She stared at the thick needle and fought every urge to blurt out her entire adventure in Duncairn. A man like Glover would never believe her, not without doing things his way. Her only hope was to drive him away from what she wanted hidden. "You took your time in arriving," she said, taking a guess. "Or was it Sir Walter Conrad who wouldn't allow you to see me?"

He paused, his eyes narrowing, the needle hovering above her shoulder. She'd struck a nerve. "I was detained by the prince. We had urgent matters to discuss, far more so than the blather of a pompous buffoon."

"I trust the prince was satisfied with your handling of the fey matter? What with all the brazen attacks and government munitions gone missing? Keeping the peace has suddenly gotten expensive. His Royal Highness must love nothing more than spending the crown's money to address the failures of your office."

Glover jabbed the needle into her already welted arm and fired the plunger. She cried out and clamped a hand over the wound when he withdrew, ducking her head into her lap until she could control her breath. Nausea washed over her, but she refused to succumb.

"Sir Walter had the gall to claim the fey were stalking him," said Glover. He closed his bag and started pacing the cell. "The man claims one of his supply trains was blown up just outside Glen Avon. Destroyed the track, carriage, and lot. No doubt the work of some local peasants' league, if there's any truth to the tale, upset with the destruction of their lands. But not to hear him tell the prince. An insult to him must be a conspiracy!"

Effie felt woozy. Her head lolled to one side, her eyelids became like two stones she couldn't quite hold aloft. She inhaled deeply, the cold air painful in her lungs, and concentrated her thoughts on the trows. She determined to speak of them and nothing else. The trows. Her mind wandered. The trows and their warren. The beach and the cave, but not the fox. She shivered as the critter popped unwittingly into her head, and the room snapped back into focus.

Not the fox. Trows. Trows. Trows. She focused on the word.

"I know your kind," Glover was saying. "Sabotage at that level is beyond your ability. Beyond your ambition." He thrust a finger at her. "Battering young girls and playing tricks on fishermen, that is your way." He leapt at her and pressed a finger and thumb against her eye lids, straining the eye behind. Her head slammed against the stone wall, jarring her teeth.

Glover released her. "We will start with something simple. Do you deny being in Montrose?"

"Duncairn," she heard her voice say. She cringed, her skull still reeling from the knock. "Trows," she added, hoping to add more, but the words just spun before her. She couldn't control them any more than she could pilot an airship.

"Yes, that dismal village. Your minions killed a fisherman there, correct?"

Effie grabbed her temple. Her flesh felt afire, sweat running down her face. "Trows," she mumbled. The pounding in her head reminded her of their cacophony.

"What is it?" Glover sneered. "What is that word you are saying?"

"Trows. Imps out of nightmares. They are the ones responsible." Her tongue was swollen and rough. She asked for water, but Glover ignored her.

"I've never heard of these things. Where did they come from?"

She giggled. "A cave. A cave of salt and sea, full of drums and death." A trickle of blood ran down her arm. She stared at it, the new puckered mark where the needle had gone in ached to the bone. The other was crusted, the flesh surrounding it purple and inflamed.

Trows. Trows. Trows. She tried to sing the word in cadence to the throbbing pain, to sear it into her thoughts so that nothing else escaped.

"And where is this cave?"

"Duncairn," she said. An image of the selkies flashed before her, the poor creatures bewitched unto their deaths. Their blood had spilled, too. She blinked. A connection snapped together. She wasn't bewitched. The thought was obvious, but it took her a moment to realize what it meant. Glover didn't control her, he'd merely rendered her simple. The man had no Craft, Fey or otherwise. He'd cast no spell over her. The way to beat him was the same as it ever was.

His own blustering ego.

"They have a laird of their own and rally to his tune," she blurted before he could ask another question. The man could only steal from her if she let him. She just needed to wrestle the reins away.

Eyes narrowing, Glover's lips pursed. "Tell me of this laird."

Effie looked up and smiled. "He's short and pale and mean."

"Yes, yes, but what of his plans?"

"Oh," she said. "He wants to kill you." She imagined it was true and believed it well enough for the words to roll off her tongue. Glover's reaction emboldened her. "Did he tell you of his Aerfenium?" she asked, not letting him speak.

"What?"

"Sir Walter." She appraised his baffled look. "No, I suppose he wouldn't."

A vein on the man's forehead pulsed. His cheeks flared the color of beets. "How dare you!" Spittle flew from his lips as he bristled.

She ignored him. The rhythmic chant of trows, trows, trows, made the feat easier. In fact, she could barely hear him at all. A shield had risen built by the knowledge that Glover had no spell over her, only a buffoon's understanding of chemistry.

"I guess he didn't allow you to overhear it as he told the prince, either."

Glover seethed. "You will not goad me into knocking you unconscious, so let us stop with this game you're playing." The words whistled through clenched teeth. "Now tell me all you know of this supposed laird."

"He wanted me to do his bidding," she began, telling Glover of her brief encounter. She rambled on, giving details of the trows and their cave, and of the dead selkies who killed Ewan Ross. But she left out parts, too, avoiding Ramsey altogether and the question of what she was doing in the village. She let Glover assume what he would of her intent, and guided him around her honest tale.

When he asked about her life before Duncairn, she told him of forests and streams and hills. She described the landscapes of her drawings, noting every last blade of grass, until frustrated, he abandoned his inquiry. Then she would jab him with another taunt, distracting him, and the cycle would begin anew. By the time he left, she could no longer keep her eyes open and found herself stretching out along the bench. Telling the truth in such a manner was exhausting work. The night was cool and sleep quickly overtook her, despite her growling stomach.

Conall Murray woke her hours later. A blanket had been placed over her, and a plate with bread and cheese lay within reach. She snuggled deeper into the blanket, wanting nothing more than to continue her slumber. Even her sore joints and the unyielding bench couldn't dissuade her. But the Sniffer's presence made her wary.

"I found this cloak for you," he said, as she sat up and dug into the food. Her head still ached, and her eyes shied from the light.

"What of my reticule? My belongings?"

"I'm afraid it won't be allowed. Mr. Glover was quite insistent none of your effects be returned to you." Murray placed the cloak, a thick, blue woolen thing, on the bench next to her. "He was mighty piqued this morning. I can't say as you gave him all he wanted."

"He got what he deserved." She frowned as she tore apart the last of the cheese, folding it into the bread. "Why would I need a cloak?"

"For the journey to Duncairn. Mr. Glover won't leave you out of sight and means to try you in front of, as he put it, 'the villagers to whom you've most offended.'"

She gagged on the bread and forced herself to swallow the last lump. "I would think the city folk would be more ardent in their calls for my death," she said. Historically, the mobs of Edinburgh had been known to turn violent on just about any prisoner, and sometimes even the guards. It was the country folk of the Lowlands and Highlands who kept a soft spot for the fey, despite their claims of vexation.

Murray shrugged, not meeting her gaze. He stepped into the corridor and gestured. The turnkey appeared, his meaty arms hoisting a tub of water. The man produced a chunk of soap and a towel, leering at her all the while. Murray sent the man out and shut the door. She eyed the soap and water, then turned back to the Sniffer.

His cheeks blushed. "I am instructed not to leave you unattended."

"For Heaven's sake," she snapped. Rising, she started unbuttoning her dress. The embarrassment would be worth it to sluice off all the grime from the previous day. She had scrapes, bruises, and cuts to cleanse as well. Murray crossed to the far corner of the cell and turned his back to her, folding his arms.

"I thought you weren't to let me out of your sight," she said, sharply.

He swallowed. "I am a gentleman first, Miss Martins."

Snorting, she let her clothes drop. "I think you Sniffers have a different idea of that term." She picked up the soap and dunked it. The cold water brought pimples to her flesh, but the effect served to waken her dulled senses. She studied Murray's back and wondered how quickly she could reach him, whether she could knock him cold with a single blow. But there was still the turnkey to deal with and the other guards, not to mention the castle wall. It would take them a day at least to reach Duncairn, and there Ramsey could aid in her escape, if the opportunity didn't present itself on the open road. She shivered but told herself it was only from the water.

CHAPTER 14

Effie embarked for Duncairn with iron shackles binding her wrists and ankles. She stood in the back of a wain, iron bars forming a cage around her, feeling like a heretic from centuries past on her way to burn at the stake. The plow horse pulling the wain did nothing to lessen that effect. It chomped and snorted as it hauled her, eyeing her as if ashamed of its part in the task. The turnkey drove it with a long whip, while Murray rode behind on an anxious palfrey.

Edmund Glover pranced his own mount aside her, his clothes as neat and foppish as ever. He wore a smirk chiseled on his lips, but refused to acknowledge her presence, glaring instead at any who dared slow his procession. Foolishly, he believed the iron of her chains worked against whatever Fey Craft she possessed, but the bars and locks welded to the wain were enough. They held her more firmly than all the charlatan's wards and charms in Scotland.

She'd expected them to take a direct route through the city, so Glover could display his prize in the Grassmarket. But they avoided the Old Town, cutting a path to the west through the village of Blackford. There, a few urchins skulking around threw rotten turnips and tatties at her, and one even ran alongside trying to smack her with a stick. But none made any great effort, and soon she was just an oddity rumbling past in the early morning light. Glover did nothing to shoo away the assailants, and she wondered why the man wasn't making a bigger spectacle.

Perhaps he feared the mood of the slums, which were known to turn violent as quickly as the wind gusting off the North Sea. Graham had once told her there was nothing as terrifying in the empire as a mob in Edinburgh. The city's history was full of occasions where the common folk meted out their own brand of justice. And when the sympathies of the disgruntled poor contradicted the pronouncements of the court, sometimes that justice was meted against the prosecutors.

She regarded the Fey Finder General. For all his disgusting faults, she didn't quite believe fear was the reason for their detour. The man was a zealot above all things and wouldn't fathom that the crowds of Edinburgh would stand against him. There was something more afoot, something not only compelling him to drag her out of the city, but to do so in a roundabout way.

"Sir Walter Conrad," she said, as understanding dawned. Glover didn't need her in Duncairn as much as he wanted her out of Edinburgh. She recalled how infuriated he had become at the mention of the geologist's name. She'd assumed Sir Walter's threats to glean information would take form from the Sniffers' hands, but none of the Fey Finders had mentioned Aerfenium. Sir Walter must've demanded her from Glover, who saw fit to remove her from the city before being commanded to hand her over. Certainly, Sir Walter held the prince's ear more so than Glover. Her eyes found the fat man again, with newfound detestation.

After another twenty minutes of trundling, they reached a wayhouse nestled at the intersection of five roads. Glover reined his horse, and the turnkey did likewise. The Sniffer's countenance twitched with dissatisfaction. He pulled a watch from his pocket and flipped it open.

Effie thought of a few choice words for her captors, but kept her mouth shut. It would get her nowhere. Already her feet and legs were sore and back aching from keeping herself balanced as the wain swayed and bounced amongst the ruts in the road. She wouldn't give them an excuse to make her conditions worse.

They waited in silence for another ten minutes, until Murray pointed down one of the roads. "There," he said.

As he gestured, a drum's steady thump reached her ears, a herald of death beating in precise time. She squinted and found its source.

Down the road, the sun glinted off the barrels of rifles and the highly polished buttons of uniforms.

The company of soldiers marched three abreast, five ranks deep, keeping time to the drummer, whose boyish face was like that of a toy. Their lieutenant rode a chestnut horse before them, stiff in the saddle, yet with an easy cast to his features. He stopped and saluted Glover, his eyes running over Effie with a steady consumption.

"You're late, Lieutenant Walford," said Glover, kicking his horse into motion. "The train won't wait for laggards."

The lieutenant moved alongside. His face remained passive and blank. "Empty bellies make for sore feet, I have found. This undertaking called for a proper breakfast, and so I commanded it. I do apologize, Mr. Glover."

The Fey Finder General's head whipped around. "Do you make a jest of me, sir? This is my command, not yours, and you will follow my instructions."

"Certainly not," said Walford, but in answer to the question or response to the statement, Effie could not tell. "But if we had boarded at Waverly…."

Glover snorted, cutting off the lieutenant. "Proper breakfast. I see the Zulus of Africa were not as fierce as the papers made them out. They have made the queen's army soft, wanting for food when they should be minding their duty."

Walford's eyes steeled, his cheeks stretching tight, but he merely nodded his head. "At your lead, General." The soldiers fell in line behind the wain, forcing Murray to move beside her.

"Do you think me as dangerous as to need such an escort?" she asked.

Murray glanced at the riflemen, then Glover. "He means to root out the trows you spoke of." Effie blanched, uncertain why she was appalled at the notion. Perhaps it was just that Glover might succeed where she could not.

The morning took them further west and a little north, until they reached the village of Uphall. Shale mining had taken over the rural area for the purpose of manufacturing oil, and already the great machines could be heard in the distant hills, shrieking their whistles, crunching the earth, their boilers engorged with steam.

They halted at the rail station, which squatted amongst a handful of factories. The turnkey unlocked her cage and pulled her out, jerking her roughly by the shackles. She stumbled, but Murray caught her and ushered her to a bench. Glover checked his watch again and nodded. It was only a few minutes before a train arrived. Once it arrived they loaded the horses into a car, all except the one pulling the wain. The turnkey pulled it around, and with a salute to Glover, started it plodding back toward Craigmillar castle.

The soldiers piled into a car at the front of the train. Glover and Walford inspected them before heading for the rear car where the compartments of the privileged were found. Murray cleared his throat. He held Effie by the arm, looking inquisitively at Glover. The fat man glanced at them peevishly, and gestured for them to follow the soldiers. Effie relaxed her hands. She hadn't realized how tightly they'd balled into fists. Having to listen to Glover's twisted tongue the entire journey would've been worse than all the serums in the world.

Murray ushered her inside and found a seat for her away from the other men. He sat across the aisle, within reach. A whistle shrilled as the train pulled into motion, and the car jerked forward. A few of the soldiers leered openly, while others studied her with curiosity. A couple glared with outright hatred, as if she'd done some harm to them in the past. She tried to ignore them all, keeping her gaze locked on the countryside rolling past, but she couldn't help from feeling unnerved. She'd lost track of the number of strangers who now knew her face, who knew her for a Sithling. It ran counter to all she had ever known, all her mother and Stevenson had taught her. She was outed. Even if Stevenson welcomed her return, she may never be able to work for him again; she would never willingly place his honor in jeopardy.

She watched the fields and hills flit past and forced dour thoughts from her mind. They were concerns for a later time and may well become moot if Glover had his way. But she refused to succumb so easily. Even a cornered mouse still had claws and teeth. Catching the eye of one of the soldiers, she smiled coyly. The man quickly looked away. The next one she caught smiled back, until her grinning stare became so prolonged the soldier paled.

Emboldened, she turned to Murray. "Are you to watch me bathe again tonight?" she asked. "Perhaps this time I will let you wield the soap." She flung the words at him like acid, hoping his insecure manner would set him on the defensive. The young Sniffer might have knowledge she could use to affect her escape.

Conall Murray blushed, but he did not reply. She pressed her tactic. "Your boss has stolen me away from Edinburgh, hasn't he? Right from under the nose of Sir Walter Conrad."

The Sniffer tugged uncomfortably at his collar. "Fey prisoners fall under the authority of the Fey Finder General," he said.

"And Glover's authority falls under that of His Royal Highness, does it not? It is a foolish game he plays, to deny such powerful men their wishes."

"That is not for me to say." He turned toward her. "But you are not far wrong."

The blunt admission shocked her. She knew Murray was not one to hide his position, but to speak of Glover's actions in such a manner was tantamount to mutiny. For the moment, she decided not to press the matter. A slow-burning wick worked better than a fast one, even in her current state. "What regiment are these soldiers from? They don't appear Scottish."

Murray's lips twitched, almost in a grin. "Does it make a difference to you?" She tried to think of a response, but her tongue tied. He couldn't contain his mirth. "I believe you already know the answer. You strike me as a rather intelligent woman."

"Don't let your general hear you say that."

"The intelligent part, or the use of the word woman?"

Both, she thought. She was woman enough in most men's eyes, yet her blood was different, and that kept her from ever truly being human. At least in the eyes of people like Edmund Glover and Sir Walter Conrad. And Murray. That thought shouldn't bother her any more than the others, but it did.

"Newcastle, then," she said.

"Northumberland Hussars brought up to quell the fey disturbances," Murray confirmed.

She smirked. The volunteer cavalry unit was well-known for putting down overly-ambitious unions of miners and fishermen. In

1831, it had even fired on its own countrymen. "To protect the interests of the Hostmen, you mean. It is their money that drives this sudden interest in the Highlands, isn't it? For centuries they have been nothing but barons of the coal trade. Why do they now back a man like Sir Walter Conrad?"

Murray blinked, an expression of surprise crossing his face. "Surely you've heard the chatter in the coffeehouses? Coal has had its day. Its supremacy won't last forever, and the Hostmen want to keep their true monopoly, that on energy. Money and energy drive the world, and there isn't one without the other nearby."

"So they fund research into alternatives."

"And work against other sources they can't dominate." He raised an eyebrow. "Namely, stardust."

The insinuation was clear—the fey were a problem the Hostmen could not control. The hatred of her entire race boiled down to a handful of men who wanted their heirs to live as opulently as they had. A flare of rage swept through her so intense it brought tears to her eyes. "You seem to have a firm grasp on the subject."

"For a time, it was more than a passing interest." He studied his hands. "The empire needs a better source than coal if it is to remain in power. Other countries already outpace our industry, and we are but a small island to compete with them. We must pursue greater technologies, push for even loftier heights if we are to remain on top."

It was a similar argument he'd made before, the last time they'd shared a train. "Do you think any of that matters to the fishermen of Duncairn? If Britain were to return to isolation, they would fish the same as they ever did. The bakers would bake, and the millers would mill."

Murray shook his head. "Not so, I'm afraid. The Zulus have demonstrated what our imperial subjects can achieve, rising up and defeating us on the battlefield."

"We've lost colonies before and the kingdom still stands."

"The reach of the world is far greater than it was then. Imagine what chance we'd stand, if alone we faced a united Germany? And now it seems the League of Emperors is to be reborn, adding Russia and Austria-Hungry to Bismarck's designs. I'm afraid, Miss Martins, we are rats scurrying to keep from drowning."

"So men pillage the land, destroying it to keep other men from destroying them?"

"That is a romantic notion, one of which poets are fond, but not one borne by science. The Picts cut down trees and hauled stone, and the land grew back. The Romans did the same, and so did the kings of Scotland. Yet look at the landscape. Its beauty is surpassed by none. The land re-grows itself."

Her eyes narrowed. "For all your knowledge of the world, you are an utter fool."

He laughed. "And you are a riddle, Miss Martins."

She bit her tongue. She was trying to earn the man's good graces, after all. The train stopped in Stirling and again a bit farther north. No one boarded their car, and by the time they struck eastward half the soldiers were asleep, the other half playing at cards or dice. Though she knew he was a couple years her senior, Murray's contemplative cast appeared almost boyish to her. His brow was never brooding as much as it was in sorrow, as if he thought on some loss. She liked it better when he smiled, and an impulse to jest with him sprang to mind.

"Tell me, how exactly does one sniff for fey?" she asked.

He spread his hands, palms open. "That is a question better asked of my superiors, and even they may not be able to answer it."

The response confounded Effie. Sensing fey blood was a rare ability, however it worked, yet it was long held that all Sniffers could do such a thing. She thought again of her encounters with Edmund Glover and how the man had trusted in his serums to expose her. Could the man not tell without them? She'd assumed if Murray truly didn't have the ability now, that it must lay dormant, and that he'd be instructed in its use in due time.

"I'd thought it a requirement of a Fey Finder. How long has it been since that standard was abandoned?"

"You have me at a loss. I'm afraid I am quite new to this profession. I accepted my appointment only after a recent sojourn in Aberdeen."

Ducking closer, he said, "I would have you believe it was the very prospect of this profession that turned me to melancholy when first we met. But that is not the truth. Not the full truth, anyway."

"Don't trouble yourself with an apology. You are much more likable when you aren't whinging. Besides, I'm sure all of your kind must loathe themselves." She cringed. She meant the words to tease, but they came out harsh. What was it about the man that made him so prone to insult?

"My father put me to this profession," he said, ignoring her slight. "A great advancement for his younger son. Something respectable, and I suppose with the state of labor in the country, he has a point. It's better than coughing to death in a mine or toiling away in the fields. I'm too big to fit up a chimney, too prone to seasickness to work on a boat, and not intelligent enough for much else."

She grinned. "What did you do before?"

"I owned a shop in Glasgow and made tools for the rail companies. Pry bars, spike drivers, tie tongs. We didn't service the big lines, but all the foremen in the city knew to come to us for the best quality. We used modern techniques to produce a good, hard steel, and fastened leather-crafted handles for a sure grip. I'd even started a line of surveying equipment."

Effie remembered his enthusiasm as he related all the tools and machines at Sir Walter's worksite. "My apologies for pressing on a personal matter, but how did it fall to ruin?" Despite their positions, she found herself liking the man.

Conall Murray's voice turned hollow. "In a way only a family can bring about, I'm afraid. My father didn't think much of my dabbling in local commerce. To him, trading with engineers and laborers is not worth a bother. One enters business to control the market and better the family position." He smirked. "A great man, he is. The Murray name is stamped on every mess kit and rifle barrel across a dozen of the queen's regiments. On the fittings of a quarter of the ships putting in around the Isles, too. If he weren't a Scot, he'd have a peerage by now, and I wouldn't bother working at all."

"But what did he do?"

"I owned the shop but not the land it sat on. When I refused to give up my livelihood, he purchased the whole block and became my landlord. Needless to say, my shop did not long survive."

"How awful!" She couldn't imagine such a fate thrust on her by her mother. Stevenson's natural son had abandoned the family trade, but even that cold relationship had never stooped so low.

"Indeed, and yet it already feels like a dream, like a life that never really existed." He swallowed and looked away. "Perhaps it never did, and all it entailed was just a lie."

She frowned, unsure what comfort she could give, but her thoughts were interrupted when the door at the rear of the car banged open.

"Insufferable man," said Walford, barging in. He strode down the aisle without more than a glance at her and Murray. She could judge from his face whom the lieutenant meant. He patted a soldier on the back and grumbled something. The men greeted him cheerily, their manner relaxed. Effie watched and was gladdened by the camaraderie. It meant if it came to it, the men would likely follow their lieutenant over Glover.

When Walford was done checking on his command, he eased onto the bench in front of Murray. He growled a few pointed questions about the Fey Finder General, but when Murray refused to take the bait, he turned the conversation to trivial things—the shite weather and cricket. He glanced at Effie a couple of times but never addressed her, giving the impression he'd rather pretend she wasn't there. She didn't know whether that meant the man was disturbed by what she was or his role in her captivity.

She spent the rest of the passage silent, listening to their chatter and staring out the window. The view was not as spectacular as it had been soaring high above the coast, but it was pretty nonetheless. Arriving in Duncairn, the train halted in a squeal of brakes, the engine sputtering to a halt. She realized her gut had clenched over the last few miles, and she forced herself to relax. Ramsey would come, she told herself. She just needed to get a message to the man.

The soldiers alighted first, and by the time Murray led her to the platform, the horses were already waiting. The wind bit against her cloak, the sea salt it carried more putrid than she remembered. She clutched her cloak tight, trying to hide her shackled hands. A mist cloaked the village, kissing everything with thick dew.

Glover strode toward them. "Take her to the constable," he told Murray. "He'll have a cell for her. We're to muster an hour after sunrise." Addressing Effie, he spat, "Let your little trow friends fall asleep and die in their slumber."

The drum started, and the soldiers fell into ranks. They marched off to their billet, leading the horses. The villagers scrambled out of their path, and Effie noted the worried glances and ducked heads. They feared Her Majesty's response as much as the uncanny attacks, and of what would happen on the morrow when their two nightmares collided.

She and Murray walked to the High Street. She kept her stride short so the chain between her ankles wouldn't tug at the skin. Already she felt so chafed that the iron might as well be sanding paper. The fishmongers stood at their stalls. She could feel their eyes fix on her. But when she glanced over, they found other tasks to occupy their attentions. She wondered what gossip had spread of her flight from the trows. Or had the Sniffer at the hotel told them of her?

The constable's office had come within sight when a hulking figure entered the street. "Calum!" she gasped. Murray's hand tightened on her arm. The fisherman started, his face blanching as if he'd run smack into a banshee.

"Bloody arse," he spat.

She had no time to explain. Murray already pulled her along. "Rabbie," she begged. "He must know I'm here."

Calum's gaze sharpened to a knife point. "Shot dead the night ye stole him from the Poet. God curse yer soul to a buggering hell!" Spittle flew into his beard. He ran a hand through it and grunted, blowing past her and Murray without glancing back.

Her gut lurched. Her legs lost their strength and buckled. She sagged against Murray while the village spun into a blur. The young Sniffer caught her and carried her the rest of the way. The only sound she heard was a distant cackling that carried on the breeze, and she vowed—if it took that last drop of her blood, she would see the end of the Laird of Aonghus.

CHAPTER 15

Guilt crumpled her into a ball on the cell's floor. She spent the night replaying her last moments with Ramsey. Each time became more painful, the weight of her decisions greater. His concerned face as she turned to leave etched in her mind. His eyes were weary and drained from the loss of blood and lack of sleep. The torment of his bewitchment was too much. She should've held strong for him, should've forced her will and badgered him until he relented. Deep down she knew it wasn't her fault, but she had little doubt her presence would've changed the night's outcome.

"I would be dead myself," she murmured to the frigid air of the cell. The words gave no comfort. She'd lost her appetite and refused to speak with Conall as he'd ushered her into the constable's holding cell. As Conall, she realized awkwardly she now thought of young Murray. Yet it suited him better. He snored now, asleep on a chair outside the bars. The early morning sun crept through the windows, casting shadows of light into the darkness. A part of her wished Glover would lend her a rifle so she could join with the soldiers in the coming assault. Remove her bonds and she would destroy the trows herself.

Shot dead, cold and alone and exhausted. Her concerns over anonymity seemed childish, an immature fear compared to the cruelty of the man's fate.

A cart trundled to a stop outside, its wooden wheels bouncing off the High Street's cobblestones. Someone banged on the door, a sturdy iron thing the constable had barred shut. Conall started awake and nearly fell off his chair. He rose and let in a man Effie recognized. The Sniffer she'd seen in the hotel nodded brusquely at Conall before peering at her with a nose scrunched as if smelling something unpleasant. He gummed his lips and snorted. His eyes were dead. They displayed no emotion, neither disgust nor pleasure. She hoped he wasn't to be her new guard. The man seemed as cold as an iceberg and twice as difficult to melt.

Conall Murray, on the other hand, was as pliable as copper. She smiled at him as he unlocked her cell and clamped on her shackles. His lips pulled slightly, under eyes that warmed when he looked at her. He smelled of the village, of sea salt and earth, and she felt an urge to lean in and feel again the strength that had held her the night before. But she resisted it; it would only get the man in trouble, and besides, she didn't need to show any of them a weakness.

He introduced the other man as Theodore Todd, and the pair led her to the cart outside. This one had no bars and was barely large enough for her to ride in. Conall helped her sit on a clump of hay, her back resting against the upright front slats.

"I feel like Boudicca," she said, "riding on my chariot to the field of battle."

Todd snorted. He and Conall hefted the handles of the cart, and they set off along the road heading north out of Duncairn. The soldiers waited for them just outside the village. They stood stiff and alert, their rifles clutched tightly. Wary eyes darted about, and more than one man shifted uncomfortably from foot to foot. Effie knew their expressions. They had yet to see their foe; they had only the frightening tales of their childhoods and the violent yarns of the locals to inflame their imaginations.

"Which way is it?" snapped Glover, already agitated despite the early hour.

Effie thought he addressed her, but it was Todd who spoke. "Along the path, sir, to a large mound ringed with stacks of stones."

Glover glared down the path. Tendrils of mist crept along the bracken, thick and sticky, as if a giant spider-web lay over the countryside. No sunlight peeked through the clouds as it had in the village. It made the way dark and brooding. "Very well," he said.

"Gag her." He thrust a pudgy finger at her when she gawked. "You thought I would leave you here in the village and allow your friends to save you? I won't have it, and I won't have you calling out and alerting them of our presence, either. You will remain silent unless I have need of your tongue. If you lied to me about this laird or his minions, I will shoot you."

Conall pulled a handkerchief from his breast pocket. He smiled at her apologetically as he fastened it around her mouth. When it was done, the Fey Finder General pulled a pistol from the holster at his belt and cocked it. He gestured to Walford, and the troop lumbered forward. Without drums, the only sound to herald their approach was the stomping of boots and the clink of buckles scraping across canteens and rubbing over bandoliers. Her cart bearers plodded along at the rear, the cart's wheels large enough to free themselves from ruts. Dew quickly coated her dress and cloak, leaving her frigid and shivering.

Waves crashed into the beach below, in a lulling rhythm. A crow pecking at a dead mouse startled and took to wing. It cawed at them, reminding Effie of the foolish omens the country folk pronounced. But whom did the crow stand for—the soldiers or the trows? Glover's ambush was ill-conceived. The laird would know of their approach, just as he was certain to know of the soldiers' arrival the evening before. It only remained whether the trows would fight against trained riflemen or flee from them.

Effie dreaded the looming violence but abhorred more the part of her that desired it—the part seeking vengeance for Ramsey, and for Ewan Ross and the young Munroe girl. She held no qualms that the laird must be dealt with, and his trows brought low, yet marking them for slaughter without any manner of parlay seemed just as wrong. If only she'd had a chance to call on wiser men than the queen's Sniffers, perhaps butchery wouldn't be the first course of action. But she'd as well wish for a rainbow in a snowstorm, in her current state.

When they reached the barrow, the procession stopped. Glover ordered a half-dozen men to form a guard while the rest began ripping up great patches of moist bracken with camp shovels. Once they had enough to fill a proper wagon, the bracken was flung over the cliff top. Theodore Todd descended after it, leading Walford and a detachment of riflemen, each with a bulging leather satchel. The remaining men held their ground, loosening the buckles on the ammunition pouches of their bandoliers.

Effie craned her neck, trying to watch Walford's progress, but it was no use. She couldn't see the beach below. It took her a moment to realize the Fey Finder General's plan. Fire. He would burn the trows from their cave and force them to fight on the open ground.

"My man found the cave from your description," said Glover, as if reading her thoughts. He pointed his pistol at her. "If it is nothing more than empty sand, I will leave your corpse to rot in it."

She looked away, refusing to be goaded. The plan was clever enough, she had to admit, much better than crawling single-file through the low passages into the warren. But it would take time to build the bonfire and generate enough smoke for it to be effective. And the laird would not sit idly and wait, if he still waited within.

Minutes slipped past. Glover held his pistol on her for some time, until he became anxious of the progress below. He peered over the cliff. "What is taking the damned man?"

"A bonfire of that size takes some engineering, sir," said Conall. "Shall I go check on the progress?"

Glover glowered. He checked the watch in his pocket and shook his head. "They must have it going by now. Each man carried two pounds of Lavastone, my own creation. The chemicals in the fumes will be enough to force the beasts out. We needn't fill the entire cave with fire."

He'd barely uttered the words when one of the soldiers hollered. The soldier pointed. "Sir!" A wisp of smoke puffed from the base of one of the cairns. Every eye fixated on it as it dissipated. More smoke slithered from between the stacked stones, filling the air as if the fire were lit right beneath their feet. Effie's heart thumped faster. Judging from the size of the cave and warren, there was too much smoke. Something had gone wrong, but there was only silence from below.

A familiar tickle started in her gut.

She bit back a yelp and managed to keep her face calm. The warning sensation intensified. Effie closed her eyes and let it pulse within her. She knew what it was this time, and what to do. She pictured herself reaching out with both arms, pulling. The sensation throbbed in response, and she yanked harder. It broke into distinct points, as it had in the Grouse's courtyard, and her eyes snapped open.

The trows were right on top of them.

Glover stared at the stones, his brow knotted in confusion. Smoke now billowed from all the cairns. It melted into the mist above and formed a dense canopy. The air darkened as if a giant hand had cupped itself around them, blotting out the light. Effie could no longer spy the far side of the barrow. She could only hear the soldiers stomping about and cursing.

"This is too much smoke!" barked Glover. "What have you done?"

He spun on her as her eyes went wide. A shadow slunk next to the barrow. One of the soldiers saw it too, and a rifle cracked. The shade squealed and jerked. More rifles erupted. A wayward shot screamed past Effie, making Glover flinch and scramble aside. She dove into the cart, trying to bury herself into the wooden slats.

"Don't let them escape!" roared Glover. He fired the pistol, but at what, she couldn't tell.

One soldier screamed. Another snarled as he hacked at the bracken with his rifle's butt. A trow ran from the barrow toward the cart. It grunted as it came, its long ears flapping. Conall stepped in front of Effie. His pistol barked, and the thing was thrown from its feet.

An eerie silence fell atop the cliff. In its wake, came cries echoing from below. They were followed by a volley of gunfire.

A soldier emerged from the smoke, bloodied, his eyes glazed over and distant. He raised his rifle at Conall. Effie screamed, but with the handkerchief shoved in her mouth, she could produce only a muffled whimper. Flinging herself forward, she kicked Conall square between the shoulders, sending the Sniffer sprawling. Unbalanced, the cart tottered on its wheels. The rifle belched. Wood splintered as the bullet smashed through the cart's wall and ripped a hole in her cloak.

Conall rose to a knee and flinched as a second shot rang out. The bewitched soldier's head snapped back, and he dropped. "The man must've gone mad," said Glover, reloading his pistol.

Tears welled in Effie's eyes. She yanked at her bonds and

struggled to shout through the gag. She had to tell them not to shoot. If any more were bewitched, the men would be innocent, their deaths senseless.

"Quiet," snarled Glover.

Conall glanced between them, still uncertain what had happened. He knelt by the fallen man, but there was nothing he could do.

"What the bloody hell?" hollered a soldier, lost in the mist and smoke. The man grunted, and another shrieked. A trio of rifles opened up in unison, sounding like a rolling clap of thunder.

And then stillness again. The smoke lessened, pulling apart like strands of cotton. Four of the soldiers held rifles couched against their shoulders, running the barrels along the bracken in a frantic search. The last of their number lay slumped in a heap, as still as the man who'd attacked Conall.

Something scrambled up the cliff. Glover wheeled and leveled his pistol. The soldier who popped into view had blood crusted on his temple. His hair ran wild, and his uniform was ripped. "He shot them!" the man gasped. "He just…He came out and shot them."

"What is this?" demanded Glover. He seethed, his veins bulging, his neck and face a red flame. "Tell me everything, and make more damned sense."

"It was Jenkins, sir. He was wounded, and the lieutenant ordered him to fall back. But he just turned his rifle on the men. Shot Mils and your man afore we could blink."

"Dead?"

The man swallowed and nodded. "Your man, Todd, sir. Clean in the chest. Mils took his to the arm and should recover, though he may lose the limb."

"And this Jenkins?"

"The lieutenant saw something wrong in the man's eye and knocked him cold, ordered us not to shoot. We have him tied up."

Glover's whole body shook. "Bring me Walford and the bodies of the trows you've slain."

"Sir?" the man squeaked. "I can bring you Walford. Only we didn't kill any trows. Only a couple shadows darted about, and then the smoke was so thick we couldn't see. Jenkins got the best look and, well, he went mad because of it." The soldier crossed himself.

His cheeks were deathly pale.

Effie worried Glover might shoot the poor soldier. His beady eyes were narrow slits, his brow pulled so tight it almost touched his chin. He spit venom as he spoke. "Tell Walford he is ordered to enter the cave. Tell him he is not to return here unless it is through the passages of this barrow." He thrust a pudgy finger at the mound. "With every trow within killed."

"Yes, sir." The soldier forgot himself and saluted before retreating back down the cliff.

Glover rounded on Effie, once the man had left. "You did this," he growled. Her heart thumped into her throat. She couldn't meet his glare and ducked her head. He stomped toward her.

"Sir?" begged Conall's voice. "You should look at this, sir."

The Fey Finder General stopped. "What is it?"

"All of me ammunition is stolen," answered one of the soldiers. "The bandolier was ripped right off me chest. Benjamin's too, and York's rifle is missing."

"You let them just take it?"

The soldier bristled. "I killed a pair of the beasts, but two more snuck up behind me. If it weren't for the damnable smoke." He left the rest unsaid, returning Glover's stare with his own fury.

"Spread what's left of the ammunition amongst yourselves. The devils are still out there, and now they are armed, thanks to your incompetence. We will hold our ground and wait until Walford rejoins us."

The men did as they were bade, though they grumbled and cast searing glances at Glover. Conall busied himself tending to the man who lay in a heap. The soldier was knocked cold but still breathing, and they moved him next to the cart. The bodies of the trows they'd killed atop the cliff were also gathered and lined up.

"Four dead trows," said Glover, inspecting the bodies with a wrinkled nose. They appeared smaller when lifeless, less terrifying. Their shaggy coats and broad snouts glistened from the mist. The reek of smoke hid the pungent odor Effie remembered. Glover tugged her gag down. "How many were there?" he demanded.

"Please," she gasped. "The men who turned their arms against you."

"Silence!" Glover snapped.

"No, you must listen," Effie yelled. She tried to catch Conall's attention, but the Sniffer had his back turned to her. "They are bewitched! Look for a—"

Glover raised his pistol and threatened to strike her with its butt. The gesture stole her breath and silenced her. "Oh, there is little doubt of it," he said. "I am not blind. Now tell me how many of your trow friends dwelt in this warren."

"I don't know," she said. She shook her head. "More than those four, a dozen at least. They've fled, certainly. They outsmarted you." She spoke in a flat tone, taking no pleasure in the statement. But it was the truth on all accounts. She could no longer feel the trows. They'd fled into the hills and disappeared from her senses.

"The queen's army has been attacked. Soldiers have died." He snarled. "Fool shrew. Your friends will not succeed. This was not a victory for the fey but a nail in your coffin. More regiments will come and root out your kind until not even the tales of your existence survive." He stormed away to inspect the cairns, kicking over the stones and nudging them about.

She held her tongue as he left. The foul man refused to listen, and besides, the trow threat had vanished. A faint smile cross her lips. Not for the mayhem the trows had inflicted on the soldiers, nor for Glover's frustration. It was because she realized now that while the fighting had taken place, when her fey senses had blossomed, she could've just as easily pointed out any of the men as any of the trows. And not just randomly. She knew them each by the way they pulsed. It was much like the horse, only she'd had no premonitions this time.

An hour passed before Walford and his men emerged from the barrow. They were covered in dirt and soot, coughing, and lumbering with fatigue. "Empty," said the lieutenant, helping the next man out. "The whole bloody thing is empty."

Effie started. "Even the gold? The treasure?"

Glover chuckled manically. "Gold? Still you play at your tricks."

"There's nothing but shite and soot down there," said Walford. "And this." He flipped a silver coin into the air. It landed in the dirt, already forgotten by the lieutenant. His eyes took in his wounded, and the dead soldier.

"Her doing," said Glover. "She played one of her wicked fey tricks and caused the man to go mad."

Walford growled. "And how from there, bound and gagged, did she manage that?"

"She must've warned them somehow with some Fey Craft or pagan charm. Regardless, I won't allow her to endanger us any longer." He cocked his pistol and marched toward her. "Her usefulness to me has ended."

CHAPTER 16

W alford's stance hardened. His muscles were steeled from years of soldiering, and his bearing commanded an aura of authority. The soldiers around him snapped their rifles to the ready. Their eyes darted from the lieutenant to the Fey Finder General. Conall stepped between the pair. "But what of the trows who fled? The stolen arms? She can give us that information."

"She will only deceive," said Glover. The fingers on his pistol twitched.

"You are tempered, sir, and acting rashly." Walford's voice was low, but the timbre rumbled like thunder. "You forget your duty to uphold the queen's justice."

"It is you who forget, Mr. Walford. I have dominion over all fey matters and will do as I please and not be questioned for it!"

Walford refused to flinch. "I have a sworn duty to uphold the realm and protect its citizens. Arrested is not tried, and it is not convicted. If you discharge that weapon, I'll place you in chains myself."

Glover's face twisted into a grotesque mask of throbbing veins and puckered flesh. Effie feared the man was insane enough to challenge the lieutenant. He was certainly petty enough to do something foolish. But finally Glover uncocked the pistol and turned to her.

"We need the cart for the slain men," he breathed so only she could hear. Cold fury laced each word. "You'll walk to the billet.

There I will shoot you and leave you to rot."

He spun on Walford. "Clean up your mess. I will go and see this cave myself." With a gesture at Conall to remove her from the cart, he started the labored descent. His polished boots were no match for the steep path, and though removed from view his curses rang out over the cliff face. Walford wheeled, ordering his men to task, setting scouts to guard while others tended to the slain and wounded. When the men were sufficiently busy, he stalked over to Effie. His stare held a heavy intensity that was more burdened than threatening.

"How was it done?" he commanded. "The trance. One moment Jenkins was rushing their murder hole; the next he was firing on us." Effie glanced at Conall as the man unfastened her ankles and helped her to stand. The Sniffer studied her, as eager for the knowledge as the lieutenant.

"Pick your words true," said Walford. "I won't have it happen again. Not to my men. I did not save you from the Fey General's wrath out of pity, or for your own preservation."

Effie swallowed hard. "An eldritch stone used as an arrowhead. The device is etched with runes. Remove the stone from the body, and he will return to normal." She pointed at the soldier Glover shot. "You can see for yourself if you search that one there."

Walford's gaze took in the dead man, and he seemed to tire. "Fey Craft runes. Bugger me, I'd rather you was a Zulu spearman."

"Mr. Glover did save my life," offered Conall. "Your man was firing on me. With all the smoke, it was as chaotic up here as it was below."

"I'd keep that quiet, if I was you," grunted Walford. He strode away, growling at some of the men who'd stopped their work.

Conall watched him. "A curious response."

"He meant you should not brag of Glover's heroics to the other soldiers," said Effie. "I don't think they'd see saving your life worth the cost of their companion, especially as it was Glover who shot the man dead."

"Oh, quite," said Conall. His cheeks flushed. "I'm not normally as thick. It's only, this was my first skirmish and my nerves are a bit ruffled."

Effie grinned. "You put yourself in front of that trow who

charged me. I think your nerves are stronger than you proclaim."

He doffed his hat and returned her grin. It barely lasted a breath before a somber countenance overtook him again. "You aren't working with these trows, are you?"

She kept his eye and shook her head. An earnest compassion worked behind his gaze. He wanted desperately to trust in her. His lips parted, but whatever he was going to say he shook off. She reached for him, but he stepped away before her fingers found his.

"I'll see you to the billet now, Miss Martins." Snatching up the discarded ankle shackles, he threw the chain over his shoulder.

The wounded were rounded up and bandaged to the best of the soldiers' abilities. The man Jenkins shot in the arm was helped into the cart along with Jenkins himself. The first held his arm in a sling, while the other's wrists and legs were bound with rope. Their dead they carried in makeshift litters; the trows they left for Glover. The Fey Finder General would follow them once he completed his inspection of the cave. The sun had not reached midday as they shuffled along behind the cart, retreating somberly toward Duncairn.

As they marched, the soldiers grumbled. The trow corpses should be burned, most agreed. Effie couldn't blame the sentiment. In death, the creatures were even fouler to look on, and she was glad to leave them behind. A few of the soldiers peered at her and Conall. When they did, their eyes narrowed in anger. But it was Glover they hated most. She heard the name repeated often, always followed by a rant of cursing.

"They blame your Fey Finder General," she said to Conall. "And they are afraid and angry. They have fought with horrific devils today and suffered the loss of friends." It didn't take her much effort to share the emotions they felt. Ramsey's loss wracked her with sorrow every time she thought of the morning's events.

"Yes," he said, not bothering to continue the thought.

He stared off at the sea, at anywhere but her. The man was lost in his own contemplation, and she decided to leave him to it. Her mind was tired enough, and her nerves worn thin from panic. A nice long bath and a good deal of wine were all she desired, but there was no hope of either.

She had a passing thought to bolt but dismissed it. With the shackles still on her wrists and the soldiers still with their rifles loaded, she'd not make it more than a stone's throw. She'd need a distraction first, a large one to allow her to gain a safe distance. But none such occurred before they reached the billet.

The soldiers boarded in a barn on the outskirts of the village. The farm's young owner laughed and jested with the soldiers as if they were longtime mates. His wife scuttled about with buttered bread and tea as they all got settled, her smile not as loosely given as her husband's. An older fellow with greased hair and a pointed moustache approached the cart, checking on the wounded. His coat and trousers were black and simple, well used to travel. "Lieutenant Walford wired the doctor in Montrose last night and bade him come south in case his services might be needed," said Conall. "Mr. Glover snapped at him for it." The Sniffer shook his head and mumbled under his breath, something about using a hammer to plank wood. He found a chair for Effie and placed her in the shade before re-shackling her ankles.

"Am I not allowed inside?" Effie asked, once the cold iron was clasped.

"Best you not," he said. "Out here will be safer when Mr. Glover returns. There are more eyes to bear witness." He gave her a frank shrug and left to aid the doctor, who was barking at the poor farm wife to fetch this pot and tear those cloths. As the afternoon passed and the sun began its steep plummet toward the horizon, the tension in camp lessened. Soldiers milled about chatting as they cleaned rifles and stitched uniforms. A guard was set along the perimeter of the farm, the men standing like scarecrows amongst the crops. But none grasped their weapons tightly, and their stares, while alert, held none of the fear they had that morning.

The mood changed readily when Glover was spied from a distance. He strode alongside Walford, each man silently staring ahead. It took them some time to reach the farm, but each strike of their boots vibrated within her, like a carrion bird plucking at her tendons. Activity around the farm halted. Death approached. Effie considered lying to Glover, deceiving him into thinking she held valuable information worth keeping her alive. But such a gambit seemed pointless. He had his serum to root out the truth, and other devices to ensure she would not last the night. Her only real hope lay in Walford, that the man's honor would buy her at least the time it would take to stage a formal trial.

Glover strode straight for her. She choked back the bile gurgling into her throat. His breath hissed through yellowed teeth. "I've watched you slither about, blinding all these fools." He yanked on her shackles, testing them. "No doubt you think yourself clever for ensnaring them this morning. Like your trow friends, it will be your last trick."

His eyes narrowed as he caught Walford staring at them. "The man forgets his place. It is no matter, he will learn. I'll have him transferred to the Australian continent. Let him guard convicts and savages for the rest of his days. There is an order to the world established by God, and only He can determine one's rank. All else is arrogance." He patted her head. "Think on that in your final moments."

Effie clamped her lips together, resisting the urge to lash out at his gnarled face and knock the teeth from his skull. Her fists clenched. Her gaze focused on the void of space between them; she couldn't look at him anymore but refused to break her gaze first. He sneered and turned away, snarling at Conall to join him as he stalked into the farmhouse. Walford kept his eyes on her for a moment before following the Sniffers inside.

Within minutes shouting erupted from the house. The words were garbled, but two voices echoed clearly, one Walford's. The lieutenant played a dangerous game. Though Glover held no military rank, he was an agent of the crown, and the crown protected its dignity no matter the extent of its folly. The lieutenant would face a firing squad as easily for disobeying the Fey Finder General as for disobeying a field marshal. Effie's chest tightened. She was reminded of something Stevenson had told her as she departed Ben Nevis: Edmund Glover was proof the queen did not take the Fey Finders seriously. If she did, such a man would never lead their ranks. The statement had given her hope at the time, yet such rhetoric mattered little now. Lieutenant Walford had best contain himself, or he might face the same pistol as she, with only a curt report penned by Glover to bear witness. Effie scanned the fields beyond the farm. It angered her to let others come to harm for her cause. It had taken years for Stevenson's kindness to melt her defensive nature, her trust earned as a glacier moves. Stevenson and cheery Graham. Poor Robert Ramsey, and now Walford. The list grew ever on, those whose debts she would never repay.

"You're not turning mad, are you?" asked Conall, startling her.

She swallowed down the hardness in her throat. "Dear Lord!" She caught her breath, then nodded at the house. "You must force the lieutenant to hold his tongue. I won't have Mr. Walford risk himself for me."

Conall blinked before catching on. "Ah, yes. Well, the lieutenant discusses the command and disposition of his men." The Sniffer shuffled in embarrassment. "It pangs me to say he has yet to bring up your current situation. He is an honorable man, but I believe the gravity of his losses weighs heavier on him than your plight."

"Oh," she said. Her shoulders sagged as if he'd dropped a yoke on them. Learning she'd misread the situation made her feel all the more alone.

"But I made an appeal on your behalf." He glanced back at the house, studying the threshold. The other men hadn't emerged. "I begged Mr. Glover to call for the magistrate. I told him I could take you back to the constable and keep you under watch until the trial."

Effie fought hard to keep her heart from racing. Such time would allow her to act, to get word to her friends. "What did he say?"

"He asked for the keys to your shackles and bade me leave his sight." Conall studied the ground. "I fear the man won't still his hand for very long. If it comes to it, he has the power to take you away from here, away from Walford and the soldiers, and once alone to do with you as he pleases."

She nodded. It was difficult for her to trust a stranger, but in the moment, studying Conall's disheartened face, she decided to ask him a favor. The young Murray was many things, but she believed he would keep her secret if she asked. She could trust him that far, at least, for he had shown her enough kindness over the past days. That he was a Sniffer was not an accurate measure of the man, who'd lost so much at the hand of his own father. In other circumstances, she might seek more of his companionship. But they were not so.

She was about to ask him to deliver a message, so Stevenson and Graham would know of her fate, when Conall spoke. "Answer something truthfully for me." His eyes pierced hers, eager with a sudden boldness. "Who is the Laird of Aonghus? Mr. Glover seems to think he is a tale you imagined to cast blame on another."

Effie paused before answering, studying the Sniffer's gaze. The dark eyes held a yearning in them, and she realized Conall wanted an escape as much as she did. That he was also trapped with Edmund Glover, even if it was only by profession, had been lost on her until that moment.

Clearing her throat, she spoke firmly. "I believe he is an older fey who may have ruled this region long ago. He is of a race called the Sidhe Bhreige, though I don't know much about them. Perhaps they are related to something called an Unseily Court, a cabal of wicked fey. He commands the trows, ordering them about as if they were his pets. He attacked me after I removed the bewitchment from a friend, but I have the feeling now he could've killed me had he wanted."

Conall relaxed, satisfied. "The doctor from Montrose removed the arrow from Jenkins. It cured him, just as you said it would. He'll recover and hopefully have no memory of what he did."

"That has been my experience with this bewitchment," she offered.

"It does not surprise me we were caught unaware this morning. When I was appointed a Fey Finder, I believed I would spend years studying your kind before being thrust into the field." He shook his head. "Two days I spent with Barnes before I was given an assignment. The few men I've met since have only spouted wild tales and gossip, as bad as any scullery maid. The government knows nothing of the fey. They are blinded by fervor and tradition, and I don't know which is worse."

His brow hardened. "You contend the fey matter in Duncairn is perpetrated by this laird, and yet the country is facing something much bigger, isn't it? There are reports of uncanny events from here to Fort William. Explosions and sabotage."

"Yes, though I'm afraid I know little on that score, only vague conversations and the same news you've no doubt read."

The Sniffer nodded. "It's a start and is more than the Fey Finders will discover on their own. They have no passion for detection or reason."

Effie allowed her heart to swell completely for the first time since Edinburgh. Her senses sharpened at once, awakening from a dullness she'd worn like a cloak. The earth around her blossomed and took root: the bitter tang of mud, the crisp kiss of the breeze, the rustling of a thousand crackling leaves. Conall looked to her, begging for assurance. It was now he who sought trust.

"I am not violent by nature," she stated firmly. "But these attacks must stop, regardless of the cost. I have friends, fey and human, who count on me, as I am counting on them. More needs to be discovered of the enemy, the true enemy, or more disasters like the one suffered today will afflict the land." It felt oddly calming to speak so brazenly. The fear that had kept her sheltered for years seemed a foolish thing compared to the magnitude of what they now faced.

"Then we are agreed," said Conall. "Only there is one problem, and Mr. Glover has the key."

Effie grinned. Iron shackles could not destroy her spirit, nor could the Fey Finder General. "Aren't you a great pugilist? You could knock him out and steal it."

Conall snorted. "That would be rather risky. Besides, I have a better solution." He reached into his coat and pulled forth a bundled handkerchief. Unwrapping it, he plucked out the sprig of a tiny flower. Its purple petals formed the shape of a bell.

"Twinflower," breathed Effie.

"Mr. Glover told me how you escaped him years ago, mixing the crushed flower with your blood to produce an acid." He shrugged, sheepishly. "He meant to warn me against you, and was rather riled in the telling."

Effie was astounded, but a part of her flared in alarm. "Twinflower is rather rare. Not even a doctor would carry it, and I would doubt you could purchase it in Duncairn."

"No, I wouldn't think so," Conall admitted. "That's why I bought this sprig in Edinburgh before we left." Effie started, trying to thank him and question his motives at the same time. He raised a hand. "When I ran my shop, I always prepared for a possible change of course. 'It is easy to keep stock for today,' my father always said, 'but a rich man sees what is needed tomorrow.'"

"He would be proud," she quipped, putting the proper amount of acid in her tone. "What of Walford's men?"

The Sniffer shrugged. "They will not care to notice. Mr. Glover never ordered them to guard your person. He wouldn't dare share his glory with the army. He wanted you solely under the authority of the Fey Finders. Besides, between a man they despise and a bonny lass they can't fathom for a fey, there is no choice." She blushed and wrung her hands together. Her fingers trembled under the excitement of it all.

"I'll come for you in an hour when it's darker," he said, tucking the twinflower into his coat and striding away.

The wait was painful. The wind blustered, the blue patches above disappearing behind a wall of gray. She had nothing to do but watch the soldiers and the road beyond. Conall never glanced her way as he busied about, and she tried to avoid him as well, but every time he marched past she yearned for him to bring her freedom.

Twilight turned the air colder and thick, and it smelled of rain beneath the aroma of the farm. Walford appeared for a time, milling around the soldiers, talking to each in turn. Effie heard none of the conversations but read agitation on the faces of the men. The lieutenant refused to glance her way, just as he'd avoided her on the train. She gathered it meant he'd remembered his station and surrendered his argument. He had other fights to press, and she was no concern for his command.

She did not fault the man, but the failing light felt all the darker for the abandonment. Now Glover would come at any time. Conall had better act soon, or all their plans of escape would become moot. She sought out his curly locks and frock coat, and discovered him emerging from the house. He held a bowl in one hand and a flagon in the other.

"Where have you been?" she snapped, a little too harshly. Her cheeks blossomed, and she mumbled an apology.

"It took me a while to find something to grind the flower. That, and Mr. Glover wanted me to run into the village. I think he wanted me out of the way. I stalled him, but only just." He offered her the bowl, which was filled with a peppery broth. The flagon held a dark beer that wafted a sweet malt. Lastly, he pulled out the handkerchief and shoved it into her hand. Folded into the cloth was a small knife, along with the crushed petals.

"Do it quickly," he said. His hand remained atop hers. It was warm and firm, lending her confidence. "Mr. Glover takes a coffee after meals, but he's almost through with dinner. After, he means to come for you."

She stared into his gaze. "You're sure the lieutenant's men won't stop me?"

Conall swallowed and shook his head. "Try to sneak away without being seen. There are only a few sentries, and they are watching outward for the trows. Wait for me a half-mile down the road, and I will bring supplies."

Her eyes bulged. "You're not coming with me. Your life would be ruined!"

"It is too late on that score, I'm afraid."

"They'll hang you!"

"I will be suspected of aiding you, regardless. Either Lieutenant Walford or I will have to stand for treason the moment you are gone. You know this is true. My only solace is if we can uncover the true danger that faces the empire. Then all may be forgiven. Nothing you'll say can persuade me otherwise. I'd rather risk my life trying to help queen and country than wallow in melancholy, watching the merciless condemn the innocent under some pretext of centuries past."

She sunk into the chair and stared at him. "You're putting your fate into my hands."

His eyes twinkled. "Well, if you're playing some fey trick on me, make it a good one." He grinned a moment more, squeezing her hand one last time, before marching away and leaving her clutching blade and flower.

She fumbled the knife and almost dropped broth and beer. The faith the Sniffer proclaimed was too much, but she had no time to dwell on it. She heaved a breath to steady her hands. Hungry as she was, she gulped down the broth, barely tasting the leeks and carrots. As soon as it was gone, she wiped the empty bowl dry and dumped in the crushed twinflower. When this had worked years before, her wrists had bled freely from large cuts on her rubbed-raw skin. Mixing the flower and her blood had produced an acid strong enough to burn through Glover's flesh, but the links of her shackles were thicker and made of iron.

She would need significantly more of the serum.

The knife gouged her palm as she drove in the tip, pulling forth a swell of blood. She gritted her teeth. Clutching her wrist, she massaged more blood into the palm before pouring it into the bowl. The mixture instantly congealed and turned black. Hissing tendrils of smoke rose from where it kissed the bowl's wood.

Panicked, she whipped her head around. The night was still. The soldiers gave her no heed. They were busy chattering over steaming cups of tea. As subtly as she could muster, she pulled her dress' hem and poured the mixture over the chain binding her ankles. It sizzled, distorting the metal instantly. She dropped the hem and waited a moment before gently spreading her legs apart. The links gave brief resistance, and then metal snapped.

Her heart thumped so hard, she thought she would need to catch it flying from her mouth. Quickly, she dabbed the mixture over the chain between her wrists, using the knife to spread it. Biting her lip, she worked carefully to avoid the acid burning her flesh. At last, the second chain broke apart.

The night shrank, the fields and house crowding in, the soldiers looming closer. The clouds above, thick and swirling, pressed down on her lungs, shortening her breath. "Be a shadow," she whispered, wrapping the handkerchief around her bleeding palm. The knife was a melted, ruined mess, and she dropped it before gulping down the rest of the beer.

Like a stalking cat, she watched and waited. She eyed her route, first against the side of the house where the shadows were darkest, then out along the sheep pen, away from the barn. She'd have to keep her head down and her feet free of the muck. Rifle shots cracked in her imagination, firing at her fleeing form, but they were no worse than Glover's pistol or a hangman's rope.

It felt like tiny crystals had formed on her limbs, trapping her in the chair. Her gut churned. But her heart fired strong. Go now, it beckoned, sending fire through her veins, and breaking the panic. She went, creeping at first before darting into the night. She forced herself not to look back until she reached the far edge of the pen, and then it was only a fleeting glance. Nothing stirred. No voices raised in alarm. She was just a shadow, a distortion in the soil.

Rain began to fall in earnest, pelting her as she hurried through the fields. Her feet splattered through the growing puddles. She'd long lost sight of the sentries but saw no movement ahead. One field passed into another, patches of bracken and wild grass sprouting here and there. After a time, her feet started to slip, and she had to slow her pace.

It was a full twenty minutes before she thought she heard a shout, and even then it was hard to tell above the driving rain. She circled north, or as best as she could tell, until she reached the road again. Trows were the furthest thought from her mind, but when she spied the lone form huddled ahead, she paused and wondered how the night could speed so fast, and yet be so dreadfully slow.

The figure rose at her movement and waved. He'd made it. She raced to Conall, shaking her head. "I could've been a trow, or worse," she said, barking out her own fears.

"Their shapes aren't as fine as yours, Miss Martins," he said, shouldering a bundle.

She huffed, trying to hide the reddening in her cheeks. "Have you food at least? Water? Horses?"

It was Conall's turn to redden. "A crust of bread and a flask of whiskey was the best I could do, I'm afraid. Doing anymore would have aroused suspicion. Though once we reach a town, I have enough purse to buy horses and any meal we desire." He peered into the dark, blinking against the rain. "If we can reach a town without being caught. Do you have a notion of which way we should go? We might have only a quarter-hour's head start, but there aren't so many of them. They can't search in all directions, and Lieutenant Walford won't risk groups too small with all the trows about. Come daylight, things will change. Mr. Glover will telegraph anyone within fifty miles he can persuade to hunt for us."

Effie thought for a moment. They needed to head west, but there wasn't a town in that direction for quite some distance. And the longer they stayed on foot, the worse their chances of evasion became. What they needed was a place to hide for the night and a friend who could help them obtain dependable mounts. She considered circling back into Duncairn, to visit the Tattered Grouse, but the risk was too great. Besides, she didn't know what they believed of Ramsey's death, and she might not be welcome there any more than the Fey Finder General.

Recalling Ramsey made her heart twinge. It seemed a lifetime of friendship had sprouted after their encounter in the Blind Poet, all related within a single night. It was shocking considering the way he'd acted at first, as if in a drunken stupor.

Or like someone kicked in the head.

Forgetting herself, she did a little hop in excitement, fists clenched, then cursed herself a fool for not seeing what was plain before her. "I know where to go," she squealed to Conall. Putting her hands on his shoulders, she almost reached up and kissed his cheek but stopped herself. She barely knew the man, despite his trust and willingness to aid her. Let them see the night through, and the morning might embolden her further. Her arms dropped, flushed in a way she'd rarely known, and she stepped back, swallowing.

Leaving him staring after, she scampered down the road, her head ducked against the downpour. "Bugger me for not making the connection sooner!"

CHAPTER 17

The worn thatch of the cottage sagged under the weight of the rain. Effie scurried along the low wall that led to the Munroe House, her hands scrambling over the stones to aid her balance. They were not far from where she'd rejoined Conall and had moved quickly over the hard-packed road. But the route left them exposed in plain sight. If riders came on them, they would be overmatched. She'd fallen once already in her haste, her feet skidding in the mud. The second time, her knee found a sharp rock, and she sucked a panged breath through her teeth to avoid crying out.

Light flickered through the front windows of the house, illuminating the door and the tiny bell that hung over it. The sprig of primrose was gone, replaced by an iron horseshoe. A good sign, at least. The man might listen to her again. Effie slogged through the yard, ignoring the pain that throbbed with every step.

"Mr. Munroe," she called through the door. She ran a hand through her hair and straightened her dress as best she could, though her cloak was sodden and covered in muck. The hand she'd gouged was stiff and cold. Blood crusted the handkerchief she'd wrapped around the wound, and stained her fingers. She looked a horror.

Floorboards creaked within. She could picture the man's round cheeks as she heard him go to the hearth and fetch his rifle before coming to stand opposite the door. "Who's calling for me?" he shouted. The rifle's hammer clicked back.

"It's Miss Martins," said Effie. "I've brought help, and I believe we can cure your daughter." On her first visit, she'd been so focused on learning of the trows and the uncanny attack the girl had suffered, she hadn't considered the poor girl's wounds. Certainly not with the knowledge she now possessed.

"Father Murphy did say to avoid ye. What kind of help can ye offer?"

"Miss Munroe has a puncture in her side, doesn't she?" It was a guess, but one that made sense.

"Aye," said Munroe, after a short pause, "a small one, a snag as she scrambled to get away. What of it?"

Effie relaxed. "She wandered about dazed and acted out of sorts, so you strapped her to the bed. She's been trying to get up, but she's been restrained since the attack. Isn't that correct?"

"She took a wicked knock to the head, Miss Martins. Father Murphy's seen other children kicked by horses and thought it best to see if she'd come round after some rest."

"And did he inspect the wound in her side?"

"Nay, it wouldn't a been decent. I stitched that one up myself. Only...." Munroe's voice trailed off.

"What is it?" Effie asked, nudging gently. The door cracked open. Munroe stood with his rifle cradled across his chest. His eyes glistened under the flames coming from the hearth.

"She hasn't changed. Not a bit since the day I found her. What do ye ken about such things?"

Effie wondered how much the man would believe but decided it best to lay her cards on the table and trust in sincerity. "The creatures that attacked your girl have bewitched at least three people around Duncairn. In each case, a thunderstone was inserted into the victim's side." She didn't need to give too graphic an account. Already, comprehension grew on Munroe's face. "I believe your daughter suffers from the same malady. If true, we will be able to cure her."

He cocked his head and studied Conall. "Are ye a doctor?"

"An agent of the queen who's seen such wounds before," answered Effie, hastily, before the Sniffer could respond. Conall's jaw snapped shut, and he nodded. "I'm sorry for calling at such a late hour," she continued, "but I thought the matter shouldn't wait until morning."

Munroe glanced between them, shifting his feet. "Perhaps I should wait for Father Murphy. He'll be here bright and early in the morning. He always comes on the Sabbath before he's needed for Mass."

"Do you at least have a horse to sell?" barked Conall. The anger in his voice startled Effie. Munroe flinched as well.

"A horse?" The man was perplexed.

Conall thrust a hand at the rain. "I've come all the way from Edinburgh to lend aid, and I don't mean to spend the night tramping about in the rain having doors shut in my face. It's bad enough you choose to leave your daughter under the spell of some fell imps, but don't keep others in need waiting any longer than they have to!"

"Don't fear, sir," added Effie, catching on to Conall's ploy. "If the trows haven't come for her yet, I doubt they'll come tonight."

"Trows? Come for her?" Munroe's voice quivered. "But you'll come back? Ye'll help my Sarah?"

"When I can," said Conall, "though if the wound closes, it'll be a much worse situation."

Munroe paled. "It festers. I tried to halt the bleeding, but it's gone black." He staggered backward and allowed them to enter. "It started small, just a wee cut compared to the knock on the head. But the head wound is now just a bruise and the other stinks of death."

"And you haven't called the doctor?" Effie strode into the house. The décor was sparse, a few cluttered tables clung to the walls, and a massive rug that spread beneath a set of sturdy chairs. A rack of cooking pots and knives lined the hearth. She kept her cloak on, the better to hide her shackled wrists and ankles.

"Nay, I haven't the money for all that, and Father Murphy did say…."

"Then we'd best have a look," said Effie, cutting him off. The old priest might harbor the best of intentions, but like as not he did more to comfort Mr. Munroe than treat the man's daughter.

Munroe nodded and led the way into the small adjoining bedroom. He kept the rifle hugged to his breast, cradling it as a baby does a doll. Conall reached for her arm as they followed, but she pretended not to notice. His alarmed face told her enough of his worry. He would need to do what he could; there was nothing more to it.

The girl lay bundled under a mound of blankets. The topmost were tucked so tight as to strap her to the bed. She was near womanhood, though it was hard to tell from her complexion. Her golden hair clung to her face; her skin was ashen and sweaty. Short, whimpering breaths came out of her pursed lips.

"How long has she been in a fever dream?" asked Effie.

"She sleeps most the day, and when she wakes it's like she's still dreaming," said Munroe. "She mumbles the most unpleasant and confused things."

"We need to uncover her," said Conall. "Can you fetch some boiling water and a sharp knife?" The Sniffer spoke with confidence, and Munroe set the rifle down and hurried out.

As soon as he left, Conall rounded on Effie. "You could have warned me," he said. She put a finger to her lips. They would still be heard, and besides, it would do no good to argue now. She moved to the girl's side and untucked the blankets. The dress beneath was sodden. Conall helped her roll the girl until they could get the dress up far enough to reveal her side.

Effie gasped. The wound was inflamed, with streaks of black running along the flesh. A handful of ragged stitches held the thing shut, though none of the skin had knitted properly.

Conall put a hand over his mouth. "It stinks," he whispered.

"Do what you can," Effie whispered. She prayed it would be enough.

Munroe returned with knife and pot, blanching when he saw Sarah's inflamed flesh. Conall accepted the items. He shrugged out of his cloak and coat, and took his place, kneeling by the girl.

"I'm going to remove these," he said, pointing at the old stitches. He dunked the knife into the scalding water and took a couple deep breaths.

With a final worried glance at Effie, he began to work. The girl barely moved as he cut the stitches, but when he began feeling for the stone, she gasped awake. Effie rushed to hold her still and begged Munroe to snare her legs. Conall prodded with deft fingers, moving slowly around the rent flesh. He ignored their struggle to keep the girl pinned, pinching her here and there until he found the lump where the stone rested.

He nodded to Effie. "Keep her as still as you can," he said. Effie nodded back and braced herself. The girl shrieked as Conall went for the stone, but her father's anguished cries were louder. The bed shook as the girl thrashed. Conall strained, keeping his concentration about the task. The stone had lodged deep, and Effie began to worry the girl wouldn't survive the ordeal.

Conall delved one last time and yanked free the arrowhead. He showed it to Munroe, blood covering his fingers and the stone, before plopping it into the pot. The man crossed himself and slumped onto the bed. His daughter stopped thrashing and fell silent, too weak to do anything but whimper. Effie moved to Conall's side and helped him wash out the wound, using the water and some whiskey from Conall's flask.

"The wound needs closing, but I'm worried over these black lines," said the Sniffer. "The doctor from Montrose is just down the road. Can't we find a way to call him here?"

Effie glanced at Munroe, who watched them once again with an uncertain gaze. But she knew Conall spoke the truth. Keeping up the ruse would only endanger the girl. It had served the purpose of getting them off the road, and of removing the bewitchment. Now was a time for blunt honesty.

"Some of the flesh may die," she said to Munroe. "It needs the care of a doctor to sew it up properly and treat the infection. As it happens, there's one down the road in the company of soldiers. A lieutenant named Walford will see the doctor is brought here if you tell him of your girl's plight and show him the thunderstone. You needn't worry over the cost."

She rose and steadied herself. "Only, if you could kindly tell them you removed the stone yourself and leave us out of your tale, we would be greatly in your debt. They are hunting for us, and I fear our lives are at risk."

Munroe jerked to his feet. "Hunting for you! The queen's army? But ye said ye were the queen's agents!"

"I am a queen's Fey Finder," said Conall, "and Miss Martins was my prisoner. But things got...." He blinked and searched Effie's face. "Confounded."

Munroe snatched his rifle and brandished it once more. "What've ye done?" A trembling hand cocked back the hammer.

Conall and Effie pleaded for the man to see reason.

"Quiet!" yelled Munroe. "I'll see what the constable wants with ye. That's what I'll do!"

Effie's thoughts scrambled for something to say. She wasn't about to let the man return her to a cell. But it was the girl who saved her.

"Father," came a meek voice. "Why are you yelling?"

Munroe melted in an instant, his arms and shoulders going slack, his jaw falling agape. He rushed and knelt by the girl's head. "Oh, me dearie Sarah."

"What's going on?" the girl asked. "My throat is terribly dry." Munroe cradled an arm around her, tears streaking down his face.

"I'll fetch water," said Effie. She found some in a pitcher near the hearth and returned with a cup. Munroe helped the girl sip it down, then bade her rest.

"This is the first she's been sensible since the attack," he said.

Conall pointed to the stone. "It was Fey Craft that stole her wits. The wound remains serious, but now it can heal. We removed the bewitchment."

Without warning, Munroe lunged at Conall and snatched him up in a bear hug, pulling the smaller man off his feet. "I didn't ken what to do. But, oh, you've saved her."

"Not yet," warned Effie, but she couldn't help but smile over the man's joy.

Munroe nodded. "I'll fetch the doctor as soon as can be. But what of ye? I'll keep your secret. I owe you that at least, but ye can't stay here."

"We would not press too much upon you," said Effie, "but if you had horses we could buy, we'd give you good coin for them."

Conall pulled out a few heavy coins. "And a hammer and spike, too," he added.

Munroe's brow furrowed, but he gave no resistance. His eyes widened when he saw the shackles Effie had kept hidden within her cloak. Conall took the hammer and spike to the locks and broke them off, finally allowing Effie to massage the raw skin beneath. The horses Munroe offered to sell were old plow beasts, but the Sniffer paid liberally for them, enough for the farmer to replace them with younger, fitter stock, and to pay for the doctor.

Effie redressed her palm and rubbed life back into her sore legs. By the time they were set to go, an hour had passed and the rain had lessened to a thick mist. She bundled herself against the chill air, straining her ears for any sounds along the road.

"I won't forget yer kindness," said Munroe, seeing them off.

"Nor we yours," replied Effie. "Fare your daughter well. The soldiers will hunt down these trows, but until then secure your doors and windows each night." She didn't know what other comfort she could offer the man. It would have to be enough for now, until she discovered the bottom of these troubles.

Flicking her reins, she set a brisk pace up the road, heading toward Montrose. Dawn was still hours away, and with the clouds and pattering rain, their movement was well hidden. Conall trotted his horse at her side, peering ahead.

"Is this the safest course?" he asked.

She shook her head. "Nothing's safe. But we can't risk the fields in the dark. The horses would stumble and break something. I'm hoping anyone searching for us will have torches, so we'll spot them from far away. If they don't, we'll just have to figure something out when we get to it." She patted her mount. "Once it's light enough, we can strike west and search for faster horses."

"And food," added Conall.

Effie raised an eyebrow. "But we've your crust of bread to sustain us. Whatever more do we need?" The Sniffer chuckled, and his teeth flashed white.

In the distance, thunder rumbled and the sea mist gusted through the trees and grass. Rain returned, lashing them across the face. It reminded Effie of when she was young, scared and alone. The nights then had been long and full of terrors. But now, despite the lurking trows and pursuing soldiers, she felt comforted by its beauty, obscured by its wrath. She'd escaped the Laird of Aonghus and Sir Walter Conrad, and with them the Hostmen of Newcastle and fiendish trows. She'd escaped Edmund Glover and his Sniffer minions. She'd aided those she could and now embarked to uncover the tangled plots that plagued the countryside.

For the first time since departing Ben Nevis, she felt like she was making a difference, and the notion of hiding no longer enveloped her thoughts. She was capable of more than allowing others to protect her. It was her turn to shelter them and foil the plans of those who wished them ill. Those who wished the entire empire ill. It was finally her turn to be the huntsman.

CHAPTER 18

Conall returned with a saddlebag full of food. He handed her a piping hot pastry stuffed with lamb and onion. She took it and held onto the heat, trying to will it into her body. The journey through the previous night had been tiresome and freezing, the rain turning into an icy frost well before sunup. But they'd covered some distance, and morning found them near the village of Kirriemuir, well away from Duncairn and the coast.

"Horses?" she asked, her mouth full of pastry.

He shook his head. "Not at this hour. I had to pay the baker double just to open shop early and sell me these pies."

She smiled, in a jesting mood. "Double for the pies, an extortion for these plow horses, and not even a second thought for your lightened purse. You certainly didn't grow up Scottish!"

He rocked his head back and laughed. "My nursemaid was French. I suppose she preferred to instill in me a fondness for cheeses, no matter the cost. That, and wine. Lots and lots of wine."

Effie chuckled and steered her mount back onto the narrow road they followed. The rain had fled the sun, and the morning had turned pleasant despite the damp their cloaks still carried. After turning west, they'd avoided the broader carriageways and larger towns, choosing instead the country lanes that connected village to village. A few game trails were large enough for the horses, though they were slower going. At first, Effie had feared an ambush at every intersection, but they'd heard no sound of pursuit, and after hours of riding, she'd relaxed. Glover and Walford didn't have enough men to cover the ground they'd made, and any reinforcements would be coming from the cities.

She hoped to make the shores of Loch Rannoch by nightfall. The brothers Croy lived there and would provide them with a warm, safe place to sleep. Ben Nevis and Stevenson lay only a day's journey beyond, and from there a plan could be formed. She'd told Stevenson of the Sidhe Bhreige in her telegram but not of Gabus' warnings. She bit her lip as her head began to spin with all the details of the past few days. It was difficult to keep them straight.

"The spell that binds them has failed," her friend had said. The news was enough to terrify the fey in the city, and those near Duncairn as well. Enough to have them flee their ancestral homes. And what of Sir Walter Conrad and his Aerfenium? The man was adamant his substance was of fey origin, claiming the uncanny attacks throughout the Highlands were an attempt by the fey to protect it.

Strange and stranger. She had no proof but couldn't fathom the two tales being unrelated. She would need to find some of the fled fey and discover more of the spell Gabus mentioned. She also needed to find out who besides the Laird of Aonghus was behind the attacks, how many were truly Sidhe Bhreige and how many were fey bent on stopping Sir Walter, if any were at all. And what did it mean if the Sidhe Bhreige were returning? She had a horrible feeling they might find out before long, and that a few trows were mere kindling in the inferno to come.

She told Conall of what she knew as they rode through the Forest of Alyth toward Pitlochry. He seemed bewildered by the news, and she had to remember how odd it must sound to someone so new to fey lore. He asked a barrage of questions but fell quiet after a time, realizing she didn't hold many answers. Sometimes she found herself watching him, wondering what it would be like if they weren't hounded by troubles. But that was the problem; the man was a Sniffer. If they hadn't met as they had, he would be the enemy no matter how many times she touched her face unwittingly, remembering the way he'd held her. No matter how his smile filled her with warmth. Long years spent near Graham's workmen had left her with bawdy tales on what to do with a man. She bit back a fit of giggles thinking on them, but her thighs gripped the saddle tighter.

A few hours passed while they walked the horses along the shores of Loch Tummel. The sun had long ago crested midday, yet they hadn't managed to exchange their mounts. She was beginning to grow attached to the old beasts. Whisper, as she had begun calling the one she rode, certainly seemed to like her too. He kept nudging her shoulder and whinnying in delight when she stroked his mane. They rose and fell as the banks ascended and descended, spotting the tranquil waters through the trees at times, and crossing over rocky shore at others. Skirting the village of Foss, Effie led them the few miles along River Tummel to Loch Rannoch, and down the winding path to Kinlochy.

A bridge spanned the river, three stone arches rising in a hump over the water. On the far side of the village, a cluster of boulders formed the shape of a head and torso. The Sleeping Giant, it was called, though Effie didn't know if the tales about it were true. The village had a public house in its center, with a grocer next door. A few other shops had sprouted over the years, but the village was too remote for any frequent commerce. Most of its inhabitants provided for themselves from their own gardens and stock.

At the edge of the village sat the MacLaren brew house. As large as a barn, it stank of yeast, filling the air with a pungent and sour scent. Effie led them passed it, down a short lane to a smaller house with a croft stretching toward the loch. From a work shed came hammering and men's voices, but the sounds stopped when the horses drew near.

A head popped out of the shed, ginger and covered in sweat. "Ah, Effie!" he said. A toothy grin broke out on his face. He came out to meet them, a leather apron worn over a pair of tartan trews: red striped with black and yellow. Another man followed, his hair a deep russet. It was clear from their chins and eyes the two were brothers.

"Hello, Donal," Effie said to the first. She nodded to the second. "Colin, how is your son?"

"Lovely, a wee bairn with his mother's cheeks!"

"Effie?" asked Conall. He sounded amused. He alighted from his horse and reached a hand to help her down.

"The Croys are dear friends of mine," she told him, ignoring his question. "I don't have many secrets kept from them." She took his hand and hopped to the ground.

"Our Good Auntie were a Maid of the Trees," said Donal, "a lady who ken the giants, our father said." He smiled, but both brothers stayed back as if waiting for an explanation.

"This is Mr. Conall Murray, of Dunkeld," said Effie, thinking it better to name him a Scot from the nearby town rather than English. The brothers would accept any friend of hers as their own, yet some preconceptions ran deep. Centuries of hatred ran even deeper. Turning to the Sniffer, she realized Colin would smell the city on him from miles away, so quickly added, "Though I'd say lately of Edinburgh. We've come all the way from Montrose on an urgent matter and seek to impose on your charity. I fear the Fey Finder General may have soldiers out looking for us."

Donal appraised Conall. "Are ye of the Fair Folk as well?"

"I was an agent of the queen," admitted Conall, "though now I supposed I am an outlaw."

Colin bristled at the first statement, but Donal barked a thundering laugh at the second. "Welcome, then! It's been nigh ten years since we've had a Murray at our table." Colin kept his distance, but both men shook Conall's hand.

The door to the house banged open and a woman strode out, an infant swaddled in her arms. Blonde hair framed a slender face. She had a lithe body, though she still showed signs of her maternity. Nora was the younger of the two wives, but Effie knew she ruled the roost. Always kind and generous, she had a worldly cunning beyond her years.

"Ah, look at ye!" she boomed.

Her blue eyes lit up as she took in Effie, then narrowed as Conall was introduced. She hummed in disapproval that Effie would travel alone in the company of a strange man, but when Effie began the tale of their escape from Duncairn, all concerns over propriety were forgotten.

Nora ushered everyone inside and sat them at the large table before the hearth. Its thick timbers were scarred by decades of use, its benches worn where each member of the family sat their rump. A bed for the children stood in one corner of the main room next to a cradle for the youngest. A private room led off on either side of the hearth for the brothers and their wives. Nora kept the house cozy and warm with cheerful sprigs of flowers spread about on shelves, and rugs full of color.

Mary, Colin's wife, worked at the brew house when they could give her shifts. Effie asked after her and found she had plucked at a thorn. Nora laid the wee one in the cradle, then fetched a platter of bread and cheese. She set a kettle to boil, muttering under her breath all the while. The brothers ducked their heads sheepishly before Donal finally spoke.

"We've had to tighten the belt of late," he said, "and the bastard was tight enough already. The machines of the cities will be the death of all craftsmanship. A man can't compete."

Effie smiled in sympathy. The brothers were coopers by trade, who turned out barrels for the brewery and local villages.

"It's said a factory in the Haymarket of Edinburgh can turn out two hundred barrels a day," said Colin. "Two hundred! What would anyone do with that many?"

Donal leaned forward, resting on his meaty arms. "It's all we can do to make a dozen in a week, and auld MacLaren wants to expand the brewery. He keeps us on because he ken our pa, but there'll come a day. He's already ordering stock from some bugger in Glasgow."

"He'd put us out, too," said Nora. She poured from the kettle into a teapot decorated with purple heather and green vines. There was a tremor of worry in her voice Effie had never heard before. Nora was always a strong-willed optimist. "Times are hard across the village. The MacTaggarts were forced into the tenements of Edinburgh so Fergus could work at a bottling factory. The Corbetts sold their sons, Gavin and Lucas, to a mining company. They might as well have made a pact with a banshee!"

"Poor wee bairns," said Colin. "My Mary used to look after them during the harvest. She was devastated to see them go." He drove a wedge of cheese into his mouth, then waggled a finger at Effie. "She'll be along soon, happy to see ye're here."

"Aye, and full of tales too," sniffed Nora, "fit to prattle your ears off. It's all she can drone on about these days."

Colin eyed her. "It isn't some nonsense about a miller tricked out of his gold by a pixie. I've seen the horses and the cattle found dead. Black Donald stalks the glen in the shape of a werebeast. He's been seen by half the village, and you've heard the hollowing at night."

Effie caught Conall's eye. The Sniffer wasn't laughing at the cooper's tale, either. "How long have these sightings been going on?" she asked.

"A month and a fortnight or so," said Donal. "Ever since that explosion up near Aviemore."

It was as if a huge fist of air pounded into Effie's chest. She reeled back in her chair, needing to grasp the table for support. The brothers lurched to their feet. But it was Conall who spoke, putting words to her thoughts. His face had turned white as a sheet. "The one that killed those miners in Glen Avon?"

Donal nodded. "Aye, that's the one."

Effie closed her eyes and took a deep breath. "The spell that binds them has failed," she whispered, and the riddle unraveled before her. The gas had exploded, consuming Sir Walter Conrad's substance in a ball of flame. And the spell Gabus spoke of began to break apart. The wards her ancestors had put in place to contain the Sidhe Bhreige were failing as Aerfenium was destroyed. She didn't understand much about such Fey Craft, but one thing was clear: Sir Walter had been correct. The fey would have to fight to protect this substance, whatever it was.

An urgent need to fetch Whisper and ride hard for Ben Nevis overwhelmed her. Graham and Stevenson had to be informed of the connection. They must work to stop Sir Walter. The man had power, influence, and wealth. In many ways, he was a more formidable foe than the Laird of Aonghus. She bit her lip, weighing the danger of traveling onward through the night.

"It is too dangerous," said Conall, reading her silence. "We haven't slept in two days, and the ascent is not an easy one. It can wait until morning. Another few hours will not spell doom, but it might for us if we don't rest and eat."

Effie glared at him. She couldn't tell what angered her more, that he was so quick to suggest resting when what they faced was so dire, or that he was right. She planted her hands on her hips, but the effect wasn't the same while sitting. Her foot tapped furiously in frustration. The brothers returned to their seats, confusion painted on their faces.

Nora came to the table as well and sat across from Effie, her eyebrow raised. "One of ye better tell us what's going on, or I'll set to you with my ladling spoon. And ye might as well add in this business in Duncairn, too. Don't think I've forgotten."

Effie exhaled but allowed it would be better to stay the night. She wouldn't reach Stevenson until morning if she left now, anyway, and there was no use fretting over what she couldn't do anything about. She picked up a piece of cheese and began tearing it into bite-sized chunks, pressing it into equal-sized pieces of bread. Her foot tapped in earnest. At least she could do that without being called to task.

She talked while she tore, relating what she knew of the troubles near Duncairn, her journey to investigate it, and how she came to be in Conall's company. She left out the parts regarding Stevenson's investors and of Gabus Säurbaum. She didn't want to keep secrets from her friends, only those weren't hers to tell. When she finished her tale of escape from Edmund Glover, she began telling them of Sir Walter, of his discovery and his belief that Aerfenium was of fey origin.

Nora rocked back in her seat when Effie finished. "So ye think this Aerfenium is the spell that binds these terrors away?"

"Something like that," said Effie. "I don't know much about the Sidhe Bhreige, nor about binding spells. But there is too much blood already spilt to deny they're both very real and very dangerous."

"So this talk of devils on the roads is true?" asked Colin. "We thought it a bunch of government bunk, an excuse to call soldiers into the Highlands. Many around here fear a new round of Clearances."

Conall shook his head. "I was with Mr. Glover when the Newcastle regiment arrived. No one spoke of anything besides the turmoil spreading across the country. However misguided they are, they do act only to thwart a fey uprising."

"What can we do to help?" asked Donal.

"I'm not sure," admitted Effie. "Tomorrow we'll speak to Stevenson and hope he has more to offer than I can. For now, keep alert and lock your doors at night. Perhaps the beast hunting nearby is more simple than the trows plaguing the coast. Perhaps it's as cunning as this Laird of Aonghus. Until we know, it wouldn't be smart to confront it."

Donal rubbed a hand over his scruffy chin. "I should go with ye in the morning. At least to hear what there is to say. I'll return here after and start spreading word."

Effie hesitated. An old part of her alarmed over inviting so much attention. She trusted Donal would keep her secrets, but to let others know that someone, even nameless, worked on their behalf felt like she was exposing herself too much. Someone might've seen her enter the village or on the road, and if her description matched the wagging tongues of Duncairn, how long would it take before she was known throughout the Highlands? And yet, the Highlanders deserved a chance to defend themselves. They deserved the right to know what she knew and perhaps lend what aid they could. The time for worrying over a government Inquiry was long past. She gave a short nod, and the matter was settled.

"All right, Effie," said Donal.

"Effie?" Conall asked for the second time, his eyes glinting with mischief. Her gaze narrowed, but it only made his grin fiercer. "I think I'll take a wee wander by the water," he said, rising. "You have other matters to catch up on, I'm sure." He nodded to the brothers Croy, each in turn, and strode out.

Nora caught Effie's attention and flicked her head toward the departing Sniffer, her eyebrow raised. Her insinuation was clear. Effie ignored her and grabbed for another bite of cheese. Suddenly, her throat felt tight. Until yesterday, the man had been the enemy, and her emotions were still crossed on the matter. She shouldn't trust the young Sniffer as much as she already had, and she knew to trust her fluttering gut even less.

"Where are the other wee ones?" she asked. She wanted to think on something else. Besides the bairn in the cradle, the brothers had three sons and a daughter between them.

"With Mary," answered Colin. "Helping tote sacks of barley and corn." He spoke a bit more about the happenings in the village before talk turned to the cities, and then to the whole of the Highlands and Lowlands. Donal and Colin were prone to a cheery manner, even when speaking in distaste, but there was a sullen mood to them now. To hear them despairing and worried angered her, and she resolved not to let her friends suffer while she had the will to aid them. They had already done nothing less for her.

They chatted until their tea grew cold. Effie's legs were stiff from days of captivity and long hours of riding. She stood and stretched, trying to rub the numbness away. "I think I'll go check on Mr. Murray," she said. The grins she received in return were enough to make her blush, and she huffed away wishing she knew a few tricks the pixies played. Donal and Colin and Nora deserved to have their cups spilt into their laps.

She found Conall sitting at the edge of the loch staring out over the calm water. His face was a mask of deep thought, and he didn't move as she approached. "You look as melancholy as when I found you on the train to Aberdeen," she said.

"Not as bad as all that," he said, looking up at her and feigning a smile.

He took a long swig from his flask. She waved the flask away when he offered it and sat beside him. The rocks and sand crunched under the folds of her dress. The wind felt warm, more than it had all day. A few rays of sun peeked out from beneath full-bellied clouds, painting the hills in a prism of brown and gold shadows.

He took another swig, licking his lips, savoring every drop. "It's been a great while since I've sat and enjoyed the beauty of a loch. With the heather in bloom and rough scars tumbling down the hillsides. It's a wonder all men should see at least once. There's nothing like it in the South."

Effie tried not to laugh. "I can smell the whiskey on your breath from here. It's bringing the romantic out in you."

"Och." He snorted. "Aren't you the pot calling the kettle black?"

She smiled, but her tone held sorrow in it. "I spent my childhood hunted by the queen's minions, casting about for a home and a family. To be called a romantic is to admit I am part of a dying race."

"But your whole life is built upon the auld folk, the auld ways. It imbues you with a greater romantic sense." He poked her arm with each point. "It is known."

"I don't dwell on either." She stared out at the loch. It made her uncomfortable to talk about such things. She kept her memories of the past as sheltered as her hopes and dreams. A part of her had always feared their revelation, as if they might float away on a gust of wind if uttered and given substance.

"I'm sorry you have risked so much," she said, to change the subject. "Will your relationship with your family suffer even more for it?"

"Nothing I will lose any sleep over." He drained the rest of the whiskey and shoved the flask into his pocket. "It is a trivial thing, the love from my father. He uses it only when it suits his whim."

"How horrible for a son to face," she said, not knowing what else to say. She had loved her mother more than life itself, and the devastation when she passed was a rift in her soul that had yet to fully mend.

"Love is not always as strong as the poets would have us believe." Conall's face became hard, almost a snarl, before he shook it off and looked away. "Did you know I was engaged to be married a mere year ago?"

Effie started but again was at a loss for words. No wonder the man was rife with fits of melancholy. Her heart turned from a budding yearning to sympathy on his behalf.

"To Miss Catherine Thorton," he continued. "She pledged her devotion to me time and again on our long country walks and merry shopping trips, but she fled to America the very week my business failed." He smirked. "Her entire family bought passage, somehow, with her father's wages as a tailor."

Effie gasped, disbelieving. "You suspect your father's hand?"

Conall's face went blank. "Does it matter? She never wrote, never even said goodbye. If that's what love truly is, then beauty is but a blindness, and passion an ailment."

"No, Mr. Murray, love is not always so cruel." She clutched his arm. She couldn't stand the pain that shone in his eyes and wanted nothing more than to erase it.

"Have you loved, Miss Martins?" He eyed her. "Or is it Effie?"

She wet her lips. His candor had opened something within her. It begged for her to relent and give in, to reveal herself the way he had done. "Effie is what my friends call me," she said. "My mother called me Aelfryth, but that is a name of history and not so fit for the common tongue. And yes, I have loved. Maybe not as a man loves a wife, but in a bond with those who will never betray me, never abandon me, whose comfort and company make life worth living." She paused to stare at the clouds gathering over the water. "Even after their time on Earth has passed."

He studied her for a long moment, his eyes glassy, before turning to the water. "You'd do well at melancholy, if you ever tried it," he said. She saw the drunken grin pull at his lips and tossed a pebble at him, feigning indignation. He laughed and knocked it away. "I stink like a Campbell," he announced, standing. He pulled off his coat and tugged his shirt. "I'm going for a swim to wash away this dour talk."

"The water must be freezing!" she exclaimed.

"Aye," he said. He dropped his trousers and stood, rubbing his hands against the cold in naught but his undergarments. "Are you joining me?"

She blushed at the sight and shook her head. Wind-milling his arms, he stretched before racing out into the water. He splashed to his waist and dove under, surfacing with a yelp of delight. With his clothes wet, she could see far more than was proper. But she wasn't the gentleman he'd been while she was bathing, and she didn't turn away. Her gaze devoured all of him. The lust within her stirred, and her body ached in response, stiffening and melting at the same time. If only it were becoming of a lass to rush into the water and embrace him, she thought she might lose herself in the moment. She had no concerns over an honest marriage, after all, and had thought about surrendering to such impulses in the past. Yet the time had never been right, on those occasions. Or perhaps it had been the man.

"Not too far, or you'll drown, you fool!" She laughed, straining to find a safe place for her trembling hands.

He slapped the water, sending a spray of mist her way. "I'd swim all the way to Skye, if I could!"

She opened her mouth to retort, but the words stuck. Something clicked in her thoughts, and all other yearnings vanished. "To the sky," she hollered. "Bless the wee German, of course!"

Conall cocked his head in confusion.

"The fleeing fey, they're all heading for the Isle of Skye!"

CHAPTER 19

E ffie wrestled in her sleep. Stevenson and Graham had always provided shelter, a blanket of safety to shield her from the unknown. Stevenson would have a plan, as he'd had a thousand times throughout her adolescence. But he wouldn't know the properties of Aerfenium. No one knew them. No human, at least. She'd waste a day or two, possibly more—the time spent ascending Ben Nevis, sharing a warm embrace with Graham, and receiving considered advice from Stevenson. Such comforts would soothe her, yet they would do nothing to solve the greater matter.

She needed knowledge, not comfort. So her path must turn toward Skye.

Punching her pillow, Effie turned over. Rorie would be cross with her. Somehow he'd know she chose not to come home. Her heart felt hollow over the decision, but her head told her it was the correct one. She wasn't a child anymore; she didn't need Stevenson's direction to tell her what was right, what needed doing. Graham didn't need to lend her kind words of encouragement. Those days were past, as were the days when her mother had done the same. She settled back and tried again to sleep, but thoughts of home wouldn't go away.

Conall lay on the other side of the hearth, wrapped in a heap of furs. His snores were a dry rasp, not loud but peaceful. The chill of the loch had seeped most of the whiskey from him, and he'd spent the evening in a more jovial mood, talking of tool crafting and coopering with Colin and Donal. She watched the furs rise and fall with each breath. His black curls glinted off the light cast by embers still smoldering in the hearth. It always amazed her. Men were such simple creatures, yet prone to lives of overly vast convolution. She could go to him, but the yearnings of the earlier evening had dimmed. Her mind raced too much to desire such things now.

Her stomach fluttered, a gentle tickle that brought gooseflesh to her arms. She frowned, suddenly alarmed. The sensation was not right. Outside, hounds began to bay. In the distance, a beast howled. It sounded like a wolf, only deeper, and stronger. It sent shivers up her arms, biting beneath the flesh and scraping at her very bones.

Then her back convulsed as if a giant had stomped on it. Sharp pain made her cry out and reach for her spine, expecting to find a bloody dagger stuck within. The room whipped in circles as her vision blurred and twisted. The heat of the agony scorched her flesh, and she crawled to the hearth, retching bile and shaking. Her eyes burned as she tried to focus, tears dropping into the embers.

An arm wrapped around her shoulder, trying to keep her still. Conall whispered soothing words into her ear, and Nora joined from the other side, pulling her hair away and pressing a dampened cloth against her forehead. Effie's body cramped from the strain of the convulsions.

The nightmare outside seemed to sense her weakness. The howling quickened with excitement. It sounded closer, stalking toward the house. Effie trembled. Black Donald came for her. She felt him creeping through the woods, could picture the shadowed demons trailing at his cloven hooves. Darkness crept into the village, voiding the moonlight. Closer and closer, the devil prowled.

And then it was done. The howling stopped. The images left her, and only a dull ache remained to torment her body. Something must've threatened it off. Men with rifles, perhaps. But she hadn't heard any shots. She struggled to come up with another answer, but her mind remained blank.

"There, there," said Nora, "If ye didn't like my cooking, ye coulda' just said as much."

Effie tried to thank her, but it hurt and her voice came out as a whimper.

"No natural beast could utter that terrifying wail," said Conall.

"It were the Beast of the Loch." Donal stood in his nightshirt, rifle in hand. "The Black Donald come to feast on our cattle."

Effie was glad the others had heard the beast, too. It meant she hadn't completely lost her wits. She accepted water from Nora and used a cloth to wipe her face. "It felt like the beast was inside me, clawing to get out." It must have some hold over the fey, she considered, only the pain had reminded her more of the night she'd flown from Duncairn. The sudden sharpness of it, springing from nowhere, was all too familiar. Had the Black Donald been on her heels that night as well? The thought made her shiver.

Concern washed over Conall's face. "Perhaps we'd best stay the morning and make for Fort William on the morrow. Ascending Ben Nevis and meeting with Stevenson can wait another day, until you've regained your strength."

She shook her head. "No, I will be fine. And I'm not headed for Ben Nevis anymore." Her mind remained set on this new course. If anything, the uncanny ailment had redoubled her determination. "You and Donal will go while I head for Skye."

The three men balked and started talking at once, until Nora shushed them. "Wheesht, let the poor lass talk. I'm sure it's not as foolish a notion as it sounds." She gestured for Effie to continue.

Effie ignored the backhanded encouragement and gathered her thoughts. "Only the elder fey will know the properties of Aerfenium," she reasoned, "and any who remain are gathering on Skye for some purpose. They're the best source for information on the Sidhe Bhreige, too. Since Edinburgh, I've been fixated on returning to Stevenson, but it's clear now the answers we need rest on the Isle of Skye. Heading there directly cuts out a couple days' delay, days we may not have."

Conall folded his arms over his chest. "Then Donal can carry a message to Stevenson, and I will journey with you."

"I thought of that," she said. "But I don't think the elder fey will present themselves with humans around. They're too scared right now. If I go alone, it's the best chance of finding them."

"And how do you plan on finding them?" asked Donal. "If they're even still there."

Effie let out a short huff. It was the part of her plan she hadn't quite figured out yet, but she wasn't about to let them talk her out of going. "The Storr," she said, firmly. "That's where I'm guessing they'd gather." It was a reasonable suspicion; the jagged crags and pinnacles were steeped in fey lore. "And if they aren't there, I'll find a way. The isle isn't overly big. It shouldn't be difficult to spy a host of fey."

"Not big?" exclaimed Colin. "It could take weeks of scouring the hills and cliffs."

Nora sucked on her gums, contemplating. "The Giant of Storr," she mused. "Me mum used to tell us of him. Sleeping on the shores of Loch Leathan for centuries, waiting for some horn to blow so he can rise up and skulk about the land again. He was a fearsome beast, not like our gentle Sleeping Giant of Kinlochy."

"It's a place to start," said Effie. She sipped more water, feeling herself again.

Her flesh had finally cooled and muscles settled. Rising, she stretched out legs that had remained crouched for too long. Dawn was still hours away, yet a part of her wanted to start the journey now. The path before her beckoned like a sweet wine on a warm summer day.

Conall saw the look on her face. "We should discuss how to relate the news to Mr. Stevenson. Perhaps you'd best write something yourself so it will be believed. I fear he'll only see me as a Sniffer come with a false tale."

"He kens me well enough," said Donal. "He'll trust your tale if I vouch for it." Effie nodded. Stevenson would take the cooper's word as her own. Guilt twinged, however, shaming her for the part that was glad Donal would accompany Conall. The Sniffer was right. That she had trusted him the past few days, even forming a friendship with the man, could not remove the years of disgust Stevenson and Graham felt toward the profession. She was asking a lot of them to heed the word of a Fey Finder and harbor him against the crown.

Conall jawed a bit longer, still unsatisfied that she was to travel on alone, but in the end he wore out and the matter was settled. They agreed to travel together to the town of Carie, where Effie could hire a coach to take her to the coast. Conall and Donal would pass through Fort William and attempt to discover the extent of Glover's fury, and any possible pursuit, before meeting with Stevenson.

Nora left to help Mary tend the children, who'd woken from all the clamor. The men huddled around the table, muttering to themselves for a time, rifles never too far from hand. Effie tried to sleep. She needed rest for the days ahead, but her mind raced. She worried she was not doing enough, that others would suffer Ramsey's fate due to her failures. She wondered who else knew of the connection between Sir Walter's Aerfenium and the wickedness creeping across the land. Was she fooling herself to believe she had any role to play in its obstruction? She felt out of her skin. She'd lived so long in the shadows, hiding from society, that the thought of speaking in front of the fey host was absurd. But she had to make them listen, or she would doom more than just her friends. The whole of Scotland would fall into war, and with it the empire would crumble.

CHAPTER 20

S he blinked against a piercing ray of sunlight peeking through the windows. The dark of morning had passed. Outside, a new day stirred, yet she hadn't rested at all. They broke their fast on warmed oats mixed with honey, while the horses were tended and provisions readied. At Arnisdale, Stevenson had built a lighthouse, one of the first Effie had ever rendered, and she knew its caretaker well. They determined to rendezvous there after their tasks had completed, hopefully in no more than a few days' time.

Goodbyes were made to Nora and Mary and the children, as the sun crested the hills and lofted into a sky smeared with foggy patches of cloud. A frost covered the bracken and grass, and a wind gusted off the loch, chilling the air. But they covered ground as quick as they could while the day remained dry. Effie kept an eye out for signs of the beast, but if it had feasted on any livestock, it had done so in the other direction. When Conall had suggested to Donal the army might come hunt the thing down, he'd bristled and sworn he'd rather die under its tooth than live under the army's rule.

Carie was a small town yet still larger than Kinlochy. They were able to find a coach willing to take her to the coast, where she could hire a boat to ferry her south to Oban. From there, a larger ferry ran to Skye. The endeavor was costly, but time was of the essence and Conall's purse never seemed to empty. She wondered if they spent his father's money or the crown's, but she was satisfied either way.

The Sniffer held the reins of his horse in one hand, the reins of

Whisper in the other, as they set to part ways. "God speed," he said, then took on a quizzical look. "Does that make sense to tell one of the fey?"

"It's good enough for Miss Martins," she replied. She smiled and patted his hand. "Fare thee well, and give Rorie a giant hug for me!" She stroked Whisper's shoulder and thanked him for bearing her on such a long journey. The old horse whinnied and nuzzled into her.

"Rorie?" Conall's expression became even more perplexed.

She and Donal laughed, and she left them there, determined not to become emotional over the parting. She would see them again in only a matter of days, after all. But more than that, she longed to join them. Longed to reunite with her family atop Ben Nevis. That her coach sputtered off in the wrong direction was perhaps the most trying cross to bear since she'd learned of Ramsey's fate.

The man who drove the coach kept to himself for the bulk of the journey, working the knobs and levers atop the driver's seat while she remained within the carriage. At top speed, Whisper could keep pace with the steam-powered contraption, at least on the rutted and uneven back roads of the Highlands, but the plow horse wouldn't manage the pace for very long.

Every now and then, the driver pulled the coach over and stomped to the rear, shoveling in another load of coal. Effie left him to his tasks, content to watch the trees and hills. The seat grew warm as the boiler labored, and musty coal-smoke billowed about them in a cloud, so much she could taste it on her teeth. Her eyes grew heavy, and she let them rest. By the time she woke, the sun had fled behind a wall of cloud. Rain pounded the coach's roof, dampening the smoke and sizzling as it struck the boiler. She peered outside and saw the waters of Loch Linnhe. The end of the loch opened into the Firth of Lorn, giving passage to the Atlantic. A village nestled along the shore, and a handful of boats bobbed up and down on their tethers, as the rain and wind stirred the water.

A paddle steamer was heading south within the hour, its owner hauling lumber to Oban. He agreed to take Effie aboard and found a dry place for her to have tea while his crew readied for the trip. The barge's wheel was twice her height and banded in steel, an old-fashioned thing but sturdy and of sound design. Effie felt a sliver of embarrassment as she paid the captain with some of Conall's coin, which she kept in a borrowed reticule from Nora. It seemed one thing to watch the Sniffer pay on their behalf and quite another to hand the money over herself. The debts she owed her friends were ever mounting.

The barge blasted its horn and was soon underway. The dreary weather rocked them a bit, yet the air was crisp and clean enough that the movement didn't bother her. The wheel groaned as it gained speed, the paddles splashing into the water, propelling them forward. They reached Oban in good time, entering the horseshoe-shaped bay just as the midday sun peeked through the clouds. The captain pointed her toward the larger ferries that serviced the western islands and bade her a safe journey.

The ferry to Skye could fit a hundred passengers, though it wasn't a quarter full as they embarked. Effie found a bench to rest on and worked to determine her next step. Even if her assumption was correct, and the fey host gathered at the Storr, she would need a means to call them out. Most fey were communal creatures by nature, who favored moving about in troops. Solitary fey had always been outcasts, and since the Seily Court abandoned the Highlands the divide had become even greater. Effie bit her lip. She couldn't rest her hopes on the host presenting itself. Even a large fey host could remain hidden to prying eyes, if it desired, and she had no assurance they would accept her, especially with all the troubles afoot. She wished Rorie were with her. He could sniff them out. Perhaps she could find another fox or borrow a farmer's hound to do the same, but that was chance. She understood little how to control such feats, despite her success in Duncairn.

She pressed her hands into her lap and took a deep breath. What had her mother told her about the Seily Court? That they laughed and danced and made mischief without a care to the wind. They bathed in the moonlight and set fire to the sun. They worshiped glittering metals more than the living soil that bundled them, more than the roots and stems that cradled them.

Effie perked up. "Chimes times three; beckon pixies wee," she said, repeating the rhyme her mother had taught her. There had to be some of the Wee Folk among the fey host. If so, all she needed to find was a silversmith, and she could bid the wee ones come to her!

The remainder of the crossing she spent trying to call up other rhymes, anything that might be of use, but no other scraps of lore provided as good a chance. Her arrival at Skye was a blur, her thoughts anxious and excited, roiling in a stomach already soured by the previous evening. She managed to reach Portree and found to her relief the High Street shops still open. The man at MacDonald & Burr eyed her curiously as she placed the unmatched spoon and serving pitcher on the counter, recommending a matched serving set as an alternative gift.

"These will accommodate," said Effie, "as long as they are a high grade of silver."

The man assured her they were and wrapped them carefully. She felt his gaze follow her out into the late afternoon light, but she had no time for feeling self-conscious. She'd spent the bulk of the coin Conall had lent her and still needed to travel another ten miles before she reached the Storr.

With not a minute to waste, she trudged north along the carriageway until she found a local crofter willing to take her along in the back of his wain. The man's Gaelic was almost as incoherent as his broken Scots, but she managed to make herself understood and was grateful to trundle along with company.

The Storr appeared a short while later, erupting from the ground as if the gods had punched the rock forward from beneath the earth's crust. A landslip had caused the ancient mountain to split asunder. Half remained upright, while the other dropped off toward the coast. Tall pinnacles stood sentinel around the crags, finger-shaped towers of stone too stubborn to crumble. The black and silver shades of the rock met the shadows of the surrounding glen, giving the place a hallowed feel, like that of a cathedral. And it was, of sorts. The locals called the base of the Storr a sanctuary, and no disciple could pray for a reflection of nature any more glorious.

The Giant of Storr lay on his back at the southern end of the cliff. He'd slumbered since the days of the druids, his mighty feet sticking up at odd angles, his nose a bulbous rock jutting from an expanse of stone. He was dwarfed by the cliffs on which he slouched but would stand five times Effie's height when upright.

She thanked the crofter and alighted from the wain. The man would no doubt spin a story or two about her to his village—it wasn't every day a stranger asked for a ride to the Storr, and a woman traveling alone no less—but the day had a need for haste. Her anonymity paled in comparison to the threat that stalked the Highlands, and the apprehension she'd felt departing Ben Nevis not so long ago seemed as meaningless as trying to gauge the distance to the end of the world.

Hill walkers often climbed the slopes of the Storr. The worn paths they left made it easy to discover a trail leading off into the forest on the southern slopes. The stretch between the crags and Loch Leathan was lush and rolling, sheltered by the high peaks above. Effie searched as she tramped through the undergrowth. Pixies were impulsive creatures, attracted to anything shiny or flickering. They loved pools of water for the reflections they cast, and the moonlight brought them near to rapture. They fed on berries and the sugar they stole from kitchens, but they were gluttonous when it came to hazelnuts.

Effie wandered for over an hour, drawing as near the giant as she could while remaining amongst the foliage, until she found the right place. The small pool lay in a clearing, allowing a view of crag and loch, yet hid her from the road. A perfume of blackberries and hazelnuts wafted from the shrubbery and trees encircling the pool. Twilight had settled in, and as darkness fell the shadows of the Storr grew deeper and longer, the gaps between the trees seeming to shrink until only a wall of forest surrounded her.

She gathered wood for a fire, thinking it prudent to prepare in case she had to spend the night alone. But she didn't let such thoughts overwhelm her. She'd come too far and was too tired. Waiting until moonlight cast across the pool, she took out the spoon and pitcher. The pair glinted under the light, as if the metal were made to drink in nourishment from the heavenly globe.

She struck the spoon against the pitcher. A hollow chime reverberated within, echoing out into the night. It wasn't loud, but in the stillness of the glen it was a clarion call befit a regimental bugler.

She struck a second time and a third after that. Each chime felt more powerful than the last, as if the Storr itself embraced her endeavor. Effie glanced around and waited. Nothing stirred. Only silence met her.

After a few minutes, she tried again. Three chimes ringing out across the glen.

Again, nothing.

With the third try, she tried to concentrate on an image of a pixie, and on the fourth she tried to will them to her summons. She tried to cast her senses out and pull in the feeling of every living thing around her, as she'd done with the trows. She tried clanging louder, softer, faster, and slower. When a dozen attempts had failed, she slumped to the ground in frustration. She crammed a handful of berries in her mouth, foot tapping away absently, and considered lighting her campfire.

It had seemed so easy. All she had to do was reach Skye, and the way would point itself. She wondered if Conall was having better luck. Was he with Graham and Stevenson now, sipping mulled wine around the hearth, developing a plan to save the empire? Planning and debating while she sat on the cold moss of a nameless hillside?

Leaning forward, she dunked the pitcher into the pool. The cool water tasted sweet, like a nectar brewed from the berries fallen into its depths. She thought about stripping down and bathing. A cold soak would help rinse the day's journey away and hopefully wipe her mind of brooding, too.

Rising, her hands worked the buttons of her dress. She reached to pull it over her head but stopped with it halfway raised. She glanced around and listened, but the clearing was as motionless as it'd been since her arrival. She closed her eyes. Something tugged at her senses, a perception at the edge of her awareness. She couldn't quite put the sensation into words, yet she had a certainty that something approached. It felt almost like that of the trows' presence, only sweeter and lighter. It didn't threaten in such a blunt manner. Dropping the hem of her dress, she clutched the pitcher tightly in her grip.

A tiny light flitted through the trees, disappearing on one side of the pool and reappearing on the other. It danced up and down, darting about like a hummingbird. Effie relaxed, her lips spreading in an uncontrollable grin. Her stomach tickled with delight.

"It was you!" squeaked the pixie.

It fluttered forward and hovered before Effie's nose. Its wee body was draped in a tunic of azure silk, its flesh pulsing with a golden glow. Amber hair sprouted from a head marked by sharp ears and rounded eyes. A black thread tugged the silk tight at the waist, tied in an intricate knot.

"I searched up high and down low, and over by the willow-do, and by the grassy-burn, and by the oak-lee, but you weren't there." The pixie spun about as it spoke. Catching sight of the spoon, it zipped to the ground and strained to pick the thing up. "Heavy!" it squealed.

"Hello, I'm Effie. It's very nice to meet you. I wasn't sure if anyone would come."

"I know!" said the pixie, buzzing up to her face. "We were expecting you. The whole court waits for your arrival. He said you'd come. And you did!"

Effie started, taken aback. "Someone sent you? I thought you'd heard the chimes."

"I did! I did! I heard them. But I was already searching for you." The pixie flew along the pool, stopping to dunk its head in the water. "I'm called Alison. The chimes were helpful!"

Effie couldn't make sense of it, and following wee Alison about was starting to give her a headache. "But who would've known I was coming?" Perhaps Gabus had told someone to watch for her. It was the only explanation she could think of.

"We mustn't tarry," said Alison. "I want to hear what he has to say. They've gathered the entire court for him, everyone who's left. Come; it isn't far!"

"But for whom?"

Alison huffed and put her fists on her hips. Rolling her eyes in exasperation, she said, "The Laird of Aonghus, of course!"

CHAPTER 21

E ffie's heart pounded. She ran from the clearing, trying to keep pace with the darting flight of Alison. She shoved down the part of her that wanted to flee the other direction. If the entire court stood against the laird, she would stand with them. And if they had joined his cause, well, it was better to discover their alliance and intent than to run to Stevenson with nothing but whiffs of theories. Knocking into trees and scraping her arms along the bracken, she was lucky her feet didn't find any loose rocks or the boggy pits scattered across the Storr. She barked questions with gasping breath, but they went unanswered. The few words the pixie squeaked were scolding in nature, urging Effie to hurry up and quit her prattling.

They reached the gathered fey host on the shores of Loch Leathan. A hundred strong huddled around great bonfires that warmed the night air and dulled the starlight. Pixies fluttered about in a swarm, like a hive of midges, their glowing bodies swirling in the wind. A handful of gnomes chattered in a group, debating some matter with a rather tall brownie who stood almost to their shoulders. Gabus was not among them, Effie observed with disappointment. Their frock coats were heavy and craftsman-like, all covered in stains and dust. The brownies were difficult to tell apart from the hogboons, except for the former's cheery, excitable nature, and the latter's gloomy slouching. Their heads wouldn't reach her waist, though they could pass for human children in their waistcoats and trousers. A sharp angle of the cheeks and eyes was the only thing that gave a hint of their otherworldly nature. The remainder of the host appeared mostly human. A few would be selkie or some other shapechanger, the others Sithlings like Effie.

Her gut soured. In the middle of the host stood the malformed fiend of Duncairn. The Laird of Aonghus stooped over his cane. His eyes twinkled at the sight of her, the only one to greet her with a smile. The reaction chilled her more than the stone-like stares from the other fey.

"I found her!" squealed Alison, whirling about one of the bonfires.

"Indeed, you have," said the laird. As he spoke, all other conversations died. "A most fortunate timing, too. Her presence will confirm the truth of my words for any who doubt them."

Effie rankled at the pronouncement. "I will do no such thing!" she hollered.

She glanced around the host. Their stares were as cold as the chilly waters of the loch, but she saw in many of them the trembling of fear. Their eyes darted toward the laird, their bodies shying away. Some had shuffled back into the shadows and watched only as shades wavering in the darkness.

Emboldened, Effie asked, "How have you allowed this wicked creature into your host? He brings peril to us all. He should be in chains and his minions hunted down!"

"Who are ye to demand such things?" asked the tall brownie, who Effie now saw was female. Wisps of ginger hair sprouted from her head. Snaggled teeth protruded from her lips.

"Effie of Glen Coe," answered one of the Sithlings.

Lithe, with a handsome face despite a hooked nose, the fey imbued a regal air. Effie thought he might be young, no more than a dozen years her elder, but his gaze was ancient. He stood near the laird, as calm as the waters spreading out behind him.

"I am Caledon, steward of the Seily Court of Righm, the last Scottish host of the Daoine Sith. I welcome you to our moot." He raised an arm, palm up, fingers extended toward her, and addressed the gathering. "This is Aelfryth, called Effie, the daughter of Adeleyde, granddaughter of Arnwyrd."

"The oathbreaker," hissed a gnome.

A ripple rode throughout the host. Effie blanched. She knew her grandfather's name but nothing more. It shamed her that these strangers knew her family's history where she did not, and even more so that the knowledge was borne with distaste.

"Accept her words kindly," continued Caledon, "as befitting a member of this Court."

The laird cackled. "Her blood has not strayed far from root. The Grundbairn contends I am false, but it was she who betrayed our kind, causing the deaths of many of my subjects. She killed one with her own hands, snatching the life from him with a club. The others she had her human friends destroy with fire and lead."

A frenzy of angered mutterings shot toward Effie. Quite a few of the host scowled at her, and the rest stared at her as if they had bitten into something bitter, their cheeks sucked back in disgust.

"Your subjects," said a hogboon. "Trows, you mean. Nasty buggers got what's coming to them, you ask me. Their kind has always been crude and fiendish."

"No one asked ye, Gor," said the tall brownie, "so shut yer gob hole."

The host erupted anew. The hogboons bellowed at the brownies, the Sithlings argued amongst themselves, while the gnomes griped at any who would listen. Alison and the rest of the pixies zipped around the bonfires like stirred up embers sparking from the wind. Effie shouted, straining to be heard above the din. Her senses spun and flickered, overwhelmed and exhausted. Support for the Sidhe Bhreige was the last thing she'd expected to find within the host. She didn't understand it. From the way Gabus had reacted, and from what she'd witnessed firsthand, fey were better off flying into the sun rather than joining sides with the laird of Aonghus. She tried to make note of who argued in her defense and who for the foul creature, but it was hard to tell in the confusion.

Caledon raised his fists. "Silence," he commanded, and Effie felt a jolt pass through her, like a sudden snap of the wind. The host staggered, also buffeted by the unseen hand. "We have given the Laird of Aonghus permission to address our court. Let us be courteous and be done with this matter." He turned to the laird. "Speak your cause, but do not presume the terrors of ages past are forgotten."

The laird's lips drew open, revealing the decaying teeth behind. He tapped his cane on the ground, studying the host. "I am blood of the Sidhe Bhreige, whom you children of the Daoine Sith banished to the Downward Fields after forming a vile pact with the humans of this land. Trapped for millennia in a realm of darkness, I have returned to reclaim my mantle of divinity." He waggled the cane at the host. "I see in your eyes a hint of mistrust. But there is no need Leaving this realm for your sweet Elphame. Do not fear retribution. A shepherd does not scold his sheep for shitting in the fields. Your kind have always been given to frivolities. Where my blood flows pure, your ancestors were ever swayed by lust and greed, diluting and degrading your stock."

Effie blanched, barely able to contain her disdain for the creature. But she managed to hold her tongue.

"You find yourselves hunted, driven from your lands by the very race who tricked you into turning on your masters. Does this so-called queen not know it is our soil she steals? Our water, our forests, our stone? She and her minions are a parasite who befoul the realm with tyranny and decrepitude. Swear fealty to me and restore what once was. Swear fealty and strike down your true oppressors. Do not flee as cowards bowing beneath a yoke created by lesser beings. Stand in majesty at the side of the Sidhe Bhreige, as was before."

Effie watched a few of the gathered host nod their heads and wondered if the laird were not using some craft on them. How could they not repulse at the thought of submitting to the creature's will?

She stepped forward, anger pushing down the fluttering in her gut. "Where are your trows? Where are your rake and bite? You claim harmony and forgiveness but bring with you murder and enslavement. What of the slain selkies of Duncairn? Did they stand in majesty?"

The laird smiled at her, but his eyes flashed in fury. "Casualties necessary to throw off the chains of human oppression," he snapped. "Already their sacrifice has produced a great boon, drawing out the hounds of the bitch queen. The very ones who threw you in a dungeon, who tortured you and bound you like a prized sow. You defend those who would kill you without a second thought. Defend those who tricked you into betrayal of your own kind." He let a heavy pause build before smirking. "Or did they not have to force your hand?"

"Enough," barked Caledon, before the rising clamor could reach open hostility again. "Violence glides from your tongue like water down a hill. It is not our way and never was, something your kind never learned. We have humored you long enough and ask for you to leave our court. Any who wish may follow." The Sithling swept a hand over the host, giving his leave.

The Laird of Aonghus sneered. "You take a Roman name and call yourself the leader of this host. You are but a pale breaking of wind compared to your forebears."

Caledon stood taller. "It is enough their blood is within me," he said. His gaze crackled with power.

"So be it." The fiend tapped his cane and hobbled away from the host. "I will wake the giants and see if their slumber has left them restless. Then any who stand against me will face doom at my hand for this second betrayal."

A chill enveloped Effie like a blanket as the laird disappeared into the night. The host held its breath, all waiting for some calamity to befall them. But nothing stirred beyond the bonfires, and soon whispered conversations broke out within the huddled groups.

Effie started as a golden light popped before her vision. She had to control her hands to keep from swatting at the pixie in fright. "He wants to speak with you," peeped Alison.

"The laird?" Dread crept up Effie's spine.

"No," the pixie droned. "Caledon. The steward." She twirled and darted away, not waiting for a response.

Breathing a sigh of relief, Effie regarded the steward of the Court. He stood straight but not stiff, his clothes common yet neat and well-made. In any village public house, his countenance would beg respect, yet she guessed he would receive a cheery welcome as well. She approached, not knowing whether she should curtsy or address him formally.

"He said you would come," said the steward. His voice was warm and friendly, not at all the same that had commanded the host earlier. Yet it still held an underlying strength of iron in it. "I did not think it true. We have not seen you since you were a wee thing tugging on your mother's skirts, but I sensed you the moment you reached our shores."

Effie blinked. "I'm sorry; have we met before? I'm afraid I don't remember."

His eyebrow rose, and he chuckled. "It is no matter," he said. His deep-blue eyes and playful grin were hypnotic, lulling her into a dreamy state. She struggled to clear her head. "I was sad to hear of your mother's passing. She was a Sithling of great skill and passion, and always a voice of wisdom. Yet in the years after your birth she seldom met with our society." He studied her with knowing a gaze. "You must wonder at the reason for this and of the story of her father, but the tale of oathbreaking is for another time. I have much to do this night and can already see the questions sparkling in your eyes."

It was true. She was overwhelmed by them and didn't know where to begin. "Alison said the same thing about my arrival," she began, focusing on the notion that disturbed her most. "But how did the laird know I would come? I didn't even know until this morning."

"The powers of the Sidhe Bhreige are mighty and varied, yet at heart they are still communal in nature, as are those of the Daoine Sith. We share a common blood, and that binds us together in matters of Fey Craft. It binds our senses together, too, and allows those with enough skill an awareness of others. The laird is weakened by the lack of fey blood in the Highlands, but he is still able to perform many feats. The better question is, why does he follow your path?"

"For vengeance?" She was at a loss for any other reason. At the steward's beckoning, she related the story of Duncairn—of her first encounter with the laird and the subsequent destruction of the trow cave by Edmund Glover.

If Caledon was shocked by the tale, he showed no sign of it. "Many see the Laird of Aonghus as a malicious foe, yet there are some who would pledge their fealty and follow him if it meant the overthrow of London's rule. The laird knows this, and he needs the fey if he is to reclaim the Highlands. It is why he's hung around this court like a creeping mold, begging for allies rather than attacking with his beastly minions."

"Because his power wanes as fey blood leaves?" she asked, uncertain she followed.

Caledon nodded. "Yes. Forgive me; I've forgotten your knowledge is sparse." Effie blushed, grateful he put it so kindly. "All of fey kind, including the Sidhe Bhreige and those of our court, share a common ancestry. Our affinity with life, what the humans call Fey Craft, is based on the power within this shared blood. The more the blood is concentrated, the greater the power becomes. Five pixies are stronger than one, and a dozen stronger even still. It is how the ancient fey troops could move about unseen, holding court right under the noses of the humans. Their amassed power could conquer this modern empire twenty times over. We few who remain pale in comparison, even when huddled together."

Her mind reeled, thinking over the events of the past week. "That's why the fox understood me on the cliffs. I was standing above the trows' warren! Their blood must've lent aid to mine. And the stable horse, too. I was surrounded by the laird and his trows, at the time." She felt as dumb as a rock to not hold such simple knowledge. For all the rhymes her mother taught her, she'd wanted her isolated from the remaining fey. Why else would she not have told her? "I had thought the Fey Craft of the Grundbairns dead, dissolved when the elders departed Sidh Chailleann."

Caledon hid his mirth, but the humor still reached his eyes. "No, not dead, just very weak. There is not much fey blood left in the Highlands. But a gathering still has strength, even a small one, as you've discovered. Even now, this host has the might to conceal itself. Any man or woman who wandered about the loch would see nothing but empty shores, and any fey with the skill of awareness would not be able to sense our auras."

She stammered, about to ask why the remaining fey didn't then live together and combine their strength, but the answer came to her as fast as the question. The fey who'd remained after the Leaving sought isolation and were willing to give up any power they might possess as a community. She herself had never sought other fey to live among, though her rationale seemed far too brittle now. There was also the queen's government to consider. A community of fey would make it easier for the Sniffers to root out, even hidden from sight.

Her mind jumped to what Caledon had asked earlier. "I know little of our Fey Craft, and yet I can aid the laird by my presence alone. He can use the aura created by my fey blood. He thinks me a simpleton to use as chattel, to bolster his own power. That's why he tracks my movements."

"He must do something to strengthen what power he has," Caledon said, nodding. "It was a shock for him to reemerge from the Downward Fields and feel so weak. The majority of the Daoine Sith left this realm for Elphame thousands of years ago, but that was still generations after the time of Sidhe Bhreige banishment. And now the remaining few threaten to follow their forebears, as did many during the Inquiry of the Potato Famine. That Second Leaving almost extinguished the Seily Court of Righm. This third will greatly reduce the laird and his brethren."

"There are other lands with fey," offered Effie. "Saxony, France, Bavaria, the Norse—would the laird not travel there?"

"Eventually, but remember when the Sidhe Bhreige were banished, this world was a smaller place. Other gods ran havoc on the continent; only this island was for the Sidhe Bhreige to rule. The laird wears blinders at present, and his schemes are contained to what he knows. Yet I have no doubt when he learns the other elder gods have retreated to their heavens, he will seek to expand his dominion. And then the entire world will be under threat."

"But you let him leave!" she snapped. "Why didn't you try to stop him?" The anger snuck up on Effie, masked by the fatigue of her long journey. Her hands shook, and she realized just how drained of energy she was.

The steward's calm tone didn't change, despite her temper. "Because it is not my place to do so," he said. It wasn't meant as an excuse, merely a statement of fact. "I am a servant of the court, and the host has decided to abandon this realm. I must work to this end alone. The Sidhe Bhreige have no power in Elphame; their nature is too corrupt for such a peaceful place. It is a fact that angers the laird's kind, for it lessons their claims of divinity. Like the Scottish fey, they are only an offshoot from the same ancient bloodline, and they do not like to be reminded of that fact. When the court has gathered its strength, we will depart, and then we will be safe from the Sidhe Bhreige."

"Safe in Elphame, leaving the Earth to destruction and misery, leaving it to face these fiends alone."

"All of our kind are welcome in this Third Leaving," he said, not denying the truth of her words.

Tears blossomed, flooding her lashes and running down her cheeks. She was surprised to feel the pangs of loneliness rising within her emotions. It was foolish—she'd never met any of the gathered host before, at least not as she could remember—and yet the thought of all these fey gone tore at her as much as the fear of impending doom. She clenched her fists at her sides, willing herself to not wipe the moisture from her face.

"I must stop him," she said. Her voice rumbled with fury. In her heart, there was no other option.

Caledon watched her for a moment before speaking. His gaze was both enthralling and unnerving. "Some would argue there was truth in the laird's words," he said. "That the whip of the Sidhe Bhreige is not much different than that of London's. You would fight only to trade one enslavement for another."

"That is not true. There are many who welcome me and all of fey kind. Those who applaud our nature and revere our lore. Not all are as ignorant as the Sniffers." She thought of Conall and amended her statement. "And not all Sniffers are close-minded gits."

She glanced around the host, taking in their numbers. "We must stand against the laird and find a way to defeat him. This realm has been our home for generations. We've bled for this land, tended to it, and made it our home. We shouldn't allow ourselves to be driven off so easily." She spoke with passion but knew the words rolled too easily off her tongue. Without allies to support her, convincing the host to remain would be like coaxing a cow up a mountain. She was a stranger to them, her word only as reliable as her family's, and apparently that wasn't good.

At least Caledon didn't argue against her this time. He stood mute, his eyes glittering with a polite curiosity. Something dawned on Effie. "The Sidhe Bhreige need our blood for their strength. So that means the laird will be weaker when this court leaves. If those who remain lie in wait, would we have enough strength to defeat him?" The plan would certainly be easier than convincing a bunch of strange hogboons and grumpy gnomes to risk their lives.

"The laird will weaken for a time after the Leaving," agreed Caledon, "but further rifts into the Downward Fields will allow more of the Sidhe Bhreige and their minions to return, and when they do, their own blood will be enough to return them to power. Already, the Laird of Aonghus is no longer alone. You have felt the tearing of the wards, no doubt." At her puzzled expression, he continued, "The wall between this realm and the Downward Fields is maintained by a substance of our making. It is of our Fey Craft and hence a part of us. As it is consumed, the wall crumbles and the destruction pulls at our blood. The sensation is quite memorable, like being torn asunder."

Effie started. "The terrible pain last night—it was from Aerfenium being destroyed?"

"If that is what you are calling the Aegirsigath, the substance that binds the Sidhe Bhreige within the Downward Fields. And I believe it was not the only time you have felt its consumption."

"No," said Effie. "When I was flying for Edinburgh, it came on me all of a sudden." She squeezed her eyes shut, feeling almost sick. "And once before that, weeks ago." She'd not remembered that earlier bout, having dismissed it as a careless misstep while tramping on Ben Nevis. Her back had jarred, and she'd spent an afternoon sipping tea and resting abed. That must've coincided with the initial discovery by Sir Walter's men, and the second, while she flew toward Edinburgh, matched the timing of the explosion spoken of by those in the city.

"A pair of the laird's brethren have escaped, as have scores of their minions, fell beasts who've reproduced into untold numbers while in captivity. One rampages through the Highlands now, while the other lurks in the shadows. As more are freed, their kind will strengthen all the faster."

Ice seized Effie's veins, blocking her blood from flowing, freezing her to the bone. She imagined a tidal wave of demons bursting forth from the deep rocks of the Highlands, overrunning farms and villages, bringing blood and fire and ruin. "They will seek to destroy the substance," she realized. "To speed their return."

"Perhaps. But the humans are doing that well enough on their own."

It came back to Sir Walter Conrad, as Effie knew it would. His great discovery released destruction on the empire, and from there it would spread until all nations were destroyed. "I can get them to stop," she said, almost scoffing at the words herself. What would Sir Walter do if she told him to abandon his profits and cover up his great discovery? Throw her in chains again, most like. He already believed the fey were behind the attacks on his worksite. Who would heed the word of a creature London had raised arms against and sworn to hunt down?

"Even if you could, the damage is done."

"Can't it be rebuilt? You said the Aegirsigath was a substance of our making."

"An undertaking of such power would need…."

"The entire court," she finished for him. She turned and examined her brethren again. A few eyed her back. Forcing a smile, she steeled herself and raised her voice. "The steward has informed me I am too late to state my cause, but I would ask you to hear me anyway."

The host quieted so that she could hear only the buzzing of the pixies.

These are my people, she had to remind herself, looking at all the strange faces. There was no time for timidity. "I feel…I think…Perhaps you've abandoned hope for this Earth too quickly."

"You want us to die for the humans," squawked a hogboon. A group of heads bobbed in agreement, muttering to each other.

"No, I only wish you to stay just a little longer and help me rebuild the wards. Not just for the humans but for the pines and oaks and burns and glens, the lochs and firths. The whole of our lands and everything that lives upon it. We've dwelled here too long to let it fall to ruin."

"What of us as sees justice in the Sidhe Bhreige overrunning London's cities and industry?" asked the tall brownie.

"Aye, and what will happen if we manage to throw back the Sidhe Bhreige?" asked a gnome. "The same as it were before, no doubt."

"You would have all our forefathers worked for, all they created, destroyed in the name of vengeance?" asked Effie, glaring at the tall brownie. How could they be such heartless fools? "I have not lived among your court, it is true, but I cannot fathom it teaches such vile baseness."

"But what would you have us do?" asked one of the Sithlings. "The Sidhe Bhreige grow stronger and time is short. Within a fortnight they will have the strength to destroy this court and enslave us all."

"Reseal the Sidhe Bhreige in the Downward Fields," answered Effie. "Only we have the power to do such a task. Let the queen's regiments destroy the creatures the Sidhe Bhreige have brought with them. That is their fight. Ours is only to protect the land and bind the enemy." She saw more than a few heads shaking in disagreement. For all it felt like her argument was sound, none raised a voice to her aid. Effie fumed, forcing herself not to snap at them. They could not all be so pigheaded. Perhaps if she spoke to them one at a time, but no, there was no time for that. If she'd known them before things might be different. But that milk was spilt. Her shoulders slumped as defeat began to weigh her down.

"Even if you succeed," said the Sithling, "the remade Aegirsigath would be a weak substitute needing constant attention. Without assurances of protection from London, it would be only a matter of time before the Sidhe Bhreige broke free again."

"But other fey can return," she pleaded. It was the first answer that popped into her head. "They can help. If it takes hundreds, then hundreds can come, remake enough Aegirsigath to seal away the Sidhe Bhreige forever, and then...." Her voice trailed off. She almost said they could decide to stay, to re-forge their lives within the Highlands. But already the mocking laughter of the court rolled at her in waves. It reminded her of the trows' chittering.

The chill of the night closed in around her. Her eyes suddenly became heavy, and all she wanted to do was rest. "I will not give up," she said quietly to Caledon. "I will stay and fight, even if you flee with tails tucked between your legs."

Caledon didn't flinch at the insult. "Our Leaving is on the new moon in four days' time." He spoke as if arranging a tea. "Get

London to concede by then, and I will stay, at least to discuss the matter further. But no more Aegirsigath can be destroyed, else the Sidhe Bhreige will overrun the Highlands before the fortnight is through."

The steward regarded her with a warm smile. Effie blinked, swaying on exhausted legs. Though his words were a small victory, they didn't feel like one. She had passed a sort of test she realized, wondering if the steward had led her to this result all along. Perhaps the man wanted to fight but was bound by the confines of his position. She hadn't the energy to consider it any longer. The next test would be more grueling, and the cost of failure more than just her life. Entire cities and clans, the very empire, depended on her.

Exhausted, she tottered down to the loch and sat in the tall grass along the shore. Moist air kissed her skin, the crackling of the bonfires played a symphony in her ears, and the sweet scent of pine filled the night. The land called to her as vividly as it ever had, and in its embrace all panic fled.

CHAPTER 22

The trek to Arnisdale took twice as long as that to Skye despite being half the distance. Effie's mind raced the entire way. She'd journeyed to Skye seeking knowledge and somehow wound up the spear point in the fight against the Sidhe Bhreige. Had that been Caledon's intention all along? If the Laird of Aonghus knew of her coming, the steward of the remaining Seily Court might have, too. How much of the evening had unraveled just as he'd intended? The thought rankled something deep within. In all her years alone, she'd never sought out the court. She'd never asked Stevenson where he received his stardust, if there were any he knew who would take her in, who would welcome her as one of their own. And yet, she never considered she'd feel as much an outsider amongst the fey host as she did within the world of men. For some reason, she'd expected something different. The naïve child in her had placed blinders over her wits.

Caledon's orchestration aside, there was no doubt the laird played her against the host. And now he roamed the Highlands, building power and worse—gaining knowledge of their modern world. She'd begged the court for aid and received only a meager sum of days. It irked her to no end, but the rational part of her knew there was no time left regardless of whether the Scottish fey stayed or fled. The Sidhe Bhreige were loosed, their tidal wave already looming above the shores of the empire. She must convince Sir Walter to stop destroying the Aegirsigath or ruin would find them all.

No, she corrected. She needed to stop him from destroying the Aegirsigath, at any cost. It mattered not whether he consented. If she could find the remaining substance first, she might have a chance to secret it away. She'd asked Caledon where to seek it, but the steward had offered little insight. "Spread throughout the Highlands," he'd said, "in secret dells and clearings. That is the best our lore can offer. Its secret was lost when the elder fey left for Elphame."

He'd spoken further, in the chill of the morning, weaving a story of betrayal and fading memory. There had been a time when the Highland clans knew of Aegirsigath. It was lore passed down by clan chieftains and held by the druid elders. But years turned to centuries, and the might of bloodlines ebbed and waned. Soon there came a time when only a handful of Scots remembered the tale of banishment and the warrior heroes who conquered the islands so long before. It was a tale not given much thought. And then the Scottish crown united with that of London. James VI became James I, and for the humans Aegirsigath was forgotten. The Daoine Sith had departed, and civil war re-forged the newly united kingdom.

"After the overthrow of the Sidhe Bhreige," said Caledon, "the chieftains of the Celts swore never to disturb the Aegirsigath, but the House of Stuart, and now of Hanover, know nothing of those promises. London has closed its ears to its Seily denizens. They create wards against us as we created wards against our cousins. Perhaps in that sense, our current fate is just."

Effie refused to believe in such cruelty. As she parted from the steward, she'd struggled to portray an air of confidence. It was far too easy to lose courage, and they had no time for wallowing. She had to believe in the strength of her righteousness. But her thoughts swirled in a circle. She had no idea how to find the Aegirsigath, nor how to persuade Sir Walter from abandoning the greatest discovery of his life.

The steam whistle of her hired carriage shrilled as they started a winding ascent. The scene out the window was familiar and comforting, like returning to a childhood home, or as close to it as she had. She knew every tree on the hillside, every ridge and gully aside the road. She had traveled this way a thousand times and run through the surrounding forest ten thousand more.

The lighthouse nestled in a shallow saddle overlooking the firth. Its approach was blocked from view on the land side until the last bend of the road, but from the water its beacon could been seen from Skye. Stevenson's simple design was a marvel, blending the structure into the surrounding nature while creating a bold profile for sailors to spot even in the dreariest of weather. The engineering within used the latest technology—sporting a weather box attached to a high balcony and an antennae for sending wireless telegrams—but it was stardust that powered the great light. The substance burned a tranquil blue, like an early spring sky set afire. Its heat was piped through a network of channels, dispersing it throughout the house. The entire dwelling never lacked for warmth.

A small garden grew roughage and potatoes on one bank of the saddle, while on the other sat a carriage house and stable. As her hired carriage passed through the gate of the low stone wall that encircled the grounds, a prickle washed up from Effie's belly and raised the hairs on her neck. It was like the feeling of someone watching her, but instead of unnerving it was blissful. She took in the sensation, knowing what it meant. The awareness was easier for her this time, now that she could recognize the signs of Fey Craft cast by her blood. She tugged, and her gaze turned to the stables. Whisper was there, as surely as she knew Conall was inside the lighthouse. Him, and another. A broad grin split her cheeks.

The driver offered to see to her things, but she sent him on his way. She was excited to be alone with her friends. A clamor of pots and spoons came from the kitchen. She heard it well before she entered through the service door, though it didn't prepare her for the sight. Conall stood covered in flour, hands on his hips, studying a lump of soggy gruel spilling across a table. His face lit up when he saw her.

She laughed, quivers shaking her body, her earlier anxiety forgotten. "Is that meant to be bread?"

"A cake," he replied, wiping a smear of gruel across his forehead while trying to tuck a wild curl of hair back in place. "To celebrate your arrival. Only there wasn't enough flour at first, so I added more. And then the batter was too thick, so I added water, and now it won't stand together."

"A lovely thought all the same." She raised an eyebrow. "But how did you get Mrs. Heyward to leave you in her kitchen alone?" The cheery woman and her husband had been the caretakers of the lighthouse since its construction.

"I sent them into town for the evening," came a hearty voice from the hallway. Where Effie had been full of glee before, she now threatened to burst in joy. Graham winked and raised his arms as he stepped into the room. She rushed into his embrace. Even sensing him earlier had not lessened the shock of his entrance. She shut her eyes and breathed in his musky smell—pipe tobacco and whiskey— for what seemed an eternity before releasing.

"I knew it was you," she said.

Graham raised an eyebrow, but before she could elaborate, a bowl clattered to the floor, erupting in a cloud of flour. "Och, that's enough lad," he said to Conall. "Mrs. Heyward would pitch heels over head if she saw her kitchen in such a state. Leave the rest to me. I've learned a thing or two overseeing the cook in the camp mess. My cakes aren't pretty, but at least you can eat them." He patted Effie's arm. "Go let Mr. Stevenson know you're okay, and wash up. There'll be time enough for catching up while we're eating."

He strode to the table. "And take this one with you," he added, with a nod toward the Sniffer. "I think I saw some blackberries about. I'll see what I can salvage of this."

"Scones?" The word yipped from Effie's throat. Graham's scones were her favorite, always perfectly moist and rich with flavor without being overly sweet. A wisp of a grin pulled at his cheeks as he began working away the mess.

Conall dusted himself, looking quite sheepish. She tugged him out of the kitchen and down the hallway that connected the rest of the house. They passed a storeroom and a pair of bedrooms before the hallway spilled into a drawing room. An antechamber on the far side held the house's main entrance and the grand circular staircase that wound its way up the tower.

She'd come to the lighthouse—then, in the final stages of its construction—the first time over a decade before, on the run from the queen's agents, desperate for anyone who would welcome her. The year after her mother's passing had been fraught with hunger, desperation, and fear. For all her cherished memories of childhood, for all the great things her mother had taught her, once alone she'd had no conception of her place in the larger world, no idea of who she was or where she belonged. Stevenson had been the first to treat her as more than a curiosity. To the Highlanders who sometimes gave her food and shelter, she'd always been an outsider, never far from being asked to move on, never trusted beyond simple courtesy. But Stevenson had given her a home, a place to live and grow. He'd found her a purpose and carved a niche for her to fill.

In the hills around Arnisdale she spent years reading the works of the Greeks, the modern poets, and the thinkers of the Scottish Enlightenment—the works of Hume, Smith, and Stewart. The painters John Constable and Richard Wilson became her idols, with their romantic depictions of the countryside. She studied Stevenson's designs and began sketching impressions of them. Her drawings became her new passion. She worked at them day and night until she'd mastered the stormy clouds rolling off the sea, the gnarled cliffs of the rugged coastline, and the brilliant colors of surrounding flora.

She drew Arnisdale a thousand times, never thinking it more than a passion, until one day Stevenson brought her a commission to render one of his new projects. Soon he had her reading blueprints and deciphering the engineer's notes so she could envision their structures and place them in the landscape. Within a year, he was giving her so many assignments that she needed to move closer to his offices in the city. He found her a cottage tucked away in the Campsie Fells where she could live in comfort. It was a life her mother never wanted for her, one Effie had never dreamed of even when times had been at their darkest. But Effie felt blessed. She'd found a home and people who loved her.

Running her fingers along the carved beech rail, she mounted the winding stair. "Did you say hello to Rorie?" she asked over her shoulder.

Conall snorted. "Aye, I met the brute. The way he glared at me, I think he knew I'd been around you."

Effie thought of what she'd learned of the fey aura. "It's possible," she said.

"Donal knew Mr. Stevenson and Mr. Graham, of course. The

moment he introduced me, they knew everything had gone askew. They'd followed part of your journey, but the trail had gone cold in Edinburgh, the bits after you'd sent them the telegram."

"You were able to fill them in?" she said.

They reached the top of the tower. The stair ended at a landing large enough for them to squeeze next to a squat table. A ladder provided access to the space above where the great light swiveled round and round, beaming across the waters and headland. Copper pipes funneled along the walls, pumping water up and down the tower to cool the stardust powered devices. The clink of gears turning echoed above the swooshing sound of the spinning light.

"I told them all of it," said Conall. "My part in your imprisonment and in your escape. Mr. Stevenson immediately sent for word on what transpired in Duncairn thereafter." He caught his breath. "Glover has returned to Edinburgh. A warrant has been issued for both of us for treason against the crown."

Effie's gut lurched at the statement, but she'd expected nothing less. Conall reached out to steady her. She drank in the touch. She'd missed the closeness they'd formed on the journey from Duncairn, and it steadied her to know his support was near.

"There won't be anyone hunting us," he said. "Two fishermen spotted a monster in Loch Fyne, and there are tales of a banshee near Aberdeen. A wailing sound has panicked the entire city. Worse, sightings of the Black Donald continue to rise, and not just ones that seem superstitious. Some creature is out there attacking homesteads and livestock; its host grows in might with each day. With all this chaos, Glover has no men to send after us. The army is taking over. Four new regiments have been called from Manchester."

"Is the queen mad? Most Scots would rather kiss a banshee than see Englishmen with rifles in their hills."

Conall chuckled. "Donal said something similar but a little less ladylike." He turned to the device on the table. "Another of Mr. Stevenson's air broadcasters," he marveled. "I couldn't believe my eyes when he used the one at Ben Nevis." A microphone sat in the middle attached by wire to the ceramic box behind it. Braided cords fed from the box to the wall, snaking their way up to an antennae affixed to the tower's peak. A bell-shaped horn protruded from the left side of the box, a lead pipe from the right. This last passed through a shutoff valve before attaching to a larger pipe running vertically along the wall.

"It's the same theory as a telegram," said Effie. "Others have presented the idea; they just don't have the refined power needed to make it work. Especially not amplified at any distance."

"And Mr. Stevenson uses stardust."

"Just so," said Effie. She reached for the valve on the lead pipe and twisted it. Gas hissed as pressure was released. It fed into the ceramic box, where a red light began to blink. "A few grams burned in the underground furnace is enough to power the light and the air broadcaster for months."

"He could make a fortune with this. He'd be richer than even the steel barons. Forget transportation; communication at such distances would give an edge to topple empires."

"And how would the world get their stardust? Do you think the fey races would be treated kindly in such an exchange?" Her last breath faltered as she thought on something Caledon had said. "That's why the steward isn't eager to show the world we can remake Aegirsigath. He fears the knowledge will be exploited."

"Who? What?" asked Conall.

"I'll explain to you both," she said, clicking on the microphone.

It was awkward speaking into the contraption. She had to remember to speak clearly and overly enunciate her words. The broadcast was relayed through the antennae and sent out to anyone with a means of listening. For now, that meant a handful of Stevenson's devices. If they'd arranged to speak ahead of time, the sound traveled fast enough for them to hold the semblance of a conversation. When no one was there to listen, a modified phonograph at Ben Nevis recorded incoming broadcasts on rolls of tin.

She leaned forward and cleared her throat. "Mr. Thomas Stevenson," she announced, and then started in on her tale of Skye. She kept her words short and to the point. Sir Walter's discovery was a fey substance meant to bind the Sidhe Bhreige within the Downward Fields. Its destruction imperiled everyone and everything and needed to be stopped at once. They had perhaps four days or hope of containing the fiends would be lost.

Conall licked his lips and swallowed. "Things are going that well for us?" he asked once she had clicked off the microphone.

She tried to smile, but the false cheeriness turned into a grimace. "We need to take a bold step, not yet a desperate one," she said. "The question is what?" Conall inhaled and started to speak, then stopped and shook his head. She knew how he felt. She'd had a full day longer to contemplate the matter and was little closer to a solution.

She smoothed her dress and felt his gaze follow her hands. Stepping closer, he spoke in a soft voice. "I hope it does not vex you to hear me say I did worry for you the past days." He swallowed. "It seems foolish now to put forward such a notion, with greater matters at stake."

Effie's breathing quickened. She remembered the urges she'd felt at Loch Rannoch and blushed. "Poor timing, us," she said.

He gave her a slight nod, his eyes returning the same mischief she knew her own cast, and offered his hand to help her down the stairs. "You are ever a pleasure, Miss Martins."

She snickered. "It is Effie, you well know, to those fond of me." She pecked his check as she passed, ignoring his hand and leaving him stammering atop the landing.

When they reached the kitchen, she repeated her news to Graham. The stocky man chuckled at sight of the abashed Sniffer, and ran a meaty hand over his chin on hearing of their dire position. "I know some engineers we could meet with. They may know how Sir Walter is prospecting for the gas. If we could beat him to the stuff...."

"It would still be too late," Effie finished for him. She shoved a bit of scone into her mouth. The berries, normally sweet and delicious, tasted tart and unsatisfying.

"What about his backers?" asked Conall. "Can we get them to halt the mining?"

"Nay," said Graham. "Promise those scheming thieves money and they'll take yours, ask for more, and still let Sir Walter have his way."

"If we can't find the Aegirsigath before Sir Walter," said Effie, "and we can't coerce him to stop, what does that leave us with?"

"Perhaps we can order him to stop," mused Graham, yanking at his chin as if trying to tug the notion out of his head, "through the duke."

"You know the Duke of Edinburgh?"

"No, but I do have a friend in Saxe-Coburg who is a cousin to the duke, Oswin von Cleve. He has the ear of Otto von Bismarck. And I've another acquaintance in France who may add pressure as well."

"Why would the duke listen to them over English investors?" asked Conall.

"Because he knows all the worldly powers need is pretense. A pretense to attack British interests in Africa and Asia. A pretense to invade the very shores of this island. With colonies sprouting up everywhere, the world has become a tinder box searching for a match. The duke would listen to caution. All it would cost him is asking Sir Walter to wait, wait on something the public knows nothing about. If he's wrong, he's at least saved the crown from total war. If he's right, he's saved us all from much more."

"But we know he's right. That we are right," said Conall. "We just have to make sure we have proof when the time comes."

"Aye," agreed Graham. He said something else, too, but Effie missed it.

A churning in her gut told her to panic. Whisper and the other horses were terrified. She could feel them as if they were right in front of her, as if she were sucking in their emotions. She stood on wobbly legs. The men, seeing her expression, bolted to their feet. Conall reached for her as Graham cast about, searching the front wall where she stared.

She could feel the horses. She sensed Graham and Conall, too. In her excitement to reunite with her friends, she had thought the awareness sprung from the power of those gathered at Skye, but she realized now how foolish that was. The host was miles distant.

There was fey blood much closer.

"He has come for me," she said, as her throat ran dry. The words fell like the weight of the sea. Then howling started. Barking yips and low, hungry cries. It came from within the garden wall, curling her blood. Graham snatched a pair of rifles from the stand near the door. He checked the load and tossed one to Conall.

"Are these the same beasts as at Loch Rannoch?" asked the Sniffer. "Did they follow us?"

"I don't think so," said Effie. Letting the sensations flow through her body, she picked out individual creatures scampering toward them, a dozen at least. They were smaller, their impressions foul and muddied. But one was too familiar. "They aren't trows, either, but the Laird of Aonghus is with them."

"I'm too old and fat to run for it," said Graham. "You two go, and hurry now! I'll hold them here."

"Never." Effie snatched up a knife. She could feel the creatures approaching the main door. "Help me block the hallway," she barked, dumping the table on its side. Conall helped her wedge it against the opening, its height still allowing him enough room to fire over it.

Graham peered out the kitchen door into the black of night. "What the blimey hell?" he spat, just before the explosion blew apart the lighthouse and deafened them all.

CHAPTER 23

T he world tilted, the blast hurling Effie against the wall. She knocked her head and spilled to the ground as a cloud of dust and debris washed over the overturned table, covering everything as Conall's flour had earlier. Her ears rung with a high-pitched squeal that made her squint. Blood trickled across her lips. The blast had come from the front of the house. The creatures there stirred in a frenzy, though she couldn't tell if it was from joy at whatever they'd done or a hunger for more blood.

Across the room, Conall struggled to his feet. A dribble of red ran down his cheek, but he gestured he was fine. Fine? Effie glowered. In the past week, the word had redefined itself.

She turned to Graham who motioned he couldn't see anything out the backdoor, but she already knew that. She could feel them gathering out front. The laird had his own plans for her and a quick death wasn't yet a part of them. She waited for a long minute just to be sure, then strode forward.

"Help me with this," she said, tugging at the splintered table. "If they wanted us dead, we'd already be so. The laird just wanted to get our attention." The Sidhe Bhreige could feel where they were in the house just as easily as she could feel them. Still, her heart pounded against her chest, and her legs refused to steady.

The explosion had ripped through the front of the house, leaving a gaping hole in the drawing room. The bottom half of the winding stair and the antechamber that fed it were gone. Smashed bricks and splintered wood lay strewn across the floor. Random shards stuck into the walls like hurled daggers.

The creatures snarling outside were smaller than trows, something in between a fox and a wolf. Their ears came to sharp points, their curved fangs drooped around blunted snouts. Shaggy coats blended them into the shadows, more than a dozen comprising the pack. One of them rose on its hind legs and shuffled forward a few steps before dropping back to all fours. Effie blanched. The movement had allowed her to see the razor-tipped claws hidden in its forepaws. She could swear it smiled at her reaction, drool dripping from its eager lips.

"Wulvers," Graham named them. He kept his rifle trained on the closest one. "Or something as similar as makes no difference."

A trio of trows danced out of the shadows, beating sticks against chimes in a clanging melody of procession. The Laird of Aonghus followed the heralds, mounted on a Shetland pony. His black cloak splayed across the mount's rump, secured by a golden clasp. He gripped his cane at the midpoint, wielding it like a field marshal's baton.

Conall whipped his rifle to his cheek and fired. As if sensing his master's peril before the shot thundered out of the barrel, one of the wulvers leapt in front of the laird. The bullet flung it to the side. It squealed and slunk off into the darkness, as its brethren snapped and howled. Conall cocked the rifle and aimed again, but was stopped short by a gesture from the laird.

"That is unwise," the laird said, "unless you believe you can reload your device before my pets are upon you. I hold them at bay for now, but do not doubt they would rather feast on your warm flesh." To punctuate his point, the wulvers crept closer, their stares delirious with bloodlust.

"Why have you come?" demanded Effie. She tried to pull Conall back, but the Sniffer refused to leave her side. Graham at least had found cover behind a pile of rubble, though he stood tall and in plain sight.

"Your aura makes you easy to track," the laird said through a cackle. "These humans call it a smell, some taint one can sniff on your body. They are as foolish as moths curious over a flame. It is your blood pulsing with energy. A true power they cannot fathom."

The ringing in her ears lessened, but she had to strain to catch every word. She recalled her conversation with Caledon and her loathing of the warped Sidhe Bhreige doubled. Here was the thing that harnessed selkies and set upon children. Here was the thing that had killed Ramsey. She snarled, her teeth showing as viciously as the wulvers. "I will never side with you. Nor will I allow you use of my blood. Take your beasts and flee, or we will slay them all." Her wrath seemed to amuse the laird for he smiled, eyes gleaming. The expression made her hands twitch. She wanted nothing more than for Conall to put a bullet in the laird's head. She almost reached for the rifle herself.

"Side?" said the laird. "Sweet child, I hold your power within my grasp whether you will it or not. It is not for you to decide which side you are on. It is only for you to concede that our enemy is mutual, that your desires are mine."

She knew his meaning on both accounts, and the realization was like swallowing a thousand gnats. It clogged her throat and churned her gut. He could use the power of her aura without consent. Proximity was enough. The knowledge made her feel soiled and abused, abhorred of her own being. But worse was the declaration that the laird's designs and her own were aligned, that they both wanted an end to Sir Walter Conrad's discovery. The dark connection was a knife slitting her asunder. Her flesh felt afire. Her head swam as she fought to find escape, a way for the truth to dissolve.

The laird studied her, starlight painting his features in silver. It made his jawline and high cheek bones almost beautiful. "You see, now you will do as I command, for it is the very plot to which you aspire. The miners must not be allowed to destroy the Aegirsigath. It shall be protected henceforth, above all else."

She wondered if it was some trick of his, the beauty of his face where only ugliness had been a moment before. "Never," she whispered, but there was no strength in the word.

Conall glanced at her sideways, confusion written across his brow. "I thought the fiend wanted Sir Walter's stuff destroyed. Won't it release his cronies? More of his brethren?"

"Yes, it would," said Effie, breaking her gaze from the laird. Her thoughts cleared, and his face returned to its devilish cast. "But the Laird of Aonghus covets something greater." She understood his intentions clear enough. The laird's thirst for power had caused his imprisonment for millennia. Why would he seek to share dominion now that he'd escaped the Downward Fields and the other Sidhe Bhreige had not? His desire to halt Sir Walter was as great as their own for a single reason. Greed drove him the same as the Hostmen of Newcastle. To dominate and rule alone.

"I offer you a gift for being a loyal pet," sneered the laird. He hoisted a satchel from within his cloak and tossed it at Conall.

The Sniffer caught it and nearly leapt from his skin when he saw what was inside. "There's enough dynamite here to blow the cliff side into the sea!"

"It is the easiest course," said the laird. "No doubt you have reached the same conclusion. Destroy the miners' searching machine and they are flies without wings. Explosions in mines are common enough. They have already killed many of their own delving where they should not, and will most like slay more."

Effie shook her head. "Such a deed would not stop Sir Walter. He would build another machine. Ten more, with all the gold in his coffers."

"By that time you and your allies will have convinced the bitch's whelp to intercede, and I will have conquered the North."

"Bloody bastard," grumbled Graham. His rifle hadn't lowered, and his arms quivered with exhaustion.

Effie didn't know what to do. If she pretended to go along with the laird's plan, would he leave them unharmed? She worried she wouldn't be convincing enough. And what if he bound her in some way? Could he place her forever under his spell, as he had the selkies? Perhaps the trick with the light was meant to panic her in just such a way, to remind her of the powers he possessed that she wasn't even aware existed.

But if she chose the other option, to reject him utterly despite their common cause, they might not survive. She counted the wulvers again. How many could Graham and Conall shoot before those sharp teeth snapped down on them? She could feel the pulsing of their bloodlust. Graham would never outrun the danger, and there was no

chance she would leave him behind. She considered her flight from
Duncairn, and the horse that came to defend her, but she couldn't
sacrifice Whisper to save her skin this time, not knowingly. There
weren't any other creatures about, either. No squirrels or martens—
for whatever help they would've been—not even a bird. They had all
fled or been driven off by the presence of the Sidhe Bhreige's
dreadful host.

Seconds ticked by, each one throbbing at her temple. The air
thickened under the tension, as if the dynamite's fuse had been lit and
they all stood around watching it burn. She saw Graham's arms
shaking, the sweat beading on his brow, and suddenly decided they
needed to trick the laird, to go along with his ploy. But the words that
spewed from her mouth didn't follow her thoughts. "You are a
monster," she spat, her tone exploding with fury.

The laird's grin faltered, but he quickly turned the expression into
mocking disapproval. "Such a fiery lass, and yet just a child, naïve of
our kind. Has no one taught you anything?" She bristled at the insult.
Crouching, she rolled to the balls of her feet, ready to spring forward
with her knife. She was determined to reach the laird if she could. She
would see what powers he had to best cold steel.

If he sensed her anticipation, he gave no sign. He gestured at a
wulver. "You meekly ask for beasts to tolerate your presence—horses
and foxes, maybe a mouse to come to your rescue. Why beg for their
attention when you can force them into submission? Controlling
them is not a Fey Craft of the Sidhe Bhreige; it is one of all fey kind."
He flicked his wrist, and the wulver backed into the shadows. "For
beasts such as these, whose will is so defiant, a trick of our blood is all
that is needed to bolster your power."

Effie blinked. The laird's reaction confused her. Why hadn't he
attacked? What game did he play at? She focused on his words, half-
remembering a rhyme from long ago, something from when she had
barely begun to talk. "Heather and rosemary, crushed yew...." Her
words trailed off. She couldn't remember the rest.

"Ah," said the laird. "Someone did show you." He dug within his
cloak and flung her a pouch. She caught it, warily. Her mind raced.
The laird pressed forward as if she were a supplicant puppy, despite
her defiance. Did he believe her so feeble? So weak of will? His

attempts at aiding her went against all reason. Opening the pouch, she sniffed it. The unction within held a hundred scents. The way they blended and confused one another, it would take her a year to figure them all out. "Mixed with your blood spilt on a totem, your power would make them quake with fear. Grundbairns were known for such skill and have an affinity for it above all other fey."

She studied his cane, making out dark splotches she hadn't noticed before, but held her tongue. It was better to tuck that knowledge away for later. She had seen Blood Craft work before. Her escape from Glover's clutches proved that it existed, but in her experience its uses had all been destructive. Did that make it an evil thing? She couldn't say, only that it didn't feel right, not coming from one of the Sidhe Bhreige. No doubt he only shared the knowledge because he wanted her to know how much stronger he was than she.

"Why do you pretend to offer aid?" she asked, desperate to understand. Then she thought of a better question. "Why don't you destroy the mining device yourself? You have enough beasts to spare."

"Because I enjoy watching you dance on my strings," said the laird.

"No," she said. There was more to it, something the laird would never admit. "You need me to carry out your foul scheme." His eyes flickered, and she knew she was right. "If the Aegirsigath is consumed after you'd raised a direct hand to prevent it, your brethren will know you betrayed them."

The laird clucked. The Shetland danced about as if sensing its rider's unease. "Your insolence grows tiresome." He pointed at Conall. "This one shackled you to a wagon and led you about like a lamb to slaughter, and yet you stand here with him and defy me? Do as I command!"

She felt the weight of the pouch in her hand and saw the fierce snarl on Conall's face. The laird promised powers and gave her weapons, but she saw no point in them if he only meant to kill her. She followed the line of thought. Nor could she use them against him. Not really. The laird was too strong for her to overcome with Blood Craft, and the dynamite would blast them all and take too long to ignite. Rifles were much better suited against their foe. She glanced at the wulvers and saw the way they lusted to surge forward and complete their hunt. It reminded her of the way the trows had danced in glee about their treasure. The notions clicked together.

Both were their heart's desire.

She studied the laird again. She had viewed his game from the wrong direction. It didn't matter what she knew of his strengths. It mattered what the laird knew of her. He baited her with the means to defeat her enemies, means that would do little to put himself in danger, despite their allure. But he grossly ignored her character. He assumed a common cause would make her forget the terrible things he'd done. He assumed greed and lust drove her, as greed and lust drove his other pets. She clenched her fists, loathing the laird even more. All his displays of strength and control did nothing to sway her. He'd erred to think so.

She caught the Sniffer's eye. "Make your aim true," she said, her voice steeled, her emotions as calm as a frozen loch.

Conall's rifle blasted fire. This time, a wulver merely reared to its hind legs. The shot took it in the head, tumbling it backward. Graham's shot followed a second later, aimed at a wulver who'd crept close enough she could smell the rot in its gums.

The laird's glare cut through the night, his gaze seething. His false demeanor finally broke. His game had ended. She felt a twitch, as if fingers caressed her scalp. He tried to enthrall her again, like with the moonlight. She threw the sensation aside and snarled back. The trows stirred into a frenzy, beating their chimes and hopping about. "So be it," growled the laird. Wheeling his mount, he trotted from sight, followed by his discordant procession.

The pack of wulvers surged forward. Released from the laird's hold, they were faster and more nimble. They danced around the gunfire like shadows avoiding the wind. Conall and Graham managed only two more volleys before being overwhelmed. Gripping the barrels, they swung wildly at the beats, trying to keep them at bay.

Effie slashed with her knife, but the wulver before her was too quick. It slunk away, then shot forward. Its claws caught her dress, tearing the fabric and scraping the flesh beneath. While it freed itself, Effie brought the knife down again. The blade ripped through the fur between its shoulders.

Yelping, the wulver spun away and rose to its hind legs. Its eyes were almost level with hers, and her skin crawled at the hunger found within them. She wished she had a club or spear, something to keep the thing at a distance. These wulvers were much fiercer foes than the trows. She wasn't fast enough with the knife, and she knew it was only a matter of seconds before claw or tooth would end her fight.

A rifle cracked and the thing jolted, falling dead. But the shot to save her cost Conall. The wulvers about him leapt the moment he stopped swinging at them. He hit one with the butt of his rifle, but another opened a gash across the back of his legs. He cried out and staggered, dropping to his knees.

Effie raced to help him, scouring the ground as she went. She needed something, but her thoughts were too scattered to focus on what. Her head pounded with regret. She'd risked Conall's and Graham's lives to save her own. She should've bowed to the laird's command despite the cost. How could she have been so obstinate?

Because it was right, a voice in her thoughts told her. It sounded like Stevenson, or Caledon, or Graham, or maybe even her mother. It came from somewhere deep within, and she found her calm again. Her vision focused.

And then she saw a dull gleam amidst the rubble and dove for it.

CHAPTER 24

The Celtic cross was made of iron, its surface a pattern of woven knots, each leaping over the other and snaking around so there was no beginning and no end. An Irishman had given the cross to Stevenson on completion of some work out in the Hebrides. It had hung above the threshold at Arnisdale for as long as Effie could remember, as much a part of the lighthouse as any piece of wood or stone. Knowing the iron did nothing to keep one of fey blood from entering was a jest shared by her and Stevenson and Graham, something that tied them closer together, as if the hunk of metal was proof they understood the daftness of human superstition.

The explosion had freed it from its perch. She dove for the cross, the world around her fading into a gray murkiness. Somewhere behind her, a heavy body crashed to the dirt and a wulver shrieked in glee. She refused to contemplate what the sounds meant. The cross was her only hope.

The blade of her knife slid across her palm near the still healing wound from a few days before. She pressed the iron to the cut and let the blood flow along the totem. The unction the laird had given her followed, which she rubbed in and mixed into a slimy mess. Her blood began to sizzle and give off a putrid stench, but she kept at it until the pouch was empty and the cross coated.

"Stop!" she screamed, rising and holding the cross aloft.

The night throbbed. Blood ran down her arm and pooled at her sleeve. Everything around her glowed with energy. Blinding light from the stars above warred against fathomless shadows. The wulvers howled and yipped, enraged by this new power. They spun in circles and snapped their fangs. She could feel them seething, the sensation crawling along the sinews of her arms. They bucked against her will like a buffeting wind trying to force her over the cliff. She staggered but refused to buckle.

Doubt nagged at her. How had she expected to control them when she had never considered such a thing before? When she had never known such a feat was possible? She had no idea what to do, but she had to try something. Eyeing one of the beasts, she stood taller, trying to make herself more imposing. Her face was vicious, her will an unbreakable steel. She focused her hatred until it was a sharp razor slashing through the air.

"You will do as I say," she commanded. The wulver leered at her, the hunger in its eyes mocking. Its need to devour strained against her invisible bond. She could taste the saliva leaking out its maw, and her gut soured.

"Flee!" she barked, but the wulver only stared with loathing.

Her fury wilted. Fatigue washed through her thoughts. Blood Craft was a fleeting thing, a burst of destruction that sapped its user. She couldn't hold the beasts at bay for long. The laird had played her, had tricked her into thinking she was powerful enough to control his minions. But was his will so much stronger? From her experience, Fey Craft often relied more on knowledge than innate strength. She remembered his threats to have her dancing on his strings. So why hadn't he, if he had that power? She knew now his words for a bluff. The Blood Craft might lend him strength, but it did nothing to allow him any control over others. It struck her that she had allowed herself to be manipulated more than forced by some unseen hand. He had led her down a path, feigning power all along, just as he had tried to do in Duncairn.

That was the game the Laird of Aonghus played.

She eyed the wulvers as the idea took root. She could do the same to them. The stabled horse at the Tattered Grouse had aided her because it was already terrified and wanted its freedom, not because she'd driven it to fight for her. She'd barely thought about it bucking free, and the beast had rampaged. She hadn't had a premonition.

She'd sent it a concept of how best to obtain its desire. It could work the same for the wulvers. She could never force them to do anything, not directly. Their will was their own. She needed to act as a current, not the dam. The Blood Craft would aid her, give her the needed strength, but it was for molding–not coercing.

She took a deep breath. Wulvers were hunters. The pack of beasts didn't hate her, not as humans hated. They wanted prey and the thrill of the kill. So she imagined herself one of them, their leader, catching scent of a doe. Its scent wafted in her nostrils, and she concentrated on its sweet odor. The beasts howled, and she felt the eagerness within them surge. One swung its gaze to the woods, tongue lolling out.

There, she thought. *Not one doe but three!* Just in the darkness beyond, panicked and about to race away. She prodded at the wulvers to go catch them, challenging them as their leader to prove themselves worthy as hunters. These men with firesticks were tough meat and not a prize to be proud of. A few wulvers bucked in confusion. They smelled no deer, sensed no easier prey. Effie gritted her teeth. *Yes, they are there.* She pushed the image at the beasts. She tried to give it as much detail as possible—the tufts of white under the does' tails, the moss coating the trunks of the aged trees, the scents of pine and damp earth. She was one of the pack, their best hunter, the best nose and sharpest fang. She wanted the kill more than any of them, would fight them all for first blood. She pushed with her will until bile gurgled in her throat. The night stood still, as if they were held fixed within a crack of thunder.

The wulvers howled, and she made the does bolt in terror. The beasts took off dashing in ecstasy toward the imagined prey. She held the image for as long as possible, taunting the pack with bait just out of their reach. Her knees gave way, her stomach cramped. Blood gushed from her hand, soaking her dress, as she crumpled to the ground.

Her sight blurred and faded. She could hear the wulvers off in the distance but no longer knew which direction they raced. She kept onto the image of the deer until her body convulsed in protest, the strain of her will too great to carry on.

When she finally stopped shaking, she took in Graham and

Conall, and what blood remained in her chilled. The Sniffer's trousers were tattered and slick, but the cuts did not appear too serious. Graham fared worse. Conall had dragged himself over and was trying to staunch a gash in the older man's chest. Graham's face was ashen. He didn't move as the other man pressed on the rent. Effie raced over, panic erasing her fatigue. The wound was deep and ragged, exposing the white of bone. Any lower beneath the ribs and his vitals would've spilled out. The thump she'd heard. Graham must have fallen and been set on by at least a pair of wulvers. Other cuts and gouges scored his arms and legs.

The older man reached up and patted her dress. She snatched his hand and let out a sigh of relief. It still felt warm. The wounds would not kill him, not this night anyway. There was always fear of infection, but for the moment it meant she had not caused Graham's death. The weight removed made her feel like she could float to the stars.

"We need to get him inside," said Conall. He glanced at the woods. "What you did, that was incredible. But will they return?"

She shook her head. "I don't know. Only that the laird and his beasts are no longer near." She didn't feel their presence anymore, and with their retreat the world had dimmed, her fey blood falling quiet.

Conall tried to rise but winced, leaning heavily on his rifle. She pressed a hand on his shoulder and settled him back down. Her hands tightened into fists as she glanced around the yard. Anger at the laird made her breath deepen into huffs. At the same time, her heart panged over the hurt the Sniffer had suffered. He had twice placed himself in harm's way to protect her, and she had rewarded him both times by begging him to risk more. She knelt and took his hand, holding it firm until her breathing calmed. She didn't know what she would've done if she'd lost either of the men.

Conall's eyes grew heavy, but he kept them on her until they closed. There was a small cart Mrs. Heyward used for the garden. Effie fetched it, and somehow she was able to get both the injured men into the kitchen. Graham she eased onto the table. On the floor, she piled blankets for Conall to rest on. Weariness sucked at her every movement. Her stomach rumbled in discomfort, twinging in pain. She ignored everything but the task at hand. Bar the door. Blockade the hallway. Boil water. Clean the wounds, stitch what she could, and set bandages. She worked in silence, keeping an ear for any stirring outside. But she didn't feel the creatures return and knew they were alone on the cliff top above Arnisdale.

When she startled awake, she was sitting in a chair, her head nestled on Graham's knees. She had meant to remain awake to ensure nothing happened in the night, and her breath caught until Graham's chest rose and fell. She relaxed. He lived still. His cheeks were a bit pale but nothing bed rest and a hearty stew wouldn't fix. Conall's snores filled the kitchen and she thought back on his welcoming just the previous afternoon. She wished now that the worst Mrs. Heyward would come home to was a little flour on the floor.

She made tea and checked bandages, trying to force the rubble and dead wulvers strewn about the courtyard from her thoughts. It wasn't as difficult a task as she'd imagined. As the sun rose over the lighthouse, the seconds began to tick furiously in her thoughts, overriding all else. Soon, she found herself with hands on her hips, her foot tapping away. The tender side of her wanted to let Graham rest, but they had no time. Mending wounds would have to come later.

Gently, she shook him awake. He licked parched lips and winced as he ran a hand over his bandages. "Lie down," she commanded when he tried to rise. "I won't have you moaning about the place. Besides, I don't think I could lift you again."

"A dram then," he said. "Just a wee one to nip the edge." He swallowed and the effort made him grimace. "No, bugger that, bring me the bottle."

"The day is already growing short," she said as she fetched the whiskey. "If you can manage to scratch a few notes, I can go into town and telegraph your contacts in Saxe-Coburg and France." She bit her lip and studied the dried blood flecked across the collar of his shirt. "We should tell them everything, openly. Time is against us, and who knows what will come this night. We may not hold them a second time. That unction the laird tossed me is spent.

"Besides...." She shuddered. "I have no wish to do such a thing again." Her hand cramped from the fresh wound, but darker were the memories haunting her of the wulvers' bloodlust. It was as if by using

Blood Craft to bond with their emotions, she had instilled in herself a part of their being, a residue left by the power she invoked.

"Och, lass," said Graham. "Enough of dour tidings. I've been dreaming of beasties and foul things through the night. Now it's time to stand and cast our fate." He glanced away sheepishly as her eyes narrowed. "Stand metaphorically, I meant."

"You rest. I'll fetch paper and pen."

Graham shook his head. "Nay, I've been thinking. The telegrams Mr. Heyward can handle when he returns this afternoon. But what that foul thing said to you. It made a kind of sense."

"No," said Effie. A cold tingling gripped the back of her head. A dread of what the man would say next. She reached out to steady herself and yelped as her injured hand flexed.

"We do have a mutual enemy, and that enemy can do more harm than a hundred wulvers. Damnation, Sir Walter could free all of the Sidhe Bhreige from their prison if he isn't stopped."

Effie shook her head. "I can't do his bidding now. I won't. We'd be playing his game."

"Aye, and we'd have to swallow the taste of it. But there's no time for anything else, no time for being stubborn. You've pointed that out clear enough yourself. We must destroy their searching machine and delay their efforts."

"An explosion would risk lives," barked Effie. "And likely kill."

"Aye."

"Sir Walter may never find more Aegirsigath."

"No." He studied her eyes. "He may not." His tone was grim yet certain. It reminded her of Sir Walter and Edward Waite, who thought nothing of the lives of men if it led to their success. Graham meant to risk the same to stop what he saw as a greater threat, even if the need was uncertain. The callousness was a side to Graham she'd never seen before, yet something she knew lived within both him and Stevenson. How else did men such as they become prominent in their professions? Fortune did not favor the meek. But to feel its brunt brought on disillusionment, as if she could never look on him with the same unhindered innocence.

She paced through the kitchen, around the slumbering Conall, unable to lock her gaze on anything for too long. Two evils crawled through her skin, making it uncomfortable to remain still. On the one side lay the hand of the sapper, an immoral act that could save millions of lives at the possible expense of a few. On the other side was a stubborn resolve not to play into either enemies' designs, to defeat them both in a righteous manner of her own making. But she had no idea how to do that, and if she didn't turn villain by necessity soon, she would be no better than the other fey who fled in fear of the Sidhe Bhreige. Those who did nothing to stop the growing violence. She felt naked before the paradox. The paths were too muddied. A dank and dreary cloud hung over everything. That men like Sir Walter wouldn't hesitate a second to sabotage her efforts didn't make it just to do the same to him. Caledon was right. There was always a whip, and it felt like all she could do was go about trading one lash for another.

"What of the will-o'-the-wisps?" asked Conall, who had propped himself onto an elbow. She started, not realizing he'd woken.

"Twinkling lights?" She didn't quite follow.

"A lure," he said. "The lights lead travelers from the road they're on, sometimes into danger but also sometimes out of it."

Effie caught on, excitement bubbling up within her. "I don't need to light the dynamite. I just need to make them think a saboteur is at work." She hopped as the plan formed in her mind. "That would give them caution and delay their progress for a day or two at least!"

"Lead them away from the road they're on, away from the danger they don't know exists. And it gives us the time we need." Conall's mop of curls was so mussed it appeared to grow and stretch on its own as he bobbed his head, but the toothy grin beneath was as charming as any prince.

"Brilliant!" She stooped and hugged him, careful not to jostle his wounds. He fell into her touch, and she squeezed him tighter, pressing her body against his, until his hand wrapped around her waist. They held each other for a moment longer, before Effie stood.

She turned to Graham, whose cheeks were abashed. The look was enough. She didn't need him to say a word. "You were right," she offered. "We need to dismantle their machine, just as the laird had said. It will buy us time for your contacts to pressure the duke."

He took a swig from the whiskey bottle. "That's a kindness, lass.

But I can't unsay the suggestion to blow the thing up. I would do it myself, if I could walk. There's no sense in pretending it ain't true. You're grown enough to see that."

"I know," said Effie. She pushed the sadness back. He was still the same man who'd tended to her, watched her grow, and protected her. He still would, when she needed him. She'd just taken the blinders of childhood off. Perhaps they'd come undone even earlier, the moment she'd left for Duncairn.

CHAPTER 25

E ffie's journey to Glen Avon was dark and brooding. Her leave-taking from Graham and Conall had left her unsettled. Her concern for their injuries tugged her one way while her anxiety and anger over what lay ahead tugged her another. The Sniffer had wanted to join her, but he'd only managed a step before the futility of that notion ruled him out. His legs were too stiff and would need a fortnight's rest before he could manage the sneaking and running she expected the night would bring. Slinking through the darkness, meddling with the lives of innocent miners instead of confronting Sir Walter directly, didn't settle well within her. It felt like she played the Laird of Aonghus' game.

The view from her hired steam coach did nothing to quell her distaste. Overnight, it seemed, the countryside had become scarred by the Sidhe Bhreige's minions. Charred cottages smoldered along the roadside. Uprooted fern and bracken spread in swaths through the forests as if a plague had trampled through the undergrowth. Slaughtered sheep lay in the fields, and more than a few villages had constructed barricades to keep the creatures at bay—overturned wagons and stacked barrels, whatever they could find. Effie saw more than just the Laird of Aonghus' work in the chaos. Two of his brethren had also escaped. The creature masquerading as the Black Donald was a blunt enemy by comparison, taking a hammer to the land where the laird would rather poison it. Of the third Sidhe Bhreige, she had no idea, only that it was undoubtedly as foul as the others.

Soldiers marched along the roads, crawling over the hills and lochs like red ants across a picnic blanket. Their presence, armed foreigners intruding where they please, heightened tensions more than relieved them. The faces of the villagers told Effie as much. She heard rifle fire, and even cannon, a few times as the steam coach rambled along, but always far off, a danger lurking beyond the horizon. They were enemies battling enemies, with other scoundrels lurking between.

It would not take much to ignite the country, and it dawned on her that she might be the one wielding the match. She'd set the satchel of dynamite on the bench opposite the one where she sat, as far away as she could within the coach. At the start, every bump and shudder had set her teeth on edge, but she'd wrapped each stick with extra linen and by mid-morning had convinced herself she was safe, at least as long as she kept the explosives away from heat. The driver had wanted to stow the bag on the luggage rack near the boiler. Her fierce resistance had left him a bit cross, and they barely said a word when they stopped for afternoon tea. His portly figure was like a sack of oats, his jowls saggy like a hound's.

She wondered where he would stay the night, in what tavern he'd spin yarns about her. Not so many days ago the thought would've consumed her, the notoriety an invasion into her private little world. She swallowed and studied her bandaged hand. Those fears seemed foolish now. She would proclaim herself from atop the towers of London if it would stop the Sidhe Bhreige, if it would bring Ramsey back and mend the rest who'd suffered so dearly.

Only a few hours of daylight remained as they crested the hills leading into Glen Avon. Immediately, Effie knew her endeavor was not well thought out. Soldiers patrolled the makeshift town, around the outskirts, and on the train platform. Of course Sir Walter's connections would ensure the army protected their interests. She spotted three dozen riflemen before she stopped counting. A pentacle of watchtowers rose above the buildings, spiked with redoubts protecting their bases, and along the road a group of soldiers watched her approach.

She thumped the coach's roof, trying to alert the driver. "Don't stop," she called.

The man slowed the coach, quieting the boiler. He shifted to holler down into the window. "This is the mining works, miss. Where ye asked to be taken."

Effie's brain whirled, trying to devise a rationale for her sudden change of heart. "Yes, it was easier to describe this place than my relative's cottage, which is just a mile on. There's no need to stop here."

"They're waving us down, miss," said the driver, in a suspicious tone.

One of the soldiers blocked the road, his rifle held across his chest and extended, as if to push them back. Effie winced as the driver worked the levers to apply the brake. Steel squealed on steel, and a gout of steam belched from the boiler. She felt naked as the soldier walked over. She almost shouted to the driver that she'd pay anything if he'd keep his mouth shut. But that would only invite greater trouble. It was better to play the naïve woman.

The soldier's front teeth pressed out between his lips, making him appear like a woodchuck. He leered at her through the window, then glanced at the road behind them as if they were the vanguard of some invasion. "What's yer business here?" he asked.

"Just pressing onward," said Effie, not letting the driver speak. She leaned out the coach's window, ignoring the billow of smoke that wafted in.

"Aye? Where to?"

"My cousin's home is a bit down the road," said Effie. "Is the road not open?"

"Open to loyal subjects." He licked his teeth. "There's danger afoot, especially for a lass traveling alone."

"She most certainly is not alone," the driver snapped. He bristled at the veiled insult. It was one thing for a Scot to act oddly in his charge, but quite another to be mocked by an Englishman.

The soldier smirked. A weighty pause passed as the men stared one another down. Finally, the soldier asked, his tone thick with scorn, "Did you encounter anything along the road?"

The coach rocked as the driver shifted. "We encountered many things: trees and dirt, mostly sheep. Now, if the road is open, I bid you good day, sir."

The soldier checked over his shoulder to see if any of his cohorts had overheard. But the other riflemen hadn't taken any interest and were huddled together, lost in their own boisterous conversation. Effie held her breath, watching the soldier calculate his next move. With a word, he could foil her entire plan. And worse, if any of the queen's men were to check her bag, she would find herself once again in shackles, any hope of delaying Sir Walter lost.

"Thank you, sir," she blurted as earnestly as she could muster, "for your warning. We hope to be indoors before dark but must press on to ensure our safety."

He studied her to see if she mocked him, and she tried to paint a mask of concern on her face, if not downright fear. The expression wasn't too hard to conjure. The soldier licked his teeth again, this time slowly, then waved them away with a dismissive gesture.

The boiler sprang to life, and the coach lurched forward. As soon as they were beyond the checkpoint, Effie sank into the cushioned bench and exhaled like the steam pipe above her head. She closed her eyes and breathed in the crisp Highland air for a few minutes, until the trees hid them from sight. Picking a suitable spot, she bade the driver pull over and let her off. If the man found her odd before, he was downright wary of her now. But he did as she asked without question, keeping a fair distance as she alighted. She couldn't think of a way to beg the man to hold his tongue that wouldn't encourage him more, so she settled on wishing him a safe journey home and handing over a few extra coins. The man peered into the woods, then shook his head and shrugged. Hauling himself onto the driver's bench, he soon had the steam coach sputtering along the road.

Effie hefted the satchel onto her shoulder and set out deeper into the forest. She tried to feel for anything lurking within the trees but couldn't sense anything. No fey blood, at least. A few creatures darted amongst the foliage and some birds chirped away in the higher branches. Sensing their presence came more easily now, as if their bodies gave off tiny vibrations that tickled her skin. Perhaps it had always been as simple, and she just hadn't known what the sensations meant. The knowledge was another debt she owed the Laird of Aonghus. It soured her stomach to admit, but the Sidhe Bhreige had taught her several things her mother had not.

Had not been able to, she amended. She was sure if her mother had lived she would've taught Effie everything—what had happened to her grandfather and why they lived in solitude, why every Highland fey seemed to know of her family but she knew almost nothing of them. Of the Sidhe Bhreige and whether Blood Craft was truly evil. The questions piled up as she tramped along, until she seethed, the hurt from not understanding taking control of her body.

"Blessings!" she spat. All the questions and doubt did her no good. They were like a sheep's bleating—an annoying noise she would never decipher, but one that could drive her crazy if she tried. She relaxed her grip on the satchel and worked some blood back into her fingers. As they tingled to life, she decided where she'd stopped was as good as any other to begin her work.

Mr. Heyward had a slight figure, the closest to her own of the men she left at the lighthouse, so it was into a pair of his trousers that she slipped. Off went her dress and on went one of his shirts, followed by a brown coat. The new clothes were much more flexible and comfortable, and she wondered why she didn't wear something similar all the time, like the female brownies and gnomes did.

"Because I'm a proper Scottish lass, not some American filly fighting her way across the plains, pistols blazing away," she told the tree next to her. It stared back without response, though she swore she felt its judgment. She bundled her dress and shoved it into the satchel, then pulled her hair into a braid. Last, she tucked a small knife into a sheath at her belt.

She picked a direction that would angle her toward the mines, skirting the edge of the makeshift town. The going was much easier without having to worry over the hem of a dress snagging on a branch or thorn, but the light was fading and she had to hurry or risk being lost in the dark. Worse were thoughts of stumbling blindly into some of Sir Walter's men. At a small ridge barren of trees, she was able to get her bearings. The dim twilight made it difficult, but she could see where machines had hammered away at the hillside, turning it into a giant scar. To the south, smoke rose from dozens of cook fires, the town alive with workers returning for the night. Carriageways had been cut between the mines and makeshift town to shuttle ore and equipment. They slashed across the land like the wounds of a saber.

Conall had instructed her on how to find the prospecting machine, and Effie traced the carriageways, connecting point to point, until she spied one that led off onto a distant slope. Not far beyond, a balloon was tethered. It was the marker she sought. Not large enough for passengers, the balloon let the engineers in town know where something important happened.

Nothing was more important to Sir Walter than prospecting for his new substance. Effie grinned as she set off, a blend of fear and excitement washing through her like a slow-moving serum. She had to slow her pace in the failing light, her orientation getting confused as she wound around pockets of dense forest. An hour slipped away, and she had begun to worry she'd passed the place entirely when she stumbled on to one of the carriageways.

Somehow her path had curved, and she'd cut too close to the mining sites. She stared down the rutted track. It was empty, but for how long? The foliage to either side would keep her hidden but would be louder and slower going. She could always dart within its folds if something approached on the carriageway. Decided, she crept along with quick steps, mindful of the pools of muck left by the rains.

The crunch of her feet echoed painfully, like the clod of a horse on pebbles, and she wondered whether she should remove her boots when the sputter of an engine stopped her cold. A steam wagon creaked and popped toward her, coming from the prospecting site. She had just enough time to dive behind some bushes before an amber hue pierced the starlight. The torches at the front of the wagon were shielded, focusing their light into beams that lit up the carriageway.

Effie tensed. Her body shrank as she pulled into a tight ball. Three men rode the wagon, one working the steering lever while the other two sat in the back, their legs dangling over the tail. It was an old contraption, its boiler made of cast iron, its copper piping rattling as the wheels trundled along. Several figures shuffled behind it carrying picks and shovels. Their shoulders slumped, their feet barely lifting from the ground.

"Please, sir," one squeaked, and Effie started, realizing those that followed weren't men but mere boys less than half her age.

"Quit yer whinging. He'll come along when he's hungry enough," said one of the men in the wagon. The other men chuckled.

"Tom don't do well alone in the dark," said a different boy.

The men chortled and roared. "Not well in the dark, he says," one repeated.

"He'd best find a different profession," said another. "Something in a dress, if he's gonna piss himself so much." Effie's blood chilled. The man's voice was familiar. She'd heard it before, but it wasn't until the light shifted that she could place it. The man's narrow face gave him away. The same man who'd accosted her on the train to Duncairn.

Her lips pulled into a snarl, and she clenched, causing the bushes to rustle. Prickles ran over her flesh at the sound, but the wagon was too loud. None of the men looked her way.

The boy who'd pleaded fell silent and stared behind, into the darkness of the carriageway. Another youth nudged him forward. "There'll be no food for either of you, you go back." After a second nudge, the first boy relented. He turned and mumbled something, trudging after the wagon.

"What was that?" The slim man hopped down and raised his hand as if to deliver a blow. "Speak up, bastard!"

"Leave it, Jain," said the man Effie took to be the boss. He had a thicker set than the others, and his tone left little room to quarrel.

The wagon passed her, followed by the troop of boys. Most wore the clothes of city urchins, though their shirts and trousers were so coated in dirt she doubted they could be removed without falling to pieces. Their bodies were stooped not only from the day's exhaustion but from endless weeks toiling underground. Life expectancy in the narrow shafts was not much longer than a turn of the seasons, and those who did survive were left bent and crippled.

Effie watched them fade into the darkness, recalling something Stevenson had once told her. "Coal miners are the grease that allow the empire's wheels to turn," he'd said. "And no matter how horrific the conditions, no one is in favor of hampering prosperity." She'd waited for him to carry on about injustice, as he was like to do, but instead he'd slammed back a shot of whiskey and thrown the glass into the fire. She'd read all his fury in the taut lines scrawled across his face.

Sir Walter used the same justification: the suffering of a few for the prosperity of the many. He used it to defend the treatment of his workers, and he used it to continue mining for his substance after multiple dangerous explosions. She pulled the satchel of dynamite against her chest. Perhaps Graham hadn't been wrong, she considered. Perhaps Sir Walter should be one of the few whose suffering grants others prosperity. If she destroyed his means of prospecting, or even the man himself, the world might be better off. But what would that make her? She couldn't live with a conscience tainted by such hubris, to become the very thing she despised. She thought again of Graham and wanted nothing more than to grasp him in a giant hug, an embrace to wash away whatever tension lay between them and carry her back to the way things were.

But there was nothing for it. The night was dark, and the road would become no easier. When the sputtering of the wagon had completely faded, she crept out of the bushes and padded down the carriageway.

It didn't take her long to stumble across poor Tom. The boy, abandoned by his taskmasters, sat in a sobbing heap. His arms were tucked beneath his legs, his head buried in his knees. He was rail-thin, barely moving except to convulse in a fit of meek coughing. Effie hunkered in the shadows, watching. She could easily edge around him in the darkness. She tried to tell herself the boy's troubles paled in comparison to the importance of her task. She gritted her teeth at the irony of that thought, and she found herself wanting to reveal herself, to find a way to heal the lad and remove him from the prison of Sir Walter's mines.

A woman's foolishness, every man from John o' Groats to the White Cliffs of Dover would call it. She looked to the stars and reminded herself she hadn't much time. She had to move. Her twinges of compassion were only a means of stalling. Crouching, she slunk into the foliage beside the carriageway. She made a dozen steps before stopping and glancing over her shoulder. The boy remained, like a withered plant.

Alone. In the dark and likely scared. Alone, as she had been all those years ago.

She'd seen some water not a mile back. It wouldn't take her long. The boy might tell her something of importance. She sighed, knowing the thoughts for her own stubbornness. Her heart was settled. Her legs would move no other direction, so she resolved to do the deed as quickly as possible.

CHAPTER 26

E ffie scooped handfuls of water from the trickling burn to press against Tom's chapped lips. When she'd approached him on the carriageway, he'd barely registered her presence. Even as she'd hefted him to his feet so they could start their slow progress through the night, he'd not uttered a peep.

He spluttered, spraying Effie's coat, then drank, lapping up the water as fast as she could scoop it. Sated, the boy stared at her with wide eyes. Blood and soot splotched his chest from the fits of coughing, but what shocked Effie more was his arms. The flesh there was seared into a tough leather, almost fire-hardened as one would do to wood. She'd heard of such atrocities occurring in the cities but had never seen it up close. The treatment was meant to help the skin resist cuts and scrapes, but the pain and disfigurement were brutal to behold. The Laird of Aonghus' voice echoed in her head. What more evidence did she need that humans were a truly vile race? But the logic failed, of course. Tom was not her enemy, no more than Caledon or Gabus.

Tom cocked his head, his brow raised as he tried to work out a puzzle. The soot streaking across his cheeks made him look like a raccoon. "The fillies they got in camp don't come this far into the mines. Are you an angel come to fetch me soul, or one of the Fair Folk?"

"I'm a…." Effie started, then paused. She'd worked so hard to remain hidden for so many years, it made the simple admission difficult. "Someone who is here to help," she said.

"For a price?" The boy's eyes softened. He almost sounded eager. "Me mum always told me of the Fair Folk. They act in kindness to lost travelers but always for their souls, or hearts, or such."

Effie laughed. "Nothing such as that." She thought for a moment, glancing toward the satchel she'd dumped beside her. "But perhaps you can tell me about some things?"

Tom nodded and leaned forward. He answered her inquiries with enthusiasm, as much as a boy starving and battered could muster, describing the work he and the others were doing, the machines the grown men used, and the guards who patrolled the night. When he finally fell silent, she told him to wait by the burn. She would return with some food, later. He nodded again and watched her sling the satchel over her shoulder. She gave her thanks and crept off toward the carriageway.

The rutted path was quiet, but something nagged at her thoughts. "A squad of five stand watch," Tom had said, "but I don't ken why. There's nothing but critters come around at night."

Nothing but critters come around.

She wasn't so certain. Reaching out with her senses, she felt, and her fey awareness kindled. Vague impressions stirred like stones pulsating a heat only she could perceive. All were small, and none seemed threatening. She focused on each, but while some were similar and others unique, it was difficult to actually identify the critters. Something to work on, she told herself. After all, she'd been able to pick out Whisper as surely as she'd known Graham and Conall, and that only after a few days' acquaintance.

The carriageway snaked around undulating hills. At each rise and bend, she slowed to listen and peer into the darkness. Only the soft calls of night birds and the glimmer of starlight greeted her, yet as the minutes passed she began to notice something that brought goose pimples to her flesh. The impressions she felt were growing more defined, as if the mist surrounding each creature were being burned away to reveal what was underneath. She could now tell bird from hare, and pine marten from squirrel.

Her muscles tightened. That her awareness was heightening meant more fey blood lurked nearby. But she didn't sense the Laird of Aonghus or any wulvers. His aura was a beacon of corrupt power, theirs a violent thrashing full of hatred. Instead, the sensations were calm and almost soothing. Perhaps it was some fey who'd happened past, or some gnome living in the hills. She shook her head, not believing either case. She feared a trap.

Tucked behind a tree, she waited for a time, letting her awareness roam. But whomever or whatever had come didn't present itself. Above, the stars faded as night started to recede. Long summer days were followed by short nights, and the sun was only a few hours from rising. She couldn't afford to wait another day. Sir Walter's men could be right on top of a cache of Aegirsigath, the fate of the Highlands resting beneath the swing of a pickaxe. Steeling her nerve, she reminded herself the power of fey blood worked both ways. Whether friend or foe, she was stronger while this other blood was about. It was a boon she should take advantage of, not cower from in fear.

Under the waning starlight, she could make out the tethered balloon barely a quarter-mile distant. She stalked toward it, trying to dampen her breath. Leaving the carriageway, she scurried up a small rise and found a cluster of fern to slink behind. Through the leaves, she spied a campfire illuminating a small clearing. Soft, rhythmic snores carried from a tent at one end. At the other, a guard blew into his hands to keep off the morning frost. His rifle leaned against the crook of a tree a few steps away. A pair of men squatted by the fire rolling dice and grunting curses at one another. They were armed but gave no heed to the night around them. The balloon was tethered to a wheeled cart so it could be easily moved. Several thin cables ran down the tether from instruments high above.

In the center of the clearing perched Sir Walter's surveying machine. Perched was the right word. It didn't look much like Conall had described it. Resting on six iron legs, with a needle-like contraption feeding a long hose into a shaft in the ground, it looked like a mosquito. Spools of additional hose wrapped around a trio of wooden wheels mounted to the thing's undercarriage, enough to delve deeper than the height of a tenement building. The shaft appeared barely wide enough for a boy. She thought of Tom and the other boys and shuddered. It would be so dark and cramped below the surface.

An operator's chair perched on the back of the machine, with dials and levers sprouting around it like a porcupine. A rack of gauges was bolted to the rear, along with a writing tray, presumably to hold ledgers and maps for the recording of data. The hose fed the gauges, and a simple engine above the needle contraption gave power to the entire machine.

Silently, she worked out a plan. She would need to spread the sticks of dynamite throughout the device. Placing the entire bag in a single place would do if she meant to ignite it, but it would be too easy for the men to remove. She wanted to make them fear they'd missed something, to make them check the entire machine nut by bolt.

But first she needed a distraction. She could be quiet when she wanted but didn't fancy her chances moving that close to five armed men. She felt a pair of pine martens foraging nearby, close enough she could pick out their chittering in the distance. Clearing her mind, she reached out with her awareness, calling to them the same way she had to the wulvers. This time she brought up images of Sir Walter's men trampling the foliage and digging holes in the earth that looked like open sores. She sent the pungent scent of burnt coal and the loud clamoring of their machines. Then she asked for the martens' help. She wasn't quite sure how she did it. It was a vague concept, not in words, but in pleading feelings of desperation. Last, she turned her thoughts to the balloon and its tether, and how easy it would be for the thing to drift off and how upset the men would be at that.

If only some friends with sharp teeth meant for gnawing would help her.

The night chilled with hoarfrost as she waited. One of the men at the fire grumbled and stretched, snatching up his rifle. He stood only a dozen yards from her, so close she could see his breath. The barrel of his rifle gleamed in the firelight. She began to fret. Had her message been clear enough? What if the martens didn't come, anyway? Though it was only a few paces, the open space between her hiding place and the machine stretched farther and farther. She would never reach it without getting caught. The satchel weighed a ton, and its heft pulled her down, buckling her knees.

She was about to abandon the plan when the martens appeared, springing lightly through the undergrowth, leaving the safety of the trees. Their shadows flitted across to the far side of the clearing. The movement released her tension. She felt them, too, eager to please, as they neared the tether and set to work. She sent them encouragement and realized she'd best get on with her part.

Lowering to the ground, her hands trembled as she unpacked the dynamite. She set each stick in a row and counted them. She'd carried eight with her, each enough to destroy the machine on its own. Studying the machine, she picked out the place for each stick, hidden enough to make the men spend time searching but not so much they wouldn't find them.

The balloon jerked. A cable snapped under the chomping teeth of the martens. She cringed at the metallic clink and urged the critters to work faster. The other cables snapped, then the tether. The balloon danced in the wind and came free. Effie felt giddy as she watched it float away. She sent her thanks to the martens, a sense of pride filling her for their wee act of rebellion, and prepared herself to rush in. But the guards gave no shouts of alarm. Lethargy had claimed them. None looked to the skies as the balloon disappeared into the clouds.

Damnation! Effie scooped up a rock, took her best aim, and launched it across the clearing. It sailed wide of the tent but managed to clang off something loud enough pull the attention of the guards.

One looked up and yelped in surprise. "The balloon!" he bellowed. He rushed to the empty cart where the thing had been tethered, another loping after. The last stayed where he was, studying the sky with a slack jaw. It was the best Effie was going to get. The sun would not wait for her. She picked up the dynamite and dashed for the surveying machine. The ground crunched under her like a cannonade. Her breathing huffed like a gale. There was no chance they wouldn't hear. She had only seconds to act, a moment before they turned and raised their rifles.

A shadow fell across her face. The rustle of feathers alerted her to duck, and she stumbled to a crouch. An owl swooped overhead in a blur of brown and white. Its wings stretched as it slowed, its talons reaching out with razor-tips. It screeched ear-splitting cries that echoed through the glen, as it banked toward the guards at the balloon cart, buffeting them and snatching at clumps of their hair.

The men shouted and swung at the tiny thing. Their companion rushed forward, raising his rifle, but the darting owl didn't allow a safe shot. Effie realized she gaped as slack-jawed as the guards had a moment earlier. She swallowed and stumbled forward, forcing herself to look away from the brazen attack. The guards she'd watched were occupied, but a fourth barged out of the tent. He was coatless, struggling to get his rifle through the tent flap. He faced her, and she dove the final step to hide behind the machine, landing hard.

Pain flared blinding hot. She gritted her teeth and waited for the wave to pass. When it did, she listened for footsteps coming her way. Across the clearing, the owl still screeched and guards cursed. Nothing approached. She peeked around the rack of gauges and found the guard who'd just emerged staring at the others with a befuddled expression.

Effie gulped and willed her hand to steady. With a delicate touch, she slipped a stick of dynamite into the wiring behind the rack. Two went behind the driver's seat, and another in a nook in the underbelly. Next, she moved to the spools of hose, and finally to the engine. She used her knife to sever as many wires as she could and punctured the hose with a couple of short jabs. The last stick of dynamite she saved to place on the writing tray. She had to ensure the men would see it before starting the machine.

Surveying her work, her face wrinkled. It would have to do. She rose and peered across the clearing.

Just in time to see the rifle swing her direction.

"On the ground!" barked the man from the tent. Effie's blood froze. Her heart stopped. But the shot didn't come. She blinked and realized the man no longer stared in her direction. He'd shouted at his own men and tracked the owl, which swooped and darted above the campfire. The other guards dove for cover.

Effie watched in horror, barely stopping herself from shouting a warning to the wee thing. Instead, she dashed toward the cluster of fern. She wouldn't let the poor bird sacrifice itself in vain. When the shot rang out, she stiffened, and for a moment she wondered if the bullet had screamed past her fleeting form. She could almost feel it whipping through the air. Stumbling, she crashed into the fern. Another shot blasted, and a third. Effie craned her neck, searching the sky. She clamped a hand over her mouth to muffle her labored breathing. There! A shadow soared away, melding into the night on silent wings. Effie closed her eyes and felt in that direction. A sensation returned of gloating joy. She returned it, adding a sense of triumph. They had done it! It was all she could do to keep from laughing in glee.

"We must've disturbed its nest," mumbled one of the guards. He picked himself up and studied the scratches on his hands. The man next to him was less fortunate. Effie could see a red line of blood streaking from his temple. "Been here for three days, though," the man continued. "A might bit strange that is."

"Yer a daft fool, Partridge. Check everything in camp," growled the man who'd been snoring away in the tent. "Disturbed its nest, the man says." He spat in disgust. "That balloon didn't fly away by itself. I don't care how rankled the damned bird was, it didn't peck through the tether. Something's amiss."

"The Black Donald," said the man who'd stood guard by the carriageway. "I heard tales he was hunting with witches in the Highlands. The village of Belwin is burned, some say, and a lad from Durham saw a horned beast with shaggy locks watching him through the trees the other day."

"Bollocks. That's just Highlander nonsense filling yer head. It was one of them ginger cows most like. All this nonsense of bringing regiments to the north is some ploy by the coal barons. The attacks are nothing but the Scots not liking us here and taking arms against the crown. See to your post, and this time keep yer damn eyes open."

The guard saluted and did as ordered, though a scowl etched his face. The others shared a worried glance, as if they were more likely to believe the tales of the Black Donald than one of an angry cow. Neither spoke their concerns, however. Instead, they watched the sky and peered into the trees. As they circled the camp, Effie ducked low into the shadows. The guards' vision was hampered by their campfire, but motion would still draw their attention. So she concentrated on the leaves in front of her nose, trying to remain as still as possible.

While she waited, she considered her tiny savior. Had it come on its own? The strong presence she had felt before was still in the distance, a murky aura she couldn't quite figure out. Whatever it was remained motionless. Again, a soothing calm let her know she was not in danger. At least, not from it.

Sir Walter's men were another matter.

The man from the tent ran a hand over his jowls. "Go fetch the engineer," he commanded. "Best wake Mr. Burton, too. Sir Walter will want to know of this, and I'm not going to be the one to tell him." The guard he addressed nodded and trotted off.

He'd barely made the edge of the clearing when another man near the machine shouted. "Bloody hell! Where'd that come from?" He pointed at the stick of dynamite atop the writing tray. The others rushed over, stopping short when they saw what the man was pointing at.

"Lanterns, now," said the one in charge. He backed away, hands tightening on his rifle. "Light up the camp. Then we set a post as far from that bloody thing as possible and wait for Mr. Burton."

The guard who'd found the dynamite shook his head. "There's no fuse. What's that mean?" Effie flushed in embarrassment. She hadn't considered that detail. Hopefully, the men would just assume the dynamite a warning or that some other means was meant to set it off.

"It means leave it be and let men smarter than you worry about it," snapped the one in charge.

The other man bristled but clamped his mouth shut. He helped his companions light a half-dozen lanterns and set them in a ring around the clearing. They made sure to walk in as wide a circle as possible around the machine.

It wasn't a long wait for Mr. Burton, Sir Walter's foreman. Effie heard the steam wagon long before it arrived. That, and the angry bellowing. The man would put an army sergeant to shame. The sun brought an azure glow to the sky, and the last stars began winking out. She wanted to watch more of what happened, but it was time to leave. The fern was dense, but she risked being stuck for hours once the newcomers reached the clearing, and even worse if the entire area was ordered searched.

She watched the guards as she slipped into the trees. Every dozen paces she stopped to ensure she hadn't been seen. But from the distance it was hard to determine anything besides Mr. Burton's arrival. It sounded like the bear baiting she'd rescued Rorie from, only all of the ferocious growling came from a single man. Satisfaction bubbled within her chest. The growling was as sweet a sound as she'd known the past fortnight. She'd delayed Sir Walter and given hope to Graham's plan.

The morning light made the going easier, and soon she fell out of earshot from the camp. Dew chilled her legs, and a gurgle in her stomach reminded her she hadn't eaten in quite some time. She would need to find something for Tom as well, she remembered. Scanning the bracken and trees, she looked for anything edible.

What she found made her start in surprise. A pair of eyes studied her from a branch. The owl's head cocked from side to side. Her tiny hero, she recognized. She tried to think of a way to convey her thanks. She sent it an image of the guards ducking and getting scratched, then of the owl gliding over a field full of tasty-looking rodents. It was meant to be a happy image to show she was pleased. The owl chortled, then took flight, banking in a slow circle and fluttering up behind Effie to perch on her shoulder.

Effie had to force herself not to flinch, but the owl didn't dig in with its talons. It rested lightly, turning its head to stare expectantly at her. She realized what she'd done and chuckled. "One more mouth to feed," she mused. It blinked and bobbed its head, cooing. "Come on, then," she sighed. As she trudged onward, she tried not to dwell on the men in the clearing, and what would happen if they didn't find all the dynamite before starting their machine.

CHAPTER 27

By the time she returned, the bank of the burn where she'd left Tom was empty. It was just as well he'd found his feet. She'd managed to forage only a handful of berries, and some of those she'd eaten while trying to find the spot again. The toils of the night had left her starving and exhausted. Still, if the boy had headed into the woods alone, he could be in danger. Or worse, if he—

"He fled to his masters," said a voice, answering the question in her head.

Effie leapt from her skin, the berries scattering in all directions. The owl squawked and took flight as she whirled in a circle. She saw no one.

"Do not look with yer eyes, Grundbairn."

Effie clenched and reached out with her fey awareness. She gasped. The distant something had now become a distinct five, a group of creatures lurking in the undergrowth just to her right.

She staggered back and fumbled for her knife. How had they moved so close without her noticing?

"Effie the Grundbairn, last of her kind. At least in the Highlands, for the nonce. Ye are an interesting Sithling to observe. Clumsy and unaware, yet crafty and powerful in yer own manner." The bracken shifted, and a face appeared with snaggled teeth and wisps of ginger hair topping an almost bald head.

The tall brownie had been at Skye arguing for the overthrow of London. Effie felt for the wickedness in her aura, the same foul sensation she'd felt in the Laird of Aonghus or the wulvers, but again she felt none, only a soothing peace.

"How are you masking yourself?" asked Effie. "All I feel from you is calm, none of the foul taint of the Sidhe Bhreige."

"Tsk, girl. I am not evil just because I disagree with ye. If that were so, ye would soon find yourself very alone in this world."

"You argued for the eradication of the human race and called it justice!"

The brownie shook her head. "Not the whole race, just for an end to London's tyranny. There are many human governments on this Earth, and it would be best if one were brought low so the others could learn a lesson—that our kind are not prey to be forced into the shadows and hunted." Effie opened her mouth, but the brownie cut her off. "Fear not. Caledon has convinced me the Sidhe Bhreige are not the way. Their race is too cruel. I now stand with ye against them and come to offer aid."

Effie stood dumbfounded. "Do you expect me to believe you?"

The brownie approached. She wore trousers like Effie—as all her race did, regardless of gender—though her coat was tailored to fit her lithe frame. Its green wool was threaded with a golden pattern at the cuffs. Tall for her kind, she reached just above Effie's waist. Her eyes were sharp. Her cheeks twitched as if fighting back a sneer. "Justice cannot be had by fleeing to Elphame. For London to fall, I must remain and see the Sidhe Bhreige fail. And I will not hide while others fight."

Effie's eyes narrowed. There was a twisted sense of logic there, but it made the brownie no more trustworthy. She thought of another tack. "You hid just now. You knew what I was about and only watched."

"I gave what aid I dared, the closeness of my blood lending ye strength, allowing you to gather allies. If I had presented myself, would ye have trusted me?"

"No," Effie admitted.

The brownie's face relaxed into something almost cheerful, though with a mischievous glint that reminded Effie of a pixie. "I am called Jaelyn. I am of Clan Kae, of the Gwynodd Forest. The trees are no more, struck down by the Romans and the Scots after them, but the soil and slopes remain. I bring ye four of Clan Hyr who have also joined our cause."

Branches rustled, and four other brownies stepped forward. Each stood only to Effie's knees, with short linen vests covering drab shirts and trousers. Their ankles and feet were bare, their hair wild and unkempt. None carried a weapon, and there was a solemn cast to the lot, as if their mothers had recently scolded them for losing the family cow.

"Caledon sends for ye," said Jaelyn. "We have little time left to us. On the morrow, the Third Leaving will take place. After, we will be alone against two great enemies."

Effie turned toward the clearing, but it was too far away to hear any of the commotion there. She had no idea how long she had delayed Sir Walter's operations. "Tell Caledon I will get them to stop," she said. "I just need to...." She trailed off. Only one answer came to her. Sucking in a deep breath, she wiped her hands on her trousers. "I just need to speak with Sir Walter." Perhaps the man would listen before he threw her in a dungeon, if he didn't have her shot on the spot. Perhaps she could get him to delay for just one more day. It was a slim chance. Sir Walter would not readily believe her. Her life was nothing to him, her word even less.

"Ye would give yerself over to that man to protect yer human friends?"

Effie nodded. "And to protect the fey as well."

Respect glimmered in Jaelyn's eyes before the mischievous grin returned. "Sir Walter Conrad has been summoned by the Duke of Edinburgh."

Effie uncoiled like a spring, bouncing to her toes. "Then Graham succeeded! Why didn't you say?"

"I do not ken of this Graham, but the humans have called a moot." Jaelyn stooped to gather water from the burn. "Gather yer tawny; Caledon awaits our arrival. He is also summoned to this moot."

Effie cocked her head. "I didn't call for the owl's aid. Wasn't that you?"

Jaelyn shrugged. "Most of the Wise Ones keep the old ways. It is not odd they would pay their respects to a Grundbairn. Consider it some luck o' the blood."

As if listening to their conversation, the owl glided past and landed on a tree branch a few paces away. It studied them, bobbing its head. "Then she isn't mine to gather," said Effie. She smiled at her new companion. "She doesn't look like a Tawny. Maybe a Gwendolyn?" The owl squawked and fluttered to her shoulder. It leaned against her head, content to rest after a long and tiresome night. The poor thing should be asleep in a tree, now that the sun was up.

Effie wished she could do the same but was certain long miles stretched before them. They remained in danger if Sir Walter's men decided to expand their search. Her back groaned as she picked up the satchel. It was lighter now in more ways than one. She slung it over the shoulder opposite Gwendolyn and gave one last thought for Tom, hoping the boy had found some food and rest.

At a gesture from Jaelyn, the brownies of Clan Hyr retreated into the trees. Effie could feel them spreading out to scout ahead as she and Jaelyn followed. They were making for Caldwell House near Aviemore, the tall brownie informed her, the home of Roderick Murray.

Conall's father.

Effie groaned when she heard the name. She didn't know whether to take the news as a good omen or bad one. Perhaps the man wouldn't be there. But if he was, she doubted she could keep the disdain from her face. Men like Roderick and Sir Walter sapped common folk like their machines did the landscape, leaving scars and affliction.

She tromped in silence as the morning passed. Turning north, the trees grew dense before thinning and giving way to rolling hills topped with heather and rapeseed. The purple and yellow flowers mixed with the browns and reds of the soil to form a layered pattern like a jester's motley. The taller peaks of the Cairngorm Mountains rose to the west, holding back a bank of dark clouds. Effie watched the storm come in as they crested a ridge, their third within the past hour. Her legs burned, and the dropping temperature threatened to turn her muscles to stone. She found more berries to eat and splashed some cold water on her face, but the pace they kept would've exhausted her even if she hadn't spent the night sneaking around.

Pride kept her mouth shut. The brownies had shorter legs but somehow managed lengthier strides. Strides that churned and churned like a waterwheel, never stopping. She would not be the one keeping them from reaching Caledon in time. Her stomach growled in protest, but she pretended not to hear it. As droplets began to fall, she tugged her coat closed at the neck and carried on.

When Jaelyn finally called for them to stop, the rain had come in earnest. They huddled in a hollow formed by a fallen tree that leaned against a cluster of boulders. The ground quickly turned into a sodden marsh, but the branches cut the wind, removing its bite. Effie's eyes drooped. The effort to keep them open was like breaking steel with her own hands.

"We can't tarry long," said Jaelyn, watching her. "Darkness will bring the Horned Host. The Piper of Ceann Rois gathers his flock to break us and claim this land as his own."

Effie thought she was nodding and gathering her strength to stand but realized her chin rested on her chest, her back leaned firmly against the boulder. Her eyes refused to open. Just a moment more. A moment more, and it would be enough rest. It would have to be.

"Here," said Jaelyn. A whiff of something acrid passed beneath Effie's nose. She jerked, inhaling sharply, and the world returned to focus. Jaelyn wrapped a pinch of white crystals within a leaf and tucked them into a coat pocket.

Hartshorn, Effie recognized. It lingered in her nose, making her eyes water, but her mind had cleared, even if her body still ached. "This piper is another of the Sidhe Bhreige? One of the three who have escaped?"

Jaelyn nodded. "He is a creature many humans call the Black Donald, though they are mistaken. Their fallen angel is not as hideous. The piper's feet are the hooves of a sheep, his arms and chest like that of a man. He calls his flock like a shepherd, whistling and leading a great host—the Horned Host. He is not one for subtlety like the Laird of Aonghus. Now that he has gathered his strength, he will stand and fight until the world bends knee before him.

"Already he has destroyed villages. Belwin and Kinkirk, they were called. A company of the queen's riflemen tried to stand against him near the River Spey. They broke apart and fled in terror, many falling under his sway before his minions cut them down. His Horned Host numbers in the hundreds and grows each day."

Effie swallowed. The rain pounded around them. Cascades of water funneled into the hollow, chilling her legs in a frigid pool. "What of the other, the third?"

"Not even Caledon knows." Shrugging, Jaelyn rose. "Perhaps waiting to see how the laird and piper fare."

"Or for the perfect moment to strike." More threats awaited them, poised to bring ruin to the Highlands and beyond. Effie couldn't fathom hope against such foes, but still she clung to it. Her mother had instilled that much in her. Whenever they'd hidden in the forest, her mother had told her they couldn't be found as long as Effie refused to give up.

A question popped to mind from the memory, one she'd considered several times over the past few days, ever since speaking with Caledon. "If Fey Craft springs from our auras, and our auras are created by our blood, how is it those without our blood are able to detect us?"

Jaelyn snorted. "Sniff us, you mean?" When Effie nodded, she said, "Who says they can?"

Effie folded her arms across her chest, mimicking the brownie's stance. "I met a woman who could do such a thing, and the Fey Finders, at least at some point, had that ability. There are others, too."

"And these folk know all of their ancestors, do they? Who sired whom three hundred years ago?"

Effie's eyes widened. It couldn't possibly be true. "You mean the queen's Fey Finders, those who once held the ability to sniff for fey, were fey themselves?"

The brownie shook her head. "What is fey, when it comes to Sithlings? The mixed blood dilutes in some and stays strong in others, as generations pass. Sometimes it reunites with its kind, other times it peters out. Most with a sliver of fey blood in them go their whole lives without knowing it. And how are they to know? Raised in cities or villages amongst other humans, as they are. The few who can recognize the presence of other fey aren't likely to guess the cause of their ability."

"And those who suspect it aren't likely to announce the fact to anyone," said Effie. She reeled. The librarian at the University had fey blood. So did some of the men she'd feared all her life. She'd lived a life in isolation to avoid such folk, only to find they were of a common heritage. Sorrow filled her, tears welling in her eyes as a lump formed in her throat.

No, she scolded herself. Regret is not the way. It would only lead to pity. She'd lived by her own choices, despite the bigotry imposed by society. There was something deeper there, too. To harbor such regret was to blame her mother for her lack of knowledge, and she would not trade a single second of her childhood.

Jaelyn watched her, the brownie's stare making her uncomfortable. As much to break the awkwardness as to steady herself, Effie said, "As long as your heart beats, it gives promise to another breath." It was something her mother had taught her. "An inhale. An exhale. And in that moment, the forests will grow, the waters rush, and the winds gust. That is the power of the Grundbairn, this knowing. The Earth tends itself. It can suffer the plagues of man and fey, and in its bleakest hour new life will sprout."

"Wise words."

"I never knew what they meant. I thought the Grundbairns had some greater Fey Craft, some power I couldn't ever learn on my own."

"There is Fey Craft and there is knowledge. The secrets of the Grundbairns may be lost to the Highlands for the trice, but that doesn't mean they ceased to exist. There are others who hold them yet."

Effie caught Jaelyn's arm. "Do you know of my grandfather?" Embarrassment had kept her from asking Caledon, though it seemed silly now.

"Aye, but that isn't my story to tell, Effie the Grundbairn. I know it only from another, and he from yet another. The truth lies with Arnwyrd himself." Her eyes sparkled with some unspoken meaning. Turning, she crept from the hollow and trudged after the brownies of Clan Hyr, leaving Effie confused.

Gwendolyn wasn't happy traipsing about in the rain. Effie agreed with the wee thing but staggered after the brownies anyway. She snuggled Gwendolyn under her coat and picked her way through the forest, all the while dreaming of a warm fire and a hot cup of tea. Darker thoughts of terror she managed to keep at bay, at least until they reached Caldwell House. At sight of its stone walls, patrolled by a full regiment of the queen's soldiers, a coldness gripped her heart and let in the storm.

CHAPTER 28

E ffie had nowhere to hide. For the second time in a week, strangers had expected her arrival. After years of living happily in anonymity, the recognition was numbing. She felt fully exposed. "As well be without clothes," she mumbled as the servants of Caldwell House ushered her away to dry off and change into warmer clothes. That those warmer clothes—a high-necked dress and roomy bustle—befit a proper lady more than a ragged coat and mud-speckled trousers was not lost on her.

After she was suitably attired, the servants led her to the ballroom. The skirts of her new dress swished as she strode along the red carpets. Caldwell House was a grand old manor trimmed in finery. Once a hunting lodge, it bespoke the wealth and recent success of the Murray family. Portraits lined the halls in gilded frames. The tables and chests were hand-carved teak polished to an oily sheen. She'd left Gwendolyn in a bedroom full of lace and silver, with velvet curtains and a bed large enough for Rorie to fit beside her.

The servants didn't know what to make of her. Fear shone in the eyes of some, though others were more curious. The brownies they kept at a distance, not wanting to fall prey to any tricks, but with her she could tell they held back questions. Held back because it wasn't proper to invade a guest's privacy, even though the strangest collection they'd ever seen had descended on their home.

She entered the ballroom, trying to keep her hands from trembling. The room was so spacious it could host its own hunt and the fox would never be found. A long table rested in front of the hearth. Around it several groups clustered speaking in hushed tones. She spotted Stevenson and Caledon, and hurried to them.

Caledon smiled warmly, offering to take her hand. "I'm glad to see you well." He looked regal in his stiff blue coat bedecked with silver buttons.

She gave her hand and let him kiss it, watching the mischief dance in his eyes. "Likewise," she said, flushing at his touch. She glanced at the pair and realized there was a familiarity between them. "I presume you know each other?"

The steward of the Seily Court looked abashed. "We have held an acquaintance for some years, but do not blame Mr. Stevenson for the omission. I honored your mother's decision in not bringing you into the court and asked him not to speak of me unless you asked."

Effie struggled to process that knowledge, of Stevenson having discourse with a fey court for years and not telling her, and decided it best to leave for later. There were far too many important matters at the moment. Her heart could only take so much. "What of Conall and Mr. Graham?" she asked.

"Resting and on the mend," said Stevenson. He dipped his head toward her, and though he stood stiffly, she could see the warmth in his gaze. She smiled inwardly at the thought of embracing him in a furious hug. The man would probably burst from the impropriety.

She glanced around the room. "Mr. Graham succeeded then? I feared I had not done enough, that he had been right to want to destroy the surveying machine. These are times when things must be done. All I risked would've been for naught, if he hadn't come through."

Caledon laughed. "Nonsense. You bought us the needed time, and Sir Walter is heaping mad over what you've done. The threat you posed seeped into the minds of those who work for him. They act more cautiously, even if their employer does not, and work progresses at a much slower rate. You couldn't have wanted a better outcome."

Effie sighed. "Slowed is not stopped. We have not yet thwarted Sir Walter. But how did you assemble this meeting so quickly?"

"Conall Murray has a lot of faith in you," said Stevenson. "He wired his father and had Mr. Graham's friends put pressure on the duke to travel here posthaste. Whatever they said got the attention of His Royal Highness. His airship arrived this afternoon."

Effie was overcome. She knew what it had cost Conall to make contact with his father. "Bless the Sniffer," she said. "The duke's flight must've taken him right over the scourged land. After what he's witnessed, he must make Sir Walter listen."

"We shall see about that account," said Stevenson. "Sir Walter senses a fight and has gathered allies. He has played games like this before."

Stevenson indicated a stuffy-looking woman wrapped in a fur mantle. She hunched next to a broad-shouldered man whose features were oddly familiar. "Abigail Crawley, Lady Fife, has the ear of many in London, and much of her estate is hedged toward the bankers of Newcastle. Roderick Murray is an ambitious man who will see much profit in aligning with the crown, whichever way the wind blows."

"But surely the duke will see reason?"

The duke conversed with another man on the far side of the table. A military man, his bearing was formal, his uniform covered in decorations. A coarse beard hid a square jaw. His eyes clung to a bold nose, staring out with the wisdom of one who commanded men at war. The man he spoke with also wore an officer's coat, but his was of the German style. The duke's cousin, Effie presumed, Oswin von Cleve. She was not surprised they ignored her entrance. Men of their station did not converse idly with those of fey blood. It would be scandal enough for others to know they were in the same room.

"He will listen," said Stevenson, "but he will tread carefully. The crown is aware the Highlands are stricken with panic and that regiments have fallen under attack. But by what, they do not yet know whom to believe. London has spent centuries disarming and pacifying the Scots; they know a weighty response is needed if they are to keep their kingdom intact, but it must be played right or they will have an open rebellion on their hands. All the same, Sir Walter will try to denounce our claims. He will steer the duke toward his own benefit. We must make them both see what is best."

A tromping of boots turned their attention to the door. Sir Walter Conrad strode in with Edward Waite trailing a step behind. Trailing them were two men who made Effie's stomach curl—the man called Jain, and Edmund Glover.

Jain's narrow face twitched when he saw her, a look of surprise clearly painted on his face. It puzzled Effie. If he hadn't expected her, why had Sir Walter brought him? He couldn't be a man of any importance, not the way the other had scolded him on the carriageway.

Glover seethed with pure hatred. His hands were clenched tight enough to turn his knuckles bone-white. He glared at her as he crossed the room, forcing himself to turn away only when introduced to the duke.

"I feel rather outnumbered, Sir Walter," said the duke, once they had traded formalities. "I had not expected you to bring an army to a clandestine meeting such as this."

"Apologies, Your Royal Highness. It is an ugly matter, but I have brought the Fey Finder General here to make an arrest. The Sithling standing with Mr. Stevenson has recently come from planting explosives on my mining machines. Luckily, my men were able to thwart her designs before any were set off."

Sir Walter pointed at Jain. "This man here can testify to the encounter."

The air sucked in around Effie, driving the breath from her lungs. She'd thought she'd escaped unseen, but now she might have ruined all their plans. Stevenson stepped forward and said something to the duke, but she couldn't comprehend the words. Her mind raced. It was an effective trap. She couldn't denounce the details of Jain's account without placing herself in the clearing. Her only recourse was to call the man a liar, but the blow to her credibility with the duke had already been made.

"Well, child," said Lady Fife. "These are serious charges. What do you have to say to them?"

Effie shook her head, furious Sir Walter had ensnared her so easily. "If such a thing happened at all, it certainly wasn't me who perpetrated it."

"She lies," barked Glover. Sir Walter raised a hand to quiet him.

"In the dark of night, one shadow looks much like another," said Caledon. "How are you so certain?"

"It was her," said Sir Walter. "I know it from multiple accounts." Effie caught something in his eyes and realized his certainty could've come from only one person. Tom. The boy had most likely rushed back to camp shouting the tale of the fey who'd saved him. Word of the encounter no doubt reached the ears of those in charge.

Jain smirked. Hooking his thumbs into his trousers, he dared her to challenge him. Effie's skin crawled. All she'd done was slipping through her fingers. She should've left the boy. Her compassion had blinded her.

"Would you have all the Fair Folk arrested, Sir Walter, as your minion desires?" asked Stevenson.

Glover bristled. "I am a servant of the crown, and you will address me with respect, sir!"

"Just this one, for now," said Edward Waite. "But assure yourself, Mr. Stevenson, the crimes of their kind, and of those who have aided them, won't go unpunished for long."

"What crimes are these?" said Stevenson with a chuckle. "Empty words are as useful as a thin sow."

Sir Walter laughed, trying to take the bite from the room. His eyes searched Stevenson's, trying to determine where the other man was leading him.

Lady Fife made a noise somewhere between a laugh and a snort. "Please, Mr. Stevenson. Don't think you can make us believe you are unaware of the madness that has claimed the Highlands. Honest folk flock to the cities in terror, or lock themselves in their estates. Villages organize militias and businessmen hire armed guards. All the while, these creatures ravage the countryside, killing and razing the fields. Your cohorts have shown their true wickedness and now must answer for it."

Stevenson nodded. "We are agreed, then; something must be done to stop these fiends. But you are mistaken on one point." He turned to Caledon. "Here is the steward of the Seily Court. He has no fangs, no claws, and no red-glowing eyes. He has risked his life to stand and fight with us against this menace you speak of."

"You do not deny the fiends are fey?" asked Edward Waite. He balked in disbelief. Sir Walter's stare remained pensive.

"I will not. They are of fey blood as surely as human blood begets anarchists, murderers, and thieves. There are sinister factions of fey who seek to do us harm, just as there are good factions who seek harmony with all living creatures."

"A touching sentiment," scoffed Lady Fife.

"My point is blunt. We are here to discuss the horde amassing at our door, the one invading the Highlands. Already it has sacked villages and commands the roads." He turned to the duke. "To fight in ignorance against an unknown enemy will only end in disaster. Your Royal Highness, I beg you heed the wisdom of the steward."

Sir Walter idly pulled at the cuffs of his coat. "If it is knowledge you wish us to have, Mr. Stevenson, we have means of rooting it out. Mr. Glover's interrogation methods are quite aggressive, as you are no doubt aware."

The duke studied Caledon before turning his eye to Stevenson. Something passed between the pair. Each held a vast ocean pooled behind their gaze, and it was as if the duke debated whether their waters should crash into one another or flow smoothly from one current into the next.

When he finally spoke, it was in a calm, pronounced tone. "Very well, we will hear what the steward has to say. It is why we have gathered here, after all. No one can doubt there is a very real threat to the empire; one only need look beyond the grounds of this house."

Sir Walter's gaze sharpened. He held his tongue, but Effie could see his mind churning.

"What of the other one, Your Royal Highness?" asked Glover. His eyes gleamed in anticipation. "May I escort her from your presence?"

"For the moment, she is not going anywhere," said the duke. "From all reports, she is as embroiled in this affair as any man here." He gestured for Caledon to speak.

Effie paled. From all reports. The duke not only knew of her, he'd read missives about her doings, enough to care whether she stayed or went. His decision should've made her happy, but somehow his words felt as sharp as a knife.

The steward stepped forward and clasped his hands behind his back, pausing just long enough to pique the interest of those gathered. "Centuries ago, the kings of these islands held a covenant to protect a set of wards called the Aegirsigath. These wards held back a race of fey known as the Sidhe Bhreige, binding them in a prison. It is these twisted fey who now raise arms against our queen. The Horned Host, the horde approaching this very house, is led by a mighty Sidhe Bhreige warrior, the Piper of Ceann Rois."

With those gathered intent on his every word, Caledon continued, speaking of the Downward Fields and the crown's loss of its knowledge. He told of the Leaving and of those fey who decided to remain, of Sir Walter's discovery and how it released three of the Sidhe Bhreige. "You have seen what havoc they accomplished. Once all the Sidhe Bhreige are escaped, their might will be too powerful to defeat. They will conquer this empire and beyond. Stopping those who have escaped, restoring the Aegirsigath, and leaving the wards unhindered is the only way to ensure that does not happen."

Waite snorted when the steward had finished. "These are your troubles. The queen's armies will defeat the fiends whether there are three or three thousand."

"Perhaps," said Stevenson, "but at its own folly. How much would you risk to defeat them in arms, when you have a means to halt their advance now? How many villages and cities would you allow to fall? How many lives? Stop destroying the Aegirsigath and you confine this disaster now."

"The Sidhe Bhreige are not contained in ambition as they were before." Caledon's voice grew stronger. For the first time, Effie saw the mischief leave his eyes. "There are no longer gods to the North and East to check their advance and keep them here. They will learn of the modern world. They will seek to expand and grow in power until entire continents bow before them."

"If what you say is true, we should seek to destroy the Sidhe Bhreige when they are newly released and weak." Sir Walter took a step toward the duke's side, as he mused in a contemplative tone. It was a subtle movement, but one that created distance between himself and Glover. "Tell us where the portals are that allow them to reenter our world. Are they near the caches of Aerfenium?"

Caledon bowed his head. "I do not have that knowledge, but I believe they reappear close to where they stood when they were bound. The Sidhe Bhreige were spread across the Highlands at the time. Once returned, they can slink into the shadows before we know their location."

The man in the German uniform cleared his throat. His mustache narrowed to thin tips, each side pointing toward the bushy sideburns that covered his cheeks. He looked to the duke for leave to speak and received it. "Saxe-Coburg will ever aid our cousins. Our combined armies can root out this menace."

"A stalwart offer, Herr Cleve," said Lady Fife, "but the queen would never suffer German soldiers on British soil."

"With respect, madam, if this *elfe* is believed, it will not be a choice of your liege. Our nation is threatened and will protect itself. Of that, I feel safe in knowing the mind of Chancellor Bismarck."

"The French will not sit idly, either," added Stevenson.

"A veiled threat, yet empty, Mr. Stevenson," said Edward Waite. "The French have not the stomach to attack us on our own soil. But let us speak of what really transpires. The fey have always sought domination and seek now to halt our progress and give over to their uncanny ways. We are told of some ancient evil but have no proof. We are told Aerfenium, Sir Walter's great discovery, cannot be mined or utilized, but I see nothing beyond a selfish ploy to wrestle a powerful tool from our hands."

He jabbed a finger at Caledon. "Here is the enemy. Let these attacks continue and the fey will feel the full might of the queen's armies, I say."

Lady Fife and Edmund Glover nodded, the one with feigned resignation, the other with a zealot's glee. Effie read the duke's face and started. The man couldn't possibly take Waite's tirade seriously, yet he tapped his lips with a finger, staring at the coal baron from Newcastle as he'd done with Stevenson.

"Robert Ramsey was not a lord but an honest man, and brave." The fury in her voice made her words tremble. "I did not know Ewan Ross or any of the other fallen, but I fight to avenge them. I fight so that no others will meet the same fate. How can you reject allies who share a common enemy?" Every eye studied her. She balled her fists, pushing back against the weight of the scrutiny. Her fear fell away like a shed skin. Anonymity had become an old clutch set aside, like a child does her blanket. Now was the time to stand up for what was right.

Glover tittered. "Silence, hag! The guilt of your crimes spittles from your tongue. We will not be taken by the poison."

She ignored the Sniffer. "The proof you desire is already known," she barked at Waite. "Sir Walter admitted as much when you accosted me in Edinburgh. Why else did you beg of me to know its properties? His great discovery is Aegirsigath. It is of fey origin. And if that is true, why bother with a charade like the Sidhe Bhreige? One that would only bring blood and death to our kind? We would merely hide the matter elsewhere, or…."

She trailed off, losing her breath, as something else Sir Walter had said came to her. "Or let it be known publicly the matter's origins." Society shunned stardust for what it represented—that the science of humans did not dominate the Earth. Why would they use Aegirsigath if the same held true? The answer was painted on the faces of those gathered. In Edinburgh, Sir Walter had asked what the world would be without greed. It appeared they would have to wait another day to settle that score.

"So it comes down to greed," she said. The words rang through the ballroom. Effie glared, daring any to deny it.

"The power of the substance is too great," said Lady Fife. "If we do not seize it another nation will, and we will be at a disadvantage to our enemies."

"You assume it exists elsewhere for those to mine," countered Stevenson.

The duke paced in front of the hearth, hands clasped behind his back. The glow of the fire forced them to squint as he spoke. "Sir Walter, do you allow that this substance is of fey origin? That it was made by the master steward's elders?" He waited for Sir Walter to nod, then addressed Caledon. "And if recreated, you assure it will restore the wards that were diminished and contain these evil creatures you say are being released?"

"It will, Your Royal Highness." Caledon's back stiffened, but hope welled in his eyes. "Yet those already returned would not be bound again. We remaining fey do not have the power for that feat. They would remain here and need to be subdued."

"Y…Y…Your Royal Highness," stammered Glover. "I would

not recommend this course of action. Let me root the truth from them. It is the only way."

"Perhaps not," said Sir Walter. Glover jerked as if slapped. "I find myself trusting the steward. Let the fey prove their merit by recreating the matter we have imprudently destroyed." His smug smile was far worse than Glover's wrathful stare. Effie feared it. The man sensed some opportunity and pounced on it. "The risk is slight. Either a great enemy is thwarted, or we will find ourselves in the same position we are presently."

Waite took his cue, pretending to recoil. He would never make the stages of London. "But how do we know it is stable? The fey have created a volcano beneath our lands that could erupt at any time. Explosions have already taken lives. It must be studied if we are to protect the empire."

Effie stood dumbstruck, watching the play unfold, knowing it was what Sir Walter had wanted all along—his own supply of Aegirsigath manufactured solely for his own benefit.

"An excellent point, Mr. Waite." Sir Walter paused to make sure all eyes were on him. "If more Aerfenium is produced, a portion should be given over to the crown for the study of its properties. It is too volatile to remain unexplored." He left the last word open, its meaning clear in its ambiguity.

"We are not your puppets." Caledon's face was a stone mask.

"If the fey truly wish to be considered a part of the realm, they should have no problem aiding the crown when called on," said Sir Walter.

"And if we choose to leave, and abandon you to the wrath of the Sidhe Bhreige?"

Sir Walter shook his head slightly, like a parent disappointed in a child. "Then you will have shown your true character." It was a simple trap, but one woven with the skill of a master. If the fey left the Highlands to the Sidhe Bhreige they would only prove the lies London perpetrated against them. But to offer aid would be to expose their secrets and become the prey of men like Sir Walter Conrad.

The Duke of Edinburgh continued his plodding. He either disdained standing still, or his thoughts worked themselves out better while he was in motion. "It is the duty of government to protect its people," he said. "Producing more of the Aegirsigath accomplishes this on two fronts at little cost. Without it, we risk great harm. That is your own argument, Master Steward."

Waite and Lady Fife beamed, unable to contain their rapture. Sir Walter bored holes into Stevenson, challenging him to speak. It was only Edmund Glover who was unnerved. The man fumed, his hands wiping against the sides of his coat as he turned between Waite and Sir Walter. Clearly, they had left him out of their plans.

Caledon glanced her way, and Effie felt a depth of sorrow she hadn't felt since her mother's passing. *He thinks he's failing his people,* she realized. She shook her head slightly and pulled her lips up, as cheery as she could make herself in the moment. He wasn't failing. There was no other choice.

"However," the duke continued. "It is not my station to create a permanent truce between our people. This matter must be taken before Parliament. To meet the current need, the fey will create enough Aegirsigath to seal the Sidhe Bhreige away, plus a portion for the crown's agents to study. In return, all mining operations will cease immediately. Any further destruction of the substance will be regarded as an act of treason."

"No, Your Royal Highness," Glover seethed. "It cannot be. The mere act of conspiring with fey is treason. Your mother, God save her, would never allow this!"

The duke leveled his gaze. "Do not presume to speak for the queen. It has never been a crime to be born of fey blood, nor is it one to enter into an agreement with them. Your task, as it has always been, is to hunt down those who cause offenses against our laws."

Herr Cleve waggled a finger. "More so, Fey Finder General, if you had been diligent about your duty, this horde of the Black Donald— or, how did you say, *Das Piper?*—would not be approaching to attack His Royal Highness."

Fire blossomed on Glover's cheeks. He snapped his head toward Sir Walter, but no aid came from his supposed ally. A low growl left his throat. "We shall see." His hands searched his belt, forgetting he had disarmed before coming into the duke's presence. Finding nothing, he yanked his coat down so it pulled tight about his shoulders. "For now, I will take this creature into custody." He rounded on Effie. His eyes were wide and dangerous, his jaw slathering like a wolf's.

Stevenson stepped in front of her, but before he could speak, Sir Walter raised his hand. The geologist turned to Jain, who'd stepped back, forgotten against the wall. "Are you quite certain it was her you saw? It was a dark night, and one fey does look quite like another." The answer he expected took no guessing.

Jain read it and shook his head. "I could be mistaken, Sir Walter." The man studied the floor, shying away like a beaten hound. "I apologize. It was dark, as you say."

"What is this?" barked Glover.

"Heel yourself, Edmund," said Roderick Murray. He had remained quiet until the matter with the duke was settled, but he now knew which way the wind blew.

Glover seethed. He stepped toward Effie. "She is fey. She conspires with other fey. Her guilt is painted on her face!"

"Guilt of what?" asked Stevenson.

"She's absconded from the queen's agents!"

Effie tried to keep the bite from her tongue, but she had had enough of the man. She would never fear him again. "If you mean I have escaped your false imprisonment, your unjust torture, and your unwarranted assaults, I freely admit I have done so. Twice."

Lady Fife snorted. Waite and Murray looked on Glover as if he carried a plague. "Enough," said the duke. "Sir Walter, take your man away."

Sir Walter opened his mouth to retort but thought better of it. He motioned for Jain to follow and strode from the room, pointedly ignoring Glover. The Fey Finder General bowed deeply to the duke and stormed away mumbling to himself. The clomping of his boots echoed down the hallway.

"An odd fellow," said Lady Fife. "One wonders whether he is fit enough to continue his position."

The duke's tone was cordial but carried finality with it. "I have no doubt you have a suitable replacement in mind, but it can wait. Mr. Murray and I have the defense of this manor to discuss, if you will excuse us."

Lady Fife nodded and took Waite's arm, leaving by a door at the far end of the room. As soon as they had left, a host of servants filed in wearing black livery slashed with the Murray colors. They carried platters of food and a decanter of wine. The haunch of lamb was blackened yet still moist, the potatoes fried and covered in pepper. Effie's stomach twisted in knots as the sweet aroma reached her. A lieutenant of the Black Watch marched in and saluted the duke. His red officer's coat and polished buttons were in stark contrast to the dark green and blue pattern of his tartan. He unrolled a bundle of maps on the table that displayed the manor grounds and surrounding area.

The duke ran a finger over some notes penciled in the margins, then waved Caledon over. "You and my cousin are correct. The horde will assault this house. This piper wants us not to think so, but I can see it in the way the creatures cut through the hills. Is it for my blood, steward, or something else?"

"It is because we give him a trigger," said Caledon. "Fey Craft is communal in nature. We must gather our blood into a small area in order to have the strength to do what we intend. But that pool of energy will be available to all. Thus, by necessity, the act of creating Aegirsigath will grant the Sidhe Bhreige more power, if they are close at hand. The Piper of Ceann Rois will wait until we have gathered our numbers and strike before we start the binding. He will seek to use our fey blood to suit his own ends and destroy us."

The duke continued studying the maps, giving no reaction to Caledon's explanation. Effie wondered how much the duke already knew of fey, and how many of his questions were a test of trust. "Then we will make our stand here and let them come. The army will dig in and defend your host while you perform the Fey Craft. How long do you need to prepare?"

"Four or five days, Your Royal Highness."

The duke raised his head, his gaze allowing for no rebuke. "Tensions escalate at a rapid pace, Master Steward. The crown wants to know if the Highlands are in revolt. Parliament wants to know how much the gathered regiments will cost them. The nations of the world are looking for an excuse to nibble at our heels and crumble our empire. You have three days, perhaps less."

CHAPTER 29

The last beads of rain dribbled from timbered eaves to the balcony's cast-iron railing. A fine mist shrouded the gardens below, though the veil was not so dense as to hide the pair of airships tethered to the lawn. One was bulbous, with tooled leather straps fringed in silver, and a deck of lacquered wood befitting a royal barge. The other was sleek and bound in iron, built for the vanguard of an army more than transport. Slim crank-guns were mounted to its gunwales, and a port beneath its bow could open for a device within to belch flame. Neither would hold more than a score of fliers, forcing the air-cavalrymen to stand double duty as crewmen and soldiers. Herr von Cleve had arrived from Freiberg the previous morning, having taken flight within hours of receiving Graham's telegram. The duke, alerted of Cleve's voyage and intent, had launched from Edinburgh not an hour later.

Effie studied the airships as she slipped pieces of roasted ham to Gwendolyn. The owl perched on the rail, hooting when the pieces didn't come fast enough, demanding restitution for missing her morning nap. Effie was equally irritated. She'd found little sleep the previous night, and when she had finally slumbered off, she'd tossed restlessly until the new day had pulled her from bed.

Four days had passed since her introduction to the Seily Court. It marked the day of the Third Leaving. Those gathered on Skye would be preparing by now, but to do what she wasn't certain. How did one move between worlds? One more question for which she had no answer. She plucked a piece of cheese from the platter someone had brought, and plopped it into her mouth. The veins of mold gave it a rather sharp taste.

She forced her attention to the far side of the lawn, trying to relax her spinning thoughts. There, the duke's soldiers constructed a breastwork. Why they had chosen that particular spot was lost on her. The grounds of Caldwell House were mostly open, except for a few hedges running around the garden and a low, stone wall. She could see no further through the distant trees from there as from any other spot, but the sergeant barking orders seemed to know his business. The detail had already mounted a small cannon on a rise behind the breastwork, and they'd covered it with a canvas to keep off the damp.

"There are other Seily Courts on the continent," came Caledon's low timbre. The steward strode onto the balcony, followed by Stevenson. "She will still be able to leave with them."

"Not and reach Elphame," said Stevenson. "Only the Scottish court knows the way. The other Seily courts have their own realms to attend. And they would not share their knowledge with an outsider."

"Which is why I can't take her now. It is a covenant of our court to keep our homeland safe. Taking her now and allowing her to return would create an unacceptable risk in the eyes of many in our number."

Effie hardened. "If I am the she, then she has no intention of living in Elphame no matter how trustworthy you deem her."

"Apologies," said Caledon. He gripped the rail and leaned against it, shoulders sagging. "No offense was meant."

"You're back in a man's clothing." Stevenson's weary tone belied his stiff posture. He had probably not slept the previous night. Not many at Caldwell House had.

"Faster to run in," she said, "in case the crown decides we aren't allies anymore."

Stevenson nodded. He sat and picked at the food platter. "Effie, I know you have no desire to leave, but even if we are successful here, you must realize it is only a short time before men like Sir Walter find a way to exploit our agreement. They envision what can be done with this substance, and until another, greater source of power takes its place, their whole lives will be bent on the control of its production."

"Those of our kind who remain will be enslaved," said Caledon. "A worse fate than being hunted. Most will leave for Elphame rather than suffer the appetite of humans for domination. Sir Walter laid a brilliant trap, and I blundered right into it. An amount of Aegirsigath for the crown to study, he asks. It is only the beginning. On this, Mr. Stevenson and I are in agreement. But the door opened for Sir Walter and his cohorts can be shut again."

"You speak of breaking your agreement before it is even sealed," said Stevenson. "It is why she should learn the way to Elphame now, lest she be abandoned later."

Caledon shook his head. "Even with the knowledge, she would still need others of our court to lend her enough strength to leave. And any others who would aid her would already know the way."

Stevenson grunted. "You are being obstinate for no cause, steward."

"The matter is settled, Mr. Stevenson."

Effie balked. She didn't want to live in Elphame any more than she would England, but the steward's insult stung just the same. His words were clear. The court did not trust her. Picking out a fatty piece of ham, she held it up for Gwendolyn. As she did, she studied Caledon's face. There was something he wasn't saying. "How are other members of the court deemed trustworthy?" she asked, trying not to sound too bitter.

The steward's hands tightened on the rails. The clang of picks and shovels rang out below while he stared off at the line of trees. "You are correct, of course," he finally said. "It is a personal matter. You are the daughter of Adeleyde and granddaughter of Arnwyrd, which changes things greatly."

"Arnwyrd the oathbreaker."

"Aye, the Sithling responsible for the death of my uncle, the steward of the court before me." He rounded on her.

His eyes held such sadness, they drained the ire from her. "Or so most believe. They were fast friends who differed on little account until my uncle, and a band of other Sithlings, decided to join the cause of Charles Stuart. At the time, the Young Pretender's quest to win London's throne ignited dreams of heroic deeds in the band. Abandoned by the French, the Jacobites needed allies and welcomed the Sithlings into their ranks. They fought at Culloden, and bled and died with the rest of the Highlanders. My uncle suffered a wound that few would survive but managed to make his way back to the house of a miller. Arnwyrd disagreed with the foolish band and had remained away from the fighting. He was older, in the twilight of life, and saw no reason to help one human claim a throne over another. But the stars had cast their fates. He had made his way to this same miller's house. It nestled in a dell, with a strong running burn flowing through its heart. The hills on either side were thick with tall pines."

Effie leaned forward. "They chanced on the same miller's house?"

"It was known to them, as was the miller. As was the man's daughter, a wee lass still with her hair in braids." Caledon frowned at something in the distance. "Arnwyrd treated this lass kindly, as a grandfather treats his own grandchild. He visited the family often, always bringing her presents and tales of fey in the woods. He had done the same for her father when he was a lad. There was some bond there."

"Until she fell prey to the wasting sickness," said Stevenson. He refused to look at Effie.

Caledon nodded. "Disease spreads like fire where men bleed and rot in the fields. Arnwyrd was exhausted of skill and knowledge by the time my uncle reached him. He had done everything he could to save the lass, but nothing had helped. My uncle was near death, barely conscious, leaving Arnwyrd facing the loss of two he loved. So he chose."

Effie blinked, the moisture in her eyes welling. "I don't understand. Chose what?"

"The blood of a steward is a powerful thing. It is bolstered by the oaths of those within the court. The power of those oaths stick, even when the court is far from the steward. It is closest to royal blood among our kind, and the royal fey have long abandoned this realm."

"He used it to save the girl? Is such a thing possible?"

Caledon studied the line of trees again before answering. "Blood Craft isn't evil at its heart. It is more of a corruption. It is for controlling and dominating, achieving power in a way that doesn't abide by the forces of nature." The steward clasped his hands behind his back. "In such a way, it can be used to stimulate life where natural methods would fail. Arnwyrd sapped the blood of my uncle and brought the girl back to health. In his despair over the loss of his friend, he told many what he had done. But instead of consoling your grandfather, they shunned him. Even the miller's family cast him out, thinking he had made a pact with the devil."

Effie wrapped her arms around herself, suddenly feeling the chill of the morning more fiercely. She understood now why Jaelyn hadn't wanted to tell her the tale. It left little room for warmth.

"Your mother faced a choice of her own," said Stevenson. "She could've disowned your grandfather but instead chose to live as an outcast, defending his name. Your own uncle did the same, though he eventually saw his way back to the court."

"I remember," said Effie. Her mother and uncle had a great falling out before she was born. It had left her mother in a bitter mood, quick to anger, whenever family was mentioned. Stevenson had told her he was part of the Second Leaving, those who left for Elphame during the Inquiry of the Potato Famine. "And now I am dubbed a traitor, too?"

"Not by my hand," said Caledon. "But the politics of the court are tricky and the location of Elphame sacred." The steward fell silent and Effie saw no reason to press him. It would be an argument snaking in circles with no head or tail. The hardships her family had suffered sunk into her bones. Her mother had never told her this tale. Had she felt guilt? Or was it shame? Effie felt only sadness, and a longing to be with her again.

"What became of the girl?" she asked.

"She lived out her years well in Edinburgh." Caledon checked on the gardens below, and his ears perked up. Rounding on Effie, he straightened his coat. "It is time."

Effie rose, but Stevenson stepped in her path. He appraised her with a proud bearing. "I have done what I could. I know you will not heed me to remain hidden, so I will say only this: stay safe, and don't do anything unnecessarily foolish." His voice rasped with emotion. She wrapped her arms around his waist, relaxing into his warmth, pushing aside the sadness of Caledon's tale.

"The steward is a good friend," he said. "Listen to him and trust his judgment."

She nodded. It was clear Caledon bore her no malice over her grandfather's actions, and keeping her from the court of Righm had been her mother's wish, regardless of the betrayal she felt from Stevenson. Besides, if she had been brought before the court as a girl and grown up within its confines, it dawned on her she would most likely be among those Leaving without a second thought for the fate of those left behind. The thought made her shudder, and she was thankful it wasn't so.

The others waited on her. She could sense them huddled in a group in the gardens. Giving Stevenson one last squeeze, she hurried through the house. Servants stopped to watch her as she passed, their bundles of linen and dusters forgotten as they stared.

Effie ignored them. She'd grown used to the scrutiny. Only the soldiers made her anxious. They swarmed about like ants, some toting boxes of ammunition and tools for digging breastworks, while others sat cleaning rifles and sipping steaming tea from tin cups.

Jaelyn stood under the shadows of the tethered airships with the four brownies of Clan Hyr as she and Caledon joined them. Two other Sithlings Effie hadn't met before stood with them. One was tall, bearded, with long golden hair; the other bulky, with the thick neck and shoulders of a blacksmith.

"We are nine," said Caledon. "It is enough."

"Can ye convince them?" Jaelyn asked.

The steward's gaze hardened. "They will come. I will return from Elphame by tomorrow's end with a party willing to create the Aegirsigath. Enough to reseal the Downward Fields. We do not need the entire court. In Elphame there are fey whose skill surpasses all those at Skye combined, even if that host were twenty times in number."

A bubble gurgled in Effie's stomach as the nine spread in a circle. They stood close but not quite touching. "Leaving is not a skill known to many," Caledon explained. "The strength needed is beyond what any can do alone, and it is only because I am among you, with a steward's blood, that we few here can accomplish the feat."

Jaelyn patted her shoulder. "I will guide ye. Only Caledon needs to ken how to reach Elphame. The rest of us will act as conduits, passing our focused auras into a pool for the steward's use."

Effie took a breath, nodding, and an awareness snapped into her senses like icy water dumped on her head. She gasped from the shock. Unseen tendrils delved beneath her flesh like creeping vines. Eight of them entwined her, each as distinct as it was foreign. She reacted out of instinct and tried to force them out. But Jaelyn beckoned with a hand, and somehow she understood. Steeling her mind, Effie opened herself. At the same time, she reached and probed into the others, following their lead.

Her senses took form, snaking from her and joining with the others. Slowly, the tendrils wrapped and twisted into a complex knot, the shock of their touch receding as they meshed. A calm settled over her, and she began to recognize the sensations flooding through the knot. Of old places, deep and dank, and of new life, ripe and blossoming. A trickle of water seeped into a bog to find roots like cobwebs growing strong within the murky sludge. Rocks as jagged as a carving blade crumbled speck by speck from a wind dancing off a loch's surface. Those held great power in them. Caledon's, they had to be. Jaelyn's were of a chase through fallen leaves, weaving across glens whose brilliant colors waned before the coming winter. But always they kept a hue of gold pushing back the biting cold, a fierce fire against the nothingness on the horizon. The others held the musk of campfires, the lapping of gentle waves on a shore, the taste of roasted hazelnuts, and the perfume of pine needles strewn across beds of pungent moss.

Effie projected the warmth of a hearth as rain pounded the earth outside. A faint voice breathed a song, a cheery reel she couldn't quite make out. It was her mother's voice, so much like her own. She strained to listen, the notes tickling along her skin. Her arm floated as she reached out, the distance between herself and the voice shrinking yet forever unclosed.

Caledon appeared before her, and the warmth from the hearth whipped into a funnel that sprayed colors like a prism. The funnel sucked in the rain and her mother's melody, drawing in leaves and roots, the scent of pine and lapping of waters, until nothing was left but a void of gray air. Effie knew she should be terrified, but euphoria gripped her. Her body was a feather drifting in a cloud. She had no weight, no feelings to ground her in the mortal world. The steward's bearing throbbed with ancient power. He was the center of the whirlwind, and its master.

Jaelyn's lips pursed in half a smile. Behind her, the gardens reemerged, painting themselves into existence from the void. The shadows of the airships crossed Effie's face, and the clamor of the soldiers milling about their work returned. Awakening from the stupor, she began to worry the Fey Craft hadn't worked when a great clap of thunder shook the ground. Its fury rang in her ears. They all staggered except Caledon. His body remained frozen like a statue, then crumpled to the ground in a pile of dust.

The shock sent Effie to her knees, crying out. She stared at the pile as flecks drifted off on the breeze. "Did he...?" she stammered. "Is he gone to Elphame?"

"Giants and dwarves turn to stone for all to piss on," said Jaelyn. "But you Sithlings aren't as boring." The brownie helped Effie to her feet. "Here," she offered, pulling a long, slender knife from behind her waist. "No sense wasting the time waiting for the steward's return. Ye'll be needing to defend yerself but soon. Best ye learn how. Have ye any skill with blades?"

Effie shook her head. "I'd prefer a club, or perhaps a wooden spoon."

Jaelyn tittered, her crooked teeth poking out. "Aye, we might get ye one of them. A solid shillelagh can be the best of friends. But a blade cuts both ways in a pinch, provided you're prepared." The brownie patted a pouch that hung from her belt.

Effie caught her meaning and shook her head. "No, I won't use Blood Craft again unless the need is dire. The last time I faced the Laird of Aonghus, I watched him force his minions unto their deaths only to please his whim. That power cannot be something to rely on."

Humor fled the brownie's face. "Ye may see some day how wrong ye are." Her head snapped to the side a moment before an ear-splitting cry rang out from the woods. The howls of wulvers answered, hundreds of them spread out in every direction. Soldiers swarmed the lawn as whistles shrilled in alarm, spilling from the house, snapping up rifles, and digging into their positions.

Suddenly, Effie felt them. The Horned Host. A mass of fey blood that crawled through the hills, too many to tell apart. Far too many, like a solid wall of ice rolling toward Caldwell House. The tall, bearded fey gasped. "Bloody hell, how did we not sense them? So close. So many."

"The piper is full of tricks," said one of Clan Hyr. His voice was high-pitched and anxious.

Jaelyn met Effie's eye, standing tall and defiant. Effie was grateful for the strength. It kept her own legs from trembling.

"Come, let's get ye that stick," said the brownie.

Effie nodded, wishing they had another battery of crank-guns instead.

CHAPTER 30

S hadows darted through the woods. Effie sensed more than saw the creatures who cast them, from her vantage on the balcony of Caldwell House. She tried to keep from fearing what lurked in the distance, but the piper's army caused everything to pulse with a vile energy. Decay crept toward the house like a corrosive sludge oozing through the forest. The trees dug their roots deeper, as if to gird themselves against the coming onslaught. The smaller critters of the underbrush had fled in a panic, the birds escaping to distant skies.

Random howls sent shivers down her arms. At first, she'd tried to pinpoint where they'd emanated, casting out her fey awareness. If she could learn something of the creatures' movements, she could pass the information to the duke. But the howls came too fast, the creatures too many. Tracking them led only to frustration, overwhelmed by the sheer vastness of the Horned Host. It gathered throughout the night and into the morning. By afternoon, it had swelled to rival a large city.

The soldiers in the garden grew anxious. Red coats covered green and black tartan uniforms, in stark contrast to the flowering purple and yellow petals. They had kept their positions through the night and half the day, pressed against the low garden wall that reached barely half a man's height. They squatted behind the breastwork they'd constructed and filled the roofline of the house. But the waiting had made them restless. A few dozed, their soft snores carrying on the breeze, while others fidgeted with their equipment, checking and rechecking their ammunition. One had fired into the trees and been reprimanded by the sergeant. Others held a silent watch, eyes strained, rifles pointed at an unknown enemy.

An officer had ordered the airships boarded, and from the higher vantage, crackshots watched the horizon. Their boots clacked on the wood as they paced the deck. Their hand signals to those waiting below were always the same: no approach sighted.

The Piper of Ceann Rois delayed, as Caledon had said he would. The attack would come when his power was greatest. The Laird of Aonghus would come, too, if things went poorly for them. Effie had deduced as much. The fiend schemed for his own slice of power but knew the other Sidhe Bhreige would not treat him kindly if they deemed themselves abandoned. He would lurk in the forest nearby and wait to spring some trap.

The duke had tricks of his own. He'd not spent the hours idle, but whatever the plans were, Effie was not privy to them. She saw only that their side was fewer in number compared to might of their enemy.

A lone howl went up, a summoning cry louder than the others had been. Effie shuddered. The piper's horde surged forward an instant before fey blood arrived on the lawn. Caledon appeared as if stepping out of a pocket of air, near where he'd departed. A score of Sithlings, brownies, and hogboons appeared with him. Most were wizened with age. The hogboons leaned on canes, long white beards dragging on the ground. The brownies were silver-haired, their jackets thick over frail bones.

Effie bolted from the room, snatching up the shillelagh Jaelyn had found. Its blackened wood felt solid in her grasp. The rounded knob at its end was slightly bigger than her fist. Her feet barely touched the steps as she hustled down the main stairs.

The assault had begun.

The piper's army swarmed, choking out all other senses. Bellowed shouts and cries of alert echoed through the halls. The boom of a cannon rattled the house. Effie grabbed the banister to steady herself and caught movement out of the side of her eye. Jain lurked in a doorway a dozen paces away. He grinned and dipped his head.

"Didn't know it was you they wanted," he said. "Mr. Burton said he had a job for me, something special for Sir Walter, something for a little coin. Couldn't believe my eyes at the luck. Never thought to see your filthy whore's face again. The Lord must be smiling down on me."

She had no response, nor any time for the foul man. A quiver of revulsion swept through her as she ducked down a hallway and fled into a sea of chaos.

The gardens were on fire. Flames burst from cannon and rifle. Smoke from spent cartridges gave the air a burnt smell, the mixture of oil, metal, and powder like a blacksmith's smelting oven. Water doused on overheated crank-guns sizzled, sending up plumes of white vapor. Soldiers at the breastwork fired as fast as they could load. The cannon mounted behind them thumped exploding canisters into the woods where the timbers cracked apart and smoldered.

Wulvers raced from the trees alongside rumbling creatures whose bodies were as fat as a boar's. Sharp horns and tusks surrounded their flat snouts, and tails as long as a hound's wagged from thick haunches. Effie started when she saw some were mounted by tiny imps who threw spears and shot arrows at the duke's soldiers. Their hair was wild like a brownie's, but their thick, bent noses looked more like what she'd learned of trolls, despite their miniature stature.

The Duke of Edinburgh stood high above, on a terrace atop Caldwell House. The Admiral of Her Majesty's fleet surveyed the fighting as if from the bridge of one of his warships. Signalers waved colored flags to those below, directing the soldiers to counter the enemy's movements. Roderick Murray and Lady Fife huddled with Sir Walter Conrad behind the duke, a few paces apart from Stevenson.

No argument from any of them could force Effie to seek shelter. Every fey was needed to re-forge the lost Aegirsigath. It was the only means to ensure the imprisoned Sidhe Bhreige remained sealed within the Downward Fields. Their only means to ensure victory. And even if that weren't the case, she wouldn't let others risk their lives while she hid, especially for a cause she had rallied so fervently for.

Caledon and those returned from Elphame worked on the lawn as if the chaos around them was nothing but a cloud of bothersome midges. Already, lines of crushed limestone wove in a spiraling pattern on the grass. How those spreading the powder kept track of the knot was beyond Effie. She could barely keep her eyes from the mayhem at the walls and couldn't follow the design for more than a moment—let alone aid in its construction—before an explosion or shout drew her attention.

A mortar and pestle were shoved under her nose, as she stood slack-jawed. She barely registered it before Jaelyn slapped a pouch of petals into her hands. "Crush these into a paste and hurry about it," the brownie snapped, staggering as a cannon bombardment rumbled the ground. Trees splintered and fell, sending up a chorus of howls and yips from beyond the wall. "And get ye down, fool lass!"

Effie didn't need Jaelyn to tug her coat. She had already backed toward the shadows of the house. An old hogboon, his face like a plump, furless marten, sat over his own mortar, tufted knuckles working at a steady rhythm. He greeted Effie warmly, as if nothing were amiss and the world around them not filled with blasted iron shot and the burnt tinge of spent cartridges. She sat next to him and set about her task, concentrating on his cadence. If she kept her hands moving, she could focus on the petals and keep her wits from crushing apart.

A ball of fire splashed over the wall, sending a wave of heat across the lawn. Scorched stone and crackling embers whipped about in its wake. Soldiers called for water as another fiery ball arced toward their position. A soldier screamed, his flesh seared by the blast. Trows, Effie felt. Hundreds of them. They came in a bold rush, hurling glass orbs from slings as long as they were tall.

The crank-guns opened up with renewed fury. At a cry from the sergeant, the same she'd seen build the breastwork the day before, grenadiers launched incendiaries of their own at the enemy, and for a moment the air shimmered from rapid concussions. Effie grabbed her ears against the deafening barrage. Her eyes teared from the heat.

A surge of wulvers leapt over the wall, driving back its defenders with fang and claw. Caledon pointed and yelled something she couldn't hear. He was trying to get the sergeant's attention. The man had ordered the cannon to fire, but the artillerymen stood transfixed. Those on the breastwork also fell silent. The soldiers there wore the same masks of fear.

Fingers danced across Effie's mind, an invisible probing touch. The Piper of Ceann Rois was stronger than the Laird of Aonghus. His touch was steel where the other's was a malleable bronze. Instead of enthralling his victims, he thrust horrors before their eyes. Her vision clouded. Giant serpents wrapped around her body hissing venom as great horned beasts rose from the ground, mangled flesh dripping from drooling maws. She focused her will against the nightmares but couldn't peel her gaze from the barbarian who strode from the trees with a giant hammer raised high like the Thunder God of the Norse.

The piper towered over his minions. Black Donald, the Highlanders called him, because his feet were sheep's hooves, just like tales of the devil. Some said he had horns. He didn't, but he stood taller than any man on the field, ginger hair falling to his waist in wild, loose strands. His chest was bare, muscles corded like a pile of boulders stuck together and come to life. A leather belt studded with sapphires kept thick, hide leggings in place. Yet it was not his imposing figure that melted the defenders' resolve. The horrors his aura exuded were much worse. Those at the breastwork tottered in a terrified stupor as wulvers ripped into them. A man shrieked, crumpling to the ground. Another turned and fled, clawing at his face, and the line of soldiers broke.

Effie shook off the horrors. Her mental will and stubbornness to disbelieve dissolved them. Her gaze fell to the mortar and pestle and the bag of uncrushed petals. How would they ever re-forge the Aegirsigath under such an assault? The duke and his lieutenants, and Stevenson and Sir Walter, had sorely overestimated their superiority of arms.

Caledon recognized the dire plight. Snatching up short blades and heavy axes, he and a group of the gathered fey rushed toward the breach. The steward's body pulsed as he ran across the gardens, sending off a cold wind that startled those it touched, snapping them from the piper's horrible apparitions. In his wake, the soldiers returned to the fight, laying down a barrage that punched gaps into the enemy ranks.

"I have to help them," said Effie to the aged hogboon.

She turned to retrieve the shillelagh just as a shadow crossed her face. Gwendolyn swooped in, shrieking, talons outstretched. Effie barely ducked in time to avoid being raked. A man grunted behind her as a pistol fired. The bullet whizzed past her head, yanking her hair with it.

She spun and chucked the mortar. It hit Edmund Glover square in the face with a sickening crack. He cursed at her, blood seeping through his fingers as he clutched his nose. He raised the pistol again, but a wulver darted toward him, and he was forced to turn and shoot the beast dead.

Panic shocked Effie into action, and she bolted. The line of battle had dissolved into an open skirmish throughout the grounds of Caldwell House. The boar-like beasts charged in herds while the duke's men rallied, forming tight circles, their rifles laying waste to the piper's trows and wulvers. Flames licked the garden hedges and trees beyond. Crackshots from high in the airships sought out any who wielded sling or bow.

Effie raced through it all, dashing around trows and ducking as explosions ripped the ground. She felt movement at her side and was not surprised to see Jain trying to head her off. The man carried a rifle but did not aim it at her. Instead, he pressed nearer, trying to corral her into a corner while Glover chased from behind. The Fey Finder General's face was flushed from the effort, but the pistol he carried was all she could focus on. She couldn't let him level it no matter how out of breath the man was.

Skidding sideways, she leapt over a dead trow, thanking the gods she wore trousers. The move brought her closer to Jain, and the gamble paid off. Her instincts were correct. The man was instructed not to shoot her. Glover would covet that satisfaction himself. His pride had failed him once again. Jain fumbled trying to bring the rifle up and swing it like a club. Effie dashed toward him and lashed out with the shillelagh. The blow glanced off the barrel and knocked the rifle aside.

She had just enough wherewithal to whip the club down across the back of his knees as she flew past. The blow struck home with a sickening crack, but there was no time to look back. She'd lost track of Glover, though from Gwendolyn's cries he wasn't far behind. Edging around the side of the house, she searched frantically for an open door. All she saw were manned or barricaded, and she couldn't trust the soldiers. Who would the soldiers believe if the queen's Fey Finder General demanded they hand her over? They had no time to fend for her, with their comrades fighting for their lives.

She could double back to Caledon. But the steward fought in the thickest part of the battle and had the other fey to defend. Where then? She found an old, gnarled oak tree and ducked behind it. Her lungs were on fire. Each breath was a spasm that barely brought in air.

Grabbing the tree for support, she peered around its girth. Glover stalked toward her, pistol raised, a mere ten paces away. His hair was torn and tangled from where Gwendolyn had done her work. Long scratches raked across his face. Blood seeped over the dried crust from his broken nose.

"Come out here, witch," he spat. His lips tugged into a grin when he saw her, but the rest of his face remained a mask of fury. His hand jerked and the pistol fired. Effie flinched. Her legs buckled as the bullet ripped into the trunk above her head, spraying bark in her face. Glover tittered with glee and shambled forward.

She eyed the house, but it might as well stand a mile distant. A heavy cloud passed low overhead, turning the world dark. Everything fell into shadows. Far behind, the odd rumbling and clinking of some machine filled her ears. Effie didn't understand either of the omens. She hefted the shillelagh, ready to give it one last desperate heave.

Glover glanced up and his jaw fell slack. Neither of them saw the boar-thing until its rider had cast its spear. The iron-tipped shaft struck the Fey Finder General in the back just below the neck, sinking deep. He cried out, grabbing for it, as he fell to his knees. The crazed troll urged his mount into a charge. Its tusks lowered as the beast picked up speed. Glover's eyes went wide in horror. He shot at the pair, the rapid cracking of his pistol like the snapping branches of a felled tree. But his shots flew wide and the creatures barreled down on him.

The pistol clicked, spent of bullets. Effie rushed forward without thought. Leaving the man to die was what he deserved, but she couldn't allow herself such baseness. She swiped with the shillelagh and missed, but the troll had to duck low, pulling the boar-thing off its course. Instead of gouging Glover, the thing knocked into him with its shoulder.

Man and beast grunted. The troll hopped off and tumbled to its feet. The boar-thing backed up to charge again. Glover lay dazed. He'd rolled onto the spear and snapped it against the ground.

Effie raised the shillelagh as the troll pulled a squat knife from its belt. The trundling of the odd machine had drawn closer. It was right on top of them. Death, thought Effie. The sound meant death. Boilers whistled, metal gnashed against metal. Crank-guns popped and cannons exploded in a deafening roar.

She whirled. The machine was twice the size of a steam carriage. Steel sheets of armor wrapped its body like a hide. Muzzles poked through its portholes, blasting away, as a swiveling hand-cannon mounted to its top thundered shot far into the distance.

Four squads of soldiers fanned out behind the contraption, at least fifty men with brilliant red coats and shining buttons. New arrivals unsullied by fighting. One took aim at the troll and another at the boar-thing, their rifles cracking in concert. Effie raised her hands to shield herself before she recognized the trio of men who detached and rushed to her side.

Lieutenant Walford's familiar face melted her fear. The other two she remembered from the march to Duncairn. As the reinforcements rushed past, she caught her breath and stared at them in wonder.

"The duke's an old rascal with some tricks up his sleeve," said Walford, answering her unspoken question. "Two more regiments are scrambling to get here, coming up the queen's highways. But we stole a march on the fiends, thanks to this new armored wagon and a little help from above."

Effie looked up. The heavy cloud was no cloud at all but a giant airship, the kind used to shuttle troops to the lower continents. Only this one was sleeker-looking, with giant hatches on either end.

"The thing flies faster than any ship I've seen and can skim low enough for men to hop out, rifles ready in their hands."

"It's monstrous," said Effie.

"Aye," Walford agreed. "I'm glad we have it and not the enemy. Imagine what they would do with such a thing."

She made to respond, but Gwendolyn's cry warned her of a new threat. Glover reloaded his pistol. He ranted under his breath, the words undecipherable, as he shoved in fresh rounds. His eyes were unfocused yet somehow determined.

"I have you," he snarled, snapping the barrel closed and raising the pistol. "Run, and I will order these men to shoot you down." He cackled and licked his teeth. "Please run. Harlot. Run."

She held her ground. Her grip tightened around the shillelagh.

"No?" Glover cocked his head. "Then perhaps I will shoot you myself. Right here." He balanced himself on an elbow, grimacing in pain.

"You will always fail, Edmund Glover," she said, her voice calm. "Because you are blinded by ignorance, unable to accept a friend you don't understand, unaware of the enemies your pride creates."

Walford stepped in front of Effie. "Arrest the Fey Finder General." The soldiers leveled their rifles.

Glover's face contorted. Shock overtook him, and he stammered. "No! This is treason! I will have you hanged!"

"We have orders in the duke's own hand to protect all fey who fight against the queen's enemies. You, General, are attacking an ally of the crown. That is treason." Walford's men stalked forward and one snatched Glover's pistol away from him.

"Confine them both in the house," Walford instructed.

The men prodded the stunned Fey Finder with the butts of their rifles, driving him to his feet. They remembered Duncairn and were none too gentle about the task. Glover stumbled away seething and cursing, his cries a mix of rage and pain. A dozen yards away, more of the lieutenant's men knelt over Jain. Sir Walter's man whimpered as they hauled him away on a shattered knee. Walford watched with more than a glimmer of satisfaction in his eyes. Then he nodded to Effie and rushed to rejoin his unit.

She turned toward the garden. The reinforcements had pushed back the piper's charge. The armored machine rolled along the breastwork. Where it went, the soldiers cheered and rallied. Caledon and the host from Elphame had gathered on the lawn and resumed their work.

Effie hurried over and reclaimed the mortar, though it barely had any of the flower paste left in it. Jaelyn came to her. Blood seeped down her arm from a gash in her shoulder. "We must do with what we have. There is little time before they come, and this host may not have the strength once the piper shows us his full might."

Effie was puzzled. "They?"

"The giants, lass. Can ye not feel them?"

CHAPTER 31

The large mass at the center of the Horned Host dissolved into a few large somethings approaching together, masking all the smaller things underfoot. Under enormous feet. An ungodly roar shook the ground. The trees swayed and bent, thrust aside as if they were blades of grass. Those in the giants' path snapped and were trodden over, the crashing sound like an Edinburgh tenement crumbling to ruins.

The soldiers had regained the garden wall and breastwork. They awaited with dazed expressions, their rifles and cannons forgotten. A lone trow tittered and hopped in glee. Its brethren huddled in the shadows with the rest of the piper's creatures, where they had retreated after the last assault. They hissed and snarled, sounding like a foaming wave about to break across Caldwell House.

A mountain appeared above them. The giant's flesh was like weathered stone. Moss coated it in large patches, hanging in fuzzy clumps, making the thing's chest look like a worn hillside. Its hands were large enough to crush a steam wagon, its legs as thick as the turrets of Craigmillar Castle. Yellow eyes and a squat nose gave it a gnomish face.

Jaelyn yanked Effie's sleeve. "Don't ye worry over him. That stick of yers wouldn't be a midge bite to the fellow. We've need of yer Grundbairn ways."

Effie stumbled after the brownie, unable to break her gaze from the giant. The airships above the lawn hissed steam as they banked, though she couldn't tell if they were closing to attack or fleeing. "But I don't know—"

"Of course ye do," Jaelyn snapped. She pointed at the design the Elphame host had painted on the grass. The complex knot snaked its way in a great circle, united so it had no end and no beginning. Copper urns had been set at seven points along the circumference, and within each was scraped some of the flower paste. "Where do ye stand?"

It took a moment for Effie to understand what the brownie was asking, but once she did the answer came to her without thought. She gestured at one of the urns. "That one there." She couldn't explain why; it just felt right.

Jaelyn nodded. "When ye felt Caledon Leave, ye were full of roots and dirt and the like, yeah? Well, it's different for the Grundbairns than the Star Readers, and them from the Spae Wives. Ye ken the ways of the trees and the earth, and the wee critters between. Star Readers, well, they think on stars, don't they? As the Spae Wives do for mending and the body's humors."

"You need a Grundbairn to seep the Aegirsigath into the earth and bind it there." Effie was sure the task needed doing but couldn't fathom how. That it might be up to her made her gut heave into her throat.

"Ha! Are ye giving me the lesson now? This is elder Fey Craft, lass. We need a Grundbairn, aye. But we must be interwoven, melded so that the power of one is the power of all."

The sergeant at the breastwork bellowed. A half-second later the cannon there boomed in response. The crank-guns started up again, and the sweet tang of spent gunpowder thickened the air. After ripping up a tree, the giant bludgeoned the garden walls, sending soldiers dashing for cover. A poor fellow wasn't quick enough. He cried out as the stones shattered and crumbled on top of him.

The sleek German airship swooped past. Its crank-guns trained on the giant's throat but fell silent as the thing stooped and hurled a boulder at them. The captain swung the wheel fervently, and the ship pitched toward the heavens. Crewmen slid down the deck, grasping for ropes or the gunwales, anything to tether themselves, as the boulder clipped their hull with a loud crack.

Wulvers rushed the scrambling soldiers who didn't know on which enemy to focus their efforts. The surge pushed them onto the lawn, close enough for Effie to read the inscriptions on their bandoleers. But the breastwork held. The riflemen there pitched incendiaries into the onrush, throwing up a wall of shrapnel and burning gas.

Effie found herself sucking in deep breaths and shook herself into movement. She wasn't there to freeze up like a stone. They needed her. The others had taken places around the knot, and she hurried to the urn she had pointed out to Jaelyn. Instantly, the jolting cold washed over her. But if the Leaving was a brief shock, what she beheld now was a tempest.

The skies rumbled. Even above the cacophony of explosions and the cries of soldiers, the howls of wulvers and shrieks of the trows, the thunder was deafening. Effie clamped her hands over her ears once again and felt vibrations coming from her throat, though she couldn't hear herself scream. Dark clouds rolled in from the hills quicker than a natural wind could carry them. They swirled and snaked, pulled along uncanny currents until they echoed the circle on the lawn.

Cold rain fell like icy daggers. Where it struck her flesh, numbness spread. Those of the Elphame host were doing something. It didn't take reading their fixed expressions to know that. She could feel it. Like before, impressions of root and bough filled her head, along with her own, but this time she did not flit between them. There was no sense of passage. Instead, the sensations were consumed as quickly as they came on.

She staggered as a gust knocked into her. Only it wasn't a wind at all. An unseen hand wrenched a piece of her aura away, melding it with others. She tried to follow where it went but became lost in a void, unable to decipher the nothingness from the gray steel roiling above her. The loss didn't make her afraid. Her aura was still whole despite the missing piece.

Pressure built in the space before her like steam in a boiler. The air bulged, pressing at the boundaries of the circle. The thrum of its rhythm beat painfully behind her eyes. She clamped a hand to her temple and felt her pulse racing. Roots sprang from her fingertips and wrapped themselves about her head, while the rest of her turned to stone. They slithered to her feet and plunged into the ground, gripping with an iron force. She delved deeper and found anchors to bind herself to the earth, crevices and fissures as old as time itself.

With a shrieking hiss, the pressure subsided. A wave of heat blossomed in the circle, wilting the grass and causing the rain to sizzle. The urns spewed mist as if they were volcanoes erupting. The clouds of vapor from different urns tangled, and where they touched blinding bursts of light shot out.

She shied away, just as movement passed overhead. The German airship had returned, this time with its forward hatch open. A gout of flame shot from the hatch, its reach three times the length of the ship. The burst smacked the giant in the face. The beast roared and flailed its meaty arms, but the captain had already turned the ship away and was rounding for another pass.

A weak cheer rang out from the soldiers, but they fell silent as the ground trembled anew. A pair of giants, not as large as the first but still as tall as Caldwell House, rumbled from the forest. The sight of them sapped the hearts of the men. Some ducked their heads behind whatever cover they could find. Others stood and searched, but the piper had spread his army around Caldwell House, and there was no path of retreat.

Effie realized they were doomed. Even if they managed to remake the Aegirsigath, the piper would just destroy it. Caledon had counted on the duke not just to defend them but to defeat the escaped Sidhe Bhreige. Wherever the Elphame host gathered the piper would come, he'd argued when Stevenson had suggested delaying and removing themselves to another location. Caldwell House, with the duke's men entrenched, had seemed as good a position as any other to make their stand.

But the Horned Host had been mightier than they'd expected. Caledon's gamble had not paid off. Effie studied the mass of trows and wulvers. Could a single Sidhe Bhreige really control so many? An oddity struck her. They were not all attacking. Groups huddled at the tree line snarling and snapping, but unwilling to charge against the soldier's rifles and incendiaries. Yet in other spots the creatures swarmed, seemingly unconcerned by death.

One of the smaller giants bellowed as a crank-gun tore into its gut from the armored wagon. It staggered back under the torrent of bullets, and for a moment Effie thought it might flee. But it stopped mid-step and bellowed again. Its eyes were fierce with hatred, yet she caught in that fleeting instant a look of pure anguish.

The look was enough. It snapped her from despair. One didn't need the knowledge of the ancient fey to see through the piper's gambit. The Laird of Aonghus had always alluded to great power, but in the end his blood shared the same ancestry as her own. The Piper of Ceann Rois was no different, and like the laird, his pride had left him vulnerable.

"Effie!" Jaelyn hollered as she scurried toward the breastwork. She ignored the brownie. The Aegirsigath wouldn't matter if they couldn't throw back the giants. And she had a notion of how to do just that.

Three thousand years ago a group of fey woke a giant in the Hebrides. In one of her mother's scariest tales, the giant had turned on the group, crushing them underfoot before marching to the shore and returning to stone while gazing at the sea.

Giants were renowned for their placidity as much as their ferocity. Those the piper had awoken did not fight due to their hatred of man. They fought despite their hatred of battle.

Because the piper willed them to do so.

Effie darted up the mound behind the breastwork. From the higher vantage, she spied the Piper of Ceann Rois at the edge of the trees, still wielding his hammer like a marshal's baton. She peered closer at it. Its haft was covered in runes, the iron head flat on both sides. The whole weapon was slathered in blood.

The piper was powerful, but not enough to control his entire host at once. He moved it in sections, nudging here and there like the duke's signalers. But that meant gaps formed where he did not concentrate. Gaps where his minions' true natures outweighed his influence. Gaps where they feared death and wanted only to flee into the hills.

Gaps she could exploit as she had the wulvers at Arnisdale.

She had none of the laird's unction to make her own totem, but she had no need of Blood Craft. She could use the strength of the piper's host against him. The gathered fey blood gave her more power than she'd ever tapped before, and she only needed to enthrall one of the trows, one of whom the piper wasn't paying any attention. A few danced about in the nearby trees, oblivious to the flow of the battle. She picked one and reached for it, isolating the aura of the creature from those around it. She had not the Fey Craft for subtlety and didn't know if the piper would sense what she was doing, so she worked as fast as she could. Her first thought was of the warren at Duncairn and all the shiny objects collected there. Into the image she added the desire to gather and covet more riches.

The trow stopped moving and stared at her. Gold and silver, rubies and sapphires, she sent it. The thing trembled in lust. Casting her gaze at the piper, Effie hesitated. The Sidhe Bhreige waved the hammer, but at his belt a small spike protruded from the leather. It was smeared with blood. She would've missed it except for her fixation on the jewels that surrounded it. A pouch hung on the piper's hip. An easy gesture would take his hand from the unction in the pouch to the spike next to it.

The belt was the totem, not the hammer! Effie shot the trow an image of a shadow stealing off with the belt, caressing the jewels, and hoarding them away. The shadow transformed into the trow, dancing in the moonlight while its treasure sparkled.

The trow leered hungrily at the belt. Effie added other trows to the image, those who would reach the treasure first and claim it as their own. The trow glanced around, wary of the thieves. It crept forward, greedy claws out in front ready to snatch the belt.

Effie held her breath. The distance between the trow and the piper stretched an eternity, each step of the creature barely closing the gap.

Fixated on the trow, she didn't see the boulder until the sergeant tackled her. They hit the ground hard enough to drive the breath from her lungs. The stone sailed past and thudded into the ground, sending chunks of dirt raining around them. Pain flared across her shoulder and down her arm from the impact.

The sergeant rolled off her and retrieved his rifle. "He's aimin' for the cannon!" The largest giant scooped up chunks of the broken garden wall and flung them in a great arc. "Take cover!" The soldiers fled the mound, abandoning the heavy cannon as stones crashed down like a driving hailstorm.

Effie rolled. Her bruised shoulders screamed in agony. But a burst of joy met her as she came to a stop. It was followed quickly by a stab of fear. She sought out the piper and found him swinging his hammer at a trow.

A trow who clutched an ornate belt dotted with jewels and a small, bloody spike.

"Run!" she yelled, blasting forth an image of a safe warren within Caldwell House. The trow ducked, barely avoiding the hammer. It sprang toward her, belt flopping over its shoulder.

The sergeant stooped at her side, about to snatch her away from the breastwork. But when he saw the scrambling trow and her fervent urging, he knelt and reloaded his rifle. His confusion was plain, but he didn't question her behavior. "I came to you not just for the boulder. The duke sends his regards and bids me to aid in whatever the bloody hell it is yer doing," the man spat.

Effie glanced to the signalers on the roof of Caldwell House and smiled. Stevenson stood at the duke's shoulder. Both men stared at her, the chaos around them forgotten. She pointed. "Save that trow!"

She'd hardly extended her arm when the sergeant's rifle cracked. The piper flinched, and the trow was able to gain a step toward safety. She felt the giants turn their attention her way. A pack of wulvers burst from the trees, closing the ground in long strides. The trow would never reach them.

Effie acted without thought. Somehow she separated the images of treasure she sent her trow and cast new images for the trows still near the piper. She sent these after the hammer. They wouldn't win it from him, but if she could distract the Sidhe Bhreige long enough perhaps the bonds he held over his army would weaken.

She didn't realize she was moving until the sergeant lunged in front of her, blasting a wulver who'd come at their flank. The piper swung his hammer in a great arc, knocking back the trows. His gaze hardened in fury.

Then the nightmares struck her. The piper was ancient and his skill was great. He didn't need a totem or Blood Craft to be deadly. Great hairy beasts, like spiders with wings, burst from the ground.

Their maws dripped with a green ichor that sizzled when it struck the lawn. Their claws were long, curved things with jagged edges. The sergeant screamed in terror and dropped his rifle. He swiped his hands across his body in a maddened frenzy, as if something terrible were crawling over him.

The ground lurched beneath their feet. The giants lumbered for them. Effie snatched the rifle and swung it at one of the spider-demons, but it moved too fast. It was like trying to swat at a foul memory. Pouncing, it drove her onto her back. A slathering maw rushed at her throat. Drips of ichor seared her flesh.

She was dead. The moment of panic started like an icy fist ramming into her gut, fingers spreading into her chest and gripping her heart. Her whole body tightened, withering into a knotted ball. She was dead. She had lost.

No! Anger ignited within her, burning away the hopelessness. She would not give up. Not even now. If she were to die, there had to be a way to save the rest. She had lost. But the others still had a chance. They were her family and friends, even the soldiers she had never met and the Elphame host she'd barely greeted. They had all come. They fought and bled because she had begged them to believe in her. Let the piper steal her last breath, and she would die surrounded by those who loved her, those who knew her, and those who would cherish her memory and not let it fade away.

She had never realized how much she wanted this very thing, how many walls she'd created out of the fear she would live without purpose. But those walls had crumbled.

She would not die alone.

She sought out her champion and poured all her energy into the trow, pushing her strength into the creature until her vision spun. She could feel the trow's heart race as it sped toward the house. The pulse of pure joy it returned encouraged her. Her instincts reacted, and she shaped the energy she pushed into a bubble around the trow. The bubble infected the piper's minions who came within the sphere, snapping their bonds to the Sidhe Bhreige. It was what Caledon had done, she recognized. She shoved harder and wiped away the piper's taint in a swath around the trow, growing the bubble to the size of an airship. She didn't force the creatures she touched. She allowed them to do what was in their nature. Instead of attacking, the trows and wulvers raced alongside her champion like faithful hounds. They were still feral, wild things, but the lust for killing had fled, replaced by the ecstasy of loping across soft ground, kissed by a gentle wind.

The pack grew. Effie couldn't see them, but she sensed them all. The spider-demon's jagged claws and fangs ripped into her. Poisonous ichor turned her blood black. She gritted her teeth and steeled herself against the pain. With a final gasp, she dug into the living things around her, sucked in the energy of root and stem, and sent it hurtling across the lawn.

The pulse exploded like a giant cloud of hydrogen lit aflame. Masses of the piper's army were wrenched from his control. Effie shuddered under the might. It was too much for her to handle. It was more than the strength of her aura, more than what she'd tapped from the roots and earth. It was a well of bliss as vast as an ocean. Even a thimble's worth could fill her beyond imagination and last beyond her years.

And she knew they were there—the Elphame host. Beside her, feeding her more energy, their life's blood, allowing her to press her will against the piper. A flickering thought, the warmth of sunlight, sheared away the spider-demon atop her. It shriveled under the heat, caught fire, and smoldered to ash. Rising, she found her body unharmed. The nightmares had grown only from her mind. She shoved the rays of sunlight at the rest of the spider-demons, and they sizzled and vanished.

She turned and planted herself before the giants. They loomed over her, moss-covered knuckles larger than her head. They were all too real, not figments she could melt away. But she had weakened the piper's hold on them, and as she cast out to sever their invisible bonds, she could see the wrath behind their eyes. Their hatred of the Sidhe Bhreige was as great as her own.

Like cracking a whip, she snapped the energy she channeled into a burst around the giants. The air twinged with static waves that prickled her flesh. Lightning flashed, and a clap of thunder boomed, staggering even the giants. Into the void that followed, she sent them images of comfort and peace. The Piper of Ceann Rois bellowed something guttural. What remained of his army rushed from the trees in a frenzied charge.

The giants roared. The largest among them lashed out with a meaty fist, pounding the ground near Effie. She fled behind the cannon and ducked low, but a killing blow didn't follow. She peeked around the cannon, and the giants roared again. One of them thumped its chest. As one, they turned their heads. The largest bent and scooped up the Sidhe Bhreige. The piper had towered over his army, but in the grasp of the giant he was like a rag doll flailing against a mountain. The giant grabbed him with both hands and pulled.

Effie looked away. The sound of cracking bones was enough. She released the torrent of energy and sank to her knees, exhausted. The Horned Host wavered in their charge, suddenly free of the piper's grasp. Around her the soldiers cheered, unleashing a barrage against the remnants of the piper's horde. The wulvers were the first to break. Fleeing in panic, they smashed into trows who blocked their escape, bolting into the trees and scampering in all directions. The trows were not as fast. They fell in droves to crackshots and crank-guns. The airships returned with a bombardment, and in moments the Horned Host was gone.

CHAPTER 32

Effie felt as if a fast-flowing river had swept her down its frothing path, bouncing her off every rock and spinning her in circles. Her shoulders ached; her lungs burned. Her arms and knees were scraped. Blood trickled from a cut on her cheek. She turned to check the sergeant, but the man had already gone. She could hear his bellowing some way off, and grinned. The aches, the bellowing—it meant she still lived.

The ground had stopped rattling from the lumbering giants, who strode away after tearing the piper to pieces. The airships kept track of them, floating high in the distance, out of reach of their gargantuan hands. Her champion had fled as well, along with the belt and all its jewels.

Effie sighed, the effort making her wince. Behind her, the wind stirred. She gasped at the sight. Within the circle on the lawn, a funnel of vapor swirled, dancing on tendrils like legs that hopped from urn to urn. Colors flared in prismatic explosions, blinding and soft, twinkling like the sun off broken glass. It took her a moment to realize the urns were no longer spewing the mist but sucking it back down. Where the tendrils met the vessels it spilled over the lip and seeped into the earth.

Half the Elphame host lay sprawled on the ground, forming a ring around the Aegirsigath, too tired to remain on their feet. The rest huddled in groups, exhaustion plain upon them. Jaelyn strode toward Effie, her normal scowl etched on her lips.

"That were a fool thing, lass." The brownie licked a snaggled tooth. "Brave, but a fool thing." Effie nodded and eyed the Aegirsigath. The brownie followed her gaze. "It will be enough to trap the Sidhe Bhreige and keep 'em tucked in the Downward Fields. Barely, though. We had a rough go of it, lending wills to both ye and the steward."

The brownie studied her. "What ye did." She shook her head. "Blood of the Grundbairns. I couldn't have done that. Your mother would be proud."

Effie beamed, some of her fatigue washing away. She glanced around and frowned. "Where has Caledon gone?"

"Up on the roof with the high and mighty. Speaking over matters transgressed and trying to quell the human lords, no doubt. It be one thing to hear tales of fey mischief, quite another to face the Horned Host. There'll be calls for our extermination before the day is through, no doubt."

"The giants will make matters worse." Effie thought of Nora and the children and shuddered at the thought of the giants storming through Highland villages. But it saddened her just as much to think they would be put down or enslaved.

Jaelyn shrugged. "They'll return to stone by nightfall. It is their way to rest and gaze out on the world, silent and peaceful."

"I saw it in their eyes," said Effie, "the way they despised the Piper of Ceann Rois. But it was the Laird of Aonghus who taught me how to turn the piper's compulsion against him. My skin crawls knowing I owe him yet another debt, even one of gratitude."

Jaelyn clucked in disapproval. "Despite what ye just done, ye are still a child in our lore. In days long past, fey held no compass to their deeds. We who remained are much closer to humans now. Our wills are tied to their sense of judgment. It is the choice we made when we sided with them against the Sidhe Bhreige millennia ago, but do not think it was because we chose a good over an evil."

She saw Effie's reaction and waggled her finger. "The Sidhe Bhreige enslaved us, some say. Words used now by fey who weren't alive when the Sidhe Bhreige roamed the isles. It hides a subtler truth. The Sidhe Bhreige's will was stronger than ours so we cast them out like bees swarming a bear who steals their honey. Does that make their will wrong and ours right?"

Effie stood firm. "From the horrid things they've done since their return, I have to believe it does."

"Bah, that is Thomas Stevenson speaking in ye. The trees don't care a tick for doctrines, nor the shores or the winds. Codes of who can do what and when, that is the domain of humans. A mouse would kill an owl if it could, not because the owl is evil but because the mouse wants to survive."

Effie warmed inside. She'd spent the past fortnight worrying over the fey part of her, ignoring the life she'd found with Stevenson and Graham. Perhaps they had bent her toward their human ways of thinking, but the life they bestowed had brought happiness. She would never give that up, no matter its name.

"It is because of humanity I believe London can be reasoned with," she said. "It is why now, when they have seen all the wickedness the Sidhe Bhreige have wrought, they should also see the goodness of our kind."

Jaelyn's eyes lowered. "The queen's army will nae care friend from foe as they pursue the scraps of the Horned Host. It'll be a savage hunt, as it always has been."

Glancing at Stevenson and the duke, Effie paused. What Jaelyn said was true. It would be a savage hunt. Many in London wouldn't care about the details of how those from Elphame aided the duke's men. They would only see what they'd always seen: a fey enemy that needed to be put down. But men like Sir Walter, even driven by greed, were men of logic. And if they could be won over, the voices of prejudice could be cut short.

"A spark can kindle a big fire. We shall have to wait and see how hard the wind blows this time."

Jaelyn snorted but held her tongue. They watched as the old hogboon moved from urn to urn, covering each of them with an earthen lid. The mist dissipated as he went, the last tendrils seeping into the ground until the air was clear.

"Sir Walter's boon," sneered Jaelyn, indicating the urns. "He will take the Aegirsigath and ask for more. Our tithe to him so we could save his scheming race."

Effie thought of Walford and the sergeant and all the other

soldiers who'd fought to protect them, but she was too exhausted to argue any longer with the brownie. It would save for another day. A long and difficult road stretched before them, as steep as Ben Nevis and tougher to climb.

Gwendolyn fluttered in and landed on her shoulder. The tawny owl screeched and nipped her ear. "Ow! What is it? I have no food for you." Effie tried to push the bird back, but it screeched again. Digging its talons, it launched forward and climbed until it soared over the trees. Its shrieks became more insistent as it circled something in the distance.

"What does she—? Oh." Effie saw Jaelyn start as her own senses found the answer. On the edge of her perception a pack of wulvers massed.

"They hunt in packs," offered Jaelyn. "'Tis no strange thing."

Effie felt the surrounding area. The Horned Host had splintered into scores of smaller groups. She could feel no more than a dozen together in any other place. "It's him," she said with certainty. "He stayed at the periphery of the battle until the outcome was known. Now he'll gather what he can and slither into the shadows until he thinks we've forgotten about him."

"It is his way," the brownie agreed. She massaged her knuckles and shook off her fatigue. "We may not find him again until he has done some great harm."

Effie judged the distance. They would have to move fast. She'd feel better if they could bring a crank-gun or some incendiaries, but those were too heavy. The armored wagon lay half-crushed along what remained of the garden wall, smashed by one of the giants. The airships were off along the horizon. They would have to mount a charge without the modern machines.

Turning, she ran toward Caldwell House, wincing with every step. Jaelyn fell in at her side. "Where ye headed?"

"To see Lieutenant Walford about a horse," Effie shot back. She refused to think about the piper's fate or what they might do once they caught the Laird of Aonghus. She would offer him a choice, but deep down she knew the Sidhe Bhreige wouldn't bow to words or human chains.

CHAPTER 33

With Gwendolyn circling above, they were able to follow the Laird of Aonghus' path. Arrows flew at the owl but fell short, arcing back into the forest's dense canopy. Effie could feel more than see Gwendolyn. She could feel the laird too, at times, at the edge of her senses. The powers of her Sithling blood felt like a coat she'd worn her entire life. But they were dim now compared to the battle at Caldwell House. The combined proximity of the Horned Host and those returned from Elphame had felt like the inside of a coal furnace. She was left now with only glowing embers and the memory of an intense heat.

Octavian huffed, clomping his hooves and straining at the reins. The chestnut was eager to run. Bred for duty among the queen's cavalry, he was a fiery beast compared to the calm plodding of Whisper. Effie patted his shoulder and settled him with a light push of soothing. Beside her, Lieutenant Walford waited expectantly.

"He knows we are after him," she said. "His path weaves back and forth like a will-o'-the-wisp."

Walford pondered the information. "He's searching for good ground to make a stand." The lieutenant's face had hardened when she told him of the laird's presence. Before she could ask, he'd barked orders for a squad of mounted riflemen to form ranks.

"Or to set a trap," said Jaelyn. The brownie had refused the horse offered her but had managed to keep pace with their canter. Even after an hour in pursuit, her breath was barely labored. She stood clutching a pair of spears.

"We need to overtake him by nightfall, or he'll slink away. Whatever trap he sets, we'll just have to spring and hope our numbers are enough." Effie was surprised at the boldness in her tone. It reminded her of the way Stevenson would command a room discussing the matters of one of his great projects.

"If he keeps an eye on our location, then it is best we gain the ground between us before his trap is set." Walford nudged his horse forward. A dozen sets of reins rattled into action behind him.

Effie urged Octavian into as fast a pace as the broken ground of the forest allowed. It was difficult to keep a straight line after the laird. Octavian darted around clusters of trees, leaping over exposed roots and crumbled stone. Effie clung to his shoulders, ducking under low branches and struggling to keep her rump balanced in the saddle. She feared turning her head to check on those behind would send her flying off, so kept her attention locked firmly forward.

After a few minutes, their path led them to a game trail. Octavian barreled down it, kicking up clods of soft dirt wetted by the recent rains. Effie's heart picked up, and not just at the surge of speed. The laird lay no longer at the edge of her senses. They gained on him.

Pounding forward, their pursuit broke the quiet of the forest—a clamor of steel shoes striking half-buried stones, the creak of leather rubbing against cloth, and the snorts and grunts of the horses. The sounds rattled in Effie's head. The jarring impact make her body numb. She focused on their quarry, trying to sniff out any traps. She'd learned the past fortnight that the simplest were often the most dangerous. The laird would be clever. He would know she could sense his movements, just as he could theirs. He would know they would overtake him, that he must either face them or design some way to disappear.

As if reading her mind, the laird suddenly stopped. His minions flocked behind him, spreading out in an arc. Effie slowed Octavian and gestured. Walford moved to her side, readying a pistol and offering it to her. She shook her head. Such things would never be for her. The weight of cold steel in her hands would be like a chain around her neck, dragging her under the sea. Still, she knew their intent and was not opposed to leveling the laird low. It was the method, not the result, that disturbed her. She pulled the shillelagh from its harness at her legs. The gnarled club felt more proper somehow. It connected her more to the world she fought for than chemical powder and lead shot.

They broke into a clearing where the game trail met an old carriageway snaking its way through the trees. The laird hunched on his pony, facing them with a hideous smirk. He held his cane halfway up the shaft, rapping it idly against the pony's flank. The beast didn't seem to mind. Its head was lowered and shoulders sagged, as if it had seen long miles in recent days. Of the wulvers, Effie could not see. But she felt them in the woods, crouching in the shadows beyond the clearing. Trows, too. The laird had no doubt gathered all who crossed his path during his retreat from Caldwell House.

His cackle was a guttural sound that left no trace on his expression. "I congratulate you on your victory, Grundbairn. Or should I say, our victory. You have made it quite possible for me to rule this world alone. Your contributions will not go unrewarded."

Walford balked and raised his pistol, but Effie stayed his hand. "Come peacefully and answer to the Court of Righm, or these men of London's queen will pass her judgment upon you." Effie moved Octavian into the clearing, allowing Walford's men to fan out beside her. Their rifles were trained on the laird.

The laird eyed the soldiers. "I've felt the judgment of the Court of Righm for millennia, in the cold, blasted hells of the Downward Fields. The court is full of noisome children who will be shown their place. Or do you believe you have seen the extent of my power?" He pointed a finger at one of the soldiers, and the man cried out, dropping his rifle and slumping off his horse. The soldier's face turned a shade of purple. He pulled at his hair and shook in a fit.

"The Piper of Ceann Rois was a fool," said the laird, "to fall to such primitive beasts."

Effie snarled. "You are a coward who hides in the shadows like a mold, a rotting sickness eating away all that is hale." Effie couldn't feel what the laird was doing to the soldier, but she guessed it was similar to what the piper had done, invading the man's thoughts with horrors so real they drew a physical response. She cast out her senses, wary of an encroaching menace.

Flicking his wrist, the laird snapped whatever enthrallment he'd held over the soldier. The man rolled on the ground, gasping. "Shadows are where the greatest power resides. Your Thomas Stevenson knows this. He has played a game of shadows with you your entire life, molding you in isolation, pulling you away from your natural instincts, never telling you the truth about anything."

The laird glared at her, head drooping slightly, eyes raised to meet her height. "Humans will never tell you the truth. They will try to lead you astray because you are not one of them." He cocked his head. "Even in violent matters that concern only their own, like in the case of your friend, Robert Ramsey."

She bristled, a sudden flare of anger trembling through her. She slid in the saddle and fought to regain her balance. The Laird of Aonghus flashed his teeth. "Shot dead at the hand of a man called Theodore Todd. Shot dead at the mere rumor of harboring and conversing with fey. Ordered to do so by London's whelp."

Octavian whinnied and shuffled a step as her body went rigid. She bit back a stammer of disbelief. It made no matter at present whether the laird's words were true. He spoke only to distract and manipulate her. But if it were true, who knew and had misled her? Her gut dropped, her bones sagged in dejection. There was no end to those who sought to use her, who coerced and misrepresented in order to pull her strings and make her dance to their whims. Even Caledon, in his own way, had done so.

Her head clouded. She was a lonely mouse scampering across a vast field of wind-blown grass. Falcons and hawks and other hunters circled above, cawing and dipping low to make a run at her. She was out in the open, no matter how far she ran or how fast. In endless directions she went seeking refuge, but there was none to be found. The hunters played with her, thriving on her fear, gleeful in the racing of her wee heart. They drove her one direction after the next, all the while fighting with each other.

One bird circled far above, higher than it should be. Brown, she thought, but kissed by the sun so it glowed a golden hue. She could barely make out its shape from so far below, with so many other birds squawking for her attention, pushing her onward in an endless race for survival. But she saw the bird and understood. It was time. Time for her to let go of the fear. She'd been running far too long. Her murine body could not handle the exertion anymore. It would give out soon.

The hunters saw her weakness and swooped lower, talons and claws snatching the air just above her supple fur. She ducked and dodged, tiny paws barely touching the ground as she scurried. An oak tree appeared in the distance, breaking the void of the field. Its solid limbs beckoned her. Its roots dug deep into the ground, refusing to be ripped away by the sudden torments of wind. The hunters frenzied at the sight of it. The oak shouldn't be there; it wasn't a part of their game.

She jumped, and the distance between her and the oak disappeared. She was at its trunk, under a thick canopy that folded over her like a protective mother. She placed a forepaw on the oak and drank in its shelter, its solace, its wisdom. The ancient tree saw her and knew.

It was time.

The paw grew and shaped into a hand. Her body formed, and the meek part of her that wanted to hide in the shadows of the tree fell away. Rising, she stepped out into the openness of the field. A hawk swooped at her. She ripped its fury from it and forced it to settle on her arm, docile as a dove. "This is not your fight," she told it, and sent it high into the air to tell the others.

Gwendolyn soared past her face, intent on some movement ahead. Effie closed her eyes and lashed out at the laird's bonds. His false dream of fear buckled and snapped apart, leaving her dizzy. It felt like she'd run for hours, but only moments had passed. She was back in the clearing with Walford, slumped over Octavian's mane. She clutched a handful of the coarse hair to steady herself.

An arrow whistled out of the shadows. She could hear its shriek piercing the air before she could see it. Gwendoline banked hard and snatched the shaft with one of her talons. The force of it sent the owl spiraling to the ground.

The Laird of Aonghus chortled. "Good, lass. You see what power is yours for the taking. The piper was a fool to doubt your will, to ignore your strength." His teeth punched through his lips, his grin so feral it was half snarl. But the roundness of his gaze betrayed a hesitancy. He hadn't expected her to defeat his Fey Craft so easily. His tongue stuck to his teeth. Whatever words he meant to speak were deafened by the crack of a rifle.

Leaves rustled and broke where the bullet tore through them. The hot lead struck a tree with a sharp thwack, and the shadows behind it sprang to life as a trow darted from concealment. A volley of gunfire tore through the forest, its retort echoing outward. The trow was flung aside under the barrage, the crude bow it clutched snapping beneath it.

The spent gunpowder billowed along the carriageway like a warm, sweet mist. Effie had just enough time to shout a warning before the laird's wulvers and trows surged forward. But Walford's men were prepared. They held tight ranks, rifles spewing death. Their horses were trained for battle, disciplined and vicious. Those wulvers who reached their line were kicked and bit and battered until they shrank back in fear.

The trows sent arrows arcing from the trees. The soldiers hurled grenades back at them. Explosions blasted the creatures from the shadows in thunderous gouts of flame and earth.

An arrow thudded into one of the soldiers, sending him reeling off the back of his horse. Walford leapt from his saddle and rushed to fallen man. As the soldier stood, Walford thrust the butt of his rifle, bashing the man back to his knees. In one quick motion, Walford yanked the arrow free. He'd ordered all to do the same before they left. The wounds might be made worse, but none wanted to risk enthrallment.

Effie tried to keep track of the laird's minions. They raced to their deaths, compelled by the Sidhe Bhreige, their numbers dwindling by the second. The Laird of Aonghus slowly walked his mount backward, edging toward the trees. She stepped Octavian closer, about to call out when a wulver darted at her from the side. Without thought, she summoned the power of the forest and brought it into a shield that protected her and Octavian. It was a twist on the bubble of energy she'd wielded against the piper. Instead of sending the wulver a soothing pulse to snap its bonds, she created a shell around herself that drew from her aura and smelled of pine and earth. The might of fey blood in the clearing was not nearly as great as it had been at Caldwell House, but it was enough. The wulver snarled at the phantom barrier, howling in frustration, its lips slathering for a kill. One of the soldiers turned and shot it in the head.

Dropping from the saddle, Effie kept the shield up as she stalked the laird. He'd almost reached the shadows. A pair of trows waited for him, protection against Walford's rifles. His old tricks were becoming obvious to Effie. The Sidhe Bhreige held Fey Craft akin to gods but neither the laird nor the piper had adapted to the modern age. They were too long imprisoned, decaying over eons into relics as brittle as felled timber left to rot.

Warping the energy of her shield, she flung an image at the laird's mount–a rampaging lion to spook it. The laird expected the attack and flared a burst of energy to deflect it, but he expected Effie's pulse to be aimed at him and realized too late his shield was useless. He'd protected only himself. The pony bucked and jerked away.

The laird cried out as he landed with a bone-jarring thump. "Always selfish," said Effie. "It makes you weak." She crouched, ready to spring aside. Digging as deep as she could, she summoned as much energy as she dared, pulling from beast and man; from tree, root, and soil; from the clouds above and the coursing waters beneath the crust of the earth.

Wincing, the laird dragged himself to his feet, using his cane to prop himself upright. He snorted at her effort. "It is time to end this. Even with your new tricks, you cannot hope to pull my pets away from me. I am too strong. You are too clumsy." A massive well of darkness sprang up around the laird. To her senses, it was like a murder of crows had swarmed around him, a storm of flitting shadows crackling with lightning. The clearing buckled. The laird's summons yanked everything toward him, demanding obedience. His reach flowed across the forest, a blaring herald pulling at the wills of all it touched.

The soldiers bellowed in defiance. Their horses reared and cried. The remaining trows and wulvers prostrated themselves, the pull too much for them to remain standing. Miles away, their brethren howled and agitated, responding to the beacon that called them forth. It was an eldritch power strong enough to topple kingdoms.

Effie grinned. "You are right, of course. That is why I would never try." She released her energy and sank to a knee. It was the signal they had prepared. The moment her knee touched the ground Gwendolyn shrieked and Walford shouted. Rifles answered the herald, firing on the laird in scattered shots that flew well high.

With a wave of his cane, the laird brought forth the trows who'd hidden in the shadows, to act as a shield. Confusion painted his face as the rifles fell silent. His gaze swiveled between the supplicant Effie and the stone-faced soldiers. He realized a moment too late their trick.

Jaelyn sank her long dagger into his back. The trow she'd replaced lay in a heap in the shadows where it had hidden, its body unnoticed by the laird. They were all pawns in his mind without need for distinction.

The laird's eyes fell vacant. He sputtered some final word Effie could not make out and collapsed to the forest floor.

"It was a good trap," said Jaelyn. She pulled her dagger free and cleaned it on the laird's trousers.

Effie rose. "All the Laird of Aonghus needed was a little distraction. His arrogance did the rest, just like the Piper of Ceann Rois."

Moving to her side, Walford checked the load of his rifle. "I still don't see why we didn't just shoot the bastard."

"We tried that way before, twice, and it did not end well." She shrugged. "Who knows what tricks he had ready to spring on us? It seemed more prudent this way."

"Cold steel is always best," Jaelyn agreed. "That, or giants."

Walford's men gathered around. None of the laird's minions remained. Those in the distance who'd turned to answer the Sidhe Bhreige's final pull had fled as soon as the laird had fallen. Effie met the eyes of each of the men and gave them thanks. They had risked everything on her word, and on Caledon's. Those back at Caldwell House had too, and she would not refuse them the right to know her now. Notorious or not, they must see her as she truly was, or she might as well be trapped in the Downward Fields. It was the final lesson the Laird of Aonghus had taught her.

CHAPTER 34

S ir Walter Conrad lifted a snifter from the silver tray and filled it with a liberal amount of brandy. His normally gaunt cheeks were sucked into an unpleasant pucker as if he were gnawing away at their insides. Crossing the room, he settled into a giant leather chair across from Effie, near the crackling fire. Effie tried to bring a pleasant smile to her lips. He was a man they must make peace with, both Thomas Stevenson and Caledon had reminded her. Graham had as well, giving her a knowing look as Sir Walter entered the small parlor within Caldwell House. A long fortnight had passed as they waited for His Royal Highness to return from London.

Graham sat beside her, feet propped on a stool, peering over a broadsheet from Edinburgh. "His Royal Highness has defeated a cult of dissident fey, it says here," he murmured. "Dissident, mind you. I suppose it is something for them to make the distinction."

Sir Walter cocked his head askew. "I'd say it was rather more than something. The masses in the cities are driven by the news contained in those tabloids. Seeding tolerance into their minds will pay its dues eventually." He sipped his brandy. "Or did you expect hundreds of years of superstition to be washed away on the passing word of a handful of soldiers?" Grunting, Graham pointedly returned to his reading. Effie thought he should take his own advice but couldn't fault his gruffness. Sir Walter was an infuriating man, especially when he spoke the truth.

Cane pounding against the hard wooden floor, Conall Murray

burst into the parlor and slumped into the remaining chair. His limp was slight and getting better with each day. In the week since he and Graham had arrived, each had grown stronger and begun returning to their normal selves. Her face pulled into a grin at the sight of him. As if sensing her need, he had made her laugh more in the past week than she could remember doing in years. It had relaxed her and helped her overcome her own injuries.

"My father will be the death of me," he droned.

"Now, young Murray," said Sir Walter, "that is no way for the Fey Finder General to enter a room."

"Only until Her Majesty appoints a permanent replacement," he said with a sigh. He tapped his cane. "I half-think the duke proclaimed me thus just to appease my father over the destruction of the house grounds."

Sir Walter chuckled. "That, and to spite Lady Fife. She did have her heart set on that cousin of hers."

Effie took in Conall with wonder, not believing she perched so close to the queen's chief Sniffer and thought more of his health than her own. Her world had indeed molded into something new. Of Edmund Glover, a smelly, crowded ship had taken him away, stripped of office and rotting in his own vile filth. At least, that's how she imagined his journey to Australia. The Duke of Edinburgh appointed him to a clerk's desk somewhere in the crippling desert. When questioned about Robert Ramsey, he'd only sneered and spat vulgarities at her.

Jain confessed he'd attacked her on Glover's orders, but there was little doubt Sir Walter's coins had brought him to Caldwell House. More of those coins had likely kept his mouth shut as well. Sir Walter saw the lecher taken away in chains before anything damaging could spill from his lips, and in that matter Effie didn't mind. Removing the pair had done as much to cleanse Caldwell House as had burying the dead outside.

A weighty stare brought her thoughts back to the present. Sir Walter studied her. "Have you considered more on what we discussed?" He swirled the amber liquid in his snifter.

Effie bit her tongue. "I am not a puppet for your games, Sir Walter," she said as softly as she could muster.

Sir Walter leaned forward. "Now that London and the fey have reconciled, there is much work to do bringing the populace in line. To start, there will be a royal progression throughout the Highlands." He waved a hand. "Something to prove the crown has everything under control, and that the recent troubles are laid to rest."

"Secretly, to have a conclave and forge a new treaty between the crown and the Seily Court," offered Conall.

"Quite so." Sir Walter sipped, his eyes never leaving her. "Such events need proper guidance. If not a figurehead in the progression, perhaps you will aid in other ways. There are still Unseily designs and other fey with fell intentions, are there not? I'm sure your usefulness would be of great worth to the crown."

Graham balked. "You'd have her turn on her own?" He tossed the broadsheet down, giving up the pretense of reading it.

Sir Walter tapped the snifter with his index finger and swirled the liquid. "A constable protects his people when he arrests a murderer and helps his people when he tends to the local drunk."

"And the only man detested more is the tax collector." Graham spat the words, shaking his head in disbelief. "Bah, by some anyway."

Effie wanted to balk as well, but her thoughts strayed to Robert Ramsey and the Munroe girl. Someone needed to account for them, and there was still the last of the Sidhe Bhreige to hunt down. The one they only knew about because of the torment its release caused in those with fey blood. Lieutenant Walford and his men were scouring the Highlands, but with no fey blood among their ranks, how would they recognize the enemy? Unaided, would they only wander into an ambush? Conall had suggested the absurd notion of fey joining the ranks of the Sniffers. He wanted to alter their creed and hunt only the Unseily, but London would never allow it. They had spent centuries preaching against her kind and could not turn the tide so easily.

Sir Walter saw her contemplation and dipped his head. A slight smirk drew at his lips. Effie scowled. "I have a profession and no need of the crown's authority to help those in need." She relaxed her grip on the armchair, twitching her foot to loosen the muscles in her legs.

"But of course, you are right." The words dripped with condescension.

Effie eyed the poker leaning against the fireplace. It was not far from her reach. Conall caught her temper and cleared his throat rather inelegantly. "Mr. Stevenson and the Master Steward argue for making knowledge of the Aegirsigath public, as a means of ensuring its protection."

"Mr. Stevenson is correct," agreed Sir Walter, finally breaking his gaze from Effie. "Public knowledge will place the burden of protection on the crown and hold them accountable."

Snorting, Graham pulled out his pipe and tapped it against the table to clean out the old tobacco. "Not to mention it would limit those with access to the substance, creating a monopoly."

The gleam from Sir Walter's face was bright enough to blind half of Edinburgh. Effie reconsidered her position. Walford hunted for a drop of rain fallen in the ocean. Conall Murray could barely handle his father, let alone a man like Sir Walter. The lords of London still loathed the fey. She would never become a Sniffer, but perhaps the crown did need someone like her involved, in some capacity for a time. It would be a long road with no certainty at its end. But she wouldn't do it for the crown, or even to spite a man like Sir Walter Conrad. She would do it to protect the fey against these men. She would do it to protect her friends. Her family. Her home.

Her foot started to tap.

THE END

Thank you for reading! For more from Craig Comer, check out craigcomer.com and join his mailing list.

Please sign up for the City Owl Press newsletter for chances to win special subscriber-only contests and giveaways as well as receiving information on upcoming releases and special excerpts.

craigcomer.com

www.facebook.com/craigscomer/

twitter.com/CraigComer

All reviews are welcome and appreciated. Please consider leaving one on your favorite social media and book buying sites.

For books in the world of romance and speculative fiction that embody Innovation, Creativity, and Affordability, check out City Owl Press at www.cityowlpress.com.

ACKNOWLEDGMENTS

I am immensely grateful to Tina Moss, Yelena Casale, and the rest of the folks at City Owl Press, whose excitement and guidance for this book has been above and beyond. Especially, I would like to thank Heather McCorkle who helped transform Effie's tale into something grander and more cohesive.

Thanks also to my wheel-of-names writing group, who read and gave notes on early chapters of the book: Garrett Calcaterra, Ahimsa Kerp, Corey Beasom, Eric Tryon, and Pete Vander Pluym. And to Ben Thornton, a great artist and better friend, who has provided me with sketches and artwork to help get Effie out into the world.

Last, and above all, I would like to thank my family for their support, and Martina for telling me to go write.

ABOUT THE AUTHOR

CRAIG COMER is the author of the gaslamp fantasy novel THE LAIRD OF DUNCAIRN and co-author of the mosaic fantasy novel THE ROADS TO BALDAIRN MOTTE. His shorter works have appeared in several anthologies, including BARDIC TALES AND SAGE ADVICE and PULP EMPIRE VOLUME IV. Craig earned a Master's Degree in Writing from the University of Southern California. He enjoys tramping across countries in his spare time, preferably those strewn with pubs and castles.

craigcomer.com

ABOUT THE PUBLISHER

CITY OWL PRESS is a cutting edge indie publishing company, bringing the world of romance and speculative fiction to discerning readers.

www.cityowlpress.com